SWIMMING
WITH HORSES

OAKLAND
ROSS

DUNDURN
TORONTO

Cover image: shutterstock.com/Fotokostic
Printer: Webcom

Library and Archives Canada Cataloguing in Publication

Ross, Oakland, 1952-, author
   Swimming with horses / Oakland Ross.

Issued in print and electronic formats.
ISBN 978-1-4597-4354-0 (softcover).--ISBN 978-1-4597-4355-7 (PDF).--
ISBN 978-1-4597-4356-4 (EPUB)

   I. Title.

PS8585.O8404S95 2019   C813'.6   C2018-903352-5
                                          C2018-903353-3

1 2 3 4 5   23 22 21 20 19

 Conseil des Arts du Canada Canada Council for the Arts   Canadä ONTARIO ARTS COUNCIL / CONSEIL DES ARTS DE L'ONTARIO / an Ontario government agency / un organisme du gouvernement de l'Ontario

We acknowledge the support of the **Canada Council for the Arts**, which last year invested $153 million to bring the arts to Canadians throughout the country, and the **Ontario Arts Council** for our publishing program. We also acknowledge the financial support of the **Government of Ontario**, through the **Ontario Book Publishing Tax Credit** and **Ontario Creates**, and the **Government of Canada**.

Nous remercions le **Conseil des arts du Canada** de son soutien. L'an dernier, le Conseil a investi 153 millions de dollars pour mettre de l'art dans la vie des Canadiennes et des Canadiens de tout le pays.

Care has been taken to trace the ownership of copyright material used in this book. The author and the publisher welcome any information enabling them to rectify any references or credits in subsequent editions.

                     — *J. Kirk Howard, President*

The publisher is not responsible for websites or their content unless they are owned by the publisher.

Printed and bound in Canada.

VISIT US AT

    dundurn.com | @dundurnpress | dundurnpress | dundurnpress

Dundurn
3 Church Street, Suite 500
Toronto, Ontario, Canada
M5E 1M2

SWIMMING WITH HORSES

In loving memory of Doris Mary Ross

No hill without gravestones, no valley without shadows.
— SOUTH AFRICAN PROVERB

THEY FOUND QUINTON VASCO'S body only a day after he went missing. Still clad in a black business suit, his corpse turned up amid a large field of alfalfa grass, a couple of hundred yards north of Number Four Sideroad in Kelso County. The site was not far from a trail that local teens had used in former days as a sort of lovers' lane.

By this time, the police had discovered Vasco's abandoned BMW nearby. It seemed he had walked from the vehicle into the field, entering by means of the padlocked gates; it was determined he had a key. He then proceeded on foot to the site of his death, evidently accompanied by a second person, his killer. There was no sign of a struggle.

Some said it was fitting that Vasco owned the property where he was murdered, although I can't imagine what difference that would make, either to him or to anyone else, unless it was for the view. The view was stunning. Still, it all came to the same thing in the end. The man was dead, shot twice in the side of the head from very close range — this, according to the police report. The police also said there was something odd about the bullets that killed him. Their calibre — nine millimetres by eighteen millimetres — was pretty unusual, albeit not unknown. That summer, the Evanton detachment of the Ontario Provincial Police had received several baffling reports of local livestock being shot while grazing, invariably with bullets of this same unfamiliar configuration. Possibly, the killer had been getting in some target practice.

Many people would later insist that Vasco's death must have been part of some deadly international plot, rife with intrigue and espionage. He was the inventor, after all, of the GC-45 howitzer, a massive cannon that was eventually sold to the white supremacist government in South Africa. But the actual verdict proved to be far more mundane. Kelso was a quiet region, you see, with little crime and few troublemakers. When acts of malfeasance did take place, suspicion tended to round pretty quickly upon a select group of known delinquents, a short list that included a certain Bruce Gruber. He was a grade eight dropout who worked as an apprentice mechanic at Weintrub's Garage over in Hatton. He had a mean temper and had run afoul of the law more than once. He was not noted for his keen intellect.

What was more, Bruce Gruber confessed his guilt almost at once, and he stuck to his tale like a dog. He insisted that he shot Quinton Vasco "because I hated him," which made sense if you know anything about human nature at all. It was said that Gruber acted in a jealous rage, which seemed on the surface to be entirely plausible.

All of this and more came out in the news and kept everyone jabbering for weeks. A murder? In Kelso County? Nothing like it had ever happened before. True, rumours would begin to spread toward the end of that summer about an alleged rape, a terrible business said to have involved that nice young Odegaard girl. Leslie was her name. For my part, I happen to have a fair idea of what was done to Leslie on that night, even if few others do. I may even have saved her from suffering worse harm. For almost everyone else, the episode was a matter of hearsay and conjecture — unproven and easily forgotten. Besides, the Odegaards quickly sold their store in Hatton and set out for parts unknown. People stopped talking about them before very long. I don't believe that anyone was ever punished for the assault on that poor child, or not officially. Still, some higher form of justice may have been at work because, one way or another, Bruce Gruber went to jail.

As for the object of Bruce's seemingly unrequited passion, she absconded, too. The South African girl, they called her. Colonel Barker drove her to the airport on the day that followed Quinton Vasco's death, even before the man's body was found. She left no message or, anyway, none for me. She just marched aboard an airplane and disappeared. Good riddance, everyone said. Her departure merely confirmed what they had believed all along.

That girl was trouble.

And she was. I know she was. I know that better than anyone.

PART ONE

HER NAME WAS HILARY ANSON, and she came up from South Africa in the late spring of 1963, armed with a Russian-made Makarov pistol that had been given to her by Nelson Mandela, or so she said. She was all of eighteen years old when she arrived in Canada — an unholy terror, according to the rumours, which were invariably lurid and quite possibly true. Her impending arrival had been grist for the mill long before she showed up in Kelso, deep in the horse country northwest of Toronto, the land where I was raised.

Supposedly, she was to remain for the summer, or possibly longer, in order to serve penance for certain heinous wrongs committed in her home country. The details were unclear. All that was known for certain was that she was trouble and that she was going to work as a groom at the Colonel Barkers' place, a rambling property with a stone farmhouse on the Second Line not far south of the hunt club. Some relative of Mrs. Barker's lived in South Africa — in Durban, apparently — and there was some kind of family connection with Hilary Anson. No one was exactly sure what it was. As for the rumours, if even half of them were true, then the girl had already endured vastly more outrage and scandal than I have known in all my life, and I am now forty-six. I was fifteen then.

"Durban …?" said my mother. She wrinkled her nose. This was the first she'd heard of Hilary Anson. "Doesn't that sound Arabian?"

"*Turban*, Mother," I said. "You're thinking of *turban*. And that would be more like India. Sikhs wear turbans."

"Oh …? Oh yes." She waggled her eyeglasses in the air like a schoolteacher to signal a pause in the conversation. But she soon came back to Hilary Anson. "Just think," she said. "South Africa."

My father had been there once, on business of some kind. He'd gone on safari, too, and had seen a lion, two giraffes, and at least a dozen elephants, all before seven o'clock in the morning.

"And that was just for starters," he told us later.

I did a presentation about it at school, featuring an out-of-focus snapshot of my father in a wide-brimmed hat slouching in the passenger seat of a Land Rover beside a bare-headed black driver. The driver had a rifle resting across his lap and was the first black man I had ever seen, or, at least, the first one who had any connection to me. Here was the black man my father had once sat beside in a Land Rover in South Africa. In the background: Kruger National Park. It was remote and exotic.

But back to 1963. For reasons not of my own making, I came to know Hilary Anson — a.k.a. the South African girl — over the course of that summer. I believe I grew closer to her than anyone else managed to do at that time, closer even than Bruce Gruber. This might not seem like much to others, but it surely was something to me. She turned my life upside down, Hilary Anson did, and I haven't got things righted yet, even though more than thirty years have passed since I last heard her plummy voice; last gazed at her wavy sable locks; last admired her as she sculpted smoke rings in the air with a Rothmans cigarette; last watched, transfixed, as she dove naked and on horseback into the quarry pond, down by the abandoned Colbys' place, where the Niagara Escarpment plummets toward the Kelso River and the broad green lands beyond.

I saw Hilary Anson before I met her. Along with my kid sister, Charlotte, I had hacked over to the hunt club in order to stable our horses there overnight, hers and mine. Our mother picked us up in our Pontiac station wagon that evening and then drove us back at six the next morning so we could water the horses, feed them, groom them, and tack them up, all before seven.

"Come on, Della," I said.

I bunched the reins in my right hand and led my horse out of the barn and into the brisk spring air. Charlotte followed with Pablo, a shaggy grey pony, a Welsh and Shetland cross. Della was short for Della Street, the secretary on *Perry Mason*, my favourite TV program at the time. As for Della the horse, she was a smallish bay mare with handsome conformation and an honest heart. But she had delicate bones, lacked stamina, and was apt to be sluggish at times.

On that first morning — the morning when I first saw Hilary Anson — Charlotte and I alternated holding the other's horse so that, one at a time, we could hurry back into the tack room to change. I took my turn second and soon marched back out to the stable yard in breeches, tweed jacket, and tie. Charlotte handed me my horse's reins, and I stood with my back to Della's head. I twisted the stirrup iron out a quarter turn, slipped the ball of my booted left foot into the iron, pushed off twice with my right foot, and swung myself up and into the saddle, joining a dozen or so other riders, all grown-ups.

The lemony sunshine pealed down through the wisps of morning mist, the hounds were bellowing already over at the kennel, and Colonel Barker appeared over the brow of the hunt club lane on his big half-Clydesdale named Rumpus. Colonel Barker had one sightless eye, a red moustache, and an English accent that was not really genuine; he had lived in England during the war. At his side: Hilary Anson.

She was riding the colonel's big chestnut stallion, the one named Club Soda, and it immediately seemed to me that only she and her horse were blessed with the gift of movement, while the rest of us were frozen in some kind of suspended animation, unable to do anything except stand back and watch as she rode by. Only then did the planet resume its customary rotation. That was what I felt the first time I saw Hilary Anson.

I remember that the chinstrap on her helmet was undone and flapped back and forth against her right shoulder. Her houndstooth riding jacket was unbuttoned, her necktie was loose, and she kept her weight back, deep in the saddle, not even bothering to post, just soaking up her horse's gait like a cowboy. She had a set of double reins dangling from just one hand, and the slack lengths of leather swung from side to side in time to the cadence of her horse's stride. Her riding boots were kicked out in front of her, and her feet were at home in the stirrups. She'd have been thrown out of any decent equitation class, no questions asked.

Oh, and about the gun, the Russian-built Makarov pistol that Hilary kept about her at all times. I know it was real because I saw it — she damned well pointed it at me — and also because of certain subsequent events pertaining to its use. But I don't know if it was truly given to her by Nelson Mandela, despite her insistence that it was. On the other hand, I have read that Mandela once possessed such a weapon, apparently a gift from Haile Selassie, the Emperor of Ethiopia. From what I understand, the gun is thought to be buried beneath a house in a suburb of Johannesburg, but it has never been found. Could it be that the mystery of Nelson Mandela's missing weapon actually has its solution in a storage facility maintained by the Ontario Provincial Police, somewhere in southern Ontario? Because that's where the Makarov is kept now. I know this for a fact. I also know that Quinton Vasco is dead and that he was shot with that same gun. And I know about those two giant howitzers — the GC-45s — hidden in the sugar bush north of Number Four Sideroad. They would later provide the focus for a major investigative series published by the *Toronto Star*, but I was aware of their existence long before it became public knowledge. Although I don't know everything, I do know a lot.

But I digress, as they say.

On that morning when I first saw her, this far-fetched creature from South Africa reached up with her right hand, clutching an uncoiled hunting whip. She looped the thong into the air, brought her arm down fast. The lash gave an unholy crack, and Club Soda first let out with a start and then raised his spine and unleashed a buck that looked spring-loaded. Hilary Anson just laughed. She absorbed the sudden commotion with the grip of her legs and the arch of her back. She barely moved in the saddle.

Colonel Barker said nothing, just glared straight ahead with his one good eye. The other eye was covered by a black patch, which gave him the appearance of a pirate who has lately joined the landed gentry. The colonel didn't even glance at Charlotte or me as he and Hilary Anson rode right past us and directly around to the kennel.

Charlotte and I remained by the stable entrance, keeping our horses as still as we could. We nodded politely and called, "Good morning," as Tiff McDermott, the huntsman, rode out on his imposing black mare, with the cub hounds swirling and careening all around him.

"Morning!" Tiff called out. "Morning all!"

A minute later, we were off.

I didn't see much of Hilary Anson the rest of that day, or what I did see was from a distance. She was serving as the whipper-in and was constantly busy, working the hounds up ahead, along with Tiff McDermott. As usual, Colonel Barker acted as the field master, keeping the other riders together and out of Tiff's way.

Several times that morning, some sudden movement would catch my eye. From somewhere off to one side, I would see that big chestnut of Colonel Barker's sailing into view with Hilary Anson aboard. They'd fly over another wall of fieldstones topped by split rails, she with just one hand on the reins. In the other, she brandished her hunting whip. The instant Club Soda landed, she peeled him off and away. "Get on to him!" she cried out in a glottal, sing-song warble. "Get on to him!" As whipper-in, it was her job to keep those maniac cub hounds in order.

Stiff-backed and stately on his noble black mare, Tiff McDermott trotted ahead in the distance, surrounded by the gambolling hounds. He chirped out short blasts on his horn.

It is no exaggeration to say that the ensuing months of that long-ago summer have determined the course of my life ever since. Sam Mitchell's my name, and here I am — a twice-divorced English professor, childless, tottering on my game hip through a cavernous house, sparsely furnished, on a narrow one-way street in Syracuse.

I sometimes wish I could refashion those three summer months into an endless loop that would play on forever. Hilary, Hilary, Hilary. But I can't. The summer ended, and she disappeared like Cinderella at the stroke of midnight.

Except, of course, she was no Cinderella — God knows she was not — unless your idea of Cinderella is a sexually abused teenage girl with masochistic tendencies who smokes, drinks, swears, and leads men astray by the dozen, married or single, while also packing a gun. She rode like an angel, though, if angels could ride. That's one thing I learned from her, for all the good it ever did me. I haven't sat a horse in thirty years, not since that summer at age fifteen, when I fell in love with Hilary Anson.

That summer is the reason I finally lit out for South Africa myself. I needed to learn what had become of her. I needed to discover what I could about her backstory, a term we in the literature

game are wont to use. God knows she'd been maddeningly inscrut-
able that summer in Kelso. One moment she would stun me with
some outlandish revelation. The next moment she'd clamp her
mouth shut, refusing to utter another word. Still, over time, she
did divulge the rough outlines of her private chronicle — the events
that eventually brought her to Canada. A scandal was what it was, a
messy, sordid affair that ended in cold-blooded murder, and Hilary
had been right there in the thick of it.

Never mind that she herself was innocent, a victim of abuse
and injustice, of terrible, unlawful deeds. People in South Africa
did not seem to care about that — white people, anyway — and
so she had come to Canada. She told me she'd been banished by
her own flesh and blood, her own father. It was expected that she
would remain until the scandal died down.

I was able to learn this much and even somewhat more, enough
to know that hers was among the sorriest tales I had ever heard. The
name of the dead man was Muletsi Dadla, who'd been her companion and soulmate. That was before he was shot twice in the head
while trying to escape the country by fording the swollen waters
of the Tsoelike River on horseback, something only a fool would
attempt — a fool or a desperate man. From what Hilary told me,
the villain of the tale was a certain individual named Jack Tanner.
He was a tough, mean-spirited cockney, and a pedophile to boot,
who worked as the stable manager at her father's farm. It was he
who shot Muletsi Dadla and then pushed his lifeless body into the
rushing waters of the Tsoelike. What was more, he got off scot-free.
You could do that in South Africa — murder a man and walk away.

This, at least, was the account that Hilary related to me, and
I had no reason to doubt it, no reason to suspect it might not be
true in every last detail. After all, there had to be some reason she'd
pitched up in Canada, and her explanation made sense to me. She
told me she was expected to change her reckless ways, something

that might be possible in a country as peaceful and righteous as Canada. This was the hope, anyway, and it wasn't wholly misplaced. But in Hilary's case, the cure somehow failed to take effect. Try as she might, she could not shake her sinful reputation. People who knew nothing of the matter still held her to blame for what they saw as her deplorable ways. They didn't know the truth. They had no idea what she had been through. Her own boyfriend shot and killed before her very eyes. Murdered by the man who had tormented her since she'd been a child. Who wouldn't go astray after something like that? If only people knew the truth, they might have given her a decent shake.

Or maybe not. Maybe there was no escape. Maybe the taint of outrage would have clung to that girl no matter what she did, or where she went, or what other people knew or thought they knew. That's the way scandal seems to work. It gets into your pores and then your bones and can't be washed away. It goes with you everywhere.

As for me, the stain of long-ago scandal is not what I most vividly recall when I think of Hilary Anson now, as I often do, as I likely always will. Instead, I remember those three indelible months in Kelso in 1963, a season in my life when suddenly anything seemed possible — anything at all — a season that began with that fox hunt in late spring, when I first set eyes on the South African girl.

The rest of us riders stayed well out of the way while she and Club Soda raced ahead, back and forth, zigzagged hither and yon, splashing or galloping through ponds and copses, flying over split-rail oxers, gathering up stray hounds and chasing them back to the main pack. Club Soda was drenched with sweat, lathered and muddy. Veils of steam swirled around him whenever he and Hilary Anson paused. But that was only for an instant. Almost immediately, she would nudge her heels against his coppery flanks and, just like that, he would burst again into a gallop, and they were gone.

"THEY SAY SHE'S AN absolute terror." My mother set her drink down on the kitchen counter and untied her apron. "Deirdre Barker is at her wit's end. No one can control the girl. Drinking. Smoking. Boys. And I don't know what else." She looked at my father, who was using a dishtowel to rub water stains from the highball glasses. "Hal . . .?"

"Yes, Mary?"

"Did you hear what I said?"

"Yes. Drinking. Smoking. The Anson girl."

"Girl is right. She's only eighteen, I'm told. Is this the way all children are brought up in South Africa?"

"I don't think all. At least, not according to my understanding. There are certain exceptions."

"Well, I can't say I'm very impressed. Poor Deirdre. She was on the telephone for hours today, telling me about it. She — *Sam!* Put that back! How many times do I have to tell you?"

I pulled my hand back from a plate of canapés — oysters or pink shrimp on small rounds of Melba toast. It was Saturday evening, a week after the hunt with Hilary Anson, and company was expected, including the Barkers. I rested my elbows on the stout wooden bar overlooking the kitchen.

"She's ebullient," I said. It was a new word that I was trying out. "Hilary Anson. I think she's ebullient."

"Ebullient!" My mother snorted. "That's not my idea of ebullient. Not by a long shot."

"Well, anyway, she can ride. You should have seen her. Even Major Duval says so." He was a former Belgian cavalry officer who taught us equitation each Sunday at the club. I made a not-very-successful attempt to mimic the major's nasal French accent. "She ride zat horse like a shenius. If I 'ad not see it wiz my own eyes, I would never 'ave believe it."

"Well, riding isn't everything." My mother tapped the side of her drink with fingernails lacquered in burgundy.

Maybe not, but it was certainly something. I had overheard the major talking to some of the parents after riding lessons at the club that week. He was saying that Hilary Anson's apparent wildness in the saddle was an illusion. In fact, she knew exactly what she was doing and was in constant communion with her horse. Normally a careless — even dangerous — jumper, Club Soda suddenly became sensible and deliberate with Hilary Anson aboard. It was a rare thing, he'd said, that kind of subtle, precise communication between horse and rider. It was certainly a gift. It couldn't be taught.

I shrugged and looked down at the canapés. I liked the shrimp ones best.

"Oh, all right. You can have one." My mother swallowed the last of her preparatory Scotch and soda. She asked my father for another — the secondary preparatory.

The guests started to show up at seven thirty, and the house was gradually transformed into a whirl and hubbub of cigarette smoke, buzzing voices, groans, clinking glasses, and peals of sudden laughter. Charlotte made a brief appearance and then waltzed back upstairs to watch TV in our parents' bedroom. I stayed downstairs.

I liked to observe the adults as they drank and made jokes and put their heads back in that strangely festive way. I watched the proceedings from the kitchen counter or wandered through the rooms, collecting empty glasses or spilling water into ashtrays from a highball glass, to make sure the cigarettes were out.

Colonel Barker and his wife were late arrivals — and they brought Hilary Anson.

She marched straight over to stand beside me near the bar. "Howzit?" she said. "My name's Hilary. What's yours?"

"Sam," I said.

She pursed her lips from side to side, as if testing the effect of my name on her palate. Then she shrugged. "Shame. There's no one here under fifty."

"Forty," I said. "My mum and dad are both around forty, I think."

"Hmm."

She wore a tasselled brown leather vest over a blue turtleneck jersey and a short denim skirt. Her thick slate-black hair was brushed back in several waves that framed her face, oval with high cheekbones. She was wearing pale-red lipstick, her eyes were preternaturally blue, and she was easily the most smashing girl I had ever seen. Or heard. She spoke with a breathy, emphatic intonation, at once singsongy and clipped, much more interesting than our flat, central Canadian drone.

"Ag, I could kill for a smoke," she said and popped an oyster on Melba toast into her mouth, followed by another. "Where's the loo, hey?" She looked at me and swallowed.

"There's three."

"Right. Where are they?"

"There's one over —"

"Shush. Don't point. Which one's yours?"

"It's upstairs. It's —"

"Don't tell me. Show me. Come." She looked around, once over each shoulder, like a spy embarking on a secret mission. "But, first, a drink."

Not a drink, it turned out. Drinks. Hilary snuck them from the bar — two for her, two for me. She handed me a pair of highball glasses, and I led the way upstairs, past my parents' bedroom, where Charlotte was perched cross-legged on the bed, bathed in milky, bluish light, transfixed by the TV screen. I walked partway down the hall and stopped.

"It's in there," I said and motioned with my arm.

"Don't point. It's not polite."

Hilary strode ahead into the bathroom and flicked on the light with her elbow, somehow knowing instinctively the location of the switch. She turned around.

"Hey …?" she said. "Aren't you coming in?" She raised one of her glasses. "I hate to drink alone."

I looked around, as if someone might be watching. No one was, so I shrugged and shuffled into the bathroom. Hilary closed and locked the door behind me, swayed over to the bathtub, set down her drinks on the rim, and lowered the lid of the toilet. She sat down and nodded at the edge of the ceramic tub. "You can sit there."

I eased myself over and huddled on the side of the tub, my knees about six inches from Hilary's.

"Here." She took one of my drinks and set it on the floor, along with one of hers. "Now, a toast." She raised her other glass. "To equality and strong drink!" She clinked her glass against mine, took a gulp, and grimaced. "Yechhh. Scotch and Coke." She shivered, shaking her head. "Tastes vile — but at least it doesn't look suspicious."

I glanced at my drink. I glanced at her. "I'm not supposed to drink alcohol," I said.

She rolled her eyes. "*Obviously.* That's why there's Coke in it. No one will know."

"That's not what I mean. I mean I'm not supposed to drink alcohol."

For a while, she stared at me without speaking. It was as if she had just discovered a new sort of primate, a species that had never been encountered or even imagined before. Then she nodded. "I see." She took my drink and set it on the tiled floor. "All the more for me."

I closed my eyes. Idiot. Moron. I opened my eyes again. "Maybe just a sip?"

"Attaboy, tiger." She retrieved my drink and handed it to me. She raised her own. "Chin-chin."

I clinked my glass against Hilary's and then raised it to my lips. I let a little of the liquid pool at my throat and then swallowed. It was sort of sweet and bitter at the same time — not good, but not terrible, either. I took another sip.

"Easy does it, my boykie. I poured it quite strong."

She took a good-sized swallow herself and then narrowed her eyes, peering straight at me, as if plotting her next move. She set her glass on the bathtub's ledge and started poking around in her leather shoulder bag. She pulled out a package of Rothmans and a booklet of matches. She made quite a business of lighting up, then closed her eyes and blew out three perfect smoke rings. One. Two. Three. She opened her eyes and smiled.

"I can only do that as long as I'm not looking. Don't know why." She tapped a bit of ash into the bathtub. "Ag. All those grown-ups. I can't stand them."

I took another sip of my drink. Not half bad, in fact. "Me, either," I said.

"Kindred spirits." She clenched her cigarette between her teeth and reached back into her shoulder bag, which now slumped on the floor. "Here, I've got something to show you."

This time she produced, of all things, a handgun. She pointed it straight at me.

"Bang!" she said.

"Whoa!" I must have ducked or done a double take, the way comedians do on TV. I had never seen a gun in my life, or not up close — not a real, actual gun. And, just as surely, no one had ever pointed any kind of gun at me. At once, my heart was racing. "Is that real?"

"Yebo."

"Why do you have a gun?"

She shrugged, turning the weapon over in her hands. "Protection. Why do you think?"

"Is it loaded?"

She squinted at me as if it had just occurred to her that I might not be in full command of my mental faculties. "Is it *loaded* …?" she said. "No, no. Of course not. I always wander around with a gun that isn't loaded. I like the way it goes with my hair." She tilted her head. "Are you serious?"

"I don't know. It's just that I've never seen a gun before, not in person. They're banned in this house, even toy guns." I took another mouthful of my Scotch and Coke. "What kind is it?"

"Makarov. Russian-built. All the Soviet police have one."

"Can I hold it?"

She shook her head. "Not on your life, soldier. The man who gave it to me is Nelson Mandela, and he made me promise never to let it out of my possession except in circumstances most dire. His words exactly. It's my duty to the cause."

"Who's Nelson Mandela?"

She closed her eyes and blew another trio of smoke rings into the air. She opened her eyes again and looked at me. "One day, my boykie, you will want to strangle yourself for asking me that." She clutched at her throat with one hand and pretended to gag. "Mark my words. Next question."

I asked what cause she was talking about.

"What *cause* ...?" Hilary smiled. "Ah, well. That I can explain." She reached into her shoulder bag again. This time she produced a dog-eared paperback book and held it out to show me. The title was *Cry, the Beloved Country.* "Alan Paton. Ever heard of him?"

I shook my head.

She riffled the pages. "Well, prepare yourself, my boykie. You're about to be transported."

She took another puff of her cigarette and began to read aloud. Almost at once, I felt my back grow rigid and then give way as a shiver ran up my spine. It was the slow, dignified tempo of the words. They gripped me from the first sentence — the rhythm itself plus the effect of Hilary's voice. She read in the mournful tone someone might use at a funeral to talk about some great person who had died. She continued reading until our drinks were emptied. Then she smoked another cigarette and read some more.

Later that night, after the guests had departed and I had gone to bed, I heard my mother totter along the hall in her high heels. She knocked at my door and edged it open.

"You awake?" she said. She was holding a drink in one hand and an earring in the other, massaging her earlobe.

"Yebo ... I mean, yup."

I raised myself against the pillows and let a book flop, still open, at my side — a biography of Sir Isaac Newton. Just now, I was feeling a bit queasy from the drinks. I looked up at my mother.

"I was reading," I said.

She nodded and stepped into the room. She perched herself on the bed, close to my knees.

"Sam ..."

"Yes, Mum."

"I have a question for you."

"Okay."

She shifted her weight. "You … you would never hurt a girl, would you?"

"Sorry … what …?"

"*Pardon.* I beg your pardon. You know. A girl. You would never hurt a …?" She hesitated. "Do I smell alcohol? Have you been drinking?"

"No."

"Oh." She shrugged. "Anyway, as I was saying, you would never hurt a girl, would you?"

"You mean like — hit her?" What had Charlotte been saying?

My mother tilted her head and pursed her lips. "No. I mean, more like —" She broke off, with a shake of her shoulders. "Oh, I don't know. Some of the women downstairs were talking. Boys will be boys, they say." She seemed to fix her gaze on my book, the one about Sir Isaac Newton, but I didn't think she was really looking at it. "I just want to say, Sam, that if you ever do hurt a girl — if you ever — then just don't come looking for help from me."

I waited, expecting her to add something more, but she didn't.

"Okay, Mum. I won't."

She'd had too many penultimates again, as my father called them. You had preparatories, then warriors, then ceremonials, then penultimates, and finally ornamentals.

"You don't have to worry, Mum. I promise."

She nodded and straightened her shoulders. There. Mission accomplished. "Well, then," she said. "That's all I have to say."

"Okay. Good night."

"Good night, honey. Lights out now." She squeezed my arm, stood up, and wobbled out of the room.

I marked my place in the book and slid it under the pillow then switched off the light. For a time I lay motionless in my bed, gazing up at the stucco swirls on the ceiling, barely visible in the near-darkness. I was thinking of Hilary, her voice, and the passages she had read from that novel, *Cry, the Beloved Country.* The high rhythm of its language reminded me of tales from the Bible that I had read, marvelling at their power, their lofty grace — the words bequeathed by God. I had never before imagined that a mere human could approach that magnificence, and yet this South African writer named Alan Paton had surely done so. It was strange to think that a man could summon such words and fashion them in such a way. Already, I sensed the world around me shifting, reshaping itself, the way tectonic plates drive skyward, forming mountains where once there had been only plains. I pulled the covers up around my shoulders and rolled onto my side. My last thought was of Hilary Anson. She was holding a Russian-made gun, a gift from someone named Mandela, and she was pointing it right at me.

THREE

Jack
South Africa, Winter 1962

WHEN JACK TANNER LOOKED back on all that happened and all that went wrong, he could specify the exact day — in fact, the exact effing hour — when the earth began to shudder and the sky commenced to fall. Granted, he hadn't recognized it at the time, but later he saw it clear.

It wasn't the kaffir. It was the girl. It had been the girl all along.

Of course, that wasn't what he told Daniel Anson, the girl's father. It wasn't what he told himself, not at first. What he told the girl's father, along with anyone else who asked, was that it was the kaffir who had caused it all. The shame. The scandal. The physical harm. This was easy enough to say because it was close enough to being true, or so it was by a certain way of thinking. But, in his heart, Jack understood that the kaffir had only been taking advantage of a rent already torn. Truth was, the trouble had got started even before the boy showed his goggle-eyed visage around Daniel Anson's farm. Of course, it wasn't long before he did pitch up — and then everything went straight to effing hell.

But first, the beginning: the time when Jack should have noticed, but didn't quite, that his fortunes were headed off the rails.

It had been late in the afternoon on a Sunday, and he had been about to tend to the feeding of the horses, a chore handled other days by the stable hands, but Sunday was their day off, so Jack chipped in. He was the stable manager at Daniel Anson's farm, but he didn't mind dirtying his hands now and then. Besides, he liked to see the horses content. He liked to be the source of their contentment. All it took was a flake or two of dampened hay in each stall and a quart or so of grain in each bin, with a chopped-up apple and maybe a tot of molasses added as a treat. That did the job.

Jack sometimes wished that people could be as straightforward as horses — but, no, not even close. Even a man of mature understanding, a man such as himself, could sometimes be flummoxed by the ways of the human species.

And so it was that time with Hilly. She marched into the barn alone. Obviously, she'd picked the moment, an hour when there would be no one else about. Just him. Just her. He heard the swish and click of her approaching footsteps, and he looked up.

"Hey," she said, not bothering to utter his name, not even bothering to issue more than a word of proper greeting. Then she just blurted it out, the thing she must have thought needed saying.

"I'm telling my father," she said, her voice strained. Nerves, probably. "It's over."

Jack eased the wooden lid of the grain bin back into place and dusted off the palms of his hands. All right, then. He'd attend to the feeding later. He turned, slow and easy, to look at her. She was wearing blue dungarees and a dark anorak, and she had some kind of woollen band pulled over her forehead, something he hadn't seen her wear before. Navy blue, it was, very striking against her raven hair. Matched her eyes, those deep pools of sapphire. What he noticed next was that her complexion was high. Nerves, no doubt about it. The blood, racing.

"Over …?" He shook his head. "I don't think that's the case. I think you'd be sorry if that was so. I think you'd regret it." He took a step in her direction. Pleading didn't work any longer. Might have to take a harder line.

"Are you threatening me?"

"Now, now," he said. "Hilly."

"Hilary."

"Ah."

"I don't want you to touch me, not ever. Not ever again. I want you to leave."

"It's feeding time. I was about to feed the horses."

"I don't mean leave the stable. I mean leave here. Quit. Go."

"Where would I go?" Interesting — she'd stopped saying anything about telling her dad.

"I don't care. Anywhere you want. Just away. It's over."

"Over? What's over?" He ran a hand through his hair and took another stride toward her. Slow. One step at a time.

"Please. Just leave."

"Hilly …"

"Let me go."

"Just this once. Can't see no harm in that. Just once more."

"I said, let go! I said —"

She turned and darted away, ran straight out of the barn, a thing she had never done before. Jack stood his ground and watched her go. Something had surely changed, and he wondered what it was. Strange that he wasn't sure. With Hilly, he sometimes thought he knew all there was to know, knew her better than she knew herself. Now he wasn't certain. But that was all right. He was not a man to rush matters. He knew there were times when it was better to stand down and keep your trap shut. Let troubles tend to themselves. There'd be a cooling out. He knew that. Still, he had a feeling she would come around in time. She was a good girl, all in all. But something had changed. He knew that, and it bothered him. There was nothing for it, though, but to go back to work, back to feeding the horses.

He didn't appreciate it at the time, but later he would remember that tussle. There. Right effing there. That was where it began, and it only got worse — far, far worse — when that bloody kaffir got involved, when it came to blows. Later, much later, after his smashed-in cheekbone had partway healed, Jack marched straight up to see Mr. Anson himself, knocked on the door at the main house, tweed cap in hand. The big man was summoned to the entrance, and straightaway Jack offered to take his leave, no hard feelings, just finished and done. He was that cut up about it. He confessed he should have known all along what was happening between Mr. Anson's daughter and that kaffir swine. By a certain way of thinking, it was indirectly his fault, what took place. After all, he was the one who'd hired the boy.

Daniel Anson nodded, his eyes glistening, his shoulders slumped. He told Jack not to punish himself. One man could not be blamed for another man's sins. Life brings its burdens and its pains. You endure them. You move on. That was what Jack should do. That was what he, Daniel Anson, proposed to do. It was out of their hands now. Jack nodded and narrowed his eyes in what he hoped would be taken as a display of sympathy — sympathy and remorse.

"All right, Jack," said Daniel Anson. He stepped back and closed the big door of the main house, never having invited his stable manager inside. Never had. Never would.

Jack replaced his cap. He turned and trudged in his rubber boots down the verandah steps, past the lunatic peacocks, across the unkempt green lawn, and along the macadam lane that ran by the poplar windbreak. He kept on walking till he reached the stables, and there, after a bit of aimless bustling about, he plunked himself in the tack room with a glass of Glenmorangie cradled in his hand. Drank it down. Straightaway poured himself another. Drank it down, too. From that day on, he'd swear to anyone who would listen that Daniel Anson was the finest man he'd ever had the privilege to know. Anyway, those were the words he used. Let no one say that old Jack Tanner was in any doubt as to which side his bread was buttered upon.

And the truth was that Jack did take some comfort from what the big man had said, to wit: that he, Jack Tanner, could not be blamed for what ensued. He liked to think it was precisely so. But, looking back, he could see plenty of signs that should have aroused his suspicions, long before any of them had. For example, the garish way the boy behaved with Mr. Anson's daughter. Damned kaffir. Why, he sometimes looked her straight in the eyes, and he talked to her without first being talked to. Cocky was what it was. Bold. It was a dead giveaway, or it should have been. An African that gets stroppy with a white man — well, that is one thing. To a point, you can tolerate it. But with a woman, it's different. You'd never know where that might lead. And yet Jack hadn't seen it. It would only be later, too late, that he would detect for a certainty what had been right square in front of his eyes all along.

Something had got started between those two, something you maybe couldn't put a name to or a finger on — not at first — but something just the same. And who could be surprised? That Hilly was a fine piece of work. Young and fancy, all that shiny black hair, and that long slim shape, not a woman's shape but a kind of stripped-down version of a woman's shape. It had an excitement all its own. She'd been maybe fourteen or so when things with Jack had first got underway.

Well, thirteen, come to think of it.

Twelve, to be honest.

"Please, Hilly," he would say when the time came, when he couldn't keep the monster down. "Please, just this once. Hil."

And she obliged — maybe not at the instant of the asking, maybe not with the alacrity he'd have liked to observe. But that was no cause for complaint, long as everything totted up square in the end. And so it did. She got something out of it. He got something, too. Where was the harm in that? You never get anything free in this life. You get only what you pay for, and he'd paid for this, invested everything, his livelihood, maybe even his life. Just think of the risk he was taking — and all for her. She owed him something in return. That was what he told her, as many times as she needed telling. Besides, he was the only one who understood her, who had ever understood her.

Twelve years old. That was her age when he first started forming some designs on her. Of course, she was away at school in Durban during the week, a boarding school. But she was home on most weekends and for the holidays at Christmas, which would be the very drear of winter in England, of course, but was near the fat of summer down here. Balmy, splendorous days. Plenty of time for riding out upon the broad green hills above Mooi River. That was where Hilly and he would go.

He called her Hilly. Hardly anyone else did. Maybe no one at all. They were a formal lot, the Ansons. Cold-like. Austere. Both their sons had grown up and gone off to add to their riches in the mining game, up in the Transvaal. So now there was just the one daughter, left on her own the bulk of the time. No one to talk to. Slump-shouldered on account of her early height. She warmed pretty quick to a man who said he understood her. Was her only friend. Called her Hilly.

Of course, he was not supposed to call her that. Miss Anson — that was the indicated nomenclature, as he was given to understand. But Hilly it was when they were out on their own. Hilly or Hil. And it didn't take Jack long to get things inclining his way. It isn't difficult at all, not with a twelve-year-old, not when you know what you are about. There's a knack to it, no denying that. And could be he had the knack. Could be that was part of the reason he left England in a mite of a rush, so soon after the war. Could be it went some distance toward explaining why he'd shortened his stay in Bulawayo, up in Southern Rhodesia. Could be. Mum's the word, though. Best to let those old dogs lie, for love is a ravenous beast that can turn on you in a flash. Eat you whole.

Besides, there was another lesson he had learned over the years. What works with a twelve-year-old won't likely work with a thirteen-year-old. And what works with a thirteen-year-old won't likely work another year on. And one dark morning you awake to discover that nothing will work at all.

As for the boy, well, that one was trouble. Trouble from the first light of morn. Jack should have seen it all along. It should not have come as a surprise. The boy was Xhosa, after all.

His name was Muletsi Dadla, and he hailed from Bruntville, the African township across the way. A township, they called it. A garbage heap was what it was. Pitiful. It was Jack himself who hired the lad, took him on to work as a groom at the Anson farm. He was twenty-two years old and a good-looking buck, good-looking for one of them. He had a strapping build and a coffee-coloured complexion, and he was fastidious about his appearance, which wasn't always the case with their kind, or so it was writ in the gospel according to Jack.

In addition, the boy wore a pair of horn-rimmed glasses with round lenses that gave him a strange scholarly air — strange considering he was from Bruntville, where few young men completed secondary school. With the females, it was even worse. But the boy had not only finished secondary, he'd gone to university, as well — the University of Fort Hare in the Eastern Cape, where the black people went, a chosen few. He'd studied English literature there. It was said he was the first person from Bruntville to achieve such a feat, acquiring a university degree.

To Jack, this was a good joke, the boy's famous scrap of paper. He'd heard all about it. English literature. Eastern Cape. Blah, blah, blah. He laughed each time the subject came up. No doubt some people considered him jealous, indignant that a black man was better educated than he. But Jack didn't give a fig about that. Not one effing fig. None.

"Name …?" Jack had said on the boy's first day. Damnedest names they had. He could never keep them straight.

"Muletsi Dadla, *baas*," the boy said. Or some such.

"Muletsi what …?" Jack shook his head and then sniggered in anticipation of what he was about to say. Had it all worked out. "Tell you what. Let's say I call you Hunt. Berkeley Hunt." It was rhyming slang for a lady's privates.

"Hunt, *baas*?"

"That's right." Jack could see the boy didn't get the connection, despite his alleged brains. Didn't have an effing clue. That made the joke all the better. Berkeley Hunt.

"All right, *baas*. If you say so."

"I do say so." Jack held out a manure fork. "Know what this is?" The boy said he did.

"And do you know what it's for?"

The boy nodded.

"Fine." Jack handed over the implement. "Get to it then. Can't stand here jaw-wagging all day." He sniggered again and said the boy's name aloud once more. "Berkeley Hunt."

The moniker stuck from the very first time it was used, or it did for Jack, who relived the joke all over again each time he said the name. The boy never cottoned on, which just goes to show how much a degree in English literature is worth on a horse farm outside Durban.

English degree be damned. What mattered was smarts, which Jack had aplenty while others came up short. Take these Africans.

They lived in a different world. A world apart. That was why it was called apartheid. Apartness was what it meant. Whites over here. Blacks over there. Not much in between.

Over here was Mooi River, where the white folk lived — in the town itself or in the surrounding terrain. This was horse country, and the people of the vicinity mostly owned big places, with houses meant to last, all surrounded by sprawling meadowland and dense woodlot. Meanwhile, the black folk lived over in Bruntville, as if on a different planet. That was the way it was.

It hadn't taken Jack long to learn the score. As a white man, you'd have to be pretty damned dense not to figure it out, and so he had, quick as you please. He'd come down from England after the war, when there was no work to be found at home, certainly not at the racetracks that had employed him in earlier times. Like a lot of former enlisted men, he first pitched up in Southern Rhodesia. Then he worked his way down to the republic and wound up here on the Indian Ocean side. Never regretted it for an instant. You could have Europe for a fiver, as far as he was concerned, and he'd throw in England for free, as a bonus. That was all she was worth. But this here, this was Africa. God's country. "Come on, Berkeley, put some shoulder into it. Like this. See? Make that coat shine. Put your English literature to work. Fat lot of good it will do you here."

These words were meant to be insulting, but the boy seemed unperturbed. He shambled about, kept his head down, always did as he was told. He must have had his reasons for that, his reasons for being here, working as a groom in the stables belonging to Daniel Anson, a powerful businessman and a parliamentarian to boot, a minister in the government of Hendrik Verwoerd. Daniel Anson was the minister responsible for national security matters, which got Jack Tanner thinking. Was it beyond the wits of the ANC to put a spy among Daniel Anson's servants? The ANC — that was the African National Congress, a plague of communists and malcontents who were stirring up trouble in the land. If they were smart, that was exactly what they would do, sneak a spy onto Daniel Anson's hired staff. Jack sometimes wondered who it might be. On the other hand, who ever said the ANC was smart?

One thing he did know was that most of the blacks here in Natal were not apt to be troublesome, unlike the kaffirs you found up in the Transvaal or down at the Cape. Here in Natal, you had Zulus, and they were all right. They were warriors, yes. That was their history. But they warred against black, not against white. And there was none of this communistic nonsense, either. No, man. They weren't so bad, the Zulus. At least they knew their place. A rand's work for a rand's pay. *Tankie, baas.* And off they'd go. Drink corn brew all weekend. Stumble back to work on Monday, flat broke again, of course. Pitiful. But at least you knew where you stood with Zulus.

But this Berkeley Hunt — he was a shifty-eyed bugger and a Xhosa to boot, not a Zulu at all. Still, looking back, Jack could see that the trouble had really got started even before the kaffir stuck his foot in things. It had all got underway that sorry Sunday evening, when Hilly first pitched up in the stables to blather about telling her pa. It wasn't the kaffir. It was the girl.

It had been the girl all along.

FOUR

Sam
Ontario, Summer 1963

BY MID-JUNE, THE rumours about Hilary Anson had spread throughout Kelso. There wasn't much she wouldn't sink to, it was said. Booze. Cigarettes. Not to mention half the single men in three different towns. Soon she'd be getting started on the married ones, it was said.

Already she'd become a sort of local celebrity, if only because she was talked about. As a result, her laughter seemed louder, more raucous, her manner more jarring, her behaviour more brash. Everything she did seemed magnified now and served only as further confirmation of the rumours swirling in the background. There she was, Hilary Anson in the flesh, laughing too loudly as she swung herself up onto Club Soda once again — so it must all be true. It was as if she could refute the gossip only by ceasing to exist. Show your face, and you're done.

Meanwhile, the spring hunts were over, but the combined-eventing season was just about to begin. I was determined to earn a place on the preliminary-level team from Kelso that would compete in the provincial championships in Cardenden at the end of August. Granted, no one expected me to qualify. People thought I lacked backbone, I wasn't gritty enough, and Della was too delicate and poky. I meant to prove them wrong. That was my goal for the summer.

As a result, I spent much of each day training Della for the trials ahead. I was up at five thirty each morning for road and field conditioning. It was still dark at that hour, but soon enough the light broke over the rolling hills and the tall maple thickets, already decorated with the lime spray of new leaves. A sharp breeze shifted the branches, and the first rays of sunshine flashed against anything that contained water — glinting from marshes, popping like flashbulbs from puddles in the road, glancing against the trickle of streams. Sometimes the mist hung so low above the fields that I could lift my head into a floating cloud simply by rising from the saddle and arching my back. One moment I'd be cantering Della along a path worn into the edge of a newly ploughed field. A moment later my face would be pressed against the pale, roseate splash of oblivion.

After that, there was more work to be done — the cooling out and sponging off, followed by a long walk on a halter and shank until Della's coat had dried, and then a rubdown for her legs with Absorbine Senior. The liniment always left my hands cold and tingling. I mucked out the stalls or cleaned tack, with the barn radio tuned to CKEY. That spring, my favourite song was "Up on the Roof," by the Drifters. Back in the house I had a bath, brushed my teeth, and dressed for the day. I gulped down my breakfast and then raced out the door. My father drove us both to school, Charlotte and me, first to Alyth and then to Hatton, before heading south to Evanton, where he had a legal practice of his own, specializing in real estate deals.

In the afternoons, after school, I worked on dressage exercises or schooled Della over fences in the paddock. On Sundays there were riding lessons at the hunt club with Major Duval, a special round of instruction meant only for the team hopefuls. There were to be three riders on the preliminary-level squad and two at the intermediate level. High above everyone else loomed Lisa D'Angelo, the club's only advanced-level rider.

Finally, there was Hilary Anson. I heard rumours she might be allowed to compete in the championships, too, and in the advanced section, but not as a representative of Kelso. Instead, if the authorities approved, she would ride for her own club — the Mooi River Equestrian Club. Mooi River was where she'd grown up, somewhere near Durban in South Africa. Whatever they thought of her morals, everyone agreed that she was a sensational rider.

I, however, was less than sensational — a lot less. This had long been apparent to me, and it became ever more evident, starting with the first of the summer's Sunday coaching sessions provided by Major Duval. This had been a disastrous affair, even worse than I had feared. When the episode was finally over, I set out with Della on the long ride home. I was in a foul mood. It had seemed I could do nothing right. I had fumbled with the reins, slumped in the saddle, and interfered with Della, who hadn't exactly helped. She'd been sluggish and lazy, a tendency of hers. Together we'd made a mess of everything, and Major Duval had noticed. In fact, he singled me out — a custom of his. He had separated me from all the other riders and proceeded to dissect my abilities with alternating doses of sarcasm and scorn. He made me trace circles in the middle of the ring while he excoriated my posture, my hands, my seat. He pumped out his chest and raged at me in his throaty French accent. Did I genuinely think I had any hope of making the preliminary-level team? Riding like *zees*? Like a robot?

The other riders kept silent during the man's tirade. They trotted along the outer edge of the ring, kicking up waves of terracotta dust and saying nothing — everyone except Edwin Duval, who snickered after each of his father's remarks, just loudly enough for me to hear. He was a year older than I was, and he was both an idiot and a third-rate rider. But he had a magical horse, an American Saddlebred named Requiem, that moved with perpetual grace, barely needing a human on board. Requiem would jump anything. Would and did.

Later, as Della and I ambled toward home, I replayed the training session in my mind, over and over. My head burned with anger and humiliation. The season had barely begun, and already I was thinking that I should just give up. I wasn't getting better; I was getting worse.

Before long, I heard a drumming of hoofbeats approaching from behind. I shifted around in the saddle and saw Hilary Anson cantering along the shoulder of the road, headed in the same direction I was. She slowed her horse to a walk and drew alongside me.

"Want some company?" she said.

I just shrugged.

"What's wrong?"

The truth gushed out of me; I couldn't help it. When I was done recounting the worst of my ordeal, Hilary reached over and gave Della a swat on the neck.

"You know what?" she said. "I have an idea. I'm supposed to be working as a groom for Colonel Barker, but there really isn't that much to do. Maybe I can give you some help. What do you say?"

School was out for the summer, and I had plenty of time on my hands. I shrugged.

"I'll take that as a yes." She toussled Della's mane. "So. We'll get together tomorrow? Two o'clock?"

"Where?"

She gazed around. "Here?"

"All right."

"Done." She gathered her reins. "Oh — and bring your baggies, hey."

In an instant, she was off at a hand gallop, heading back the way she'd come, kicking up long bursts of gravel.

"My what ...?"

"Your bathing costume!" she shouted. She glanced over her shoulder. "Bring your bathing costume!"

HILARY LEANED FORWARD, STUBBED out her smoke in the clay pot. What was it, her twentieth of the day? She had to quit, an absolute must. Once again, she promised herself she would, just as soon as she'd sorted matters with Jack Tanner. She stood up, wandered over to the balcony railing.

It was nearly a week since she'd last spoken to him, since she'd put matters in what she thought was their final form, an ultimatum. Just to be on the safe side, she hadn't ventured anywhere near the stables since then. She wanted the finality of her absence to sink in — or, anyway, that was what she told herself. Maybe it was true. But if it were really true, then by now she'd have made good on her threat to speak to her father. Tell him everything. The whole ghastly tale. But she hadn't done it. She had never really intended to, despite what she'd told Jack. The truth was she was afraid of her dad. In some ways, she was.

That was no surprise, really. Daniel Anson was surely a formidable man, with a head the size of some large boulder, his brow riddled with worry lines. His greying hair was swept back across his scalp, and he wore at all times an expression of undifferentiated disdain, barely seeming to register anything that anyone else said or did. Still, everyone knew when he was about, for his voice boomed through the house. Even the rasp of his breathing could be heard in the next room. His presence seemed to agitate Hilary's mother especially. Each evening Sharon Anson ventured out onto the balcony adjoining her bedroom, wrapped in a nightgown and a blanket. Out there, she smoked a pair of cigarettes and put away a double shot of Scotch, neat, before retiring to bed. She did this to settle her nerves so she could sleep — a daily regimen that was the most her husband would grant.

Daniel Anson did not readily tolerate weakness in others and not at all in himself. He raged against the infirmity in his right leg, the result of a rugby injury in his youth. During that long-ago golden time, he had played for South Africa on the international stage, and his Springboks jersey was now mounted in a glass and mahogany case in his study on the second floor, along with the many other trophies accumulated during his sporting and business career. He'd made his fortune in mining. Each Christmas his gifts to family members consisted exclusively of gold coins. Hard value, not sentiment — that was the thing. Yet he had reserves of passion.

His great love now was for horses — the larger the better, for he required a sturdy beast to bear his weight. He insisted his mounts have legs like telephone posts and dray blood coursing in their veins, Clydesdale or Belgian or Percheron. Jack Tanner was under orders to remain on a constant lookout for just this kind of horse, for Hilary's father went through them at a hellish pace.

Hilary's heart quailed at the thought of coming clean with the man. Horses were one thing, and her father's affection for them was strong, but he betrayed no similar reserves of kindly feeling when it came to his female offspring — that is, to Hilary herself. For reasons she had never been able to fathom, her very presence seemed to cause him little but discomfort. Well, she wasn't a man;

possibly, it was as simple as that. Not that the reason mattered. Whatever the cause, the result was the same. It was a lie what she'd said to Jack. She wasn't going to tell her dad about what she had suffered these last few years. Not on your life. Not on anyone's. It might be different if she'd had someone to back her up, but there was no one. She wondered whether Jack knew that. Probably. He seemed to know everything.

Now she gazed off into the distance. Beneath her, and beyond the stables, the land pitched sharply away, swept down into the Mooi River valley and then rose again in the far distance, the panorama interrupted by scattered windbreaks of poplar trees and the dark-grey ribbons of narrow hardtop roads. The river known as the Mooi meandered through that broad trough of land, flashing silver here and there in the afternoon light.

Something in the foreground caught her eye — Jack Tanner, emerging from the barn, or not so much Jack Tanner himself as the horse he led on a leather shank, a majestic chestnut with a white blaze and three white stockings, a horse she hadn't seen before — a massive beast and a beautiful one. A big, dancing showboat. She watched as Jack guided the animal out to the paddock. Why hadn't she seen this creature before? Just now, the horse was in a bolshie mood; he sidestepped and skittered, tossed his head, reared around sideways, and tried to pull away. Once or twice, he lifted Jack clear off the ground.

Even from this distance, she could see what a beauty he was, this horse, and she could tell that he knew it, too. He was making a big spectacle just in case someone was watching. Get a load of me! She couldn't do much else. She pressed herself closer to the railing, fumbled for her smokes. Just look at the size of that horse. She knew he was a stallion — couldn't have been anything else. Jack was definitely having trouble holding him. At times, he had to let himself be dragged along, careful to keep his feet clear of those scattering hooves. Now and again, he dug in his boot heels and jerked back on the shank, but to little effect. This horse was too strong. When they reached the paddock, Jack swung the gate open, unclipped the shank, and let the beast loose.

At once, this chestnut demon arched his neck and surged forward at a bold trot. When he realized for certain he was free, he drew in his haunches, and released them in a fearsome buck, hooves flashing out behind him, his white stockings glinting in a spotlight of sunshine that beamed through a gap in the clouds. He shoved out one shoulder and cantered around to the left, halted, and broke into a canter the other way. He was a gorgeous piece of work; huge, yes, but wonderfully proportioned. He didn't have that mountainous bulk of many large horses. He looked fine and light. Just big. She wondered where this big handsome hullabaloo had come from. He was brand spanking new; she was certain of that. If not, she'd have seen him before. On the other hand, it wasn't so surprising that she hadn't. Her father was always buying new horses.

She forgot about lighting her smoke and instead shifted her gaze over to Jack Tanner, something she should have known better than to do. Habits. Old habits. He was walking back to the barn now, slapping the clip of the shank against the side of one of his rubber boots. At first, he didn't look up, and she thought maybe he didn't know he was being watched or by whom. But, of course, she was wrong there. You'd have thought that she would know better by now than to underestimate that man after everything he had put her through. You might think she'd have him sorted by now. But no. No, sir. Not by a long shot.

Sure enough, before he slipped beyond the stable entrance, Jack Tanner slowed, then halted. He turned and looked up at the house, shielding his eyes with his left hand. Even at this distance, she could tell what he was doing. He was looking at her, looking straight up at her. He didn't even need to cast his eyes around. He just directed his gaze upward and set it right square on you-know-who. He had known she was up here, known the whole frigging time. That was why he'd brought that big new horse out of the barn and let him loose in the paddock. Why else? What other purpose would it serve? He wanted her to see that horse. That horse was the bait. He knew she wouldn't be able to resist an animal such as that.

She shifted her gaze a notch and again peered at the beast in question as he darted back and forth in the paddock, neck arched like an emperor, tail hiked and feathering. He suddenly bolted straight for the high panel fence as if he was determined to lift off and sail clear over that barrier, only to jam his forelegs into the dirt, slither to a halt, turn, and gallop away.

She didn't need to look back at the barn now. She knew Jack Tanner was still there, still watching her. She could damned well feel the weight of his gaze on her skin, beneath her skin, in her bones. She knew, as well, that he would keep right on watching until she had returned to her chair and gathered her things and retreated into the house. So that was what she did.

"BECAUSE WE'RE GOING BATHING," she said. "That's why."

Hilary was riding Club Soda and wore a pale-blue T-shirt, faded blue jeans, and a pair of canvas running shoes — "takkies," as she would say. She also had a canvas backpack slung over her shoulders. She shifted the straps to rebalance the weight. That done, she gathered the reins and started east along Number Four Sideroad, heading for the old Colby place, where no one lived anymore. Quinton Vasco had bought them out.

I nudged Della into a jog to catch up. Swimming? Swimming where?

Soon we were striding at a brisk trot, two abreast, on a route that took us right past the Quinton Vasco estates — the most beautiful land in the county, hundreds of acres of sugar bush and grassy egg-carton hills bordered by a plunging rock-face escarpment, all of it fallow, all owned by a millionaire who refused to allow anyone to set foot on his property.

"Jerk," I said. "Thief."

"Beg pardon?" said Hilary.

I told her about Quinton Vasco, or at least what little I knew. He didn't even live in Kelso. It was said he lived in a town called

Letham, a good distance to the west. Meanwhile, he had purchased all this land, and now, because of these endless fences, no one else could go near it. Worse, he was buying up more land all the time. God knew what he had in mind. Real estate development — that was what people said. But so far there had been no sign of workmen or construction or anything of the sort. The land just stood there, fenced off and vacant, off limits to everyone. For decades that land had been available to all in the county, for walking, hacking, rock climbing — anything. Now the entire terrain was sealed off, and men in Mr. Vasco's pay routinely came out to scour the perimeter for trespassers. They carried walkie-talkies and, it was rumoured, guns. People said it would be worth your life to sneak onto Quinton Vasco's lands without first receiving permission, and there was no chance of obtaining that. Kelso had once been a kind of paradise. Now Quinton Vasco was destroying it.

"Shame," said Hilary, when I was done. "Surely he can't be as bad as all that."

"Worse," I said. "He's evil."

"Ag. Evil. Well, now I can relate."

In fact, I meant it. The man truly was evil, and I'm sure I wasn't alone in saying so. In Kelso County in those days, there were two kinds of people. There were those who'd lived here practically forever, working their farms or running small local businesses of one sort or another, in Alyth or in one of the other towns — a bakery, a dairy, a lumber mill, a hardware store. To these folk — people whose families had lived in this county for generations — the land was a birthright, a sort of shared heritage. True, it was mostly owned privately and, yes, the territory was marked off by fences. But those were normal fences. You could climb them. You could hike across that land. You could even traverse those acres on horseback, using wooden panels or stiles that had been constructed exactly for that purpose. But now Quinton Vasco had come along, and he was breaking all the old rules. He was preying on people's weaknesses, buying up viable farms and letting them rot in order to drive real estate prices down. Then he bought more land and built more fences. It was impossible to climb these fences, the ones that he was putting up. They were too damned big. They were meant to keep people out, full stop. Nothing could justify the existence of those fences, not if you'd lived here all your life, like your ancestors before you.

Lately, however, a different set of people had begun to settle in Kelso, professional people who had moved up from Toronto or other big towns. They were mostly well off, and the men commuted daily to their high-paying jobs back in the city. They purchased horses for their kids, renovated the old farmhouses they'd bought, and partied among themselves. There was no rule about that, about not socializing with the old rural stock. It was just the way things were. At first, the city folk resisted selling their properties to Quinton Vasco but, as prices started to decline, some of them began to panic and break ranks, or that was what I'd heard. I'd listened to my father talking about it on the phone, speaking to clients or colleagues of his.

As for my own family, we were an exception to the rule, bridging both of Kelso's two worlds. We Mitchells had lived here for gener-ations — my grandfather and my great-grandfather and maybe my great-great-grandfather before him. Farmers, all. But with my dad the tradition stopped in its tracks. He said, no sirree. No thanks. He saw small-time farming for what it was — a back-breaking ordeal with little pay and no security. So he went off to law school instead and later met my mother at some party in Toronto, where he was living at the time. By then he'd reinvented himself as a city boy but, still, the pull of the countryside was strong.

When my grandfather died, my father returned to Kelso with his bride, meaning to plot a new course. I was just a child then, and Charlotte could barely walk. My dad went straight to work. He tore out most of the interior walls in the old red-brick farmhouse. He put down a slate floor and lots of oriental rugs. He installed French doors and an open-concept kitchen. Then he got started on the barn, ripped out those old cattle-feeding rigs, and put in horse stalls instead, big boxy affairs. Pretty soon, he bought my sister a pony, and me a horse, and we were on our way — partly newcomers and partly old-time country folk. My father drove down to his office in Evanton each day and returned each evening, not a farm boy anymore, though not quite a squire.

Let's just say we had a split identity. But, when it came to the land, we weren't in any doubt at all. I wasn't, anyway. The land belonged to everyone. It was my grandfather who imparted this conviction, and he made me repeat it every time we visited in the years before his death. The land belonged to everyone. He called this the basic law of Kelso County, said he'd believed it all his days. I believed it, too. So, of course, I hated Quinton Vasco. Had to. What choice was there? I wasn't so sure about my own father, though. The basic law might have skipped a generation there.

Hilary and I slowed our horses to a walk. Just ahead, the gravel road plummeted beneath us, zigzagging down the face of the escarpment. We followed that steep, downhill route for a time, and then she swung Club Soda off to the right and followed a slender trail that snaked through the sugar bush, tracing the wall of the escarpment. I had ridden this way once or twice before, so I knew where the trail led — to a wide bench of rocky land set halfway down the descending wall. Once there had been a quarry works here, but the pits had been abandoned long ago. Pretty soon we reached the limestone banks of an old quarry pond, the largest of several. I was surprised Hilary had found this place so quickly, but I was to learn she had an explorer's instinct for discovery.

Now she called a halt, and we both dismounted. I had to duck behind a stand of cedar trees to change into my swimsuit. When I emerged, Hilary had already unsaddled both horses and was standing by a sandstone ledge, holding Club Soda and Della by the reins. She was wearing only her running shoes now and a navy-blue one-piece suit that she must have had on beneath her T-shirt and jeans. I noticed two features right away: the plump roundness of her breasts and the faint evidence of several pubic hairs slinking out of her swimsuit, down there. I looked away.

"Now what?" I said.

"Here ..." Hilary handed me Della's reins. She dug into her canvas backpack and produced a leather halter, then another, along with a pair of nylon shanks. She handed me one of the halters. "I brought a spare," she said. "Put it on in place of the bridle."

Already my heart was beating pretty hard. Partly, it was the being down here, alone in bathing suits, with Hilary Anson. At the same time, I had an anxious feeling about what was coming next — something to do with horses and deep water. I was not a strong swimmer, but I tried not to think about that. Instead, I held Della's reins and looped the nylon shank over her neck. Next, I unbuckled her noseband and throat latch, pulled the bridle over her ears and forelock and slid the snaffle bit from her teeth. She shook her head and tried to rub some of the itchiness out, pushing against my side.

"Hey, Della," I said. "Take it easy."

I slipped the halter on and snapped the throat latch to the side ring. Hilary was doing the same with Club Soda. I clipped one end of the shank to the offside ring on Della's halter, ran the shank over her neck, and knotted the far end to the near-side ring. The result — a crude set of reins.

When I looked up, Hilary had already vaulted onto Club Soda's back. She braced herself with her knees and long upper legs and then squeezed with her heels. At once, Club Soda clattered ahead, scrambled up onto a ledge of rust-coloured stone suspended a good four feet above the pond's sleek surface. I realized she meant to leap from the top of that rocky ledge, along with her horse, straight down into the water. But Club Soda wanted nothing to do with the plan. His ears were pinned back, and he gnashed at the air with his teeth. Hilary urged him on, but he did not obey, not at first. Instead, he settled his weight back onto his hind legs, bending his hocks, switching his tail, and even trembling a little. It was horse against rider — a battle of wills.

But Hilary didn't seem concerned in the least. She leaned forward and murmured to him with words I could not make out, just a lot of soothing mumbo-jumbo, probably. She stroked his neck and shoulders, and pretty soon she got him calmed down. He relaxed his stance and stopped quivering, anyway. The two of them remained motionless for a time, and then Hilary reached back with one hand. She squeezed her legs and gave Club Soda a slap on the rump, the gentlest contact you could imagine, and that was it. It was clear she had won him over. He took one stride forward, followed by another, and then a third. He lowered his stance just a little and then launched himself into the air, seeming to hang in place for an instant before dropping toward the flat, forest-green surface of the pond. Hilary's thick onyx hair flared behind her, there was a huge splash, and they both went straight under. I couldn't believe it. I jumped up onto the ledge and peered down.

Almost at that instant, Hilary and Club Soda broke into view again. Club Soda thrust out his head, horizontal, his jawline parallel to the surface of the pond, his ears darting back and forth like a pair of crazy metronomes. I had never seen anything quite so amazing. With only a few subtle moves, Hilary had completely reversed Club Soda's intentions, persuaded him to do something no horse had any business doing. Now his body remained submerged, with only his head visible above the water. He snorted and blew out through distended nostrils before surging through the shadows, bearing away from shore. A choker of wavelets churned at his neck, and

Hilary clung to his mane, floating behind, her legs outstretched in the translucent water.

"Whoo!" she shouted. "It's freezing!" Then she began to sing some song I didn't recognize — an African song, it sounded like. The lyrics were in a foreign tongue, strange sounding to me, and she didn't seem to know them all. She hummed and sang and started to laugh.

Club Soda swung around with what seemed to be a desperate look in his eyes, but that couldn't have been right because he didn't really appear to be in any hurry to get back to shore. He seemed perfectly at home, swimming in large loops and figure eights. Hilary guided him every now and then, pulling on one side of the shank or the other. She raised one arm and waved at me.

"Come on, Sam! Come on in!"

That took some doing. I wasn't even going to think of diving into the pond as Hilary and Club Soda had done. That was plainly nuts. Instead, using that same large slab of limestone as a mounting block, I climbed onto Della's back and guided her around to the opposite shore, where there was a grassy embankment and a gradual descent into the pond. I meant to head Della into the shallows near the bank, so that she could get her bearings before she ventured in deeper. But she wouldn't go in at all, just danced from side to side, refusing to move forward.

I looked over at Hilary and shook my head. "She doesn't want to."

"Yes, she does."

"No. I mean it. She doesn't. Look." I tried again to urge Della down the grassy bank and into the water. Again, she refused. "See? She just won't."

"Sam …" Hilary guided Club Soda closer to the shore. "There's no diplomatic way for me to tell you this. It isn't Della who doesn't want to go in the water."

I rolled my eyes. I knew what she was going to say. "You're going to say it's me. That's what Major Duval always says whenever something goes wrong."

"Well, I'm not Major Duval. I'm just saying you should try something different, hey. Don't try to make Della go into the water. Just let her."

It didn't happen right away. In fact, it took about fifteen minutes, maybe more. But eventually I managed to do what Hilary had said I should do, which was more or less nothing. I just let Della do as she wished, and it turned out that what she wished to do was hit the water at an eager trot and keep right on going until she was all the way in. Even then she didn't stop.

"She's swimming!" I shouted. "Look, she can swim! Wow. I can't believe it."

I clutched Della's mane with one hand as she struck out for the centre of the pond, where Club Soda and Hilary were already circling. Hilary waved us off.

"Not too close!" she said. "They'll tangle their legs."

That made sense. They could easily clip one another with their hooves. Using the shank, I steered Della off to the left, and she seemed to understand at once. I felt calm enough to start laughing, and only then did I fully register the temperature of the water.

"Yikes! It's freezing!"

"But it's divine."

It was also the best form of physical conditioning there was, or so Hilary said — far more effective than road- or fieldwork, with little of the strain. Just watch, she said. I'd see a difference in Della's fitness in only a week or so. But that wasn't the best thing, she said. The best thing was this: this being in the water with horses. Soon, Hilary began to croon once more, a strange, happy song. Later, when the swimming was done — when we were dressed and our horses were saddled once more — I asked her for its name.

"*Lalelani*," she said.

She told me the word means "listen" in Zulu. She confessed she didn't know all the lyrics, much less what they meant. But she had a book of songs that she had brought with her from South Africa — songs made famous by a singer named Miriam Makeba — and she was trying to learn them, one by one. She said she played them from time to time on an upright piano in the Barkers' living room. They reminded her of home. She hummed this particular melody once more. It might have been my imagination, but her voice seemed to break. She swallowed and shook her head, as if to get a grip on things, and then she clapped me on the back.

"Come on, hey," she said.

She turned and swung herself into the saddle, reined Club Soda around. She headed off the way we had come.

"Wait," I called out. I hurried to catch up. For a moment there I could have sworn she'd been about to cry.

"SOUTH WIND," SAID JACK. He glanced over his shoulder — so quick you'd barely notice — and then he smiled. "Name of this one's South Wind."

Hilary knew what he was thinking. He was thinking he'd been right, after all. Once she'd seen this horse, she would come straight down, or she would come soon enough. And here she was, just a day or so after he'd taken this big strapping beast out to the paddock on a shank. He'd known at the time that she was up at the house, out on the wooden terrace on the second floor. She was sure of it. He'd done his due diligence, as he always did. Now here she was. She stood at the entrance to the stable, reporting for duty as you might say. Again, he peered around at her.

"Southey," he said, "for short."

He leaned in so that South Wind would raise another of his hooves, permitting Jack to claw the muck out with the pick. He went around like that, till all four hooves were done. He rubbed the pick clean on his leather apron and tossed it back in the equipment box, wiped his hands on a towel. Everything just slow, methodical. He was being careful, she could tell. It seemed he was near to trembling himself.

She knew what he wanted, what he always wanted, times without number. She could almost feel the blood fizzing through his veins even now, could sense him trying to tamp the urges down. He fished a dandy brush out of the box and went back to this proud new horse, started up at the animal's neck on the offside — quick, clean strokes. Didn't look at her. Commenced to hum.

She advanced a step. "Can I take him out?"

She knew how he'd react to that. There now, he'd be thinking. There you are. She's said it already. Easy as pie. He moved down along South Wind's shoulder. She watched the coat shimmer in the morning light, the skin rippling beneath the strokes of Jack's dandy brush.

After a time, he shrugged. "This one here's your daddy's. You'll have to ask him."

"My da— I mean, my father. He's in Durban today."

He knew that, of course. A few strokes across Southey's withers, then along his back, down the croup. Jack didn't say anything more, started up his humming again.

She put out her arms. "Well, I can hardly ask him for permission if he's in Durban."

"Oh ...?" said Jack, pretending to be surprised. "You were wanting to take this fella out — today like?"

As if this weren't obvious. She knew what he was up to, bargaining for gain. They both knew it, which would be just fine in his book. In the gospel according to Jack Tanner, bargaining was just the job. It would get her mind working in the proper way. She understood that full well. She damned well should. She'd been down this road a hundred times, and now here she was, stumbling along the same old route again, barely a week after she'd sworn to break it off for good.

Jack tilted his head, all understanding and co-operation. "You'll be wanting to ride him today then?"

At first, she said nothing. Then she sighed, more in exasperation than anything else, knowing what this conversation meant — that old sinking feeling, all over again. "Yes. Today."

"Ah." He watched her from the corner of his eye.

She took another step inside the barn, shuffled over to the big wooden equipment box, took out a curry comb, started to pluck stray hairs from the teeth.

Jack was over on Southey's near side by now, looking at her. She could imagine what he saw — a young girl with her knees locked, pouting down at a curry comb, a spoiled young girl wanting to have her way.

She cleared her throat. "My father won't mind."

Jack clenched his teeth and whistled through them. "Won't he now? New horse he just bought, not a week ago? I don't know."

She didn't say anything at first. She just waited, and then she said the same thing again. "He won't mind."

Jack smiled because she was wrong there, as both of them knew. In fact, her father certainly would mind. He took a distinctly proprietary interest in things. He was liable to act as if he owned a thing that wasn't even his, if it suited him. She knew this, and Jack Tanner knew it, too.

She set down the curry comb. She nodded at South Wind. "What is he?" She meant his breeding.

"*Selle Français.*" Jack gave this strange new term a flat anglo pronunciation and a casual tone, as if it were a thing you came across every day, the same way he might say thoroughbred or Arabian or mention the colour of someone's skin. But this was different. *Selle Français.* He knew she wouldn't have heard of it.

"What's that?"

"Warmblood. From France. This here South Wind, he's one of the first ones to come down here. And he didn't come cheap — Lord knows, and your daddy does, too. Big animals, they are. Strong but graceful. Just look at him, would you?" Jack stood back and ran the dandy brush against the heel of his palm to clear the dust. He acted as if he were on a stage, as if this horse were the centrepiece of some grand production he alone had brought to fruition. Jack gestured at Southey with both his hands, inclined his head in the same direction. "He's a beauty, all right. Look at the legs on him. Like trees. Yet have you ever seen anything finer? Just look."

She couldn't stop looking. She didn't say anything, though. She just ran her eyes over this creature's sleek, strong legs, his elegant shape, his gorgeous lines. Then Jack said it, the thing they'd both been thinking. He said it slow and offhand, as if the words carried no more than their ordinary meaning, which wasn't the case at all.

"Course," he said, "your daddy don't need to know."

And she flinched. It was involuntary, just a little tightening of the shoulder muscles, not something she could control. But Jack would have seen it; she knew he would. He'd expected this, of course — hoped for it, anyway. She imagined he might be feeling something else, too. A species of dread. What if he'd gone too far? *Your daddy don't need to know.* Those same words — how many times had he used them with her before? How many understandings had he secured between them with just those words? Those words were like a covenant between them: she and Jack, agreeing to keep a secret from her father, betraying her own flesh and blood. That was the strongest card Jack had to play. Now he waited for her to respond, no doubt fearful that she might say nothing, that she might simply turn and march out of the barn. But she wasn't going to do that, not right now. Right now, she was going straight back to square one. Again.

She shoved one hand into the front pocket of her jeans, dug out two cubes of sugar. She walked over and offered them to Southey, who gobbled them both, nuzzling the palm of her hand with those big supple lips. She reached up with that same hand and stroked Southey's broad chestnut forehead, with its startling blaze.

"No," she said, her voice deliberate. She knew full well what she was saying, what it meant. "He doesn't need to know."

And she could sense some easing of tension in Jack. There you are, he was thinking. He'd been right, after all. This was the way it went — a good turn, a favour, another good turn. It was like a dance of some kind. Before long, you had the girl eating out of your hand. You just had to get her there, guide her into place. Step by step. Turn by turn. Stride by careful stride. Then pull the cinch, tight.

She understood it by now. Hell, she bloody well should. She'd been through it a hundred times — and, now, a hundred and one.

"All right," Jack said. "I'll saddle him up."

EIGHT

Sam
Ontario, Summer 1963

"HANG ON," SAID HILARY. "Look."

We pulled our horses up short. I followed Hilary's gaze, off to the right, where a pickup truck was turning off Number Four Sideroad. Normally the way was blocked by tall chain-link gates, secured by a sturdy-looking padlock. But now the gates were open. The vehicle lurched inside, then rocked and tottered along a rough access route that meandered upward through an open field. A large number of heavy vehicles must have lumbered along the same improvised route in recent days, judging by the wear and tear on the ground.

The truck slowed to a halt partway up the hill. Two men clambered out and started poking around in the truck bed. They produced what looked like a tripod, as well as some other equipment, and they got to work. One of them set up the tripod in the centre of the trail while the other stumbled off through waves of grass that reached up to his waist. He held something aloft, some surveying device. It was evident what they were doing. They were surveying the Quinton Vasco lands — but why?

Hilary and I waited and watched, but there wasn't much else to see. The two men in the distance went about their assigned tasks. Once, one of them peered down the slope, and he waved at us. I waved back and immediately wondered if that was the right thing to have done. Probably, it didn't matter one way or the other. I decided to ask my father what was going on. He knew pretty much everything there was to know about real estate in Kelso. After a while, Hilary and I gathered our reins and continued west along Number Four Sideroad, riding at an extended trot.

"Something's up," she said, in a voice that seemed too glib, as if she knew more than she was saying.

That evening I asked my father what was going on. This was half an hour or so after he'd got home from work.

"Dad …" I said. "Do you know what?"

"What, what?"

From the kitchen tap, he poured some water into a glass of Scotch and took a generous gulp. He had already changed out of his business suit and had on baggy brown pants and a navy polo shirt streaked with blotches of white house paint. These were his chore doing clothes. He'd said he planned to attend to a leaky eavestrough after dinner. He wanted me to hold the ladder.

Now I was squatting on the slate floor near the kitchen entrance, surrounded by spread-out sheets of newspaper. I was shining my stirrup irons and Della's snaffle bit.

"Surveyors, that's what," I said. "Over at the Quinton Vasco lands. We saw some men surveying there. What's going on?"

My mother looked up from the kitchen table. She was going over the monthly bills and eating macaroni and cheese with ketchup. Her glasses were suspended halfway down her nose. "Who's 'we'?"

"Me and Della." With a clump of steel wool, I gouged a bit of grime out of the snaffle joint.

My mother set down a wad of bills.

I corrected myself. "Della and *I*."

"Thank you."

"That so?" said my father. He ambled out of the kitchen and perched himself on a stool by the bar. "Hmm."

He wanted to change the subject; I could already tell.

The front door slammed, and Charlotte sauntered in, wearing cut-off jeans and a halter top. She was working on a raspberry Popsicle.

"Hi, Pumpkin," said my father.

"Your shoelace is undone, Daddy."

"Oh …?"

"Ha. Made you look."

"Charlotte," said my mother. "Your dinner's in the oven. Put your Popsicle in the freezer."

"It'll get too cold."

Charlotte heaped her plate from the casserole dish in the oven and carried her dinner over to the counter. There, she climbed onto a stool beside my father and took alternating bites of macaroni and cheese and raspberry Popsicle while reading an adventure novel by Arthur Ransome.

"Let me try that," said my father.

Charlotte let him.

"Not bad." He puckered his lips and nodded. "The macaroni could use a touch more Scotch, though."

"Daddy — yuck." She turned a page.

"So, why do you think they are?" I said. I dribbled some silver polish onto a rag and began to rub the surface of the bit.

"Who's *they*? *Are* what?" My father was up again already, getting himself another drink.

"One for me, too," said my mother. "Please."

"The surveyors. Why are they surveying the Quinton Vasco lands?"

"Uh …" Before long, my father emerged from the kitchen and paused at the bar to glance down at the book Charlotte was reading. "Good book, Pumpkin?"

Charlotte turned another page. "Shh. I'm at an important part."

"Da-ad. Why do you think they're surveying that land?"

My father carried a glass of Scotch and soda over to the dining table and set it down in front of my mother. She raised her chin, pushed her glasses back up, and gave him a look.

"*What* ...?" I said.

"What, what?" said my father, again. He walked back to the counter and settled himself on one of the wooden stools arrayed there.

"She gave you a look. I saw."

"Well, she's my helpmeet and paramour."

"Tell me, please," I said. "Why are they surveying the Vasco lands?" By now, I was positive he was hiding something. When it came to real estate in Kelso, he knew just about everything there was to know. It wasn't conceivable that he wouldn't be fully aware of something this big, as big as the Quinton Vasco lands.

My father drummed his fingers against his glass and then took a final swallow of his drink. He shrugged. "Not sure." He set down his glass and put out his hands, examined the back of them. "Guess we'll just have to wait and see."

"Dad," I said. "I know you know."

"I know you know I know ... you know?" My father cocked his ear and raised his eyebrows. "Eavestrough? I think I hear an eavestrough that's calling my name."

"Hal ..." My mother called after him. "Your dinner."

"Bring it out to me," said my father. "I'll eat it on the roof." He headed outside to fetch the ladder.

I finished cleaning the irons and the snaffle bit and put everything away. I could tell that my father knew more than he was saying. He was keeping a secret; that much was certain. What I wanted to know was why. I headed outside to steady the ladder, but I didn't say anything more about the Quinton Vasco lands. There'd have been no point.

NINE

Muletsi
South Africa, Winter 1962

MULETSI DADLA HAD BEEN working at the Anson stables for more than two weeks before the girl, Hilary, first spoke to him, spoke to him properly, that is — something more than *do this, do that*. Kitchen kaffir, that sort of speech was called, a language of dominance. The girl spoke that way sometimes, but he could tell she meant little by it. It was a matter of upbringing. In most of the ways that counted, she was respectful of black people. She just didn't take much interest in their affairs.

Besides, he was a servant, after all — nothing remarkable, unless you spoke to him. To look at him, and Muletsi knew this full well, you would think he was just another black groom who travelled in from the township by *bakkie* to do his job each day, then travelled home by *bakkie* at night. At least in the presence of Jack Tanner, that was exactly what he was. He did not say much, and what he did say was merely a dutiful mumble. When Jack Tanner was about, he slouched and kept his eyes down and did as he was told, did whatever Jack instructed him to do — same as the other stable hands. Like them, he shunted through the barn in his dark-blue overalls with wisps of straw in his hair, nodding and assenting. A spectre. A ghost. Inevitably, during that first couple of weeks, this was the way Hilary saw him. Before they spoke, that was. Spoke properly.

On this particular day, Jack Tanner had gone off in his Land Rover to run some errands in town, and Hilary had shown up at the stables on her own and announced that she meant to go out riding, alone. She asked Muletsi if he wouldn't mind tacking up South Wind for her.

"No, Miss," he said. He just stood there.

She waited, but still he did nothing. He could imagine what was going on in her mind. Why was this fellow not doing as he was told? Oh … he must have misunderstood.

"South Wind," she repeated, louder this time. "I want you to put a saddle on him for me, hey."

Muletsi adjusted his glasses, shook his head. He said he would not be able to comply in this instance, very sorry, Miss.

She peered at him again, as if seeing him for the first time. It was his manner of speech, no doubt. Precise. Correct. Fully formed. She wouldn't have expected anything of the sort. Now she was thinking: a boy from Bruntville? Talking like some kind of headmaster? That was odd. But what she mainly noticed, he could tell, was his failure to do as he was told.

"The *Selle Français,*" she said. "The new horse. My dad's."

He nodded. "I know the one you mean, Miss. Your father's horse. That is the problem. I will get in trouble."

"Nonsense. I'll take responsibility. Besides, my daddy's in Durban again. Coming home tomorrow."

Muletsi shook his head. "Coming home today, Miss."

"What …? Why do you say that?"

He shrugged, thinking he might have said too much, partway regretting it now. He had a reason for being here, working as a groom on the Anson farm, and that purpose involved the girl, but he was determined to advance by stealth, so as not to alarm her.

The last thing he needed was an enemy. What he needed was an accomplice.

"I asked you a question. What makes you think you know when my father will be home?"

"It was just something I heard, Miss. I could be wrong, but it might be better to be safe."

"Well, Jack lets me ride him ..."

Her voice trailed off, and she closed her eyes, grimaced, no doubt appalled by this clumsy double entendre. She opened her eyes again. "I mean, *Jack lets me ride South Wind*. Anytime I want."

"That's fine," he said. "But the *baas* isn't here now. I'll get your own horse."

He meant Pascal, the gelding she normally rode, a fine horse but stolid, familiar. For a few moments, she was silent, as if considering what he'd just said. And what he'd said was true. He — and not she — was the one who would bear the blame if Daniel Anson pitched up and found South Wind was gone. As for his claim to know better than she when her father would return — that was insolence on his part, no doubt about it. It had been a risk, his saying that. But it seemed that she realized it would be better to give in. Better all around.

She sighed. "All right. Bring Pascal out. Saddle him up."

At once, he set about doing as she said. He led Pascal into the grooming bay, cleaned out his hooves with the pick, went over him quickly with a dandy brush, plucked a blade of straw from his tail. He worked briskly and efficiently, wanting to show Hilary that he knew what he was about, that he wasn't intimidated by the horse, the way some are in the presence of a big animal. He was careful, but he was confident, too.

Hilary fetched a bridle, saddle, and martingale from the tack room and carried the lot out into the grooming bay, something she normally would not have done, chores she would have left to the hired help. She set the gear down by the equipment box, turned, and stood back, watching him work.

He reached for the bridle and lifted it up by the headpiece, then slid the snaffle bit between Pascal's teeth, easing the headpiece up and over his ears. He cinched the latches and bands on the bridle. Next, he swung Hilary's Stubben saddle up over Pascal's back, settled it there. He ran the girth under Pascal's trunk, then ducked his head beneath the saddle flap, and fixed the buckles of the girth. Only now did he speak again.

"So, you're going out riding alone?"

She said yes and nothing more. She was probably thinking, wasn't it obvious? He could tell she was unsettled by the question just the same, simply because it *was* a question. You didn't often get a newly hired black stable hand addressing a white lady like that out of the blue. But he had already defied her on the matter of South Wind. Plus, there was the matter of his claiming to know, better than she, when her father would be coming home. She would have trouble knowing what to make of that.

For a time they both were silent. Then he spoke again.

"You'll want to be careful. It can be dangerous out there, riding alone."

He could tell that these words were also unexpected. Yet what he said next must have been more surprising still.

"But I think you're better off alone than —" He lowered his voice. "You know ... *with him.*"

He pulled his head back and let the flap of the saddle drop into place. He ducked down to check the girth, to make sure Pascal's skin wasn't pinched anywhere. He didn't look at the girl, did not seek to observe her as she formulated a reply.

She clearly did not know what to say. It was so unexpected, what he had just done — spoken to her about South Wind, about her own father, about Jack Tanner, too. Still, he could tell she

73

took his meaning, at least when it came to Jack. Yet why would he warn her about that? What business was it of his, a black groom whose name she didn't even know? She stood up and pulled on her felt-covered riding helmet, fastened the chinstrap.

He reached into his hip pocket for a towel and ran the cloth over the bridle's leather straps. It was an unnecessary flourish — the bridle had already been rubbed to a fare-thee-well. He tucked the cloth away and, then, he did look at her. His words must have been simmering in her mind so that she said what seemed to be the first words that came into her head.

"You wear glasses …"

It sounded silly, a childish remark, but he just nodded, kept looking at her. "I do," he said, as if the wearing of glasses were exactly pertinent to the subject at hand. He kept looking right at her, his heart now pounding in his chest. He wanted to say just enough but not too much. Slowly, he nodded. "That's why I can see."

The words hung there between them, meaning whatever she took them to mean. He turned and led Pascal out of the dim grey glow of the stable and into the glare of the yard.

She would tell him later that it was only then that the spell began to break, the spell Jack Tanner had worked on her. She had tried at least once before to break it off, but Jack had reined her back in. He was a genius at that. Now things were different. She realized she was not alone. It was no longer a matter of Jack and her and no one else. The full meaning of it didn't hit her at once, but a first semblance of it did, and she understood that she would have to take her time, have to think about all of this, let the meaning of Muletsi's words sink in. It must have seemed awfully strange that her only ally might be a young African groom from Bruntville, a kaffir … or not a kaffir. She knew by then not to use that word. An African.

Out in the stable yard, he gave her a leg-up. She practically flew into the saddle, but quickly steadied herself, found her stirrups, gathered the reins. She peered down at him.

"Thank you," she said.

He nodded and smiled. "It's all right." He ran the palm of his hand down Pascal's shoulder. "My name is Muletsi."

She shifted her weight. "Mine's Hilary."

"I know."

And that was not all. It turned out he was exactly right: her father did indeed come home from Durban that same day, a day earlier than expected. What was more, he brought with him an English gent, an Englishman who lived in Canada and went by the name of Quinton Vasco. He dressed entirely in black and was thought to be something of a champion in the ballistics trade, from what Muletsi had been told. A day later, more men showed up — South Africans all, powerful men, politicians and titans of industry.

As a lowly stable hand, it wasn't likely that Muletsi would be privy to these goings-on, the meetings and telephone calls, the discussions about weaponry. But there was an outside chance that Hilary would, and it was that very chance that had brought him here, to work as a groom in Daniel Anson's barn. Of course, Hilary had no inkling of this, not at first. She would come to understand it soon enough, though, after their circumstances had changed and he could speak freely. Still, what must have surprised her most, that first afternoon, was her father's early arrival, unanticipated by her, a day in advance. Muletsi was sure she must have wondered about it then. She must have asked herself: Was it possible that the boy had known?

Not *the boy*. Muletsi. His name.

TEN

Sam
Ontario, Summer 1963

HILARY AND I MET at the corner of Number Four Sideroad and
Second Line, near the Quinton Vasco lands. Two days had slipped
past since we'd last seen each other. Now she was wearing a pair
of blue jeans and what I realized was the top piece of a two-piece
bathing suit, the fabric checkered in green and blue. Madras plaid?
Was that right? At her waist, her tummy rippled a little against her
jeans and then broadened into her hips. She had her hair pulled
back in a ponytail.

"*Lekka*'," she said.

"What ...?"

She smiled. "It's a word in South African. It means 'good.'"
She spelled the word out — l-e-k-k-e-r — but she pronounced it
without the *r*. "Better than good."

"*Lekka* ..." I said. I liked the sound. "*Lekka* day."

And so it was. Another *lekka* day in summer. We both reined
our horses around and set off for the quarry, riding at an extended
trot parallel to the Quinton Vasco lands. Off to the left, beyond an
overgrown ditch, the same endless chain-link fence stretched against
a green background. Before long, Hilary began to pepper me with
questions about this guy, Quinton Vasco — his age, his marital

status, his wealth, his nationality. I wondered why she wanted to know. She didn't even live in Canada, at least not permanently. It seemed strange, her interest. It puzzled me even then. Of course, I had to admit that I couldn't answer most of her questions. The man was a mystery; that was about all I could say — a mystery, and he was tearing Kelso apart. People assumed he was buying up the land for financial reasons, as an investment. Probably he was planning some big housing estate. What else could it be? But it was a disaster, no matter what he had in mind.

Hilary pointed off to the left. "Look."

I did as she said and saw at once what she meant. The improvised trail we'd noticed two days earlier? The one that wound through a field of alfalfa and up to a broad ridge? Already, in only a couple of days, that trail had been worked into what was practically a road, covered with gravel, the long grass worn entirely away. Even now a couple of hefty-looking trucks were stationed near the summit. I didn't see any workmen around, not just now, but something was going on; that much was sure.

Hilary and I kept riding to the east. Eventually, the road began its sudden descent, twisting down along the escarpment wall, dropping toward the rolling lands below. Here we slowed to a walk. Our horses had to square up to keep their balance on the steep, serpentine road. Partway down the escarpment, we bore to the right along a narrow plateau, tracing the trail that led to the quarry ponds. It was a trek that we were to make countless times in the weeks that followed. That day, as on so many days that summer, the sunlight washed down through a blue sky strewn with high, rafting clouds, scattering through the latticework of maple branches that criss-crossed just above our heads.

When we reached the stone ledge overlooking the largest of the ponds, I shook my feet free of the stirrups, threw my right leg over the cantle of the saddle, and dropped to the ground. This time

I had worn my swimming trunks under my jeans. I had only to kick off my shoes, pull off my shirt, and shimmy out of the jeans. I tossed my clothes onto a flat sandstone ledge, leaving them there to bake in the sun. Hilary did much the same. Next, we unsaddled the horses and replaced the bridles with halters and shanks. That done, we vaulted back on.

This time Club Soda barely hesitated before plunging from the rocky ledge and careening into the water's green surface, with Hilary crying in delight as her horse vanished beneath her and as shards of spray exploded all around. Once again, Della and I scrambled into the pond by means of the grassy embankment, a far less dramatic route. Before long Hilary began to sing a song I didn't recognize in an unknown language with strange glottal popping sounds. When I asked, she told me it was called "The Click Song," made famous by the same South African singer she had spoken of before.

"I can't do the clicks properly. I wish I could."

"What do the words mean?"

"Ag. That's the mysterious part." She cleared her throat. "Diviner of the roadways — the knock-knock beetle. It just passed by here — the knock-knock beetle."

I waited for her to continue, but she didn't.

"That's it?"

"Yebo."

"What does it mean?"

"Nobody knows." She laughed and said she would teach me the words if I wanted.

I said I did. I tried to make a popping sound with my tongue, the way she had done, but my effort didn't amount to much.

Later, as we were preparing to ride home, I started to pull on my jeans over my swimming trunks, but Hilary said to stop.

"Just take your bathing costume off. It's wet, and ... I don't know. You'll be uncomfortable."

I started toward a grove of cedars, but she stopped me again.

"Not over there," she said. "You don't need to go over there."

"I don't?"

"No. We're practically brother and sister. What difference does it make, hey?"

"You want me to take my trunks off right here?"

"Why not? Go ahead. There's no one here but us."

I stood where I was, didn't move.

She closed her eyes and said nothing. After a few seconds, she opened her eyes again. She wore only a two-piece bathing suit herself — that and a pair of canvas shoes. Takkies. She shook her head, pursed her lips and made a clicking sound, same as in the song. "The knock-knock beetle," she said. "That little demon. He makes us what we are."

Something had just happened — I knew that much. I just wasn't sure what it was. I nodded and ducked behind a row of cedars and changed into my jeans there. Before long, we saddled our horses and set off. When it came time for us to part company — I to continue west and homeward, she to head south to the Barkers' — Hilary pondered for a few moments and then asked why we didn't ride to the Barkers' together. I could leave Della in the barn for the night, she would drive me home, and tomorrow we could start working again, preparing for an upcoming competition, a one-day event near a town called Falkirk. It was the first in a series of horse shows staggered through the coming weeks. The results would determine who among us made the team for the provincial championships. I said that was fine with me, and it was. It definitely was.

Early the next afternoon, Hilary picked me up in Mrs. Barker's Peugeot and drove us both back to the Barkers' place. This time she seemed to be in a foul mood and smoked one Rothmans after another, complaining about Mrs. Barker non-stop.

"She's like a shadow, follows me everywhere, as if I were a thief or something, as if I would steal the first thing that came to hand, the moment she takes her eyes off me. I'm sure she thinks I'm having an affair with her husband."

I found that hard to imagine. Colonel Barker was about three times Hilary's age.

She blew out a plume of bluish smoke. "Anyway, she acts like it."

I noticed she didn't say whether it was true or not, her having an affair with Colonel Barker. I wanted to ask her, in a way I did, but something made me stop. It was the rumours, I guess. According to the rumours, she was having an affair with just about every second male in Kelso. I knew this to be a huge exaggeration, but I didn't really want to know much more about it than that.

When we got to the Barkers' place, Mrs. Barker was traipsing up the dirt lane from the barn. She was wearing a wide-brimmed bonnet and a pair of gardener's gloves, clutching a bunch of uprooted weeds.

"Trimming," she said. "Tidying up. Setting the world to rights."

I wondered what she was talking about. I pointed up at the sky. "*Lekka*' day," I said.

"What …?"

"Uh. *C'est une belle journée?*"

Mrs. Barker just looked at me, swaying slightly. Something was wrong; I could tell that much right away. For one thing, she didn't even acknowledge Hilary's presence. She kept her gaze fixed on me.

"Everything all right, Sam?" she said, as if we shared some secret code, she and I.

"Yes." I had no idea what she was getting at. Why wouldn't everything be all right?

"You'd tell me if there was a problem?"

I nodded but didn't speak. Mrs. Barker continued to glare at me, as if the Anson girl didn't exist. I now realized what her

questions meant, more or less. They had something to do with
Hilary, as if Hilary might be causing me harm.

"You're sure?" she said.

I nodded again.

"Well, good then. That's a relief." She held up her clump of
weeds and suddenly seemed to lose her balance. She nearly fell right
down. Somehow, she managed to recover her footing. She took a
deep breath. "To the compost with these," she said. "*Adieu, adieu.*"

We both watched as she tottered up the drive, in the general
direction of the Barkers' stone-walled house.

"She's drunk, you know," said Hilary.

I hadn't known, but now I realized it was true. I could have
read the signs myself, but maybe I didn't want to. It made me
uneasy, the whole idea of adults going off track. There'd been a
time when I had thought that grown-ups could do no wrong. I was
beginning to understand that it wasn't always so. In some cases, it
wasn't even close.

Hilary and I headed down to the barn to saddle and bridle
Della and Club Soda. That done, she set off at a canter, leading me
on a roundabout route that ran through a succession of ploughed
fields and maple fencerows until we reached a large, grassy clearing I had never seen before. A grove of crabapple trees bordered a
large paddock, scattered with high wooden standards and striped
rails that could be assembled and reassembled into different sorts
of jumps. Just to the south, someone had erected a dressage ring,
marked off by low split-rail barriers, with alphabetical markers set
out at regular intervals along its perimeter. The place had everything
you needed for schooling a horse, or just about.

Hilary released Club Soda to run loose in the paddock and
then positioned herself in the middle of an open expanse of grass.
She told me to ride in circles around her, the same procedure I had
followed countless times with Major Duval.

First, I kept to a walk. Then Hilary said, "Trot," so I rode at a trot. She said, "Extended trot," and I got Della to lengthen her stride. When Hilary said, "Canter," I did that, too. By this time, Major Duval would probably have been roaring at me, practically livid. Head up! Shoulders back! Legs straight! Shorten zee reins! Where in zee name of Got did you learn to ride a 'orse!

But Hilary just shuffled in small circles, her eyes on me. She barely said a word except "Walk," "Trot," or "Canter." I said nothing, just did my best to follow her instructions.

"Okay," she said at last. "Come in here."

I slowed Della to a walk and guided her into the middle of the circle. Hilary gave me a clap on the lower leg and said I was a good rider, all in all. There were just a few wee things that needed work.

"I'm round-shouldered," I said. "I slump when I ride."

Hilary nodded. "That's true. You also slump when you walk in case you hadn't noticed."

I hadn't, but it was the riding part that bothered me.

"Okay," she said. "Anything else?"

Plenty. I embarked on a chronicle of the many deficiencies I exhibited while mounted on a horse. The list was long and, to me, sadly familiar. I kept on going until she broke in.

"Whoa. Take it easy. Don't be too hard on yourself."

She started walking around Della, frowning in concentration. Finally, she stopped. "Okay, my boykie. I'll tell you what we're going to do. But, first, one question. How important is this?"

"Making the team ...?"

"No. Riding well."

That stopped me. To tell the truth, I hadn't thought in those terms before. I'd thought about *doing* better, not necessarily *being* better.

"Because the thing is, I can't guarantee you'll make the team. That's not in our hands. Besides, it's the wrong reason to be doing this. The best reason for doing a thing well is ..." She paused. "Why do you think?"

I sort of scrunched up my face, because I knew where this was going. I forced myself to speak slowly and deliberately. "The best reason for doing a thing well is to do the thing well?"

Hilary nodded, as if I had just said something deeply significant.

I rolled my eyes.

"Anything wrong with that?"

"It's known as begging the question."

"Say what?"

"The conclusion is the same as the premise. It's logically meaningless."

"You're way too young to be using that kind of language."

"Yeah, I know. Sorry."

She nodded. "I admit, it does sound kind of spacey, but that's the gist of it. Do a thing well, and everything else more or less falls into place. One way or another. So ... how badly do you want it? Scale of one to ten?"

"Eleven."

"Let's make it ten." She stepped back a pace and gestured for me to dismount. "Okay. Off your horse."

I kicked my feet free of the stirrups, swung my right leg over the cantle, and dropped to the ground. At Hilary's instruction, I led Della into the paddock, where Club Soda eyed us from the far end of the enclosure.

"Right," said Hilary. "Now take off the saddle."

I did as told. I balanced the saddle atop the paddock railing.

"Same with the bridle."

"What ...?"

"You heard me."

This was crazy, but okay. I draped the bridle atop the saddle. "Now what?"

"Now you get back on."

I just stood there.

Hilary nodded. "So get back on."

"You're serious?"

"Yes, my boykie. I am."

"You mean, ride like that? With nothing?"

"Not 'nothing.' You've got legs, haven't you? A pelvis? A voice?"

"I guess." I stayed where I was.

"Okay," she said. "So get back on."

IT WAS AS IF someone had turned a switch at the back of Hilary's noggin. One moment, she was set to *off*. The next moment ... well, she wasn't sure what happened. But she definitely wasn't set to *off* anymore. She was set to something else, something that didn't seem to have a name. It was as if a whole new world had opened before her, filled with questions she had never considered, much less asked, till now. For example, when you went out for a meal at a restaurant, why was it that all the people sitting down were white, while those on their feet were invariably black? Obvious, hey? That's just the way it is. But *why* ...? You had to ask yourself that question, and then it didn't seem so obvious anymore or so innocent.

Or *Slegs blankes*. Why did you see that sign all over the place? You didn't see signs saying *Tall people only* or *Thin people only*. Why *Whites only?* If you didn't question it, you'd never know there was anything to question. But if you did, then everything changed, as if someone had turned a switch at the back of your frigging head. Now, suddenly, she could think. She could see. Granted, much of what she saw was cruel and unjust, but still it was better to see than to be blind. Welcome to the world — such as it is.

Just now, she was at the wheel of her mother's Vauxhall Victor, and they were driving to Bruntville, she and Muletsi. Bruntville. It was a place she had never set eyes on before, not in all her seventeen years, even though it was located only a few miles from her family's home. Muletsi wanted her to see where he had lived all of his life, apart from the time he'd spent attending university over in the Eastern Cape. Also, she was to meet his mother. That was in the plans, too.

The other good news was that she had taken to avoiding Jack again, a thing that had proved less difficult than she had feared, in part because he was often away from the farm these days, a pattern he had followed in years gone by. It was Muletsi who told her what was behind Jack's frequent absences. She couldn't say she was shocked by the explanation — sickened, yes, but not shocked. She had imagined something of the sort before.

Girls. Underage girls.

No doubt as a nod to discretion, Jack avoided the local towns, instead driving up to Ladysmith in his Land Rover or down to Howick, even as far south as Pietermaritzburg. He had to be careful, for he was in violation of the Sexual Offences Act, after all, and on two counts — age and race. She wondered how he avoided being caught.

"Money," said Muletsi. "Money and threats. Those are the usual ways. No one will dare to testify against him. Besides, he also has an understanding with the police."

"Is it?"

He explained. It seemed Jack always kept his eyes peeled for any hint of seditious activity. Once he suspected anything of the sort, he was on it like that — here, Muletsi snapped his fingers. Jack took his information to the police in Mooi River, specifically to a man named Walter van Niekerk, who was the captain there.

Hilary braked the car, geared down into third. Jack ... an informer ...? Jesus frigging Christ. What wouldn't the man stoop to? It was horrible but not entirely unexpected. She had some direct knowledge of the man, after all. She knew that no one would call him a faithful servant of the common weal. But what most impressed her now was something else. Not for the first time, she marvelled at the range and extent of Muletsi's knowledge. He seemed to know everything that was going on.

By now she understood what had drawn Muletsi to this menial post, a groom at her father's farm. On the face of it the arrangement made little sense. A graduate in English literature working in a barn? To a certain degree, you could chalk it up to the inequities of life for young black men under apartheid. But in this case other factors were in play. He had explained it to her late one afternoon when they both were lying on their backs upon a bed of straw bales in the stable loft. Swallows darted overhead, flashing through the vertical shafts of light that shot between the wall planks. There'd been some graunching done and not for the first time. It was nothing serious, just hugs and nibbles, wholly different from the ordeals she'd been put through by Jack. *Wholly* different. Muletsi kept everything light, more talking and joking than actual touching. He seemed to understand, without her saying so, that she needed time to get her head clear. Clear of Jack.

Besides, this was all too ridiculous, what was going on — she and Muletsi. Could there possibly be a more tired plot device than this: stable hand appears out of nowhere, meets rich man's daughter, wins daughter's heart? That story must have been written a thousand times before. She laughed aloud.

"What ...?" He shifted onto his side and peered at her, a few stray motes of straw spotted through his hair.

She told him what she'd been thinking just now. Him. Her. Two players dispatched by central casting to act out this ancient charade yet again.

At first he said nothing, but then, after a few seconds' pause, he laughed, too — a warm and comforting sound, but a sound with a certain edge. "A charade, is it? Is that what you think?"

"Not a charade, exactly. Just an oft-told tale."

"You think so?"

"I don't know." She was unsure what to say. His tone was more serious than she'd expected. She brushed several flecks of straw from his hair and nuzzled her cheek against his. "It's just that this story has been told before, or something very much like it. I've been reduced to a cliché. We have. You and I."

He shrugged. "And what if we have? Is that so bad? Your great Shakespeare wrote in clichés, too. Practically nothing else but. All of his comedies — they all end in a wedding. Every single one — or almost every one. But so what? The task is not to avoid clichés but to fashion them anew."

Anew — was that even a word, a word that people actually used? "Mister English Professor," she intoned. She made a genuflecting sort of motion with just her head, and both of them laughed. They did some more in the way of graunching, and then she raised herself onto her elbows and gazed into his eyes. "Weddings," she said, "is that it?" She frowned. "Difficult to see us ending that way."

He nodded. "Difficult is right. Illegal, too."

They were silent, both of them thinking of that. After a time he cleared his throat. In a hushed voice, he told her he had something else to say. It was time to come clean, time to fashion another cliché anew. She waited, no idea what he would say, and it was on that memorable afternoon in the stable loft that Muletsi told her he was himself with the ANC, a daring admission in any circumstances, but especially dangerous now. The African National Congress had recently been banned by the government. Mere membership was a crime. At first she didn't believe him. She thought that this was a pretty good joke, so she joked about it, too.

"How's your mind?" she said. "Are you utterly mad? I could turn you in, hey."

"But you won't."

"Not just now." She gave him a kiss, smack on the lips, then rolled away and said nothing for a few moments. Then she frowned. "Is it true?"

"It is."

"And you are here, right now, as a spy, is it? Not as my suitor at all?"

"Must I choose? I cannot be both?"

"That depends."

But it didn't depend. Not really. That was just a joke she made, and it was no longer time for joking. She could tell that much. Now it was time to listen and not to speak, so that was what she did. She listened in silence while he told her what was what. The more he revealed to her about the ANC and the struggle, the more agitated she became. She knew perfectly well that there were tensions in the land. Of course she did. Anyone capable of drawing breath was surely aware of that. She wasn't quite an idiot, you check? But to her the troubles had always seemed like so much background noise, something happening a good distance away rather than right bloody here. She had never regarded South Africa's conflicts as a force affecting her own life, but now that began to change, thanks to Muletsi, who explained to her how the land really lay. No, she would not be turning him in. That was the exact opposite of what she had in mind. The transformation was not immediate. There would be more such discussions, more revelations, and more new takes on old clichés. In the end, however, she came around. She saw her country anew. Not only that, but she followed that same line of thinking, followed where it led. What she had in mind was to damn well join the man. Join the struggle. Nobody had ever accused Hilary Anson of half measures.

Just now, Muletsi pointed ahead toward a small grassy space near what seemed to be the edge of Bruntville. "Turn left here," he said. "You can park the car here. Don't worry; it will be safe. People will see me getting out."

"Oh …? You mean that, otherwise, they would scale it? Is that what you mean to say?"

"Not scale it." He chuckled. "But strip it bare? Could be."

She didn't know whether to believe him or not. She didn't know whether to be afraid or not. She'd never ventured into a world of black people before — this in a country where black people were practically everywhere.

"All right," he said. "Let's go."

They climbed out of the car and entered Bruntville on foot, picking their way down a narrow lane flanked by squat cinder-block dwellings with zinc roofs that were held in place by bricks or rocks. Goats pranced ahead, and pigs snuffled through smouldering mounds of litter scattered at uneven intervals along the way. A man in a brown fedora tottered past on an ancient bicycle. Small flocks of children suddenly appeared and, just as quickly, scrambled out of view. She had a sense that people were peering at her from beyond a multitude of windows — curtains pulled open for a time and then quickly drawn shut.

"Is it all right?" she said. "Is someone going to shoot me?"

"Not shoot," he told her. "We don't have guns in Bruntville, or precious few."

She looked up and realized that something else was missing. At first, she wondered what it was. Then she knew. Power lines. There were no power lines overhead. The people here would have to improvise their own sources of heat and light. She wondered how they managed it. Meanwhile, she kept close to Muletsi and tried not to show how unnerved she was.

In all her life, she had never encountered a place such as this, or not at such close quarters. She knew that black townships existed — everybody knew that much — but they were always tucked beyond a ridge or a hill, places you sped past in the back seat of your father's car, places you barely noticed — several filaments of smoke seen spiralling from a few tin chimneys, a fleeting image that quickly vanished as your father drove on. Now here she was, the only white person in a place that was evidently reserved for the exclusive use of blacks. Never in her life had she found herself so vastly outnumbered.

For an instant, maybe two, she wanted to turn around, go back. "Muletsi …"

"Here," he said. With one hand on her shoulder, Muletsi guided her to the left, pointing toward yet another of these low, weathered hovels, one that was indistinguishable from the rest. He smiled. "My humble domain — or my mother's domain, I should say."

Mrs. Dadla proved to be a slender woman, smaller than Hilary had expected, given her son's considerable height. She had a penchant for quoting from the Bible, which she seemed to have committed to memory, word for word. It seemed she held a position of some importance at a local church, an evangelical congregation. If the woman was put out in any way by having a white person as a guest, she contrived to disguise it. Immediately after making Hilary's acquaintance, she invited the two of them to be seated — ordered them, really — and promptly set about boiling water for tea, setting the pot on a small charcoal stove. *Charcoal,* thought Hilary, *in place of electricity.*

The visit did not last long — an hour or so, no more — but it was to be repeated on three more occasions in the weeks that followed. During those visits Muletsi would show her around the place, pointing out the local landmarks — the school he attended as a youth, the outdoor market where his mother did most of her shopping, the medical clinic that was always understaffed and ill-equipped, the dark, grotto-like shebeen, which he insisted he did not frequent.

"Just special occasions, I suppose?" said Hilary.

He nodded. "And Sundays, of course."

"Of course."

On each of her visits, he walked with her back to her car and then rode alongside her until they were once again on the main road to Mooi River. Then she was on her own, driving home to her father's farm and thinking about Muletsi, her lone confederate. She didn't bother to think about Jack. She would think about Jack some other time.

Where Muletsi was concerned, she had already decided what she would do. Collaborate. It was that simple. He required information, and she had the means of providing it. In fact, she had already begun. A month or so after she and Muletsi first met — met properly — she had seen her first chance. That Canadian man had returned, the one who dressed always in black. True, he spoke with an English accent — Liverpudlian, she thought — but he insisted he was Canadian all the same. He was introduced as Quinton Vasco. One weekday afternoon he rolled up to the main house in the back seat of a hired car that had brought him up from Durban. This would be his second visit. Soon, more men arrived.

Long meetings ensued, fuelled by tobacco, single-malt Scotch, mounds of fried potatoes, and planks of braaied steak. She didn't sit in, not exactly. That would not have been welcome. But she wandered through the living room, more or less at will, munching on buttered toast and Marmite. No one seemed to object. For half an hour at a time she curled up in an empty chair and paged lazily through a magazine. *Horse & Hound.* No one said a word. She yawned, stretched, stood up, and struck off to the kitchen before returning a short time later, maybe with a mug of coffee — that and a novel by Nadine Gordimer. She repeated these or similar manoeuvres at least a half-dozen times.

Not even her father registered a complaint about her comings and goings, assuming he even noticed her whereabouts. It was quite likely he did not. He rarely took stock of her — she being a girl and so on. He doted on his sons, Colin and Trevor, but they were gone, both living up in Joburg now, both bolstering their fortunes on that reef of gold. As for his only daughter, the man probably would have required a daily memo just to keep him cognizant of the fact he possessed such a creature. Sometimes he seemed to stumble when pronouncing her name, as if he'd only just heard it for the first time. This was her impression, anyway. Possibly, she was wrong.

But it seemed that her very invisibility had its advantages, too. Merely by ducking in and out of the room, armed with a book or a magazine, she managed to inform herself about the cannons — the GC-45s, as they were called — that the Canadian, this Quinton Vasco, meant to sell to the Republic of South Africa. The weapons were still in the experimental stage, he admitted. But they would be operational soon. He explained that his company was building a testing range even now, in a place called Kelso, in a Canadian province called Ontario, somewhere northwest of Toronto. He himself had made his domicile nearby and was overseeing the entire show.

But these were details. What was of primordial import, according to the man from Canada, was the question of South Africa's national survival. He repeated this point, laying stress on certain terms. *Primordial import. National survival.* The plain truth, he said, was this: the country faced an existential challenge, one that could not be denied but only confronted — and he could provide the means. Guns. Big guns. The biggest there were. Best to arm now, he said, for the writing was already on the wall. Majority rule was coming to the region — coming sooner rather than later — and everything would change. The Portuguese would be ousted from Mozambique and Angola. Meanwhile, the blacks would take power in Rhodesia, in Bechuanaland, and beyond. Why, they had already taken over in Tanganyika, where they were imposing socialism even now. Dear God. The red tide was on the rise and, very soon, South Africa would stand alone. There was no denying it, not any longer. Time to get your heads out of the sand. The Canadian was on his feet by then. He held out his arms and raised his voice. War was coming, war on a multitude of fronts. Best to prepare for it. Prepare for it now.

"Is it?" said Muletsi when she told him what she had learned.

"What ...?" She groaned. "Is that all you have to say? Just: 'Is it?' Frigging hell."

He looked at her with what she thought of as his steely gaze. Then he relaxed, smiled. "I'm joking. You did good. Better than good. You did great, hey."

That didn't hurt too much, hearing him praise her like that.

They were standing in the grooming bay in the stables, and they both started to graunch, just a little, nothing much. She felt love and revolution, all at once.

Just then, she heard footsteps, a man clearing his throat, spitting. She knew right away it was Jack, returning after doing some chores in town. She'd barely seen the man in days. Muletsi pulled away and hurried off, back toward the stalls, while she turned around to hear what Jack might have to say.

"BIG DAY," SAID HILARY.

I already knew what that meant. We'd be doing groundwork again, no saddle, no bridle. To be honest, I didn't truly believe it was possible, what she was asking me to do, but Hilary swore it could be done. All I needed was practice.

"I suppose *you* can do it?" I said. "Ride a horse without a saddle or bridle?"

I was taking a sarcastic tone, almost always a mistake in my experience.

"It happens I can," she said. "It depends on the horse, I'll grant you that. But, yes, I can." She furrowed her brow. "Look. I know it's difficult. I'm not pretending otherwise."

I didn't need to hear Hilary say so. I already knew all about it. In a way, it's just simple physics. There's a far greater chance of falling off a horse if you are riding without a saddle. One brief error in balance can land you on your head whereas, with a saddle, you've got stirrups, you've got knee rolls, a cantle. You're more stable. There's more to it than that, but it comes down to the same thing. Riding bareback is hard, and riding without a bridle is harder — impossible, if you asked me.

"Not 'impossible,'" said Hilary. "It can be done. It takes some practice, I'll grant you. But what doesn't? Come on. Let's saddle these two."

Ten minutes later, we both were riding out to the paddock at the back of Colonel Barker's property. Once there, we untacked the horses. Hilary clipped a shank to Club Soda's halter and looped it in a safety knot around one of the wooden panels that ran along the perimeter of the paddock.

"Okay," she said. "I'll tell you what we're going to do."

I already knew — ride with nothing but hope and faith. I couldn't help thinking that today was as good a day as any for putting an end to my residence on earth. I was dressed for a casual sort of death — sneakers without socks, blue jeans, a pale-blue polo shirt. Of course, I had brought no crash helmet. What possible purpose would a crash helmet have served? I anticipated a perfunctory flight through the sparkling air followed by a head-on collision with some large rock. Behold: a lethal concussion or a broken neck, one or the other. Either would do.

Now I stood at Della's side, expecting Hilary to give me a leg-up, the way she sometimes did. But she just stayed where she was, a few yards away.

"You're on your own, my boykie," she said. "Really. It's important to do this yourself."

No problem. I took a step back, bent my knees, and vaulted into the air, twisting around so that I ended up straddling Della's back, immediately behind her withers. She shied to the side, but I managed to stay on. I kept my balance, not by gripping her mane or by clutching her neck, but by reaching out with both my arms like a tightrope artist. That seemed to be right, judging by Hilary's reaction.

"Good," she said. "That's perfect."

Stop the presses. The kid's fifteen years old, he's been riding horses for most of his life, and he can actually propel himself onto an animal's back without immediately falling off. I shrugged. "If you say so."

"No, I'm serious. That was really good. And there's another thing."

"What?"

"Look at you. You're sitting straight, with your weight deep and stable. The difference is amazing. Now squeeze your lower legs, then release."

I did as I was told, and Della immediately perked her ears and began to walk along the perimeter of the paddock.

"Weight deep," said Hilary. "Keep your weight deep. Pretend you're just one creature, you and Della."

I did my best.

"Now close your eyes."

"What ...?"

"You heard me. Close them tight."

"I won't be able to see."

"You don't need to."

Fine. I did as she said.

"Now, turn left. Ninety degrees."

"What ...? How?"

"Just do it. Don't think about it. Do it. Della's just waiting for you to tell her what to do. You should see her right now — her ears and her neck. She's arching her neck. Sure sign. She's just waiting for you to give her a hint. Now turn left."

I tried. I really did. "This is crazy," I said. "I don't know how."

"Yes, you do. Use your pelvis. Use your legs."

"But I don't have any reins."

"You don't need them. I'm telling you. Just shift your pelvis. Shift your weight, just the way you would if you did have reins."

"But I don't."

"Exactly. That's the whole point."

"But I can't see anything. This is crazy."

"No, it isn't. You can do it. Don't think about it. Just feel it. Left. Turn left."

It was like some kind of magic. Without thinking, just relying on I don't know what, I shifted my pelvis so that the pressure of my weight changed. I altered the direction of my body, if only slightly. Everything happened at the same time in a single coordinated movement. And Della turned left. I wanted to open my eyes, to see, but I fought down that urge.

"Okay," said Hilary. "That's great. Now straighten out. Let her know what you want. She'll do it. You both will."

And it worked. It actually worked.

HILARY STOOD AT THE entrance to the stables, afraid to step inside. She'd just caught sight of Jack. He was standing in the dim light of the grooming bay, running his hands up and down his leather apron. She didn't think that he had seen her, not yet. Already two weeks had passed since she'd told Muletsi about the Canadian named Quinton Vasco. During that time, and for some unknown reason, Jack had pretty much curtailed his former wanderings. These days he stalked the barn from dawn till dusk, which meant that Hilary had little choice but to keep away. That was exactly what she'd done, until now.

Now she meant to have it out, put an end to all this once and for all. She'd told Muletsi what she intended to do, and he'd said to be very careful. There was no telling how Jack might react this time. Muletsi said he'd be somewhere nearby. He'd keep close. Just in case.

Now, only a few steps shy of the stable entrance, Hilary felt her legs grow heavy, or so it seemed to her. She sensed a tautness in her throat, found it difficult to swallow. Nerves, of course. She'd already rehearsed the words she meant to say, a dozen times at least, but she knew Jack. She knew enough to be afraid of him if he turned mean. She took a breath and stepped into the grooming bay.

He looked up, not at all surprised to see her — just the opposite, in fact. His expression seemed to suggest that he'd been standing there with nothing else to do, just waiting for her to show.

"Hil."

She didn't bother to correct him. Not Hil. Hilary. She didn't even bother to say his name. Instead, she launched straight in, said what she'd said that time before, the same hollow words — but words just the same, words that could not have been pleasing to him.

"It's over. D'you hear? Over."

She told herself she meant it this time, and, even if Jack did not believe her, he must have foreseen trouble ahead, on account of her even saying these words. They showed she had a will of her own, a will that clashed with his. No good could come of that, not in the gospel according to Jack.

When she'd said what she'd come to say, she stopped, uncertain what else to do. At first he said nothing, just let his silence do the work, let it weigh upon her shoulders like a physical thing, like some lifeless animal abandoned there. He held a curry comb in his right hand and now patted it against his leather apron, setting off a swirl of blond dust. After a time he leaned to his left and spat, wincing as he did so. Still he said not a word.

She cleared her throat. "I'm serious."

He nodded, but not in a way that signalled agreement. Truth was, it likely didn't matter to Jack whether she was serious or not. His worriment would lie elsewhere, with this challenge to his rule. He would not be pleased about that. After all, a man can tolerate only so much resistance before he is obliged to act; it was Jack himself who'd taught her so.

She crossed her arms, trembling a little. Deep down, she had always been afraid of him. She was afraid of him now, afraid of what he might do. "Aren't you going to say something?"

Jack shrugged, grimaced, and finally he did speak, though it didn't amount to much.

"Nothing to say."

Because this was not the time for words: his instincts would tell him that. A curtain seemed to lift, and it seemed she was having some species of revelation. She found that she could tell what Jack was thinking, just by observing him, something she'd rarely managed to do before. It was as if she could read his mind, predict what he would say even before he said it. It was as if they both were characters in some weird, real-life comic book, with thought balloons that appeared beside a person's head.

Words were no use anymore: that was what he would be thinking now. He'd said all the words there were to say, so now he'd have to try a different route. He would need to come up with some explanation, some credible tale, something about a horse shying at an antelope, letting out with a buck. The girl had been thrown, and here was the result. Something along those lines. He'd have to ensure she backed him up, and he must have known she would. Fear alone would take care of that. He set the curry comb down in the equipment box. His right hand was already clenched in a fist, and she steeled herself for the coming blow. She could almost feel the impact of his bare knuckles against her own flesh and bone, but it never came.

"Don't do it, man."

Jack didn't look up to see whose voice it was. Didn't have to. Deep voice. Man's voice. He knew at once. At first he seemed almost amused. His eyebrows went up in mock surprise. "Why, if it isn't my old pal Berkeley Hunt. Mr. Berkeley Hunt himself. Well, well." He kept looking at her, though — at her and at no one and nothing else. "Who's this, then? Your new protector?"

She still had her arms raised, to defend herself. She'd been that sure he'd meant to hit her, bring down a rain of blows. But he'd lowered his fists by now, so she let her arms fall. Meanwhile, Jack ignored Muletsi — she could tell — shutting him out like he wasn't even there, kept his gaze fixed on her. He was angry, no question about that, and now, finally, his anger seemed to loosen his tongue. "I've been missing something here, have I? You and the kaffir gone sweet on each other, have you? Well —"

"Shut up," she said. "Just you shut up and go or —"

"Or what? You'll tell your old dad? No, I don't think so. I've heard that one before. But I don't think it's something you'd be willing to —"

"I'm warning you. Leave her alone, man. Just leave this place. Leave this place now."

Jack Tanner put a hand to his forehead and let out a low, theatrical sigh that was like a succession of words. Here was something new — a kaffir boy issuing instructions to a white man. Jack sniggered aloud and reached toward Hilary with both his hands, gripped her shoulders, and sought to hold her still. She stiffened and arched her back. He let his right hand slide downward till it clutched her left breast through the woollen jumper she wore. He smiled at her, as if he couldn't be held responsible for any of this, for any of what was happening now. She turned away, twisted her shoulders, fought to break free of his grip, something that seemed to thrill him all the more. "Why you little —"

"I said *now*. Let her go *now*. I won't say it again."

Jack just rolled his eyes, as if to say, Well, this is quite enough of that. He let his right hand drop from her breast, but still he gripped her shoulder with his other hand. She managed to pull loose and slide away from his grasp. Now Jack turned to have a look at Muletsi, who stood at the gate between the stables proper and the grooming bay, his large shape hard to discern in the gloomy light. Jack reached out with his right arm and pointed with his index finger, dead centre, at Muletsi's forehead. He raised his thumb and drew back his third finger as if he were squeezing a trigger. He made a clicking sound with his tongue. "You," he said. "You shut your bloody gob or I'll have your neck."

And what happened next, well, she herself could barely believe it. She doubted Jack could believe it either. Without warning, Muletsi took a run at him, swinging a bridle with a big pelham bit. That was what caught Jack on the side of the head, drew blood and broke bone at the first impact, stunned him for a time, long enough for Muletsi to drop the bridle and get in a flurry of blows all over — face, chest, belly.

Before Jack could recover his balance, get his feet set, it was already too late. She knew what he must have been thinking as he felt his legs give way. This never would have happened if he'd had time to prepare. Never in a dozen lifetimes. Never in a thousand years.

Or so Jack might have said, if he'd been of a mind to speak, or if he hadn't blacked out.

As for Muletsi, he kicked the bridle away as if it were a noxious thing. He took one look at her, turned, and hurried out of the barn, moving at a brisk walk that soon turned into a run. She could tell how shocked he was. He hadn't intended this — but, oh Lord, how he hated Jack Tanner. Meanwhile, Jack was out cold. She did what she could with the blood that was all over the man, the blood and the snot and the drool.

Even after Jack came to, his mind was a blur. Still, even in that foggy state, he must have known that he'd been bested by a good-for-nothing kaffir, as he would put it. That would rankle in his gut, torment him forever — or at least until he'd settled scores. It was lucky for him he hadn't been killed.

Later the ambulance came, and they took him to the clinic in Mooi River and then to the hospital in Pietermaritzburg, where the doctors had to perform reconstructive surgery on one side of his face. More than two weeks passed before he returned to the farm, mean-tempered and bitter as piss. He tottered about the grooming bay and the corridors that ran between the stalls, swearing to himself, cursing the stable hands, and throwing things at the walls.

She knew what he wanted — wanted more than anything else on earth. He wanted to exact revenge on his own terms, which was the way things were usually done after a white man and an African came to blows. But by then it was too late. The authorities had already intervened. It was assault, they said — assault with a deadly weapon. Granted, it hadn't been a knife that Muletsi had wielded, much less a gun. It had been an expensive leather bridle with a disciplinary bit. But, still, you could kill a man with less. And that was just for starters.

The police made straight for Bruntville, and they found Muletsi there. Straightaway, they clamped him in jail. Next, the chief had his plainclothes men pay another visit to the township to ransack Muletsi's house — really, his mother's house. What did they find? Whatever they wanted. There could never have been any doubt about that. In this case, they found incriminating documents by the score. It seemed Muletsi was a member of a banned organization after all, a subversive. More charges were laid against him, political charges. Agitation. Sedition.

But what were most damning of all were the indictments that never got put down in writing, the ones that got hushed up by her father, who had his ways — the morality accusations that Jack lodged against Muletsi. Rape. Miscegenation. Carnal knowledge of a minor.

As for Hilary, she was deemed to have been hysterical the whole bloody time. Teenage delirium — that explained why she made all sorts of outlandish charges against Jack Tanner, why she said so many hideous things. He was the one all along, she said. He'd done this, done that. It hadn't been Muletsi at all. She ranted and stormed.

But Jack denied every word, never raising his voice, used logic and lies to dismantle the truth. His version was that he'd come upon the two of them together, Muletsi and the girl, and the black devil had attacked him then, with no warning whatsoever — the shock of being discovered. This was what Jack told her father, apologizing after almost every word, as if it had partly been his fault. Ag, but the man was slick. In the end, he was believed. It was a white man's word against a black man's, and there was never any contest in that.

As for Hilary, nothing she had said seemed to count for anything at all — the ravings of a girl, out of control, teenage hormones. Her own father failed to credit her words, and what her mother said or thought didn't come into the picture. In the end, Daniel Anson disbelieved his own kith and kin, put his faith in his cockney stable manager instead. And so it was that Jack came out on top, despite the beating he'd suffered. Still, he didn't gloat. Well, he wouldn't, would he? He was far too smart for that.

As for Muletsi, he was tried, convicted, and sentenced to a prison cell in Pietermaritzburg, there to live out his punishment at hard labour, in durance vile. And Hilary? She was bundled off to a girls' academy in Johannesburg. As far as she could tell, her father never wanted to see her again. He didn't say so, didn't have to. She could sense it in his tone when he said how very disappointed he was in her.

Disappointed! Dear Lord, it was vastly worse than that. Disgusted — that was what he meant. He could no longer bear having her near, and Johannesburg was a good long trek away. He must have calculated it would be difficult for her to get into more trouble up there, especially under the watchful gaze of Colin and Trevor, his two sterling sons — all of which just went to show how little he knew of his one and only daughter. He had something wrong in his head if he thought that a little obstacle like geographical distance would put things right or that she would carry out a single, solitary task that anyone else wanted her to perform as long as Muletsi Dadla remained in jail. Did he not understand that? When it came to his daughter, did he not comprehend the first and simplest thing? Jesus frigging Christ. Frigging bloody hell.

PART TWO

PART TWO

ENTER BRUCE GRUBER.

I knew him well. I had known him for years. After all, he had
bullied me for what seemed like ages when we'd both attended
primary school in Hatton. He had needed roughly twelve years to
complete those eight grades, and he spent much of that time preying
upon the smaller or younger kids, including me. When he finally
bottomed out and abandoned school completely, he went to work
as an apprentice mechanic at Weintrub's Garage. Now and again
he got into trouble with the law. It was small-time stuff, from what
I understood — issuing threats, minor theft, resisting arrest, that
kind of thing. But it gained him a reputation.

Probably Hilary knew this. I imagine Bruce's prior record figured prominently in her calculations. It must have done. How
else can you explain her attachment to the guy? What on earth
did she see in him? It baffled me from the start. As it happened, I
was on hand the first time Hilary met Bruce. That meeting took
place on what I recall as a cloudy afternoon, following two straight
days of rain, a rarity during that sun-coddled summer. When the
downpour finally let up, Charlotte and I both rode our bikes into
Hatton. I meant to buy a Big Turk chocolate bar and a Tahiti Treat

at Odegaards' General Store, as was my custom, and Charlotte insisted on coming along for the ride. I told her I had only a few dollars to my name, but she said it didn't matter.

"You don't want anything?" I said.

She shrugged. "Some jujubes? If there's any money left? I don't have any money."

"You never do."

"It's because I'm a girl."

Fifteen minutes later we wheeled our bikes onto the verandah at Odegaards' store.

"Why's it spelled *Odegaards*?" Charlotte shoved her right foot down onto her bike's kickstand. "You know, with two *A*s?"

"Nobody knows." I let my bike topple onto the concrete walkway. The kickstand was broken. "Maybe it's a mistake."

"Weird. Wee-urd." She skipped ahead several steps, like a cantering pony. "Look. It's Mrs. Barker's car. What's she doing here?"

Mrs. Barker's green-and-white Peugeot — green body, white roof — was parked alongside the store's long verandah, adjacent to a series of rectangular wooden pillars, the beige paint peeling away. The car's engine was still running.

"She's buying something," I said. "It's a store. What do you think?"

"This world is making me crazy. That's what I think. Cray-ay-zee!"

Charlotte pushed the door open, the bell jingled, and she marched inside. I followed. Right away, I saw Mrs. Barker. She was standing at the counter, with her back to the entrance. She was wearing a white blouse and a pair of emerald trousers. What are they called, the short ones? Capri pants? I think that's the name. I wondered whether she had dressed to match the colour scheme of her car. Leslie, the Odegaards' daughter, was waiting on the other side of the counter. She had her hand pressed against a book she'd been reading, holding it open at a certain page. At the peal of the bell, she looked up. She was wearing those heavy glasses she always wore, with lenses like bottle bottoms. I think she was borderline blind.

"Hi," she said.

"Hi-ho," said Charlotte. "Hello there, Mrs. Barker. What's cookin'?"

"Hello, children." Mrs. Barker looked back at Leslie and waved impatiently. "Oh — why not make it Du Maurier? I'll have a pack of Du Maurier. King size."

Almost at once, I realized the woman was drunk — drunk again. There was something not quite right about the way she steadied herself against the counter to keep from swaying. She had to work at it just a little bit too hard. She was having trouble with her money, too, fumbling with the bills. But she managed to pay for her cigarettes, and she hurried out of the store.

Charlotte and Leslie began chattering to each other; they were pals at school. Meanwhile, I wandered over to the candy counter, where the chocolate bars were displayed. Leslie looked up. She had her dark-brown hair knotted in a ponytail, which was a switch. She mostly wore braids.

"The usual …?" she said.

I stiffened at once. "The what …?"

"You know — Turkish delight and a Tahiti Treat? That's what you always get."

She'd noticed? Why had she noticed? I was tempted to select something different now, just to prove her wrong. But in the end I got the same things I always did. As it turned out, there was enough money left over to buy Charlotte a small brown paper bag of jujubes and a half-pint carton of chocolate milk.

I slid the change into the pocket of my shorts and looked up. "Why are there two *As* in *Odegaard*?"

Leslie frowned for a few moments, then brightened. "Why are there two *Ls* in *Mitchell*?"

When I didn't say anything, she tilted her head, and her glasses wobbled on her nose.

"Well ...?"

Just then, we heard a huge roar outside, followed by an even louder metallic crash. The three of us hurried out onto the verandah. The disturbance had come from the direction of Weintrub's Garage. Mrs. Barker had somehow managed to drive her car backward across the street before piling straight into another vehicle in Weintrub's earthen parking lot. Steam sang from the radiator of the car she'd hit — the engine must have been running at the time — and the Peugeot's wheels spun in the dirt, making a high-pitched whine. It seemed Mrs. Barker still had her foot pressed down on the accelerator. Mr. Weintrub hobbled out of the garage and managed to haul the woman from her car. At once, the whining stopped. Then he went back and switched off the ignition of the car she'd struck.

We remained where we were, watching events unfold. It wasn't long before Hilary showed up. I guess she must have been the only one home at the Barkers' place when Mr. Weintrub trudged back into the garage and got on the phone. He was reporting what had happened, I guessed. Hilary arrived behind the wheel of Colonel Barker's old pickup. It was clear that she had come to collect Mrs. Barker, who was pretty hysterical by now, not to mention drunk, but otherwise unhurt. Hilary climbed out of the truck. She was wearing blue jeans, a beige T-shirt, and a pair of cowboy boots. Her hair was tied back in a sort of bun. Mrs. Barker immediately started to shout at her.

"Harlot! Slut! Home wrecker!"

Hilary barely acknowledged the woman. Instead, she kept shifting her gaze to take in Bruce Gruber, who had shuffled out of the garage and now stood in the parking lot, chest thrust out, wiping his greasy hands on a towel. He kept trading glances with Hilary. Twice, he did something with his eyes, something I had never seen

anyone do before — not a wink but a kind of wowing of the eyes.
It was both subtle and brief, so brief as to be almost imperceptible,
but I noticed it, and it struck me as something significant, like a new
and important word in a foreign language I was just beginning to
learn. I wasn't completely sure what it meant, that expression, but
I did not like it one bit. I wanted to get out of there.

"Come on, Charlotte," I said. "Let's go."

"What ...? Now?"

"Yes, now."

And we left before Hilary could say anything to me. I had a
feeling she wasn't going to anyway. She was too busy making eyes
at Bruce Gruber. She didn't even look at me. It was as if I weren't
even there.

For three days following that afternoon, Hilary failed to call.
There was no explanation, nothing, just silence. It was only after
those three days had crawled by that the telephone on our kitchen
wall consented to ring. My mother summoned me down from
my room and handed me the receiver. I recognized Hilary's voice
at once, and I felt a pressure building in my chest. I expected her
to tell me why she hadn't called. I expected her to suggest something to do with horses, about resuming our lessons. But she did
neither. Instead, she asked if I wanted to see a movie that night at
the Newburgh Drive-In, and I, idiot that I was, thought she was
asking me out on a date. I already knew what movie was playing
at the drive-in — *Son of Flubber.* It was a stupid children's movie,
but I didn't care. I wanted to blurt out yes, but something held me
back. I was supposed to be angry, because of Hilary's failure to call.

"Look," she said. "I don't have much time. Do you want to come?"

"Yes," I said. Weakling.

After Hilary hung up, I replaced the receiver in its cradle. I
turned to walk away and immediately felt a sense of weightlessness.
Then my hands started to shake.

"Who was that?" My mother was sorting laundry in the dining room. "Was that who I think it was?"

"Hilary Anson," I said. I shuffled out of the kitchen and slumped down in a chair at the dining table.

"Hmm. I don't think much of that. What did she want?"

"To go to the movies."

"When? Not tonight?"

"Yes. I think. I wasn't really paying attention."

"Oh, you weren't?" My mother struck a paper match and lit a Matinée. She blew out the flame and took a puff of her cigarette. She looked at me, smoke fluttering out of her nostrils. "There will be how many of you going?"

"I'm not sure." Going, she had said, as opposed to not going. "I don't know. A bunch."

"And who will be driving?"

"Hilary. I guess."

"I don't trust that girl. No one does." She blew out a contrail of smoke. "Well, we'll see."

I knew what that meant. It meant I could go. She even gave me some money to cover admission and snacks.

Hilary showed up at eight o'clock that evening.

"Don't be late," said my mother. She was the one in charge. It was my father's bridge night — out playing bridge with the boys.

"No worries," said Hilary. "We'll be back in a jiff."

She made a pantomime of clutching me by the scruff of my neck and marching me along the walkway. There was no one else in the car, a rental. Mrs. Barker's Peugeot was down for repairs. Possibly Bruce Gruber was working on the car right at that moment. I didn't really think about that. Nor did I pay much attention to the reddish bruise on Hilary's cheek, the result of a scrape or something — or maybe someone had hit her. I should have asked her about that, but I didn't. I was going out on a date with Hilary Anson; that was all I could think about. I decided — right then, right there — that this evening marked the moment in my life when I finally entered adulthood. I would no longer concern myself with childish things. I would set them aside.

That was what I told myself, but I was to be badly disappointed. Instead of heading straight north along Sixth Line, the most direct route to Newburgh, Hilary turned left and drove into Hatton. She pulled up at Weintrub's Garage, which was closed. At once, I felt a grim premonition — Bruce Gruber. I might have known he would be a part of this. And, sure enough, here he was, leaning against the side of his own car, a shiny black Ford Thunderbird that he'd bought second-hand and was fixing up, judging by its glossy new paint job and the custom wheel rims.

I looked at Hilary. "What ...?"

"You'll be my bodyguard tonight, hey," she said. "I need reinforcements." She rolled down her window, looked up at Bruce, and smiled, batting her eyes. "Howzit?"

Bruce glared down at me. "What's with the kid?"

FIFTEEN

Hilary
South Africa, Winter 1962

IT WAS WINTER IN NATAL, and Mrs. Anson was laid up with the
flu. From her bed she wrote to Hilary at least three times a week,
recounting a litany of woe. By now Hilary was toughing out the
early winter in her new place of confinement, a boarding school in
Jozi — a species of prison in its way. Here she plotted her escape.
First she would break out of school, which would not be difficult at
all. The problem lay in figuring out what to do next. Rescue Muletsi,
yes. But how? There had to be a way. All day long she racked her
brains for an answer, but she wasn't coming up with much.

Meanwhile, she read her mother's letters, long, meticulous
accounts of gossip and sorrow. It was winter now, Mrs. Anson
wrote, and the days sloped past, unusually inclement, abnormally
wet. Miserable as it was, the unseasonable weather suited the mood
at the Anson farm. To take his mind off his troubles, Hilary's father
spent much of his time these blustery days roaming his large estate
on horseback. Hilary could easily imagine him galloping across
the crests of hills, thrashing at things with a polo mallet while
groaning in perpetual discomfort. She wondered whether the man
would ever be able to look her straight in the eyes again, assuming
he ever had.

Only once had he even broached the subject of her disgrace, and that had been to reject her claims, the charges she had levelled against Jack — all lies, as far as her father was concerned. Likewise, he avoided speaking of the matter to anyone else. It was too painful to dwell on, finished and done. Instead, according to Hilary's mother, he had returned with a vengeance to the labours he knew best, filling the long days with his professional dealings, his mining interests, and the strange vagaries of politics. When there was time to spare, he rode.

Mrs. Anson wrote that the new horse he'd got, the stallion named South Wind, was a rare source of consolation, helping to take his mind off his family troubles — in other words, what his daughter had done. But this provisional peace was not to last. Instead, the phone rang — a telephone call from an old friend of his, now serving the republic as a judge in Pietermaritzburg. That call upended everything.

Hilary's mother related what little she knew. It had been late morning when the phone rang at the Ansons' home. After fielding the call, one of the maids had been obliged to haul on a pair of tall rubber boots and stomp up into the wild meadows where her master was staggering about, on foot this time, destroying things with his cane, slashing at weeds and wildflowers, at errant blades of grass that had had the effrontery to grow too tall for his liking.

"The telephone, *baas*," she said.

Without a word, Daniel Anson lumbered back down to the great house, where he thudded inside and wrenched the receiver from another servant. It may well have occurred to him to wonder, as he often did, just how many domestic workers he employed. No bloody idea. He could never keep track of the lot. Hilary's mother listened in on the bedroom extension, as was her common practice. She shielded the mouthpiece with her hand.

Hilary's father stood in the vestibule downstairs and bellowed into the apparatus. "Go on. Speak, damn it."

It was Benjamin Greene on the line. Justice Benjamin Greene. Friend of his youth.

"The boy is out of jail," the judge said.

"Boy ...? What boy?"

"The Dadla boy. The one that took a run at your stable manager."

"What? They let him go?"

"No. He broke out, he and some other men."

"Broke out ...?"

"Yes. You know — escaped."

"You don't say." Hilary could picture her father worrying at his forehead with the heel of his free hand. "And this is of interest to me, why?"

"Just thought you'd want to know, that's all. Well, of course you would."

"*Of course* ...?" She could almost hear Daniel Anson's voice rising, his mood testy as ever. "Why *of course*? What are you insinuating, man?"

"Forgive me," said Justice Benjamin Greene. "I over-spoke. Please. My regards to your dear wife."

Hilary sat up on her bed at once, clutching the notepaper in both hands. She peered back down at the paper's surface, scribbled with her mother's faint and spidery script. She had to read the passage two more times to be certain she understood it right. Bloody frigging hell. All this time she had been tormenting herself, struggling to come up with some means of achieving this very result, and now it had happened without her having to lift a finger. Who could explain it? Still, there it was. Muletsi was free, whereabouts unknown.

As for the phone call from Justice Greene, Hilary's father didn't even both to say thank you. He just slammed the receiver back into its cradle. Hilary could imagine what he was feeling — a need to sit down, all his bulk suddenly more than he could manage, sweat prickling at his brow, diverse organs churning in his gut. She could imagine what he was thinking. All of a sudden, it would seem to him as if no time had passed at all. It would seem as if he was only just now learning about his daughter and the kaffir boy, as raw as if he were hearing about it for the very first time — as raw and, to him, as odious.

Not so for Hilary. To her, these were details — minutiae either observed or imagined but unimportant either way. Beside the point. The point was this: Muletsi had got out of jail. A day later she received a letter from Muletsi's mother, imparting the very same news. Mrs. Dadla said she was reluctant to burden Hilary with troubles not her own, but felt she had no choice. Not to share would be worse. The next day, after emptying an emergency account that was kept in her name at First National Bank, Hilary boarded an airplane bound for Durban. When she got to Durban, she would take a taxi up to Mooi River. Her father would have to pay for that, too.

SIXTEEN

Sam

Ontario, Summer 1963

"WE'RE NOT GOIN' TO the fuckin' movies with him," said Bruce, pointing at me. "I'm tellin' yuh straight out."

But he was wrong about that. After a brief but heated discussion between Hilary and Bruce, the three of us wound up driving to Newburgh in Bruce Gruber's car. We left Mrs. Barker's rental in the parking lot beside the garage. Bruce was fuming mad — or not fuming, exactly. It was the colder kind of anger. The silent kind. He drove as though he were piloting a racing car. He kept his foot heavy on the gas, gunning the engine while overtaking slower vehicles. At every intersection, he squealed his tires, leaving dark skid marks on the pavement.

A worthless runt — that was the way he saw me. And I was a runt, compared to him. He was eighteen years old, give or take, and had a large, slab-like frame. His hair was dark, oiled, and combed into an exaggerated duckbill at the front. His eyes were squinty and narrow, frequently bloodshot. When he wasn't dressed in a mechanic's coveralls, he generally wore blue jeans and a white T-shirt, usually with a package of cigarettes tucked into a roll in the right sleeve just below his shoulder. Export "A"s. He had a vocabulary of approximately twenty words, about half of which were variants of the verb *to fuck*.

I settled myself against the door in the back seat and peered out the window at the green countryside streaming past. *Compensating.* That was the word. The guy felt embarrassed because he hadn't stood up to Hilary, and now he was compensating by showing off at the wheel. Pretty soon, we would all be killed.

"What's the show?" Bruce said.

We were about halfway to Newburgh. This was the first coherent phrase he'd uttered since we'd left Hatton.

Hilary told him. *Son of Flubber.* She said she was sorry about that. It was the only film playing.

"Whadayuh mean?" Bruce blasted the horn at an oncoming vehicle. He shook his fist at the driver as the two cars sailed past each other. "It's suppose to be fuckin' A. Even better than *The Absent-Minded Professor.*"

"Well, it's all there is. I don't choose the films."

"*Films* ...?" he said, as if this were a word from a foreign language.

"Films. Movies."

"Fuck."

Things went downhill from there.

At the drive-in, I offered to buy snacks and drinks for everyone, a sort of peace offering. But this turned out to be a mistake. Possibly, whatever I did would have been a mistake that night, but the food run did not go well. First, I didn't have enough money, and so I had to hurry back to borrow some from Hilary. Next, when I again returned to the car — weighed down at last with hot dogs, french fries, and drinks of pop, all arranged on a cardboard tray — it turned out I'd mixed up the condiments.

"I can't fuckin' stand relish," said Bruce. "Makes me sick." He opened the door and tried to scrape the offending substance away with his fingers. When that was done, he bit into the hot dog, which was cold by now. "Cold as ice. Jesus fuckin' Christ."

Even worse, I had got vinegar for the french fries instead of tomato ketchup. I thought everyone put vinegar on their french fries, everyone in the world. Bruce Gruber seemed to be an exception. He opened his door again and spat a mouthful of french-fried potato onto the gravel.

"Eeee-yew. What the fuck was that?"

After a while Bruce reached over and fumbled for something near Hilary's feet. When he straightened back up, he was clutching a liquor bottle — Hiram Walker Special Old Rye. Rye is a poor man's drink. I knew that much. My parents and almost all their friends drank Scotch. Bruce twisted off the cap.

"Here," he said to Hilary. He splashed a generous portion of rye into her paper cup and then poured some more into his own — quite a bit more. He glanced at me in the rear-view mirror and held up the bottle. "You ...?"

"Uh. Sure." I reached forward with my cup, which was about two-thirds full of Mountain Dew. "Thanks."

Bruce tilted the bottle and laughed, shaking his head. "Little prick. A drinker. Hah."

"That's enough," said Hilary.

"Don't spill it, you retard."

The large paper cup was now full to the brim, and some of the liquid splattered onto the seat. I raised the cup to my lips and tried to slurp a little of its contents, careful so that no more would spill. It tasted awful. But I kept sipping from the cup all the same, and after a while it didn't seem so bad. We stayed like that for a time, slurping our drinks and picking at what remained of our food, no one saying anything. The trailers were flashing on the huge screen.

Soon Hilary began to laugh. "Do you know the word in Afrikaans for a *liquor store*?" she said, seemingly out of nowhere. I guess the rye made her think about alcohol in general.

"Afri-cans?" said Bruce. "What the fuck is that?"

"The language that Afrikaners speak. The Dutch people in South Africa. Where I'm from." She laughed again. "Liquor store," she repeated. "Do you know what the word is for *liquor store* in the language those people speak?"

"No," said Bruce. "I don't know what the word in whatchama-callit is for whatever you said. People."

"No. For a *liquor store*."

He frowned. "Huh ...?"

"What I'm asking you. I'm asking if you know the Afrikaans word for a *liquor store*. It's a rhetorical question."

"A what ...?" He didn't seem to be keeping up.

She giggled and said something. It sounded like "drank-vinkel."

"Drank-what-el?" I said.

"*Vinkel*." She laughed and swallowed some more of her drink. Orange Crush and rye. "*Drankvinkel*. I think it's the funniest word."

I laughed, too. "I vink it's the vunniest vord. I vinkel it's the vunniest vord." I took another sip. Actually, I was starting to like it.

"Christ," said Bruce. "Jesus fuckin' Christ."

I was quickly coming to the conclusion that Bruce Gruber would always be hampered in his professional pursuits unless he took urgent and comprehensive measures to enrich his vocabulary. I was about to say something to this effect but managed to stop myself. It was at this point or at a point slightly later that Bruce topped up my paper cup, again, with more rye.

I sipped some more of my drink. First it had seemed gross. Then it had seemed surprisingly good. Now it was seeming gross again. I fought off an urge to belch, but I belched anyway.

"Excuse me," I said.

"Fuckin' hell." Bruce rolled down his window and reached over for the speaker that was mounted on a steel post and connected by a spiralling cable. He rolled the window halfway back up and balanced the speaker on the top edge of the glass pane. "Fuckin' bloody hell."

123

The movie trailers were still playing, but now they had sound. I hunched in the middle of the back seat so I could watch the screen through the gap that separated Bruce and Hilary. That didn't last long. First, Bruce's outsize shadow loomed up out of the darkness, blocking my view of the movie screen completely.

"Where's your fuckin' cup?"

I held up the large paper container, and Bruce sloshed it with rye. Then he swung back into his seat and topped up both his own cup and Hilary's. For a time, there was silence, except for the tinny sounds that yammered through the speaker. We sipped our drinks and peered out the windshield at the succession of movie shorts being projected onto the giant outdoor screen. Finally, Hilary spoke.

"My, what long arms you have," she said, speaking in a sort of Little-Red-Riding-Hood voice, a girlish voice.

As far as I could make out, Bruce was massaging Hilary's left shoulder with his right hand. He had to reach a long way, though, because she was scrunched up against the passenger door. I sipped from my drink again, and my head lolled to one side. I felt as if I were gaining weight fast, all of it on one side of my cranium. It was the rye. I didn't think I could swallow much more.

Right about then, several things happened in quick succession. First, the feature presentation began: *Son of Flubber.* Next, Bruce seemed to fling himself across the front seat as if seized by the force field of a powerful magnet. He landed almost right on top of Hilary. For a time, no one said a word. The only sound was the metallic reverberation of the movie speaker — recorded actors' voices, loud and very thin.

Then Hilary spoke: "Get off me."

A little later: "I said get off me."

Later still: "Stop it. I said stop it."

All I could hear from Bruce was a lot of heavy breathing and the occasional grunt.

"Ow," said Hilary. "Christ, stop it. You're hurting me, hey."
Then louder: "I said you're hurting me."

I tried to move. I wanted to do something to stop this, whatever it was, but I was having trouble turning my thoughts into action. My balance was shaky, and everything seemed kind of blurry.

A few seconds later, Hilary's voice rose almost to a scream: "You're hurting me!"

Immediately, Bruce seemed to vault backward, landing in the driver's seat on the other side of the car. His elbow punched the horn, which blared a couple of times. "What the fuck ...?"

I managed to lean forward, and I turned my head toward Hilary, to see what was going on. I couldn't believe what I saw. Hilary was holding a gun. Even in my woozy state and in the unsteady light cast by the giant movie screen, I could clearly make out that much. She was huddled with her back pressed against the passenger door, and she was clutching a gun, obviously the same weapon she had shown me that night in the upstairs bathroom at our house — the Makarov she'd got from Nelson Mandela. She was pointing the gun at Bruce, who had his hands raised in surrender or something like it.

"Jesus, are you crazy?" His voice was weak, an octave or so higher than normal. "Put that away. What the fuck are you doing?"

"You wouldn't get off me, shame," said Hilary. Her voice was steady, gone flat and cold. She kept the gun pointed at Bruce. "When I say get off me, I mean get off me. It's that simple."

No one budged. No one said anything. I remained in my seat in the back of the car. I tried to move, but I couldn't seem to do it. It was as if I were glued to the upholstery. A gun! She was pointing a gun at Bruce Gruber, and I fully believed that, next, she was going to shoot him. But that wasn't what happened next. What happened next was ... I threw up.

SEVENTEEN

Jack
South Africa, Winter 1962

JACK LEARNED ABOUT THE kaffir's escape from a report in the *Witness*, the Pietermaritzburg paper. Right away he guessed that Hilly would be returning from Joburg. Of course, she would. He knew exactly how her mind worked, part of the skill he had, what he liked to call "the knack." The girl was loyal to a fault, and now the direction of her loyalty had shifted to an unspeakable degree, migrated to a dirty black-skinned cheat named Muletsi Dadla, a.k.a. Berkeley Hunt, now a convict freshly escaped from jail.

Jack was passably sure he knew what was next in store. One way or another, Hilly would soon be on a plane to Durban, and then she'd take a taxi up here. Her dad would pay the passage, of course, cursing all the while. Jack doubted it would be long before she arrived, a couple of days maybe, not more than that. She would be fixing to find the boy, which meant that she would bear watching herself. That was all right. Jack knew a man in Bruntville who would keep him well informed in the event that Hilly was to venture over there.

Now he got up from the little table, to fix himself another cuppa with chicory and to cadge himself a smoke. That done, he settled back into the creaky old Fred Astaire and took another drag.

Strange. Here he was, puffing on a fag and sipping a nice cuppa molten toffee on a drizzly morning in Natal while reading the paper from Pietermaritzburg — and already he knew the future. Already he knew what was to come. He reached up and gave his forehead a tap. Many a man would trade his right arm to possess a portion of grey matter such as Jack Tanner had got, right effing here.

Still, he couldn't help wondering how this foreknowledge made him feel, emotion-wise. He was not exactly sure. It was hard to get a fix on his feelings some days. He'd encountered this trouble on previous occasions. At times his feelings would swill together into a rowdy blur that left him woozy on his feet, made him do things he didn't fully intend. But at least he could say this: he felt a cracking lot better now than he'd been feeling of late. That much he could say. He'd been missing Hilary Anson something terrible, more than he'd ever imagined he would. He'd been wanting a chance to put matters straight between them, to square accounts, you might say. He'd have liked everything to be back to the way it was before. If that wasn't possible — and, with her away in Jozi, it surely was not — then maybe something else was, some sort of agreement, a truce of some kind. Just the thought of it raised a warmth in his gut.

But back to the question at hand — the boy's escape. According to the newspaper report, three men had got away together, this Muletsi Dadla and two others. Already, he'd forgotten the other men's names. A search was on, the police said. As always, the constabulary wished to assure all and sundry that the miscreants would be apprehended in short order. Until that happened, the public should exercise caution, as the individuals in question were possibly armed and surely dangerous.

Jack stubbed out his smoke in the small glass tray and cadged himself another, took a drag. Outside, the rain was pelting down at a dismal pace. It was the dry season, supposed to be, and look at the weather they'd got. He glanced back at the paper and reread that last sentence. *Possibly* armed …? He could well believe it. It was more than likely the three malefactors had simply lifted their guns from the prison guards while the guards themselves had nodded off and were having themselves a comfy little Sooty and Sweep. On the other hand, he also had reason to wonder if the escape hadn't been staged from the start — staged for his own benefit. He hadn't heard from Walt van Niekerk on the subject, or not as yet, but it was possible that old Walt — captain of the local police, no less — had put out the word. Let the boy walk free so's old Jack Tanner can have his fun, have a go of his own at the miserable wanker. Wouldn't be the first time that something of the sort had transpired. Of course, it was also possible that the convicts had managed to liberate themselves on their own initiative. Jack couldn't rule it out. The rank incompetence of the civic authorities in these parts was sometimes hard to believe. And what of the likelihood that the fugitives would soon be caught? Not as likely as all that. A kaffir can hide a good long while in a country of kaffirs. These three buggers might manage to keep themselves scarce for weeks on end, maybe longer. They could simply disappear.

But Jack didn't figure his old pal Berkeley would be venturing down that path. Jack had an idea the boy might be casting his shadow around here before very long. Berkeley had his old ma to think of, for one thing. Besides, at the end of the day a black man is a dog. You take him away from his customary haunts, and the moment you turn him loose he'll be on his way back home again, tail between his legs. That was what Jack's instinct told him. He had a feeling old Berkeley Hunt would be showing up around Mooi River sooner rather than later. The boy's mother would have sensed it, too. Maybe even Hilly would see it, once she was apprised of the boy's escape. Could be even the police comprehended it, but Jack had some doubts in his mind on that score. The police in this country? Powerful long on muscle. Pitiful short on brains.

Besides, if Jack had any say in the matter at all, it would not be the police that imposed a punishment upon a certain escaped convict known to some as Mr. Berkeley Hunt. No, sir. Where would be the justice in that? Why, there would be no justice at all. Jack had a different idea. To wit: he would take the helm now, Captain, and steer the ship from this point on. Who was more entitled than the man who'd withstood the attack? Damn that kaffir to hell. Even now Jack could feel a sting when he reached up to touch the left side of his face. He could feel the rough pebbling of skin, the unnatural contours where the bone had shattered. His face was still scarred and misshapen from the time when that Berkeley Hunt whipped a bridle at him. That was a misdeed he could not forget — a kaffir boy taking a run at a white man like that, throwing his weight into the fray before an honest bloke had time to get his own self set, his balance square, his arms up, his fists cocked. No righteous dog would ever have done such a thing. You fight a man, you fight him fair. That is the rule for gents. You don't blindside a good man and kick him to the ground. Cowardice is what that is, what that boy had done — dirty black cowardice — and it stuck in Jack's throat like a bone.

EIGHTEEN

Sam

Ontario, Summer 1963

"I OVERREACTED." HILARY frowned at her cigarette. "I shouldn't have pointed the gun at him. That was wrong."

"But he was attacking you." I hesitated. "Or something."

"Still, no need for a gun, hey."

"I would have saved you."

She laughed. "Truth is, you did. I don't think it was the gun that chased Grube away. It was —"

"I know. I know." Still, she did have a gun, and she had pointed it at the guy. As for my part in the drama, all I could do was apologize, which I did yet again.

"Never you mind." She closed her eyes. "Frigging hell. Let's not talk about it. Any of it."

We were hunched side by side in the playground by the snack bar at the Newburgh Drive-In, each of us squeezed into a seat that was part of a children's swing apparatus. There were no kids anywhere nearby; all were gathered with their parents, safe in their family cars, paying rapt attention to the movie. But neither Hilary nor I had any interest in watching the show.

A gun. She'd pulled a gun on Bruce Fucking Gruber. It seemed unbelievable, and yet I knew it was so. The knowledge seemed to open an endless span of possibilities, more than I'd ever dreamed of. The dimensions of my world seemed to stretch as far as infinity, to the point of bursting. Anything seemed possible now. Everything that had once seemed ordinary had now been transformed into something larger, more powerful, with consequences I could barely imagine.

As for Bruce Gruber, he was gone. After Hilary had put down the gun, he ordered us both out of his car. He roared away in a fury, kicking up torrents of loose gravel and leaving us both stranded at the drive-in. I wondered why Hilary had anything to do with a guy like that. What did she see in him? Maybe it didn't take much. He was stubborn, he was slow, and he had never in his life met anyone like Hilary Anson. Put those factors together, and they were all she needed, I guess — or I do now. But just then I wasn't thinking along those lines. I was thinking, *Screw you, Bruce Gruber.*

Meanwhile, Hilary and I were still shipwrecked at the drive-in. By this time, I had got myself cleaned up in the snack-bar washroom. For her part, she had smoked about nine cigarettes and drunk about three cups of black coffee, supposedly to calm her nerves. Next we'd called Colonel Barker on the pay phone, pleading with him to come fetch us. He grumbled for a time but finally said he would. What choice did he have?

Concerning the gun, at first Hilary would say only what she had told me before — that she didn't feel safe without it, or not in South Africa. Things were different back there, different for everyone. Why, even Nelson Mandela was behind bars now, a prisoner of conscience, incarcerated for his beliefs. She was silent for a time, and then she sighed. She said she owed me a bit of explanation. We were friends, after all, and that meant something. To her, it did.

"Me, too," I said, thinking that now she was going to come clean. Now she would tell me everything there was to tell about her past.

As it turned out, she did not do that — not even close. But she did recount the broad outlines of what occurred: the conflict between Jack Tanner and her boyfriend, an African named Muletsi Dadla; the times spent with his mother in a place called Bruntville; Muletsi's imprisonment and, later, his escape; a mysterious individual named Everest Ndlovu. Tensions mounted until she and this Muletsi were forced to make a run for it on horseback, aiming for a place called Basutoland. As it turned out, their attempted flight came up short, and Jack Tanner shot Muletsi dead by the banks of the Tsoelike River. Hilary had been there, at that very spot, and she had witnessed everything — her own soulmate murdered right before her eyes. After that it had been too dangerous for her to remain in South Africa, so she now found herself in Canada, where she would be safe, or so it was thought.

"So here you are," I said, "hiding out at the Newburgh Drive-In."

"Yebo."

I let out a long breath. "That must have been horrible."

"What was?"

"Your friend. You know." I tried to say his first name.

"Muletsi," she said. "Dadla." She nodded. "It *was* horrible. Worse than horrible. Just imagine."

I wasn't sure I could. "Why did that guy shoot him?" I meant the other man, the white man. Jack Tanner.

She shrugged and shook her head. "Because Muletsi was black. In South Africa, that's all the reason you'd need."

"But he went to jail, right?"

"Not on your life. A white man who kills a black man? Jail? Not bloody likely. In South Africa, it's all part of the agenda."

She stared down at her shoes for a time, and I wondered whether she might be crying.

"Anyway," she said, "it's done now. It can't be undone in any way."

I listened but said nothing. Never in my life had I known anyone who'd been associated with a murder. It was like a Perry Mason show brought to life, a Perry Mason show set on the other side of the world. Just think: a friend of hers, more than a friend, shot dead right before her eyes. I had more questions to ask, plenty more, but some instinct made me stop. Hilary was still staring at the ground, and now I really thought she might be crying. Before long she started to glide back and forth in her swing, humming another of her South African tunes.

"What's that one called?"

"'Yini Madoda.'" She told me its name means "Why Men?" in Xhosa. She swayed back and forth in the swing.

I preferred to remain motionless. I was still feeling pretty groggy. I kept glancing over at Hilary's leather shoulder bag, where the pistol was hidden away.

"He beat me up once," I said.

"What ...?"

"Bruce Gruber. Well, he beat me up a million times, but this one time was the worst."

"Tell me."

Hilary brought her swing to a halt, leaned closer to me. She scrunched up her forehead, as if she really did want to know. I remember being surprised by that, her degree of interest. Why would she care? But I told her the story, anyway — about that time with the football. It had been a gift from my dad, something special, a genuine leather football. It wasn't made of rubber, the kind of football you normally see. This one was made of real pigskin.

One time I had taken that football to school — to show off, I guess. A few of us spent our recess and lunch break tossing the ball around. No one bothered us. But at the end of the school day, Bruce Gruber and a couple of his pals showed up. They included Davey Odegaard and a boy named Tony Wills, a guy with yellow skin and buckteeth who was from England. First, they took the football away from me, and then they started throwing it among themselves, just to taunt me. I ran to one guy, and he threw it to another guy, so I ran to that guy, and he threw it to the third guy. It was supposed to be fun.

"And this went on for how long?" Hilary lit a cigarette, put her head back, and blew out a spiral of smoke that quickly vanished, swallowed by the shifting half-light cast by the huge movie screen.

"Fifteen minutes, maybe? Give or take."

"Hmm."

I believe now that she was still gauging Bruce, still trying to get an idea of what he would or would not do.

"Anyway, I finally figured out that it was useless to keep chasing my football. I was never going to get it back. So, instead, I ran straight at Bruce Gruber, and I didn't stop, even after he threw the ball away to one of his buddies, Davey or Tony. I kept right on going until I almost ran right into him. I had to look straight up to see his face. I told him to give my football back, and I gave him a push, with both hands."

Hilary tossed her cigarette away. "And what happened then?"

"I guess he must have knocked me out. When I came to, they were gone. Bruce and the other guys."

"And you …?"

"Bloody nose. Black eye. You name it. I don't remember what else."

"And the football?"

I shook my head. "That's the funny thing."

"What is?"

"I never expected to see it again. Once it's gone, it's gone. But he gave it back."

"Bruce did?"

I nodded. "Uh-huh. About two weeks later, he walked into the schoolroom and put it on my desk. Didn't say a word."

"That seems gallant."

"To you, maybe."

She shrugged. "Interesting, though. Honourable, in a way. Even bullies have their virtues."

"I guess."

To me, Bruce Gruber was a bully, plain and simple. But it seemed that Hilary thought otherwise. I also had the feeling she was storing this information away, this new insight into Bruce's character, an unexpected flourish of chivalry that might prove useful someday.

"That doesn't mean I'm defending him," she said, maybe just a bit too hastily. "I hate bullies, too, hey."

And I thought I understood what she meant: she hated Bruce Gruber. But that wasn't the point. In fact, it was the very opposite of the point. She didn't hate Bruce Gruber. Instead, she needed him, just as much as she needed me — more, even. But I didn't understand that, not then. Back then, I didn't understand anything at all.

After I had finished my story about the football, Hilary and I stayed where we were, drifting back and forth in our swing seats until Colonel Barker showed up, driving his Cadillac straight onto the drive-in grounds. He rolled too fast over a mound of gravel, and the car's chassis crunched down against the hard, rough texture of it, making a grinding sound, almost a screech, scattering flurries of sharp pebbles out to the sides. Hilary and I both stood up.

"Prepare yourself," she said. "This could be just a little bit wretched."

But it wasn't so bad. Either Colonel Barker wasn't angry anymore or he was too angry to speak. Either way, we rode back to Kelso in silence. Halfway home I fell asleep.

NINETEEN

Jack
South Africa, Winter 1962

"WELL, HULLO, THERE. THAT you, Jacko?"

The voice was deep and very loud, the voice of Daniel Anson. At once, Jack looked up. He watched as the great man lumbered into the grooming bay, putting about half his weight on his knobby wooden cane. Large as Anson was, his clothes always seemed too big for him, everything loose and flappy. He'd be wanting to go for a ride.

"Jack," he said. "How's that old bay gelding of mine today? I've got a mind to take him for a workout. Can you saddle him up for me?"

"Not South Wind?"

"No, not today. Too much work, that one. The bay will do. Tack him up for me now, there's a good man."

"The boy'll do it." Jack called for Innocent, the new Zulu groom, and told him to saddle up the bay gelding, the one named Welshman. "Saddle him up for *baas* Anson." The boy nodded, turned, and hurried away.

"Be out here in a minute," Jack said. "You'll do well on him today, guv. I had him out just the day before yesterday, and he was nice and easy. He'll have his wind back up by now, and his legs are top nick, clean as a whistle."

Mr. Anson nodded. He took a seat on the bench by the horse blankets, kept both hands clasped in front of him, resting on the knob of his cane. He peered out at the grooming bay as if examining the place for the first time, taking it all in — the big equipment box, the strings of faded championship ribbons, the brown bottles of liniment.

"Saw in the paper, did you, about that boy? He broke loose. You saw that?"

Jack ran his hand up the side of his face, felt the stinging and the damage yet. "Yes, guv. I did."

"Don't think he'll be showing up around here, do you, Jack?"

"No, guv. I expect he'll keep pretty clear of this neck of the woods. If he's smart. Course, you never know."

"That's true," Mr. Anson said. "You never do. Mind you watch out for him, Jack. He'll have taken a scunner to you."

"Will do, guv. Keep our eyes peeled — that's the job. Ah, here he comes now." He meant Mr. Anson's horse, Welshman, which worked out to Taff in English slang and was rendered in cockney — as per usual — with a rhyme. "Well there, Riff-Raff. Don't you look bright today?"

They both watched as Innocent attended to the task of saddling and bridling the master's horse. When the task was done, Jack took the reins from the boy and led Welshman out of the stable. Mr. Anson followed, moaning at the effort.

It took the combined strength of Innocent and Jack to give Mr. Anson a leg-up, to get him aloft and into the saddle. That done, they both stepped back. Mr. Anson grunted and squared himself away while Jack shoved his hands into his pockets and hunched his shoulders against the chill.

He hesitated before he spoke again. Unsure, that was what he was — unsure of how much he should say or how it would be received. In a low voice, casual like, he said, "Not heard from Miss Anson of late, have you, guv? She okay?"

"Fine. She's fine. A-one. Up in Joburg, as you know. Thank you for asking, Jack. I appreciate that." He gathered the reins.

"You give her my best now, guv, when you next talk to her. It'd give me pleasure." Jack held his breath. Bold, that. Maybe too bold.

Mr. Anson spoke over his shoulder. "That's kind of you, Jack. I will. I'm glad to see you bear no grudge. She's a good girl. She meant no harm."

"I know that, guv."

The great man kicked Welshman into a trot and bore down the macadam lane, past the poplar windbreak, with the grey hills and valleys beyond.

Jack watched Mr. Anson go, his heart racing in his chest, a ringing in his ears. That Hilly — she'd be here again soon. He was nigh on sure of it. He felt a warm glow spreading out from his gut, just thinking of that, just thinking of her.

THE NEXT TIME I saw her, Hilary was wearing a pair of sunglasses, something she normally did not do.

"Got a shiner." She eased the glasses down the bridge of her nose. "She's a beaut."

I saw at once it was true — a broad rim of purple discolouration under her left eye.

I whistled. "How did that happen?"

"Trust me. You do not want to know."

"No, really."

"Let's just say I walked into a door, hey."

I knew that wasn't so. I also had a pretty good idea who was responsible for that shiner, but I didn't know what to say, so I said nothing. By now, we were trotting along the south shoulder of Number Four Sideroad, not far short of the escarpment's plunging wall. After a few minutes a car raced past us, kicking up waves of dust, practically forcing us both into the ditch. I recognized the vehicle at once — Bruce Gruber's black Thunderbird.

The driver hit the brakes, and the car yawed in front of us, drifting sideways on the dry gravel surface. Both our horses were spooked, and it took some time to calm them down. Meanwhile, the car came to rest on a diagonal in the middle of the road, as if Bruce meant to block the way. That was stupid. The Thunderbird might have presented an obstacle to other cars, but a horse could easily go around. It was all for show.

The driver's door swung open, and Bruce climbed out of the vehicle, adjusting a pair of aviator sunglasses with one hand. The car's engine continued to grumble, like a cat's purr amplified a hundred times. I realized Bruce wasn't alone. I could make out two passengers in the Thunderbird — Edwin Duval, I thought, and Davey Odegaard. They seemed to be Bruce Gruber's current acolytes; he almost always had a couple of those. They remained where they were, smoking cigarettes and staring out the windows at Bruce and at us.

Hilary said nothing at first. Then she shrugged. "Howzit?"

"Fuckin' awful," said Bruce. He didn't so much as glance at me. He cleared his throat and spat off to the side. "I came to say I'm sorry."

"Is it?"

His mouth fell open. Already he seemed to be losing the gist. "Is it what?"

"Sorry. Is it that you are sorry?"

"'Course I am. I just said it. I been lookin' for you everywhere."

"Oh. So this is an apology, hey?"

"Somethin' like it."

"An apology for what?"

"You know." He nodded at her. "For that."

I guessed he meant the black eye. I guessed he was responsible for whatever it was that had led to that.

"Ag. Shame. Well, I'll take your apology under advisement."

"What?"

"Advisement. You know. I'll give it some thought, seek counsel, weigh up options, stuff like that, hey."

Bruce flexed his arm muscles, cracked his knuckles, and lit a cigarette, all in what seemed to be a single, coordinated motion. Calming rituals, I supposed. He breathed smoke out through his nose. "I'm only tryin' to say sorry. If you don't wanna hear it, then ..." He shook his head. "Ah, fuck it."

He clamped his cigarette between his teeth, turned on his heels, and climbed back into his car, slammed the door. Immediately, he gunned the engine. The Thunderbird fishtailed away in a cloud of umber dust that slowly cleared beyond the maple trees near the edge of the escarpment.

"He'll be back," said Hilary. "Sooner than you think. You just wait."

She touched her heels to Club Soda's flanks, and we continued our ride toward the quarry ponds.

When we got there, Hilary started to laugh.

"I'll have to swim in my *broekie*," she said. "*Broekie* and bra. I've got nothing else."

I could guess the meaning of that word, *broekie*. "That's okay," I said. Well, of course it was.

"Easy for you to say."

She ducked into the grove of cedars and emerged a minute later, wearing only her underwear, with the rest of her clothing draped over her arm or clutched in her right hand. Her bra was white and lacy. Her *broekie* — the word itself was enough to make my forehead start to prickle with sweat — was also white and spare. There wasn't much to it.

"Your turn," she said.

I had already seated myself on a rocky ledge, where I was trying to pull my riding boots off. This was never an easy task. Her *broekie*. Usually, at home, I'd use the bootjack that rested on the slate floor, just inside the front door. I could pry my boots off that way. Or I'd get someone else to help me. She was wearing only her *broekie* and bra.

141

Once rid of my boots, I pulled off my socks and immediately felt the heat of the rocky surface beat up through the soles of my feet. Somehow the warmth made me feel even more shivery than before. I slipped behind the cedars to change into my swimming trunks. That done, I gathered my clothes and hobbled out from the bushes. Hilary vaulted onto Club Soda. She was holding Della by a shank and reached down, handed it to me. She'd removed her sunglasses now, and her black eye stood out, a lurid welt of purple spilt across the soft fold of skin beneath her right eye.

She reined Club Soda around and, as she'd done countless times before, she tucked her bare heels into his flanks. Soda took three strides across the granite ledge before hurling himself into the air. An instant later they both crashed into the green element below, the water exploding around them like fragments of crystal. The pond seemed to swallow them both. A moment or so later, they resurfaced, Club Soda snorting, sneezing, and darting his head from side to side, his ears like small separate beasts, twitching first this way, then that. It amazed me how much that horse must have trusted Hilary to obey her like that.

Hilary rolled over onto her back and held one arm in the air as Club Soda drew her out into the middle of the pond. They both turned slow semicircles across the speckled green shell of the water, strewn with patches of gold. I started to lead Della around to the far side of the pond, meaning to stumble in by way of the grassy incline as I always did.

"Not that way," Hilary shouted. "Same way as I went. You can do it."

On another day, I might have refused, just as I had declined many times before. But something about this day was different. Her underwear — could it have been as simple or stupid as that? Or maybe it was our encounter on the road just now with Bruce Gruber. Whatever the reason, I turned Della toward the limestone ledge, then tried to coax her into a trot. At first, she wouldn't do it. She moved backward instead of forward. But I stroked her neck and shoulders and made gentle cooing sounds, and eventually she gave in. By now my heart was pounding. I couldn't believe we were actually going to jump. She squared her shoulders and tucked in her head. She took one stride toward the ledge, then another. I'll be damned if she wasn't gathering herself to jump, when I made a huge mistake. Instead of staying with her, following her movements, I pushed myself forward, anticipating what would come next — Della launching herself into the air.

That was all it took. At once, she dug her hooves into the rocky surface and skidded to a halt. Next thing I knew, I was sailing into space all on my own, with my arms and legs flailing until I hit the water and went under. For a couple of seconds I let myself sink. Then I struggled back to the surface and looked straight up. I found myself peering at Della, who still stood on the brink of the limestone slab, apparently as stunned by what had just happened as I was myself.

"Uh-oh," said Hilary.

It was too late for me to do anything. I could only watch helplessly as Della tilted her head in a vaguely interrogative pose, almost as if she were asking permission to do what she was about to do. After a few seconds she seemed to decide she didn't need anyone's say-so — certainly not mine. She took several steps back, turned to her right, and set off at a brisk trot, back along the wooded trail that led to Number Four Sideroad. A few moments later, she switched to a canter, judging by the fading beat of her hooves. Then she was gone.

I clambered out of the pond and up onto the slab of limestone. At first, I just stood there, dripping water onto the rocky surface. Then I looked at Hilary. "Now what?"

"It's too late to catch her," she said. "Wait. Let me get dressed."

When she emerged from the cedars, Hilary looked a mess, her hair stringy and sopping, the dark bruise around her eye. She'd put her breeches and blouse back on, but they were both patchy with dampness. Now she pulled on her boots and scrunched up her underwear, stuffed it into her backpack. By this time, I had pulled on my jeans and T-shirt, my riding boots.

"No sense in tacking up," she said. "It'll be easier this way." She swung herself up onto Club Soda. Next, she reached back down to give me a hand. "Let's go."

I took her hand, retreated a step, and then swung myself up so that I straddled Club Soda, right behind Hilary. At once, he shot forward a pace or two, indignant at this unwelcome addition of weight.

"What about our stuff?" I said. I meant our saddles and bridles, Hilary's backpack.

"We'll have to come back for everything later."

Hilary clicked her tongue and squeezed her legs, and Club Soda set off at a trot. I wrapped my arms around her waist and did my best to post, pivoting on my knees. After a few jittery strides, Club Soda broke into a canter, a smoother gait. At each twist in the path, I expected to see Della lurking just ahead, but I saw no such thing. It seemed she was well and truly gone.

TWENTY-ONE

Hilary
South Africa, Winter 1962

DANIEL ANSON WAS OPPOSED on principle to surprises, so he was not greatly pleased when Hilary pitched up in Mooi River unannounced. She was riding in a taxi that had brought her from the airport in Durban following an early morning flight from Joburg.

"Hilary …?" He shuffled out onto the verandah and clumped down the wooden steps, leaning heavily on his cane. "You're home?" It seemed to be all he could think of to say.

"Yes, Daddy." She closed the taxi door and approached the foot of the verandah steps. There, she allowed her father to place one hand on her shoulder and give her what, between them, passed for a kiss. She could tell he was sorely put out. "Where's Mummy?"

"Upstairs. She's in bed. BGR."

She knew what that meant. Bug going 'round. But it was probably only partly true — the being in bed, yes, but not the cause. Hilary's mother almost always took to her bed when her husband was about, generally emerging only after he'd set off on yet another of his many business trips. Business or politics.

Now Hilary's father pulled out his wallet to pay the driver. He muttered under his breath, displeased at this unanticipated expense. Hilary watched as Simon, the houseboy, lugged her suitcase up onto the verandah. With a pained expression, Mr. Anson waved off the driver's offer of change — a passive-aggressive gesture if ever there was one — and turned to scowl at her.

"I won't have this, you know. You were expected to remain in Joburg until the end of term."

"Yes, Daddy. I'm sorry. I know." She started up the stairs, heading for her mother's room.

The following day Daniel Anson departed Mooi River for reasons left unexplained, as usual. Hilary waited till the government limousine disappeared beyond the poplar windbreak and then promptly asked her mother for the use of her car.

"Please, Mummy. I won't be gone long. I promise. Please. Please."

Still in her dressing gown, Sharon Anson lit a cigarette — unusual for her, so early in the day. She gave a shrug. She said she knew there would be no peace until she said yes, so she might as well save time and bother by saying yes right away. Hilary clapped her hands and would have given her mother a hug, except the woman backed away. Such overt displays of affection only aggravated her nervous condition.

A half hour later Hilary was at the wheel of her mother's little Vauxhall Victor, heading for Bruntville, where she meant to learn what she could from Mrs. Dadla. She clutched a smoke with one hand and steered with the other. Meanwhile, the sky shone down, electric blue, and a gusting wind agitated a row of eucalyptus trees that slumped above the little township like so many raggedy giants. When she got to the edge of Bruntville, she stopped, cut the engine, and ratcheted the handle of the parking brake. She swung herself out of the car. This was the first time she had found herself in Bruntville without Muletsi to show the way and, for a few brief seconds, she felt an urge to climb back into her car, reverse engines, leave this place.

Instead, she gritted her teeth, got a grip on herself. The hell with that. She hadn't come all the way down from Jozi just to turn tail. She slid the car keys into the side pocket of her skirt and set out on foot. It was almost noon, and school had let out for the morning. Children dawdled along the rutted lane in their uniforms — black jerseys and tan shorts for the boys, navy skirts and jumpers for the girls. They alternately stared at her and looked away, covered their mouths, giggling. Here was a white woman in their midst. They found it embarrassing or funny, or they didn't know what to think.

After a few minutes' walk, she reached the Dadla house and … oh, dear God. The place was abandoned and smoke-charred, the doorway and windowpanes smashed and now blocked with cheap scraps of lumber nailed into place. What on earth had happened here?

Before long a man approached, wearing a baggy grey suit and a battered trilby. "Yes, Miss …?" he said. He removed his hat.

Not for the first time in Bruntville, she had the feeling of being under surveillance. She had the feeling this man had been watching her — or maybe someone else had, someone who had informed this man. Why else would he show up just now, out of the blue, just when she had come upon Mrs. Dadla's house? But now here he was.

"Good morning," she said. "Are you well?"

"Yes, Miss. *Tankie.* And you?"

"Very well. Thank you." She gestured toward the house, what was left of it. "Can you tell me what happened here? Who did this?"

Before venturing to reply, the man proffered his hand. He said his name was Mr. Ndlovu. She took his hand in a brief but firm grip. Ndlovu. The word meant "elephant" in Xhosa. Zulu, too. Even she knew that much. Now, with the requisite courtesies acknowledged, the man drew his forehead into the shape of a frown, considering what else to say. After several moments, he pointed at the ruined house. "Them come and burn it down." He shook his head and made a sombre tsk-ing sound with his tongue. "Very sad. Them very bad."

He meant the police most likely, or people in the pay of the police. A warning — that's what it would have been. She could easily imagine that. A warning to Mrs. Dadla.

"Where is she? Mrs. Dadla? Is she all right?"

His eyebrows arched up. "You're the same one who came before?"

She knew he meant with Muletsi. She nodded. "Yes."

He said nothing, evidently waiting. She realized she had yet to state her name or explain her business here. She hadn't wanted to, hadn't felt safe, but the hell with that, too. "I'm Hilary Anson," she said. "I'm looking for Mrs. Dadla. I'm a friend. Is she all right?"

At first, he said nothing, just tilted his head from side to side several times, as if debating in his mind. After a while, he seemed to reach a decision. "Come." He replaced his hat and turned to retrace his steps along the dirt lane. After a few strides, he turned to look back at her. He waved. "Come."

And so she followed, and she wasn't alone. Stifling their laughter by cupping their hands to their mouths, at least a dozen of the children tagged along as well.

Apart from the obvious reason — to see Mrs. Dadla — she wasn't certain why she'd come to Bruntville, or to Mooi River for that matter. Ever since leaving Joburg, she had worried the question over and over in her mind. In the end, she had decided that her exact purpose didn't matter. She had to follow her instincts, and her instincts had brought her here; that was all she could say. Now here she was, tromping along a dirt lane through Bruntville on the brightest, most bracing kind of winter midday. What was more, she had a dozen kids in those gorgeous school uniforms bringing up the rear. A frigging procession. So bloody cute, those kids. Their cheekbones shone like patches of silver in the overhead sunlight. If you spoke to them, they'd turn all earnest and grave. "Yes, Missus. We are well today. Thank you so. And you, please? Are you very fine?"

"Down this way, Miss," said Mr. Ndlovu. He pushed open a squeaking scrap-board gate. Just beyond the gate, a narrow path led to a sagging, ramshackle dwelling with an old floral sheet draped across the opening in lieu of a door. With Mr. Ndlovu's encouragement, she stepped from the bright sunshine into the murk within. Almost at once, a voice piped up from the semidarkness.

"Good Lord, daughter."

Hilary let her eyes adjust to the gloom until she could see — and there she was, Mrs. Dadla, seated at a table with a yellow plastic cover. The woman staggered upright. She was wearing that long purple cape of hers, the one with the scarlet lining. So she'd just come from church. She took both Hilary's hands in her own.

"And here I thought you were in Joburg still."

Mr. Ndlovu stood near the doorway behind them, hat off, clutching its brim at his waist. He exchanged a few words with Mrs. Dadla, speaking in Xhosa, it seemed. Hilary could understand nothing of the exchange, but it seemed clear to her now that this Mr. Ndlovu was a man of some standing in the community. Probably, he had been delegated to ascertain her business, her purpose in being here. She'd come to see Mrs. Dadla. He knew that now.

"Goodbye now, Miss," he said. He turned and shuffled away.

"Goodbye," she called after him. "Thank you."

Once the man had departed, Mrs. Dadla was immediately up and doing. She hurried over to a deep basin made of tin, with a bucket of water standing inside. "You'll have tea?"

She nodded. "Yes, please, Auntie." It was the term Mrs. Dadla had requested she use. Now she settled herself onto one of the rickety wooden chairs.

Eventually, the kettle whistled from its perch atop a charcoal stove. Mrs. Dadla served the tea in two mismatched cups. She lowered herself into a chair across from Hilary and raised that large face of hers with its strong, rounded features. She'd been a handsome young woman once. You could still tell.

"You must inform me all about Joburg," she said. "I want to know every little thing."

But, of course, Hilary had not come to speak about Johannesburg, and Mrs. Dadla was only being polite. Still, it was best to proceed gradually, for this was the way of the people here. She described her school in Jozi, recounted a few details of her journey back to Natal. Next, she broached the subject of Mrs. Dadla's house, and the woman replied with a description of the attack and her narrow escape, clad only in a nightgown and a pair of woollen socks. Eventually, Hilary sensed that it would be acceptable to bring the conversation around to its real purpose.

"And what of Muletsi?" Did the woman have any news?

Mrs. Dadla fell silent and seemed to grow sombre. She was thinking, of course. She was weighing carefully the words she would next say. And those words came as a surprise. It turned out that he was right here in Bruntville after all. He was here, and he was all right. But he had to lie low.

Hilary couldn't bloody believe it. "Can I see him?"

Mrs. Dadla set down her cup. "Of course you can," she said. They set out at once, Mrs. Dadla leading the way through a maze of twisting lanes and alleys. They were followed by the same entourage of children as before. Despite her age, the woman walked at a punishing pace, clad in her flowing purple cape, like a prophetess from the Old Testament. Presently, they reached a small earthen enclosure surrounded by slouching matchbox houses, their stucco veneer peeling away as if the buildings were moulting a surface that no longer fit.

A dozen boys, give or take, were kicking a makeshift ball in a game of pickup soccer. The ball itself was a primitive affair, made of bunches of paper bags compressed and encircled with layer after

layer of twine. Something caught Hilary's eye, some familiar movement, and what she saw next nearly struck her down. It was Muletsi
himself, sans eyeglasses. He was roaming the edge of the pitch,
calling out instructions to the boys. "Run. Turn. Get back. Cover
your man."

Something caused him to stop and peer up. With his poor
vision, it took him a while to make out what he was looking at.
When he realized it was Hilary across the garbage-strewn pitch, he
raised both his hands to his face and covered his eyes and did not
move. He remained in that position for what seemed a frigging
eternity. Then he eased his hands away from his eyes. When he
apparently understood that what he saw was just what he thought —
not a mirage, not an illusion — he nodded and swung on his heels
and walked away. He slipped past a clutter of crouching buildings,
turned down an alley, and disappeared. Just like that.

TWENTY-TWO

Sam
Ontario, Summer 1963

WHAT WE NEEDED NOW, Hilary said, was a car. That way, we could retrieve our tack from the quarry pond and then drive to my family's place, hoping that Della was already there and that she was safe.

"Come on."

She reined Club Soda to the left, bearing southward along Second Line, and we made our way to the Barkers'.

After we'd put Club Soda out to graze, Hilary hurried into the house, meaning to get the keys to Mrs. Barker's rental car. When she re-emerged, Mrs. Barker was in close pursuit. The woman stormed after Hilary, demanding further explanation of some unnamed circumstance and promising severe retribution if anything that Hilary said turned out to be a whit less than the truth.

"You've had your way too long, little Miss South Africa," she said. "Now you're on probation. I've had it up to here with you."

Hilary bore the onslaught without a word. She slid into the driver's seat of the rental. Mrs. Barker was still hovering on the flagstone walkway. I started to open the passenger door to get in, but something made me stop, some stupidity.

"Hi, Mrs. Barker," I said. "What's cookin'?"

That stopped her. She tilted her head and glared at me, as if I had just said something cogent and arresting, when in reality I was only aping the words Charlotte had used that time in Hatton.

"Get in the car, hey!" This was Hilary.

I did as she said. Pretty soon, we were back on Second Line, heading north. Hilary punched the cigarette lighter. "God in heaven. That woman will be the death of me. 'Probation!' I don't even know what that means."

The lighter popped back out, and Hilary lit a Rothmans. I kept quiet. Before long, we reached the old quarry trail, the way ahead overgrown with milkweed and wild grass. Hilary stopped the car, and we both climbed out and hiked a short distance farther along the now familiar path, through thickets of birch and maple. We clambered down to the rocky ledge that overlooked the main pond. This was where we'd left our gear, but it wasn't here anymore. It was gone, all of it — both saddles, both bridles. Hilary's canvas backpack was missing, as well. She and I poked around some more, making a show of conducting a proper search, even though it was pointless. Someone had pilfered everything; no great mystery who.

Just about then, we heard the approaching rumble of a car, followed by male voices, laughing. The ruckus came from behind us, back on the gravel road where we'd left Mrs. Barker's rental. We both listened — outbursts of laughter, the clatter of metallic objects, a male voice swearing, more laughter, then what sounded like a gunshot. I swear — a gunshot. Next I heard car doors slam, two or three in rapid succession. An engine roared, then faded, then roared again, accompanied by the guttural thresh of tires fishtailing in loose gravel.

"Ag, perfect." Hilary turned and started to march back along the trail. "This is just perfect. Thank you, Lord."

I hurried after her, half expecting to find our car gone, too, but it was right where we'd left it with just one difference. Now the left front tire was flat. At first I thought that someone must have punctured the side wall with something sharp and solid. Then I remembered the gunshot. That made more sense. On some instinct, I glanced down at the ground nearby, the gravel surface, and soon noticed a glint of coppery metal. I'd seen enough Perry Mason episodes to recognize what it was — the shell casing. Without stopping to think, I scooped it up and tucked it into my front pocket.

Meanwhile, Hilary settled her weight against the side of the car and put back her head, as if pleading for divine intervention. You'd have thought a flat tire was a disaster beyond repair.

She looked at me. "*Now what ...?*"

"It's no problem," I said. "I can change a tire."

"You can?"

"Of course."

And I could, too. It was one thing my father had taught me. I had a few false starts with the jack, but in the end the job got done. We were still without saddles or bridles or Hilary's backpack, and we still had to drive over to our place, where God knew what disaster awaited, assuming Della had even found her way home. But at least we had four working tires.

Hilary dug the keys out of her pocket and then stopped. "Damn him," she said. "Damn him to hell."

It was obvious who she meant, but I asked anyway.

"Who do you think?" She slid the key into the ignition and turned it. The engine caught at once. "He acts like such a bully, but he's a kid at heart, a stupid little kid. Who else would do something idiotic like this?"

A stupid little kid ...? That had never been my impression. But it wasn't what bothered me now, or not really. What bothered me now was the tone of her voice as she said it. She sounded almost affectionate. And maybe she really was — affectionate, I mean. Or maybe that was an illusion too, an act that she was putting on. One way or another, we got back on the road, and pretty soon we were driving through Hatton. I peered off to the right toward Weintrub's Garage. Bruce Gruber's car was not where you'd normally expect to see it, parked over at the north end of the small packed-earth lot. So he was still off cruising around somewhere, causing trouble. Probably Edwin and Davey were with him. None of this surprised me.

About ten minutes later we reached my family's place. Hilary swung right and drove up the long laneway. She stopped not far from the willow trees in front of the barn to let me out.

"Look," she said. "I've got to make a phone call — right away. Can I use your phone?"

"Sure. It's —"

Just then, Charlotte stormed out of the barn in what looked to be a state of panic, her twin braids flailing around her head.

"Sam," she shouted. "What happened to Della?"

I got out of the car. "Where is she? Is she all right?"

"She's in the barn, but I can't catch her. She's too jumpy. What happened?"

"I fell off. She got away. I don't know." I turned back to Hilary. "The phone's inside, in the kitchen. You can use it."

"Great. Thanks." Hilary was gone like a shot.

Calling Bruce, I thought. I doubted he was home. I brushed past Charlotte and made straight for the barn.

"Wait," she said. "Wait up." She turned to follow me. "She's only got a halter on. Where's her saddle and bridle?"

"Charlotte. Just shut up."

"You're not supposed to say that. I'm telling, just as soon as Mum gets back."

I remembered that our mother was out playing tennis at the Finlaysons'.

Once inside the barn, I paused to let my eyes adjust to the dim light. The combined scents of horse and leather, hay and molasses, wafted all around. The air was damp, much more humid in here than out of doors. It took a moment or two for my vision to adjust, but soon enough it did, and there was Della, standing loose in the grooming bay.

"I tried to catch her," said Charlotte. "But I couldn't. She's all fidgety. I thought you'd fallen off. I thought you were hurt."

"I'm fine. I already said."

"I know. I meant before."

Something wasn't right, though. Della was trembling, her sweaty coat rippling in places. Her legs quivered. She was standing with her head away from me, facing her stall, its door closed. She couldn't get in.

"It's okay, girl."

I tried to sound soothing while I eased myself to the left to squeeze past her. I reached out with my right hand to pat her on the rump. No sooner had I made contact with her coat than she squealed and let loose an unholy kick.

"Hey, easy. Easy, Della."

I slipped past her, drew back the bolt at her stall's half-door, and pulled the door open. At once, she scrambled inside, but I could tell her movement was laboured, stiff. I looked down at my hand, and I saw blood.

"BASUTOLAND," SAID MRS. DADLA.

Hilary looked up. "I'm sorry ...?"

The woman leaned closer. They had returned to her temporary home, and she looked slowly from side to side, as if to reassure herself that no one was listening. "Basutoland," she repeated. It was the only word she said.

Hilary knew what Basutoland was, a small territory perched high in the Drakensberg, a British protectorate enfolded on all sides by South Africa. She nodded at Mrs. Dadla, encouraging her to proceed. "Basutoland, yes — what of it?" But the woman simply adjusted the folds of her purple garment and said nothing more.

Hilary took the older woman's near silence as a sign of her discomfort, an indication that this discussion had reached its end. "I'll come back," she said. "Would that be all right? Tomorrow or the day after?"

"Yes, daughter," the woman replied. "You will be most welcome."

It wasn't true. She would not be welcome at all. Muletsi's vanishing act down by the soccer pitch had unnerved his mother badly. God knew what she meant by that cryptic, one-word message. *Basutoland.*

Hilary said her goodbyes and then set out on her own through the slanting light of the early afternoon. The earth glowed red underfoot, and loose braids of smoke unravelled from an array of rusty stovepipe chimneys, melting into the blue depths overhead. The bleat of goats stuttered from somewhere not far off, carried on the cool breeze. Eventually, she reached her mother's car. She climbed inside, turned the ignition, and let the motor idle for a time.

She put back her head. Basutoland …? What did the woman mean? She reached up with one hand to massage her forehead, as if this would somehow help to order her thoughts — and maybe it did because the explanation hit her with the force of a revelation. One moment, bafflement. The next moment, she understood what the woman meant. She saw that it wasn't enough for her merely to want to see Muletsi, to be on hand. What good was that? What good to him? What good to her? Had she travelled all the way from Joburg for that? A frigging social call? Well, it wouldn't do. What Muletsi needed was help — concrete, actual help. And now she saw a way to provide it.

She had half a mind to hurry back into the heart of Bruntville, find Mrs. Dadla, and tell her she understood — understood and agreed. But she could see that it would be better not to say anything now. First, she had to think this idea through. Already, she had a sense that her sudden revelation — *Basutoland* — was not quite as straightforward as it had seemed only a few moments earlier.

She took a deep breath and gazed out through the windscreen. Clustered along the track in front of her, a flock of children had paused in their play or their errands, and now all were watching this white stranger in their midst. Several reached up with their long-fingered hands to shield their eyes from the sun — like a platoon of miniature soldiers coming to a desultory salute. An adult or two glanced over at the car, as well, just for a moment, then quickly looked away.

Never mind. She had an idea, one that might — just might — enable Muletsi to go free. She jostled the gearshift into first and released the handbrake. Carefully, she manoeuvred the car along the dirt lane that wound ahead. She crept out of Bruntville, past the children, who parted like the sea, calling out and waving. She did not wave back, suddenly wishing to avoid drawing any additional attention to herself, to avoid that above all. She kept both her hands clamped to the wheel and did not wave at anyone — though God, in his infinite wisdom, must have known how much she wanted to.

TWENTY-FOUR

Sam
Ontario, Summer 1963

I SUSPECTED AT ONCE that Della had been shot. For one thing, she was trembling with pain and what must have been trauma. She certainly wouldn't let me get anywhere near the wound, but I didn't need to. I could tell just by looking. The injury looked the way I imagined a bullet wound would look — like a lot of blood.

"You keep a watch on her," I told Charlotte. "I'm going to call Dr. Feasby."

He was the local veterinarian and regularly came over to our place whenever Pablo or Della had some medical problem that required a vet's attention. I ran from the barn and up across the lawn toward the house. Along the way, I practically ran smack into Hilary, who was striding in the opposite direction.

"Della's been shot," I said.

"She ... *what?*"

"Shot. I think. In the rump. I'm going to call the vet."

Hilary headed for the barn while I got on the phone. I spoke to Dr. Feasby's wife, who said she would contact him on the two-way radio, tell him to drive straight over. A half hour later he turned up, wearing rubber boots, a pair of gigantic blue bib overalls, and a leather cowboy hat. It turned out I was right. Della had been shot. She'd been hit in the croup section of her hindquarters by what Dr. Feasby said was either a spent bullet or a ricochet. Luckily, it wasn't as serious as I had thought. She'd suffered a fairly shallow flesh wound, he said, not overly dangerous, not something to get too worked up about.

"Except that someone out there is taking potshots at horses." Dr. Feasby chewed on a stick of hay. "We might want to get worked up about that. Any idea who might have done it?"

I said no, none.

By this time Hilary had driven off in Mrs. Barker's rental car. I was pretty sure where she was going. She knew as well as I did who had shot Della. That idiot. First he'd stolen her gun — not to mention our tack — and now this. The theft was bad enough, but this was incomparably worse. What kind of person would shoot a horse? I pictured myself smiting Bruce Gruber's head with a great thudding rock. That seemed like an appropriate response. Why I didn't name him now, I couldn't say. I was thinking of Hilary, I guess.

As he treated Della's injury, Dr. Feasby kept up a running commentary, explaining what he was doing. He first administered an anaesthetic — not as easy as it sounds — and then removed the bullet with a pair of forceps. That done, he washed the area with a saline solution. Next, he applied a disinfectant and a sealing gel to keep the injury clean. He said he would come back in a couple of days to stitch the wound closed, but for now it was probably better to let it drain.

I reached into my pocket and pulled out the shell casing I had stuffed in there. "Look," I said. "I found this."

"What ...? Where ...?" The vet plucked the casing from my hand and peered at it with one eye closed. "Where did you get this?"

I shrugged. "On the ground. It was lying there. Someone shot out the tire on our car ... just now. Maybe it was —"

"The same idiot?" Dr. Feasby was still inspecting the casing. "I'd say that's a good bet." He looked at me, both eyes open now. "Can I hold on to this?"

I shrugged again. "Sure. I guess." I figured it couldn't do any harm.

As for Della, it wasn't long before she settled down. Pretty soon, she seemed almost back to normal, gazing out at us with those deep liquid eyes that horses have. Every couple of minutes, she ducked her head down for a gulp of water from the galvanized pail in her stall. All her adventures that day — setting off from the quarry, finding her own route home, being shot along the way — she seemed to have put all of it out of her mind by now. Horses are like that. They don't brood about the past, or not any more than they need to, not if they can avoid it.

JACK PUSHED HIS WALLET back into his hip pocket and marched out of the Mooi River feed store. He yelled at a pair of those bloody kaffirs to get a move on. They were loading burlap sacks of oats and bran into the bed of his Land Rover, but they were taking their own sweet time about it. Lazy so-and-sos. "Get on with it!" he shouted. "I haven't got all the goddamn day."

"Yes, *baas*," one of them said, and the other one nodded. Both of them were shirtless, coated in grain dust, with oat pellets scattered through their hair. They scuttled over to the ramp to lug another hundred-pound sack between them. "No," said Jack. "Each. One to each. For Chrissake, get a move on." He watched as they did as he said. Each of them heaved a sack, wrapped both arms around it, and staggered over to Jack's old bus. They were getting a move on now; you'd bloody well better believe it.

He turned to the side and spat. The truth was he was raw with anger, felt a raging in his gut. He knew the girl was back. Everyone knew about it, all over the farm. Hilary Anson — home from Jozi. Among the servants it had been the primary subject of discussion for a couple of days now. He knew the girl had driven off in her mother's Vauxhall, too, and he had a fair-to-middling idea as to her destination. He hawked his gob and spat again. Fair-to-middling — hell. He knew exactly where she'd gone.

It was sickening, was what it was. Unnatural. People have different coloured skin — and they have different noses and different kinds of hair and different ways of going about their business — for just one reason under God. It's so you can effing well tell them apart. Simple as that. So that each can stick to his own. It enraged him that anyone could think otherwise. It made him sick. Physically ill. Case in point. He'd been up in Lourenço Marques one time. Twice, really. That was where a lot of white men went, South African men, up to Mozambique, where they had cheap black women you could buy with a mug of gruel. Do with them as you pleased. No laws to prevent such goings-on up there, under Portuguese command.

He had seen it with his own eyes: big pink-fleshed, baldpated Boers slamming their beer flagons to the table and running their paws up those black women's short, tight skirts. Then off they'd go, upstairs or outside, staggering and guffawing, with their spectacles all cockeyed and with beer stains on their paunchy shirts, a squaw under each arm. Three times, Jack had gone up there, to see for himself.

Well, a man is a man.

But this was different, this business with Hilly. She was a white girl, and she was his by rights. In a manner of speaking, she was. The more he thought about it, the more he regarded matters in this very light. He was the one that loved the girl, the only one that ever had. He'd taken care of her when care was the one thing she'd most required. Attended to her needs. Reassured her when she was forlorn. Damned well taught her to ride. Had he not?

By Christ, he had. By Christ, he bloody well had.

He told the two kaffirs to keep on working. He had some errands to run. He hitched up his trousers and headed around the back of the feed store and out onto Lawrence Road — a big wide street, wide enough to bring a team of twelve oxen around

180 degrees in one good swing, or so he had heard it said. When he reached the first corner, he veered left. He did indeed have some errands to run, among them a commission of a personal nature. He had it in mind to buy a present for Hilary Anson, damned if he did not. He would bestow her with something to take note of him by, a coming-home gift for the homecoming queen — a plant of some kind, a flowering plant. That would do the job.

As for himself, he was going to buy a gun. A gun, you say? Why was that? Did he not have a firearm in his possession already?

Well, yes — a rifle. He had himself a rifle all right, the one that Daniel Anson had supplied him with for use in emergencies or to put away another one of those big horses when they pulled up lame with a shattered fetlock or a tendon bowed past all hope of repair. But a rifle wasn't quite the thing for the business he had in mind just now. Too hard to conceal, for starters.

A gun was what was needed. A revolver, there you are. You hold a revolver in your hand, people take note. They listen to what you have to say. They don't come crashing through the barn with a bridle and a big pelham bit swinging in their hand. That was as shameful a piece of low animal cowardice as he had ever seen. It didn't bear repeating, and he had it in mind to ensure that such a thing would never be contemplated again.

When he reached Henk Viljoen's store — Viljoen and Son, Firearms and Munitions — he turned and marched inside. The bell rang, and he said, "Henk, how you keeping?"

"Like a pig in muck." Henk Viljoen peered over a pair of half-lenses that were balanced on his nose. "And how about yourself?"

"Splendid. If I could only breathe." He had a cold in the head.

"Ah, that's the winter for you. Be over soon. Be summer again soon, Jack."

"So they say."

"Now, what can I do you for?"

"Well, I'm looking to buy myself a gun."

"Smart lad. You came to the right place." Henk Viljoen laughed and patted his belly. "Now, would that be a revolver, Jack, or a semi-automatic? I've got a fine lot of new Browning pistols. Nine-millimetre jobs. But, then, it depends. What do you want it for?"

"Just a little protection." He nodded back over his shoulder, toward the broad main street. "These days, with the lot you've got out there, a man can't be too careful."

"Ain't it just so," said Henk. "Now, would you like to look at one of those Brownings?"

"Why not? A look won't kill me — or anyone else, either." He smiled, all innocent-like. "And maybe you could show me some of your revolvers, too. It was a revolver I carried in the war, a Webley top-break."

"Fine machine," said Henk Viljoen. "Got none in stock at the moment. How about a Smith & Wesson? Could be you might like one of those."

"Could be." He thrummed his fingers on the wooden counter, like a drum roll. "Could be I just might."

I WAS AT HOME, walking from the house down toward the barn, when I heard a car crunching up the gravel lane behind me. Two days had dragged past since Della had been shot. I turned around and saw Hilary at the wheel of Mrs. Barker's rental. She pulled up beside me.

"Howzit?" I said.

She just shook her head, didn't say a word. I waited as she killed the engine and climbed from the car. She looked awful, pale and washed out. Her eyes were bloodshot. Her hair maybe could have used a wash. A cut of some kind had slit the left side of her upper lip, as if someone had hit her there. Her black eye hadn't fully healed yet.

She saw me looking and shrugged. "Could be worse."

She wore blue jeans and a white cotton blouse, and now stepped around to the rear of the car. She popped open the trunk — "the boot," as she would say — and lo and behold: my saddle and bridle.

I looked at her. "Where did you find them?"

"Don't ask."

"No, really."

"I'm serious, my boykie. Just be glad you got your gear back, hey."

"What about you? Did you get your stuff, too?"

"I did."

"And your backpack?"

She just shrugged. I wondered about the gun. What had happened to the gun? I didn't say anything, though — not about that. I just wrinkled my forehead and looked at her and didn't stop looking until finally she spoke.

"What's wrong?"

I shrugged. "You don't look very well."

She pulled her sunglasses down from her forehead so they covered her eyes. "Let's make a deal, Sam. When the other person doesn't look well, chances are that she doesn't feel well — and the last thing she wants to hear is that she doesn't look well. Got it?"

"Okay."

"It's not 'okay.' It's much more than that. Half the secret to a successful life is knowing when to shut up. All right?"

"*Oui.*"

"Good. How's Della?"

"Better, I think. It must have been a spent bullet that hit her. It just went in and stopped. There's no infection. Dr. Feasby said I can start riding again anytime. He told me ..." I hesitated.

"What?"

"He told me there's something weird about the bullet."

"Weird, how?"

It turned out that our veterinarian knew quite a bit about guns — guns and munition. I started to tell her what Dr. Feasby had said to me just that morning when he'd come back to stitch Della's wound.

"He said the shell casing —"

"The *what* casing?" said Hilary.

"Shell," I said. "The shell casing. I found it by the car — you know, after they shot out the tire." I told her what a shell casing was, something that even I knew thanks to all those *Perry Mason* shows.

She stared at me with a look she had, a skeptical look, so I told her I was just repeating what Dr. Feasby had said. He said that thanks to the shell casing he'd managed to calculate the bullet's calibre — nine by eighteen. He had never encountered those dimensions before, so he'd looked them up and learned that this round was all but unique to a Russian-built pistol called a Makarov. It was the standard-issue weapon for Soviet police. Anytime it was found outside the Soviet Union, it was almost surely illegal. He wondered who in Kelso could possibly be in possession of such a gun — and why.

Hilary didn't say anything at first. Then she said, "I see." She adjusted her sunglasses. "That's interesting."

"Yeah. I thought so, too." I looked at her kind of sideways. "Did he give it back?"

Again, Hilary paused. She seemed to be weighing her options. "Not so far."

I nodded. "Hilary. Why do you have a gun?"

"I don't. Not now."

"Yeah, but still. Why *do* you?"

"I already told you, hey. Protection." It made her feel safe, she said. Now it was gone.

"Okay." I gazed back at the open trunk, at my bridle and saddle. They seemed to be in decent shape, none the worse for wear. I looked back at her. "Why did he do it? Shoot Della? Why would anyone do that?"

"He didn't."

"Oh, right."

"No. I mean it. I'm sure it was one of the other two."

"Davey? Or Edwin?"

"One or the other."

I just shrugged. Maybe she was right. Who knew?

"So ..." she said. "Della can go right back to work, bullet wound and all?"

"Crazy. But yeah."

"How about tomorrow, then? In the afternoon? I might be free. I'll give you a call."

Might be free …? "Okay."

Hilary shoved her hands into the front pockets of her jeans and leaned against the side panel of the car. "What about your parents?"

"What about them?"

"Did they say anything? About Della?"

"Just the usual. I have to be more careful. That kind of stuff."

"They didn't call the police?"

"No. They said there'd be no point. It was probably some hunters who thought she was a moose."

"Hah."

"I know."

I looked away. There was definitely a mystery here, and not just regarding the identity of Della's shooter. There was a mystery about Hilary and Bruce, too. I wondered what else she wouldn't talk about.

"Okay," I said.

I hoisted my tack from the car, and Hilary closed the trunk. The boot. I could tell she was restless and wanted to get away. I thanked her for rescuing my saddle and bridle, and then I stepped back from the car. She walked around to the driver's side.

"I'll call you," she said. She climbed into the front, pulled the door closed, and turned the ignition key. In a cloud of dust, she was gone.

For an entire week after that she failed to call, never mind her promise. One day drained slowly into the next. I kept on schooling Della, did roadwork, cantered or galloped through the high fields north of our place. By then Della's wound had pretty well healed, and the stitches were gone. We could easily have resumed our afternoon forays down to the quarry ponds or our bareback training over at the Barkers'. But Hilary didn't call.

You'd have thought I didn't exist — that was what it felt like, like not existing or not mattering. It felt like torture, or a kind of torture, like being deliberately subjected to pain.

And then she called — a week late, but she called. She said that we should get back to work, that we should meet that same afternoon. It was just past ten o'clock in the morning, and I'd been eating a peanut butter and banana sandwich while reading a book about Einstein's theories of relativity. Not theory. *Theories.* There are two. As for Hilary, she sounded perfectly normal on the phone, as if nothing out of the ordinary had happened, as if we'd been in close contact all along. I couldn't understand why she was doing this to me. I wanted to ask her, but I was afraid of what she might say. So I just said, "Fine, see you."

Early that afternoon I hacked toward the Barkers' place. Hilary met me by the Quinton Vasco lands, and we rode the rest of the way together. She looked a lot better now than she had a week before, not so pale or worn out. The cut on her lip had healed, and her bruised eye looked better, or maybe she had just covered it with that stuff. Mascara, I think. Once again we took the long way around, cantering through a succession of cornfields while skirting the main entrance that led to the house at Colonel Barker's. When we reached the paddock at the back of the property, I saw that a course of jumps had been set up, a half-dozen fences, mostly about three feet high — Hilary's doing, probably.

"Watch," she said.

She removed Club Soda's saddle and bridle and vaulted back on. What I saw next, I could barely believe, then or now. Right away, I could tell that Club Soda was completely alert to Hilary's signals, every change in the pressure of her legs, each shift in the distribution of her weight. His ears twitched in different directions but mainly pointed forward. He arched his back and tucked his head into his chest. He was listening, waiting, expecting — and somehow

Hilary made him understand what she wanted, as if by some kind of telepathy. She guided that difficult creature around the course, jumping each fence cleanly — and not just cleanly but beautifully, in perfect balance. She kept her arms outstretched at her sides, like an acrobat or some sort of gliding bird. I watched as closely as I could, but it was impossible to tell exactly how she did it. When the round was done, Hilary brought Club Soda to a halt, through only the guidance of her legs and her body's weight, and even that was a kind of magic, achieved without apparent effort. Next she straightened up, and Club Soda broke into a canter, making straight for me. He stopped just a few feet away — and bowed his head!

Hilary put up her hands in a kind of shrug. "There," she said. "That last bit was just for show, hey."

"The head bow?"

"Yebo."

I was deeply impressed, with or without that final embellishment. Of course, I was. I didn't know how to describe what I'd just seen. Remarkable? Miraculous? Impossible? Any one of those adjectives might have served, or all of them together, all of them squared. It was as if Club Soda was not a separate being, as if he were simply an extension of Hilary's will, or as if they were two parts of a single creature.

"I can't believe you did that."

"Just for the record, I wasn't showing off, not really. I only wanted you to see what can be done."

"Just don't tell me it was easy."

"No, it wasn't. It isn't. You need to practise and practise. But, bit by bit, it comes. You'll see."

Somehow I doubted that.

Hilary threw her right leg over Club Soda's neck and dropped to the ground, a completely irresponsible dismount, but what did she care? She clipped a shank to his halter and tied the shank to the paddock railing in a quick-release knot. Next she slogged around the course on foot, lowering the rails at each of the jumps so that they were no more than two feet high. She marched back to me. She told me it was my turn. No bridle. No saddle.

By now I was more or less resigned to my fate, which was to perish after being thrown from a horse, so I did as Hilary said. I tried my best — and I managed to get around the course. In a way, I did. I fell off three times, Della refused twice, and she knocked down two of the rails. But we got around.

Hilary clapped her hands. "Bravo!"

I couldn't help smiling, never mind the falls. Despite the missteps and the refusals and the knocked-down rails, it had felt sort of ... almost ... *good.* I was getting better — more stable, more consistent, gentler. Della and I were working as a team, and it showed.

Just then I heard another pair of hands clapping, not Hilary's but someone else's — a slower pace, with a sarcastic rhythm. I looked around. Sure enough, it was Bruce bloody Gruber. He strutted toward us, past the crabapple trees. He was wearing a grey T-shirt, blue jeans, and workboots, with a cigarette dangling from his lips. I noticed he had a few scrapes and cuts on his face, too. That made me wonder. I realized he must have hiked all the way here, all the way from Second Line. How did he even know about this place?

"Good job, buddy," he said to me. He clapped a couple more times, squinting through the smoke from his cigarette. Then he thrust out his palms and cracked his knuckles in rapid succession. "But next time, try stayin' on the fuckin' horse, why dontcha?"

I ransacked my brain, hoping I'd think of something to say, something really pointed and clever, something that would humiliate the guy. Of course, I came up with nothing. Just silence. Meanwhile, Hilary marched over and gave Bruce Gruber a kiss on the fucking lips. I'm not kidding. Next he enclosed her in his arms, as if they'd been lovers for years. What the hell was going on? It was as if he were a new yearling of hers, one she'd finally broken to saddle but only after a bitter struggle, and now they belonged to each other. The mere sight of those two — it revolted me. It made my head burn, as if there were a fire inside my skull.

TWENTY-SEVEN

Hilary
South Africa, Winter 1962

IT WAS LATE AFTERNOON when Hilary turned onto the service road that led into Mooi River. She'd just come from Bruntville, where she'd spoken to Muletsi's mother. The conversation hadn't lasted long, hadn't needed to. "Basutoland," she'd said. They would ride to Basutoland. It was the only way out of this fix. Mrs. Dadla had nodded, just a gesture, nothing more. She didn't mention Muletsi's name at all. Still, it was as if she had been expecting this, Hilary's words. It was as if some circle had been closed. After that, Hilary hadn't stayed long. There was no point in drawing more attention to herself than necessary.

Now there were a couple of errands she wanted to discharge. She wanted smokes, and she wanted to pass by the bottle store. Neither transaction would take long.

First, she bought a carton of Rothmans at the café, and then she stopped by the bottle store across the street, the *drankvinkel*, for a quart of Scotch. That was when it happened. She was walking out with her purchases and bearing along the pavement toward her car — her mother's car — when frigging bloody hell if she didn't blunder straight into Jack Tanner. She damned near dropped everything she was carrying, the carton of smokes and the quart of Bell's. It was the first she'd seen of him since she'd got back.

"Hilly ..." he said. He didn't seem surprised. He didn't seem to show any emotion at all. He just said her name, or his preferred approximation of her name, and then he said it again, with that faint question mark at the end. "Hilly ...?"

She didn't bother to correct him. *Hilary*. She didn't say anything. All she wanted was to get away from here, far away. She took a sideways step and made to walk past him.

He moved to block her. He was carrying a package, too, what looked like a box or a carton inside a brown-paper bag. It was impossible to say what it was. He had several days' growth of beard, and his skin looked as though it had been rubbed with sandpaper. It was raw — reddish in patches, where it wasn't sallow — and there was a scar just below his right eye, a rib of proud flesh, along with a faint indentation that hadn't been there before, minor but perceptible. That was Muletsi's doing, no question.

He said, "I heard you were back. I was looking right forward to seeing you." He spoke, for all the world, like a frigging old beau.

She stood where she was, didn't move. She was afraid of making a scene. She didn't want anything to do with this man.

"How was Jah Rule?"

He spoke as if they were at a braai, making conversation, except she hadn't the faintest notion what he meant. *Jah Rule ...? What was that?* Then she remembered — rhyming slang. It was a habit of his. He meant school, probably. She didn't reply.

They were both silent for a time. Then he said, "I've got a cousin up in Joburg. I ever tell you that? Damned if I can remember his name. Nigel, is it? Nigel Whatsit?"

She glanced away. What was this? Small talk? He wanted to engage in a give-and-take of polite drivel? To what conceivable end? Sometimes she couldn't figure out what was in his head. Now, without quite meaning to, she must have motioned in a way that showed her impatience, because his posture stiffened. He took a step back.

"I'm late," she said. Again, she moved to walk past him.

Again, he shifted his body, the adjustment ever so slight, barely detectable. "Late …?" he said. "Late for what? I haven't seen you in ages, and here we bump into each other quite by accident, and so soon you've got to go? Haven't you time for a coffee?" He glanced at the two bags she was carrying and then behind her at the bottle store. He narrowed his eyes. "Or a Castle maybe? Wouldn't that be better? What's the harm in a pint or so? You don't have to be running off now, do you? Not from your old mate, Jack."

She watched as he shifted his own parcel to his right arm and then ran his left hand up the side of his face again. He was worrying at that scar, drawing attention to it, too.

"You're not my mate," she said. "You've never been my mate. Please. I want to go." She tightened her jaw. That was a mistake — to have said please. She knew it at once.

He was smiling already. He'd noticed it, too. His manner changed at once, no hint of aggression now. Now he was all lightness and ease. "Oh, by all means," he said. "By all means." He stood aside, to let her pass. "*Miss Anson.*"

And she knew what he was doing — he was letting her go. He was frigging well granting her permission to leave. But what choice did she have? None whatsoever. She walked past him and kept right on walking. She walked all the way to her mother's car, halfway down the block. She didn't look back, didn't need to. She could tell he was watching her, could feel it in the ripples running up her spine, as if the twin beams of his gaze were boring into the small of her back.

When she got to the car, her hands were shaking so hard she damned well dropped the keys. She had to set her parcels down on the pavement so she could retrieve the bloody things. Then she had to use both hands to pry the door open. She placed her purchases on the passenger seat and climbed in herself on the driver's side, pulled the door shut. She shoved the key into the slot, turned the ignition, and swung the car around, stalling it twice. Then she sped away, knowing all the while that he was watching her go. Christ, she could still feel the force of his gaze, hot against her spine.

HILARY AND I WERE riding north along Second Line, just having completed another of our schooling sessions at Colonel Barker's. She was in a triumphant mood, much as she tried to pretend otherwise. At a competition in Dunturn the previous weekend, she'd taken top honours in the advanced division.

For my part, I had done all right, I guess — better than my previous showing in Falkirk, where Della and I had been eliminated during the cross-country phase. This time I got through the competition without being thrown out, and that was progress of a sort. I had also managed one other feat. I'd beaten Edwin Duval in the dressage event, if not by much — my seventh place to his eighth. Still, no one had expected that even if, overall, Edwin had done far better, finishing in third place. Another Kelso rider, Janet Hünigan, had won first prize in our division. All in all, it had been a very good showing by Kelso — just not by me.

Pretty soon Hilary and I reached Number Four Sideroad, where I meant to turn left and ride home on my own. There'd been a time when I would have kept heading north along a slender trail that ran through a succession of grassy meadows and maple woodlot, a shorter and more beautiful ride, but Quinton Vasco's fences now blocked the way.

I reined Della to the left.

"Hang on," said Hilary. "I know a different route. At least, I think I do. Come on. Let's see if this works."

She urged Club Soda off the road and down through a ditch overgrown with timothy grass and daisies and that other flower — goldenrod, I think. Club Soda scrambled up the opposite side.

She glanced back at me. "Come on."

"That way's closed off."

"Not anymore."

I wasn't sure what she meant, but I went along anyway — curious, I guess. I soon caught up and then followed Hilary as she traced the chain-link fence. A thicket of maple trees stood on the far side of the barrier, partly obscuring a large open hillside rising to the east.

"Look. I told you." Hilary pointed just ahead.

I saw what she meant. Someone equipped with a powerful set of wire cutters had opened a large gap in the fence, providing more than enough space for a single human to pass through. Even a horse could manage it.

I whistled. "Who did this?"

"Who do you think?"

I didn't bother saying the guy's name. What would have been the point?

"Don't tell anyone, hey."

"I won't."

"I mean it."

"Right. I won't."

Hilary dismounted and drew the reins over Club Soda's head. Without hesitating, she slipped through the gap in the fence, then paused while Club Soda lowered his head and sprang through the opening right behind her.

She turned back to look at me. "Come on," she said.

Wasn't this illegal? What about the men with walkie-talkies and guns who were said to patrol the Quinton Vasco lands, not always but sometimes?

"Come on."

I took a deep breath. I realized that, all this time, I'd been misjudging my fate. I would not be killed by falling from a horse. Instead, I would be shot for trespassing — but at least I would not die alone. Hilary would perish, too. We would succumb, the two of us, together. I found this prospect oddly bracing, so I took another breath, dropped to my feet, looped the reins over Della's head, and led her through the gap in the fence, as easy as that.

Once inside, I stopped and looked around, thinking there must be someone nearby — some guards, some sort of security. But I saw no one. "Now what?"

"Now we're free. Come on."

We remounted and picked our way over a fencerow of field-stones sheltered by maples before emerging into an open meadow of alfalfa that rose sharply to the east. Hilary touched her heels to Club Soda's flanks, and he sprang into a canter. I hesitated for an instant and then followed her lead. The tall grass shoots peeled away like pages riffling in a book, and we raced toward the summit of a broad green ridge. Hilary was well out in front and was already waiting by the time I pulled up at her side.

"Look at that." She pointed off to the east, where the earth seemed to plummet away before rising again in the distance, a view of cascading hills that extended for what must have been miles, one emerald wave after another. "Reminds me of Natal," she said.

"South Africa looks like this?"

"Parts of it." She fumbled for a cigarette, lit it, and put back her head. She blew out a cloud of smoke. "I can see why what's his name wants this land. This must be the best view in Kelso."

A couple of heavy trucks were stationed not far away, one with a crane mounted on its bed, but there were no humans around, or none that I could see. I told Hilary there was a trail near here that was famous as a lovers' lane, or it once had been. You couldn't see it from here, but it ran across the meadow below, down to the east. People used to drive along a rutted trail and then park somewhere, in order to do whatever it was they did.

Hilary dragged on her cigarette. "Where do they go now?"

I had no idea. I was about to say so when I heard a voice calling up from the west, from the fenceline we had just crossed — a man's voice.

"Hey, there!" the man shouted. "Hey, you!"

A lone figure strode out into the long grass. He was too far away to make out clearly, but something about him caught my notice, something about the way he walked, an awkward limp. I could swear it was Mr. Odegaard, from the general store in Hatton. What was he doing out here? Whoever he was, the man now stopped and called up to us again.

"This is private property, you!"

Hilary laughed. She rose on her knees, upright above the saddle. "Bugger off!"

The man seemed to stumble and then rebalance himself. He was carrying something, and now he held it up. A rifle? He was carrying a rifle? Seconds later, I felt something bite into my left arm.

"Hey!" I felt it again, another sharp pain in my chest. "Hey!"

The man was shooting at us with some kind of air rifle. Della feinted and ducked her head. She'd been hit, too. I reined her around to the right and dug my heels into her sides. We scooted down into the shelter of the ridge, out of sight. I drew Della to a halt, then swivelled in the saddle and peered back up. What was Hilary doing? There she was, she and Club Soda, both silhouetted against the blue sky near the peak of the ridge. She was looking back down toward the man with the air rifle, and she wasn't moving. For a moment, I wondered whether she had a gun herself, that Russian pistol. Had

Bruce Gruber given it back? I worried that she might pull it out now and shoot Mr. Odegaard or whoever was down there. Why would I think that? Only a fool would do such a thing, a fool or a murderer.

"Hilary," I shouted. "Come on. Let's go."

She didn't budge. For several seconds at least, she didn't move at all, except to scrunch out her cigarette on the sole of her shoe.

"I said, come on!"

This time, she did. She shifted in the saddle, and Club Soda exploded, darted over the green crest of land and scrambled down into the lee of the ridge. We were both safe now, safe for the moment, but Hilary kept right on going, galloped right past me. She veered across the downward slope, aiming toward a dense barrier of sugar bush that bordered the meadow to the north.

I dug in my heels again, and Della broke into a gallop, just five or six lengths behind Club Soda. We soon reached a trail that bisected the meadow, the old lovers' lane, I guessed. It was newly worn. A large number of vehicles — heavy vehicles from the look of it, big trucks — had rumbled through this field during the past few days. That seemed odd. We galloped along the same trail, eventually slowing to a canter and then loping into a gap in the wall of sugar bush as if we were entering a vast natural church.

Before long, we slowed the horses to a brisk trot. We had put plenty of distance between ourselves and the man with the gun. Surely we were safe now. But we kept moving all the same. The trail through the sugar bush was newly gouged, with deep tire tracks dug into the earth. I didn't remember seeing any trucks entering or leaving the Quinton Vasco lands these past few days, and both Hilary and I had ridden along the fenceline several times. Probably, they had come and gone by night.

Before long, Hilary slowed to a walk, and I did the same.

"That fellow was carrying a bloody gun," she said. "What was that about?"

183

"An air rifle, I think. I think it was Mr. Odegaard — you know, from the store in Hatton."

"Air rifle …? Never heard of it."

"It's not a real rifle. It shoots little plastic things. BBs, they're called. They're not bullets. They're just …"

I must have winced or grimaced or something like that because Hilary reined Club Soda over to my side.

"Let's take a look at you," she said. "Here, take off your shirt."

"What …?"

"Take off your shirt."

I eased my polo shirt over my head and slung it across the pommel of the saddle.

"Let's see." She leaned closer, whistled. "You've bloody well been shot."

At least, I think that was what she said. The truth was, I had stopped paying attention to her voice because, suddenly, I could see her breasts, both of them. As she leaned toward me, the fabric of her bikini top cupped outward, and I could definitely see something, the pale tone of her skin, its soft milkiness, a sudden contrast to the bronze suntanned sheen of her shoulders and arms. I wasn't sure I could see everything, but I could see a lot. I was pretty sure I could make out her nipples. I couldn't stop looking.

"My God," she said. "You really have been shot. I can't believe it. That man shot you."

"With a BB gun."

"All the same. Dear Lord, you'd think we were in South Africa. Are you all right?"

I wasn't sure. My chest stung in a couple of places, but it didn't matter. I was thinking only about Hilary's breasts. If she would just stay like this, leaning toward me in this way, just like this, I would be happy forever. But the view did not last long.

"Well, there's not much we can do now," she said, shifting away from me. "We should keep going."

She gathered her reins, eased Club Soda around, and set off along the trail at a brisk trot. I pulled on my shirt and hurried to catch up. My arm and chest still stung where I'd been hit, but already the pain was easing. I tried to ignore it. After a while, we slowed back down to a walk.

I brought Della alongside Club Soda. "Can I ask you something?"

"Ask me what?"

"Why are we here?"

"You mean here, on this planet?"

"No. I mean here, now. You and me. Why do we spend so much time together? I'm only fifteen."

"Ag, shame." She laughed and rooted in the pocket of her jeans for another cigarette. When she'd got it lit, she blew a plume of smoke into the golden light, riddled with dust motes and skittering insects. "The reason we spend so much time together is simple. I like you."

My heart lifted at once, as if a balloon were expanding in my chest.

"And the main reason I like you — not the only reason but the main one — is you're the only male that I know, and I do mean the only male, who doesn't want to have sex with me."

"Oh."

"Cheer up, hey. That's a good thing."

"It is?"

"I'd say so."

I swallowed, then blinked several times, trying to screw up my courage. I wanted to say that she was wrong, and I would have said so, except that I wasn't quite brain-dead. I knew it would be a mistake. I could see it was better to keep things as they were — aimless and confusing — rather than take a risk and probably ruin everything. We kept riding along the same trail, aiming northwest

it seemed, not that I was paying much attention. I was still thinking about Hilary's breasts, I guess, and so I wasn't fully attuned to
our surroundings. It caught me completely unawares when Hilary
abruptly drew back on her reins and swore aloud.

"Frigging bloody hell," she said. "What on earth is *that* ...?"

PART THREE

ALL THESE YEARS LATER, I still vividly remember the weekday afternoon, during that long-ago summer, when Hilary Anson and I ventured onto the Quinton Vasco lands. I clearly recall the images of what we found there. Nowadays, the experience makes me think of a certain philosophy lecturer of mine, a Professor Lisgard, who taught an undergraduate course I would one day take, with a section devoted to the notion of causality. Bear with me. I'll explain.

If you were hiking through the wilderness, Professor Lisgard told us, and you stumbled upon a huge geodesic dome shimmering beneath the forest cover, you might well entertain a variety of different thoughts. You might suspect that this was an elaborate trick being played on you by your old pal, Kevin. Or you might believe that Martians had landed here, leaving behind one of their signature glass-and-steel structures. Or you might interpret the dome as evidence of an ancient, highly developed civilization, previously unknown and now extinct, that had built a temple here.

What you would *not* think was that this otherworldly structure had materialized, as Professor Lisgard put it, *ex nihilo*. Out of nothing. It might well be mysterious, but it would be a mystery with causation. You would not doubt that someone or something must have brought the dome into existence. It had not simply appeared of its own accord. Or, as Professor Lisgard would have put it, an action requires an entity.

Well, the same principle applies to the two great thumping cannons that we discovered hidden away in the sugar bush on that distant afternoon. Cannons. I swear to God. What possible explanation could there have been? And yet, I understood at once that an explanation must exist, a conclusion based partly on instinct, I suppose, and partly on the principle of causation. I accepted at once that these machines had not assumed physical form on some random whim. An entity of some kind had produced a force that had brought them into being. These two colossal guns were the result of something even if I had no idea what that "something" was. There had to have been a cause in order for there to be a result.

I wondered: Had Quinton Vasco put these weapons here? And, if so, why?

Freshly painted in olive green, the two cannons rested side by side, surrounded by sugar bush and sheltered by canvas awnings. Nearby, someone had stacked a dozen or so crates atop wooden skids, all protected by another awning. Each of those crates bore a pair of inscriptions stencilled in black: *SRC* and *GC-45*. At the time, I had no idea what either of those abbreviations stood for. Now, for what it's worth, I do understand what they mean.

Hilary's reaction was almost as much of a mystery to me as the guns themselves, if that's possible. Almost from the moment she first set eyes on those great, gangling machines, she busied herself taking pictures of the damned things, along with the neighbouring crates, which appeared to hold shells for those two massive guns. She used a small Kodak camera that she'd pulled from her backpack, a gadget I had never seen her use before. "Souvenirs," she said. "Souvenirs of Canada."

Souvenirs of Canada ...?

What did she mean? What was she talking about?

What sort of souvenir fodder were these huge mechanisms, each mounted on three sets of tires, with barrels that must have been thirty feet long? In some strange way, they reminded me of giant praying mantises. Their presence here certainly explained the tire tracks we'd seen along the improvised road, to say nothing of Mr. Odegaard's appearance that day. His air rifle seemed almost laughable now. It seemed extraordinary that there weren't more men on the lookout, more men armed with guns. But this was Canada, I suppose, so whoever had placed these cannons here had not envisioned a need for overwhelming security, not in this peaceful land.

Still, I figured there was a good chance of our being discovered, and God knows what the consequences of that would have been. I told Hilary we should leave, get out of there. But she seemed in no hurry. Despite her initial reaction — her expression of astonishment — I now had the weird sensation that she wasn't exactly surprised to find these massive guns hidden away in this forest. You might almost have thought she'd expected to find them all along. In any case, she pretty much ignored me until, finally, she stopped taking pictures and put her camera away.

"Yebo," she said.

With Hilary in the lead, we left the clearing and its otherworldly weaponry. We rode off in the same direction as before, aiming to the northwest, toward what I guessed was Hatton. The trail beyond the cannons was old and disused, so badly overgrown as to be almost invisible. We barely spoke to one another, just kept plodding through a thick maze of tree trunks, saplings, and shadows. Eventually, we reached another chain-link fence, or really a distant extension of the same fence we had snuck through before. It blocked the trail at what must have been the western extremity of the Quinton Vasco lands. Without a word, Hilary rode off to the right on a short detour through the bush that took us down a slope of moss-covered rocks and rotting tree trunks to another improvised gap in the fence, large enough for a horse to pass through.

"Well done, Gruber," she said. She meant Bruce Gruber, of course.

Again, we both dismounted and ducked through the opening in single file, leading our horses by the reins. Hilary swung herself up into the saddle again, and I did the same. I felt dazed, as if under the effect of some hallucinatory drug. The fence. Mr. Odegaard. And then those cannons. Who could explain any of it? This was Kelso County, a large tract of meadowland and woodlot in rural Ontario. This was horse country. It was not a war zone; it was the furthest thing imaginable. What in the bloody hell was going on? I kept thinking that Hilary would volunteer some information, explain what we had seen. But she was silent. She seemed distracted, occupied by thoughts of her own. It was dusk by the time we reached Fourth Line, the road that led to Hatton. Here, Hilary pulled Club Soda to a halt.

"You're almost home," she said.

I had all sorts of questions I wanted to ask. What were those cannons? Why were they hidden amid dense bush on that fenced-off land? Why had Hilary taken pictures of them? What was going on? But I knew she wouldn't tell me merely because I asked. She'd only tell me because she wanted to, and I could sense that she did not.

"You're not coming?" I said. I didn't really know what I was saying. "You could put Club Soda in our barn for the night. No problem."

I had an idiotic image of the two of us — Hilary and me — clomping into the house after the barn chores were done and then both of us spending the night in my room, in my bed, with my parents' permission, of course. We could read to each other from books of hers, books by Alan Paton or Nadine Gordimer. These were insane ideas, of course. My parents would have had a coronary; both of them would. Never in a thousand years could such a thing happen. Not ever — and not only on account of my parents.

"No, thanks," she said. "I'd better get a move on. Martin will be furious."

"Martin …?"

"Colonel Barker. He's always furious these days. It's his wife, I think. She drives him mad. Anyway, I'd better go. You're all right, hey?"

"Sure," I said. She called him Martin? "Why wouldn't I be?"

"Because of that gun —"

"The giant ones?"

"No. You know, the pellet gun. Mr. Odegaard."

I shrugged. "It's no big deal."

"If you say so." She narrowed her gaze. She told me not to say a word to anyone about what we'd seen back there, those cannons. That was a secret.

I wasn't so sure that I agreed. I thought we should report what we had seen. I squinted at her. "Why were you taking pictures?"

"Ag, who knows? Curiosity, I guess. They were so strange. Cannons, in the middle of the woods — hard to believe, hey."

"Yeah, but shouldn't we tell someone?"

"Are you serious? We were trespassing. We were in a place weren't supposed to be."

"So …?"

"So that would be bad for us both."

As usual, I gave in. "Okay."

Hilary nodded, evidently satisfied. I guess she knew me pretty well by then, knew the authority she had over me. If she told me to keep something quiet, I would. Now she just smiled at me and said goodbye. She reined Club Soda around, set off at a canter, bearing south along the gravel shoulder that traced Fourth Line. She rode the way she usually did when she didn't care who was watching, weight back in the saddle, feet at home in the stirrups. I watched her go, watched her fade into the dwindling light. Even after she had vanished, I still kept looking — searching, I guess, hoping to catch sight of something that wasn't there.

At last, I reined Della around, and I urged her into an extended trot. We kept to the gravel shoulder of the asphalt road, aiming toward Hatton. My head still buzzed from all I had seen that day. The cannons, yes — but also, and maybe especially, the contours of Hilary's breasts. The road to Hatton wound to the west past a ruined barn and an old disused silo. I entered the village itself and slowed Della to a walk. I rode past Weintrub's Garage, where a few outdoor security lamps shed hazy cones of light onto the dirt parking lot below. I wondered about Bruce Gruber and what was really going on between him and Hilary. I guided Della to the left and rode at a walk by Odegaards' General Store. I guessed that Mr. Odegaard was probably up there now, in the second-floor apartment where his family lived, all crowded into that little space. I looked up. The second-floor lights were on. I saw shadows ripple and swirl against the blinds and wondered whether Mr. Odegaard even knew who it was he'd been shooting at that afternoon. Probably not. Probably, he didn't even know why. He probably had orders to shoot at anybody, any trespassers, and that was what Hilary and I had been.

I was soon clear of the village, and now the roar of crickets surged up from the woodlands on either side of the road, chirping like church organs, chattering like trumpets. It was practically deafening, that sound — eerie and relentless. I pushed Della into a canter, and we headed for home.

DAMNED IF THE FRIGGING idea didn't make sense. Never mind the way it sounded. It sounded mad at first. Of course it did — because it *was* mad. But that was the beauty of it, its very madness. It was crazy, and yet it made sense, too. Hilary was sure of it. Or maybe not quite sure. It wasn't a question of being sure. Who is sure of anything? In this frigging life, you have to take your chances.

And this was a chance — hey, was it ever.

She was hunkered down on the broad second-floor terrace of her father's house in the sunlit coolness of the afternoon. She had worked everything out on a sheet of notepaper, after referring repeatedly to a road map of South Africa, one she'd liberated from the cubbyhole of her mother's car.

She had the map unfolded on her lap right now, with the notepaper set out on the plate-glass surface of a wicker coffee table. In addition, she had a mug of coffee, now gone cold, and a small china tray about half full of cigarette butts and ashes. She was smoking like a dock hand, but what did it matter? Daddy wasn't around to disapprove. He would be away for at least a week, on government business of some kind or other. Before leaving, he'd told her he wanted her back in Johannesburg by the time he returned.

He wouldn't stand for this insolence and impertinence. Did she understand? Did she? The school in Joburg — it was costing him a packet. Did she have an inkling how much? At the time, she'd merely nodded and mouthed, "Yes, Daddy." But that wasn't what she'd been thinking. Far from it. The man had no bloody idea what was truly going on. This was war. This was revolution. In her mind, it was. Meanwhile, Hilary's mother was finally up and about again, a circumstance not unrelated to her husband's absence.

She peered at the map once more. She ran her index finger southwest from Mooi River and then down and around toward the Drakensberg and the rose-hued oblong of Basutoland. This, in its simplest form, was her plan. She had worked out a way to get Muletsi into Basutoland. She was certain this was what his mother had meant by mentioning that word, that day. She'd been putting the idea in Hilary's head, more by suggestion than anything else. But that made sense, too. That way, nothing could be pinned on her.

Basutoland.

It was crazy, maybe, but there was no choice. There was no other way. And this route was possible, more than possible. Already, she had worked it out.

Fact: Muletsi had to leave South Africa.

That was a given. He was a wanted man, a criminal, and an escaped convict to boot. What was more, he'd been branded a member of the ANC, a banned organization. So there you were. Plain and simple. He had to get out. The only alternative was jail, or worse.

Second fact: He couldn't get out by car. The security forces kept roadblocks outside all the main cities and along the perimeter of certain black homelands. It was standard procedure. They were permanently on the lookout for anything that struck them as abnormal. You'd never know what that might be, what might make them look at you a second time. Even if you were white, they could decide you had something to hide. Sympathetic whites often served as shields for ANC activity. That was well known. No — Muletsi could not get out of South Africa that way. There had to be another route. And there was! The solution was simple.

She and Muletsi would ride out of South Africa on horseback. They would bear south and then northwest, up through the Transkei, over the Drakensberg, and into Basutoland not far from a place called Qacha's Nek. Nothing to it. She'd already traced out the route, first on the road map and now in her mind.

It wasn't so very far, not really. She had calculated the distance — two hundred miles or so, a five-day journey, not more than that. Not much more. In Basutoland Muletsi would be a free man, a refugee from South Africa. There would be possibilities for him. Other ANC exiles were already holed up there; she'd heard it on the news. Many had fled South Africa after the ANC was banned. By now they'd know what was what. Maybe Muletsi could go into hiding there. Or maybe there was a way of smuggling him from Basutoland to … oh, somewhere. She didn't know exactly where. Bechuanaland, maybe. Or, better yet, Dar es Salaam. Tanganyika was independent. It would be safe for him there.

But first Basutoland. She had worked out how to reach the place. She and Muletsi would travel most of the way through Natal and then enter the Transkei, which was a black homeland where the people did their farming in a communal way. That meant there would be few fences, if any. Eventually, they would cross over the Drakensberg into Basutoland, far from any border posts, if border posts there were. Maybe it seemed crazy. But it made sense. It really did.

All she had to do was communicate her plan to Mrs. Dadla, who would tell Muletsi about it. And then she would just wait and see. Maybe he would turn it down. Probably, he would be doubtful at first. But she had a feeling he would go along in the end. He didn't have any frigging choice. None. His mother saw it. Now Hilary saw it, too.

She shivered with excitement, just thinking about her plan — or maybe it was on account of the afternoon cold. It was turning seriously chilly out on this deck. Who knew what was going on with the weather this year? She refolded the road map with the sheet of notepaper inside and tapped it several times on the arm of the wicker chair. She'd need money, of course, but she could get that from her mother. One way or another, she would. She would think of something.

COLONEL BARKER WAVED OUT the window of his Cadillac, almost as if he were a member of the royal family on a tour of the colonies. "Hip, hip!" he called out.

He rolled up our driveway in his bronze-coloured Eldorado with his Rice two-horse trailer bringing up the rear. The car and trailer tottered past the lilacs and the weeping willows, proceeding toward the barn. Green trails of foliage swirled down, like a shower of pale-green confetti.

"Hip, hip!" the colonel hollered again. As usual, he was wearing a black patch over his bad eye.

Hilary rode beside him in the passenger seat. She and the colonel had come to collect Della and me so that we could all drive to Letham for the final competition prior to the provincial championships in Cardenden. My heart had been galloping since the night before, and I had barely slept. Already this morning, I had been up for several hours, fussing in the barn, getting Della ready for the day ahead. Now she was bandaged and blanketed, all set to go. Hilary and Colonel Barker lowered the trailer ramp while my father ambled up from the house, with Charlotte riding on his shoulders. She was getting too big for that.

"Morning, Hal," said Colonel Barker. "Morning, Charlotte."

"Morning, Colonel," said my father.

Charlotte saluted. "Hail, Britannia," she said.

Della could be a troublesome loader, but this time she marched straight up the ramp, tossing her tail as she went. I ducked under the horizontal steel bar at the front. Club Soda nickered and nipped at the air. The two horses each yanked a mouthful of hay from the net suspended at the bow of the trailer.

"That was easy," said Hilary. She and Colonel Barker raised the ramp and shot the bolts.

I gave Della a swat on her neck and ducked out through the small hatch at the front. I hurried back into the barn to collect my gear — saddle, bridle, clothing, and a small box of grooming equipment. Most of it fit in the trunk of the Cadillac. My Stubben saddle went into the back seat with me. Colonel Barker started the engine, and off we went. I waved at my father and Charlotte, and they both waved back. Charlotte shouted something, but I couldn't make it out — wishing me good luck, probably.

During the drive, Hilary kept a map unfolded on her lap and took charge of navigating. The colonel kept insisting he knew the way, but it was apparent that he did not. Two hours later we reached the fairgrounds in Letham a little before nine o'clock in the morning.

"What ho!" said Colonel Barker. He eased the car off the road and into a broad meadow, already half-filled with trailers and cars and riders and horses. "Great Scott!"

He manoeuvred the trailer into a free space at the edge of a field of freshly mown grass. I had nearly an hour before my dressage test, and I spent most of that time schooling Della in a practice ring. With about fifteen minutes to spare, she abruptly tucked in her hindquarters, arched her neck, and began to work the bit with her teeth, foaming with concentration. She remained in this pensive state from the beginning to the end of the dressage test. When it was done, Major Duval himself marched over to congratulate me. An hour or so later, they posted the results for the dressage portion of the event. I couldn't find my name at first, but it turned out I was looking too far down the sheet. Della and I had not merely done well. We had won. In the advanced division, Hilary had taken first place, too.

The cross-country phase followed, starting early in the afternoon. This was usually my worst stage, not only because it was long and physically demanding, but also because it scared me. There was good reason for that. The courses were difficult and often dangerous, and I worried about Della. At times she seemed to lack the stamina for cross-country. She started well but tended to lose strength before the course was done, so she made mistakes or I did. This time I was hoping that all those hours spent swimming in the quarry pond had toughened her up without wearing her down.

With Hilary's help I got Della tacked up and ready. She didn't look at all the way she had during the dressage phase that morning. Now we'd fitted a sheepskin pad beneath her saddle and strung a running martingale through the reins near her chest. I'd bandaged her legs and worked a pair of orange bell-shaped rubbers over her front fetlocks to protect them against clips from her hind hooves. She was keyed up, frothing at the bit, her flanks already stained with sweat. She knew what was coming.

I'd also shortened the stirrup leathers, two notches up from their dressage length. I wore tan breeches and a navy turtleneck jersey under a bib inscribed with my number, competitor 34. I tried to keep Della calm, but it was no use. She shied at nearly everything in sight, whether moving or stationary — trees, cars, the sudden darting of children. Every minute or so, without warning, she wheeled around on her hindquarters, reared up and pawed the air, unusual behaviour for her. She knew exactly what was coming.

"She'll be all right once you get going," said Hilary. She jogged alongside us on foot, in running shoes and riding breeches, and with a pale-blue cardigan over her blouse. "You've got the time straight?"

I nodded. I was aiming for the maximum bonus-points time. Twenty-one minutes, thirty-two seconds. The time was set on a Tissot wristwatch that Janet Hünigan's mother had loaned me. Just then the public address system crackled, and a woman's voice called out my name. Sam Mitchell. Number 34. I was on deck.

"Just stay calm," Hilary said. "You'll be fine. You'll both be fine."

In the starting ring I waited as the rider ahead of me set off on the course. The seconds dragged by.

"Won't be long now," said the starter, a big-bellied man with a ski-jump nose, wearing a panama hat. He spoke briefly into a walkie-talkie, nodded, and said, "Away you go."

I pressed down on the knob of the stopwatch and off we went, sailing down a broad green slope at an easy canter. Immediately, Della arched her neck and tucked in her haunches, all business. Meanwhile, my heart slowed to a steadier beat, as I'd half known it would. It's true what they say: the doing is easier than the waiting to do.

Nicely in hand now, glad to be on course, Della reached the narrow flat at the base of that inaugural hill. She lengthened her stride and galloped toward the first fence, an imposing wall of cedar brush. I counted down the strides — three, two, one, and off. I leaned into the rise and arch of Della's flight. My hands shifted forward with the pull of her head, and I braced myself with my knees against the landing, felt Della's forelegs shudder against the solid ground, sensed her hindquarters gathering beneath her. A dozen or so spectators reacted with shouts of approval and scattered applause. Della surged ahead at a smooth hand gallop.

I started up my customary chant. "Okay, Della. That-a-girl. It's okay. What a girl."

The sunlight drifted down through a veil of wispy clouds, thin as a film of milk on glass. The air was muggy and close, but the course was green and well marked, and the footing was just about perfect — fairly dry but also soft, almost spongy. That was a surprise after these nearly rainless summer months.

Della galloped down a gentle decline where the trail ran through a thicket of maples. We burst into an open field, rounded up a sudden rise, and made straight for the next obstacle, a hog's-back oxer with a sharp drop on the far side. I slowed Della to a canter, then a brisk trot. She took the fence in stride, an easy pop, so that she could more easily absorb the steep descent that followed. Next she scrambled down a long clay slide with another obstacle at the bottom — a pair of horizontal telephone poles. Della checked herself once and then took off, too soon, catching me by surprise. I felt my weight drift back, but I gripped the saddle with my knees and held on. We landed in near unison.

"Way to go," I chanted. "Way to go, Della!"

She was thickly lathered already, but her stride was steady. Her wind was good. She wasn't labouring. Better yet, she was moving on boldly at every fence, not hesitant or doubtful at all. And our pacing was about right. I was pretty sure we were running just a little bit fast, and that was what I wanted, to be a little bit ahead of the clock.

I guided Della past a fencerow of poplars and slowed her to a canter before peeling off to the right, clattering down a rock-strewn decline stippled with thorn scrub. A large glassy pond loomed ahead. About two-dozen spectators had gathered on its banks, many with cameras at the ready. I focused on the earthen ramp that descended toward the edge of the pond where a log jump stood, followed immediately by a drop into the shallow water.

"C'mon, Della. That-a-girl. Okay. Easy now."

I drew her down to a collected trot and then settled deep into the saddle. I braced myself for the jump, held my breath — and dropped the reins, just let them go slack. Worst mistake in the book. I'd anticipated the jump before it happened. Della stopped dead. She didn't know what to do, to pull back or go ahead, to refuse or jump from a standstill. Her haunches started to quake.

"C'mon, Della. C'mon."

I dug my legs into her sides, hoping she would respond — and she did. From a standing start, she launched herself over the barrier of horizontal logs. Next thing I knew, I was thrown way back in the saddle, and we both plummeted toward the pond's dull green veneer, the reins slack. We hit the water one after another, the spray flew up around us, and Della's hooves met the bottom of the pond about three feet below the surface. At once, my full weight thudded into the pommel of the saddle, square on, colliding at my groin. The pain roared up through my abdomen and into my chest, and I thought I would be sick or even black out, right then and there. I felt myself sliding out of the saddle. Della ploughed ahead, churning through the pond, kicking up clots of mud and spumes of water. I struggled to hang on. I'd lost one stirrup and now clung to Della with one leg and one hand. The pond water splashed at her chest in great squelching belts.

Somehow, I hauled myself back up and into the saddle. I'd lost both stirrups now, my grip on the reins was far too long, and I could barely breathe, but I managed to get Della straightened out for the climb out of the pond. She staggered through the muck, found better footing, broke into a canter, gathered her weight, and flew over a big oxer, taking me along for the ride. At least we were out of the water now, and we were still clear — no jumping faults at all.

We cantered across a gravel road, slithering down a steep bank on the far side. With the stirrups still flailing, I settled myself in the saddle, urged Della forward, and she sailed over a pair of split-rail fences separated by a single stride.

"Della! What a girl. What a girl. You beautiful girl."

I nattered away, the sound of my voice serving to block at least some of the pain in my abdomen. Della cantered ahead along a narrow path through a stand of maples. I managed to regain the stirrups and shortened my grip on the reins. I got my weight forward, out of the saddle. If I didn't think about the pain, maybe it would go away.

I gave Della her head, and we galloped along the perimeter of a broad, sloping meadow, freshly mown. At a flag marker located about two-thirds of the way along the meadow's length, I slowed her to a trot. We swung to the right and scrambled down a grassy incline toward a fence-ditch-fence combination. I counted out the strides — three, two, one — and we soared over the first element. Della checked herself, bounded over the ditch, took one long stride and easily cleared the second fence. We galloped into an adjacent field that swooped downward like an amphitheatre. Only a few obstacles remained.

"That-a-girl, Della. Come on, baby."

We raced across the field and then clattered along a rocky path that snaked through a spindly thicket of thorn trees. Beyond the thorns, Della swerved to the left along a narrow ridge, leading her straight toward the next obstacle — a Y-shaped log raised on a pile of rocks. We had to approach the jump at an acute angle, and it would be the easiest thing in the world for a horse to run out, miss the jump entirely.

But Della charged ahead, and I settled my weight deep in the saddle, counting down the strides. I eased forward on my knees as Della soared over the log. She touched down, thrust ahead with her forelegs — two long strides — and then checked herself before popping over a low rail fence followed by another steep slide down a slippery clay pitch.

We were almost done. Della clattered through a bit of rocky footing, and we swung right to gallop along a grassy lane that ran between two fields, maple trees on either side. I shortened the reins again and braced myself with my knees.

"That-a-girl, Della. Yay, Della. What a girl."

I twisted my wrist to glance at the stopwatch. Just under three minutes left. I held Della to a hand gallop, and we sped through an open field of alfalfa, bounding up a gentle rise and rounding another marker flag. I tried to steady her pace, aiming for the second-to-last obstacle — a series of steep embankments. Why did they put something this difficult so near the end?

"Okay, Della."

I straightened her line and then drove her forward at a gallop, practically flat out. There was no choice but to hit the first element at top speed and then hope for the best. Della flung herself at the initial embankment. She landed squarely, gathered herself for another stride, and leapt again, following with yet another stride, another leap. I thought for sure she would snag her front hooves on the final barrier, but she cleared it somehow and managed to clamber up onto the grassy incline above the obstacle.

We cantered on across the hill's narrow brow, rounded the crest at an easy pace, and followed a trail of mown grass to the left. I turned Della toward a gap in a windbreak of maple trees, blocked by a tall earthen mound crowned by a pair of split rails.

Della seemed to crouch slightly, and then arched into the air, flying over the earthen wall and the rails. She bobbled slightly on the landing but quickly recovered herself, and we headed toward the finish, through a meadow choked with Queen Anne's lace, aiming for an opening to the left of a large black barn. I glanced at the watch again and urged Della on. I wanted to hit the time exactly right, so I readjusted her pace every three or four strides — a bit faster, a touch slower — until we cantered across the finish line.

Clear.

IT WAS A SUNDAY, the stable hands' day off, and Hilary was nearly ready. She had been up late the previous night, stuffing a pair of saddlebags with gear they would need. Earlier that morning she'd hidden the satchels among a stack of straw bales in the stable loft. Now she was pulling on the warmest clothes she possessed, wondering how cold it might turn in the Drakensberg. She hoped that she had made sufficient preparation, but how could she possibly be sure? Anyway, it was too late to fuss about it now. Done. She hurried out of her bedroom and clattered down the stairs.

"Howzit, Pretty?" she said to Pretty, the maid. "Hey, Mummy." She gave her mother a peck on the cheek and snatched an apple from the bowl. She bit through the skin and into the flesh. "I'm off."

"Off where?"

"Don't know. Just off. For a ride. A long one."

"You've had no lunch, darling. You've got to eat."

"No worries. I'll have something extra for dins."

"That's ridiculous, dar—"

"Mummy. I need some money."

"Not you, surely. For what?"

"Things. I don't know. Just, you know, things. At school."

"But you're not at school."

"I soon will be. Mummy. Please."

"What …? You want it now?"

"If you've got any."

"How much do you need?"

Hilary pretended to conduct an elaborate calculation in her mind. In fact, she'd worked it out beforehand — one figure for what she wanted and another for what she thought she might actually acquire. She'd start at the top and work down. "A thousand," she said.

"A thousand …!"

"Yes, Mummy. Please, please."

"Rand …?"

"Yes, rand. What else?"

"Dear God. You can't be serious."

"It's to last all term. The other girls all have pots of money. I feel like a pauper, hey. You can't imagine what it's like."

"Well, I don't know …"

"Please."

In the end, it was the pleases that did it. Her mother said she thought she could manage eight hundred. She trudged upstairs to find her bag. Hilary watched as Pretty shuffled through the dining room, dusting things. A scarlet-leaved poinsettia rested on the sideboard, and she grimaced at the sight, shut her eyes. Bloody Jack Tanner. It was a gift he'd sent, addressed to her, with a card that bore his signature, a clumsy scrawl, and the word *Welcome*, nothing more. She'd have turfed the plant at once if she'd had her way. It damned well gave her the creeps. But her mother had crowed at the sight of it. "How thoughtful! It will look lovely here." And so, here it was. Hilary had to look away.

She returned her attention to Pretty, still absorbed in her labours, dusting, straightening. She felt as if she'd been watching the woman go about these same duties all her life, mainly because she had. Pretty had been working for the Anson family since before Hilary was born.

Now Pretty hesitated. She turned to face Hilary. "You be careful, Miss Anson."

"I'm sorry …? Pretty …?"

"It's cold this time of year in the mountains. Deadly cold. And you don't know the way."

Hilary's throat felt suddenly dry. She struggled to swallow. Pretty *knew* …?

Later, in the barn, after she'd got the money from her mother and after she'd promised to be back for dinner, cross her heart, she kicked herself for not having anticipated this. Of course, Pretty knew. The bush telegraph, they called it. It had its own ways and means. Probably no one could understand the true workings of it. But word got out and, one way or another, news got around. You had to be so damned careful. Muletsi had told her that.

Well, it was done now, and there was nothing for it but to saddle two horses. She'd have liked to take South Wind but wondered whether that would be entirely wise. Absconding with her father's most valuable horse? It seemed excessive, even to her, the mistress of extreme. On the other hand, no other beast in the stable had either the legs or the stamina that South Wind possessed in spades. She would need all the horse she could muster, so she reversed herself on the spot. In for a penny, in for a pound. With luck, all would work out well, and her father would have his horse back in the end, none the worse for wear. South Wind it was. For Muletsi, she had already decided on a spare horse named Welshman, a large, sturdy creature that'd be able to support Muletsi's size and weight. He was a poky, deliberate beast, but he was honest and strong.

She stood by the grain bins for several moments, brooding. She was having second thoughts, the last thing she could afford. More than anything else, she worried about the cold. Almost every year people perished in the blizzards that raged up in the Drakensberg — herd boys mostly, young lads charged with keeping watch over flocks of sheep or goats or small herds of bony cattle. They bloody well froze to death. Beyond that, she was feeling guilty about her parents. They were going to suffer paroxysms of worry.

But there was no way around that, none that she could see, so she got to work, saddling both horses and latching the saddlebags in place. She had just cinched Southey's girth when she had another thought. Magnificent beast though he was, he had a maniac tendency to throw his head. She'd taken more than one hard knock square on the nose thanks to a backward toss of Southey's head and his giraffe-like ability to contort his neck. She decided to fetch an extra piece of tack — a standing martingale — guaranteed to keep his frigging noggin more or less where it belonged. She ran the leather collar over Southey's head before unhitching his girth, feeding it through the martingale's lower loop, and cinching it again. That done, she joined the upper loop of the martingale to the backside of his noseband. There. Normally, she hated using any more artificial aids than were absolutely necessary, but Southey was uncommonly strong, and his will was fierce. Given time, she would have sorted this head-tossing business of his and without the benefit of so restrictive a device. But time, she had not. Now she gave him a swat on the neck. "There you go, my beauty."

Once both horses were tacked up and ready, she led the pair of them clopping along the corridor and then out to the mounting station in the courtyard in front of the stable. She had Welshman on a braided leather shank and South Wind by the reins. She climbed onto the mounting block and swung herself onto Southey's back, straightened herself in the saddle.

Once she'd got both horses organized, she urged South Wind forward, and they set off at a trot, Welshman tagging along on the shank — just a girl and a pair of horses making their way down a paved road past a span of poplars. To the right, the land plunged sharply away into the Mooi River valley, clad in the dull winter colours of Natal, all browns and muddy greens. Grey clouds rafted overhead. She took a deep breath, slowly filled her lungs. Just as slowly, she let the air back out.

Immediately, it began to rain, which was a curse — an insult from some rude god. Winter is supposed to be the dry season in Natal. What in the name of heaven was going on? She hiked up her collar and let the rain fall.

By the time she rode into Bruntville, it wasn't just raining. It was thudding down. In torrents. Already, she was frigging well drenched — drenched and damned near freezing. This was a magnificent start. She dismounted in a small open space among the shanties and peered around, looking for some place that was dry. There wasn't much on offer. In the end, she huddled in the shelter of a slender overhang of corrugated zinc — the best cover she could find. Some boys were moping about in the mud, just as soaking wet as she was herself, with no more than short pants and torn jerseys as protection against the chill. She called to them, and they hurried over as if attached to her by an elastic band.

"Howzit?" she said.

"Very fine, Miss," said one.

"Topping," said another.

God knew where he'd picked that up.

She asked if they were acquainted with Mr. Ndlovu, and they nodded. All the while, they bounced from bare foot to bare foot, their arms clutched around their slender, shivering torsos, their teeth chattering in the uncustomary cold.

"Good," she said. "I want you to find him for me. Tell him Miss Anson is here. Have you got that? Miss Anson."

"Miss Anson," repeated one, the one who'd spoken first. "Miss Anson is here. Miss Anson is you?"

She said that it was.

Off they went, scampering through the rain and the mud. She waited, gazing around herself at the cinder-block dwellings with their tin chimneys, now sputtering filaments of grey smoke into the winter air. They were poor, these people. That was for bloody sure. But they were trying. You could tell as much at a glance. Most of the little houses had small, hand-fashioned flower boxes arrayed outside. The boxes were drenched now, of course, and the flowers bedraggled. But there they were, just the same.

She glanced down at her watch. Three o'clock. She wondered whether it made any sense to set out right away, now, today. Wouldn't it be better to wait till tomorrow? Get a fresh start? She decided she'd leave that to Muletsi. He would know much better than she how far they could expect to travel in a given time and where they might spend the night.

Just now all she had to do was wait. She regarded the horses, who silently peered back at her, as if posing questions without words. *Why are we here? Why are you doing this to us? Why are we not someplace warm, in a barn somewhere, enjoying a hot bran mash?* They brooded, eyeing her, not blaming her exactly, but not letting her off the hook, either.

"Ag, South Wind," she whispered. "Ag, Welshman. You poor beasts. We'll soon get you dry. I promise."

"Hilary ..."

She started and looked off to her right, toward the sound of Muletsi's voice.

He ducked under Welshman's head and stood before her — Muletsi Dadla in the flesh. Except for that one time on the soccer pitch, it had been months since she'd seen him.

"You're soaking," he said. "Come. We'll put the horses away. We need to talk."

And it was true. They did need to talk — and they needed to do a lot more besides. They needed to figure this whole thing out.

AFTER THE CROSS-COUNTRY event, the stadium-jumping competition was almost an anticlimax. Della and I went clear, as did Edwin Duval and Janet Hünigan, not to mention several riders from other clubs. But my edge in the dressage made the difference. I finished in first place overall, and they gave me a large red rosette and a silver tray.

"Not real silver," I said. "Silver-plated."

This was later, when Hilary and I were tending to our horses beside Colonel Barker's trailer, preparing for the long drive home. Hilary had a champion's trophy, too, a platter that was even grander-looking than mine. As usual, she had easily won her division.

Soon Colonel Barker tottered over, issuing congratulations of his own. He was slurring his words a little, so it was clear he had been drinking. He announced he would not be driving us directly back to Kelso. Instead, we would be paying a visit to an acquaintance of his, an investor of some kind who had invited some people to drop by for drinks and whatnot.

"Won't take more than a tick," he said.

Neither Hilary nor I had any desire to make a detour to a cocktail party, not at this late hour on this long and happy day, but we were not in charge. We loaded the horses into the trailer and packed our gear into the trunk and back seat. Now we had to face a more delicate matter — the colonel's obviously inebriated condition.

"Egad!" he said.

He climbed behind the wheel and turned to look at Hilary, who had settled herself on the passenger side, bridling with displeasure.

"*What* ...?" he said.

"I didn't say anything."

"Don't need to. It's that look."

"Just drive carefully, then. Slowly. The horses."

"I'm aware of the horses."

"All right, then."

Colonel Barker started the engine and eased the car across the undulating meadow, weaving past the other vehicles and trailers, past the riders on foot and the blanketed horses. He switched on the right-hand turn signal and drove out onto the paved road that ran alongside the fairgrounds. The car lurched from side to side as the horse trailer rocked on its tires, but it seemed that Colonel Barker had matters under control.

Hunched in the back, I stared at my trophy, silently reading out the names of past winners. Soon my own name and Della's would appear alongside the rest. I'd be immortal; we both would. Colonel Barker crept through the town, his brow furrowed in concentration. He made only one or two wrong turns along the way, and eventually we pulled up in front of a mock-Tudor mansion, surrounded by similarly large houses, all set on rambling green properties.

Hilary whistled. "An 'acquaintance,' you say."

Colonel Barker straightened his eye patch. "You may have heard of him. Name's Quinton Vasco ..."

Silence. Complete and utter silence. *Quinton Vasco ...?*

Looking back on those few moments now — the three of us seated in Colonel Barker's car, parked outside what I then realized was Quinton Vasco's house — I recall a plummeting sensation, a kind of vertigo, as if I were aware even then of all that would soon follow, although I could have had no idea. But there we were, suddenly immersed in what I later took to be an irresistible tide of unfolding events. This was the moment when Hilary Anson would meet Quinton Vasco for what I then believed to be the first time. In that moment, the encounter seemed a matter of purest chance and, in a way, it was. But now, all these years later, I'm convinced that this meeting, or one like it, would have taken place no matter what, if not on this day then on another, if not at this place then somewhere else. Nothing important would have changed. Everything would have happened more or less as it did. One way or another, Quinton Vasco would soon be dead, his corpse abandoned in a large field of alfalfa grass, a couple of hundred yards north of Number Four Sideroad in Kelso County. It sometimes seems to me now — as I look back on that moment, our arrival at Quinton Vasco's mansion — that I was even then able to foresee everything that would later take place. But that's an illusion, a trick of time and memory. Of course I didn't know; I couldn't have known. I merely eased my silver tray aside, as the colonel climbed out of the car, still a little unsteady on his feet. He asked if we would like to accompany him to the party.

Hilary shrugged. "Why not?" She turned to look back at me. I saw nothing unusual in her gaze. "This should be interesting."

And it was. It surely was.

The interior of Quinton Vasco's house swelled with guests, and the air was practically blue from cigarette smoke. Men and women in dark pinstriped servants' uniforms shuttled through the living room or out onto the terrace, bearing platters of canapés or trays of drinks. Colonel Barker immediately took a first libation and then a second.

"Colonel ...!" A man approached. He was short of stature, slim of build, and looked to be about thirty-five, which seemed pretty old to me but not quite ancient. He had a square face with brush-cut hair, and he wore thick-framed eyeglasses. I especially remember that he was dressed all in black — black shoes, black trousers, and a black turtleneck sweater.

This, it turned out, was Quinton Vasco. He didn't look anything like the man I had imagined. I had envisioned an overweight oaf, thickly bearded, with dark, searching eyes and cavernous features — a stereotypical villain, straight from central casting. But this clean-cut and possibly somewhat glib individual was nothing of the kind. He clapped Colonel Barker on the back and then thrust his right hand toward me.

"Quint Vasco," he said.

He spoke in a somewhat high-pitched, slightly aspirated voice with what I took to be an English intonation, although it was very different from Colonel Barker's pretend accent.

"Liverpudlian," he said, sensing my confusion. "From Liverpool. Home of the Beatles. You ever hear of them?"

I shook my head. The British musical invasion of the early 1960s was still a way's off, and few people in Canada had heard of the Beatles yet.

"Don't worry," he said. "You will."

I nodded, but I didn't reply, not at first. I was too busy thinking about Quinton Vasco, his physical presence, nothing else. I couldn't believe I was standing in front of him, talking to him, actually taking up space inside his house.

Quinton frigging Vasco.

I said my name was Sam Mitchell. He nodded and looked at me for a time, in a way I didn't like. Then he turned to Hilary, who was at least a couple of inches taller than he.

"And you are …?"

She told him her name, pronouncing the words with care, as if it were important for Quinton Vasco to get them right.

"My, oh, my," he said. "Aren't you the ravishing creature." He took in her clothes — riding breeches, tennis shoes, white blouse with necktie, light-blue cardigan. He glanced again at me. "Are you both jockeys of some kind?"

"We were at a horse show," Hilary said. "We've got two horses in front of your house right now."

"Is that some sort of a threat?"

"Not at all. You find me threatening?"

He laughed and shook his head. "Of course not. But horses ...?" He shrugged. "Never understood the appeal myself. Damned things take up too much space. All that grass. Financially unsound."

"You're one to talk," said Hilary. "I mean, when it comes to empty space."

I half thought she was going to say something about the cannons we'd seen. I was half hoping she would. But Quinton Vasco changed the subject.

"Don't tell me. South Africa — am I right? Your accent?"

"Yebo."

He seemed to flinch at the sound of the African word. "No relation to Daniel, I presume?"

"You mean the minister Daniel Anson?"

He tilted his head, more curious now. "Yes. I —"

"He's my father," said Hilary. "What a coincidence, hey. You know him, then?"

"Oh, by reputation."

"But you have been to South Africa, I think?"

"No, no. Always wanted to. They say it's marvellous. All those wild beasts." He laughed. "Of course, with my luck, I'd wind up in a large pot of boiling water, being cooked by cannibals." He laughed again.

Hilary shook her head. "I doubt that very much. No cannibals in my country. Anyway, I'm sure we've met. In Mooi River? At my father's place? I'm positive I've seen you there."

"Not possible."

"And yet you know my father?"

"By reputation, as I said." He glowered, not quite so charming now. "Or perhaps we've crossed paths somewhere else. Damned if I can remember." He arched his back, as if trying to make himself taller. "I say, would you care for a drink?" He raised a hand, beckoning one of the servers.

"No, thanks. We should probably check on the horses."

"Oh? What a pity. Will I see you again?"

"If you like. I'm staying at Colonel Barker's. Ask him."

"I believe I will."

"Steady on," said Colonel Barker, a little groggy from drink. "What's all this?"

Quinton Vasco simply smiled and took Colonel Barker by the arm. "Come, Martin," he said. "We have much to discuss." He nodded toward Hilary, a sort of goodbye, and then stole a glance at me — a leer, really — before leading the colonel out onto the terrace, which overlooked a large swimming pool, bordered by several stately elms.

"I'll bet I know what they're talking about," said Hilary. "He wants to buy Martin's place. Colonel Barker's, I mean. I've suspected it for a while. Come on. I can't bear it in here. Let's see about the horses."

I followed her out of the house. As soon as we were outdoors, I turned to her.

"You *know* the guy? You actually know Quinton Vasco?"

"Not *know*," she said, marching ahead. "Know *of*."

"But still. You've met him?"

"I'm pretty sure."

"In South Africa?"

"Yes. Despite what he seems to recall."

"Why didn't you tell me?"

She stopped and looked at me, frowning a little, impatient. "Good question. Actually, I wasn't sure it was the same person, not even with a name like that. Quinton Vasco …? There can't be too many of those. So no surprise, really. It's him." She let out a long breath, shaking her head. "Look, let's forget about this, okay? Forget we ever spoke of it."

"Forget, why?"

"Because I say so. Besides, we've got horses to attend to, hey." She headed for the horse trailer, shaking her head and running her hands through her hair. "This is so unjust."

"What is?" I thought she meant something about Quinton Vasco.

"This," she said. "This party. Shame. Why should we be going to a party?"

"Because we won?"

"Ball dust. Club Soda and Della won. We were just along for the ride, you and I. And here they are, the real champions of the day, suffocating inside this bloody horse trailer, while the humans smoke and drink. I don't call that fair. Come on."

She strode toward the trailer and drew back the bolts that secured the ramp. I hurried over to help her lower it. Pretty soon, we had both horses out on the pavement, both blanketed, with their legs wrapped in bandages to prevent injury. I followed Hilary's lead and guided Della down the street to a grassy hollow near a brook, a small green park where the horses could graze and drink.

Hilary stroked Club Soda's neck. "God, I love horses. Sometimes I think I've never loved anything else."

I knew what she meant. I felt the same way; sometimes I did. I loved the rich, earthy scent of them, their strength and size, their air of concern, their mostly gentle ways. When you speak to a horse, you really think they are listening. Maybe they can't understand the words, but they are trying to. You can tell. You can see it in their ears, the way they perk toward you. Despite their heft and substance, horses won't hurt you, or not on purpose, or not unless it's your fault.

It turned out that we were the spectacle of the day in Letham — Hilary and I, Club Soda and Della. Passing cars slowed to a crawl so their passengers could peer out at this unfamiliar sight, a pair of horses in bright red blankets, casually grazing by the roadside in a posh neighbourhood of the city.

After a while we began to sing, both of us together. By this time, we had memorized the words to "Yini Madoda" or at least the sounds of the words. Neither of us knew what they meant. We sang the song through three times and then did our best to sing "Ndamcenga." Mostly, we just hummed that one. When we were done singing, Hilary suggested she read to me some more. By this time, we were about halfway through another Paton. *Too Late the Phalarope,* it was called. She had the book in her handbag in the car, so I held on to both horses, while Hilary retrieved the novel. She settled herself at a picnic table, smoked a succession of cigarettes, and read aloud the tale of an Afrikaner policeman named Pieter van Vlaanderen and his tragic downfall. Soon I was aware of nothing but the snuffling breath of horses and the grey skies that lowered over Natal in South Africa, pierced by gaps of blue. The spell ended only when Colonel Barker appeared, swaying along the street, his eye patch awry. There was no question now about whether he was drunk or not. He was potted.

"Must be off," he said and promptly stumbled and almost fell, barely recovering his balance. "Chop, chop." His eyes were red, his face puffy, his nose inflamed. "Can't wait all day, you know. In you get, you lot."

I didn't know what to say or do except to go along. Hilary first returned the Paton to the car, and then she and I got the horses loaded and squared away. Now she straightened her shoulders before walking around to the driver's side of the Cadillac.

"Martin ..." she said.

Right away, I detected a double-edged quality to her voice, a tone I hadn't heard before, not from her; a quality at once teasing and beseeching and yet hard as rock.

"I'll drive," Colonel Barker said. He reached for the door handle, tried to ease Hilary out of the way, but again his balance faltered. Again, he almost fell right down.

"Martin ..." She steadied him with one hand. "Aren't you forgetting something?"

"Nonsense. Not forgetting anything. Said get in. Get in, damn it. Do as I say."

"I said, aren't you forgetting something?"

Some movement caught my eye, off to the right, and I looked up to see Quinton Vasco standing alone at the edge of his driveway, hands in his front pockets. He said not a word, simply remained where he was, observing Hilary and Colonel Barker both — but mostly Hilary. I was pretty sure of that. He seemed content just to watch, as if there were something he wished to learn, and here it was.

Hilary leaned toward Colonel Barker, and he stood quite still. She brought her lips close to his ear and whispered to him. I couldn't make out what she was saying.

"No, no," Colonel Barker said. "Must do as I say."

Still she whispered.

"Well ..." he said. His shoulders slumped. He nodded. "Yes. Yes."

She raised her hands to rest them on his shoulders and kept her lips pressed close to him, still whispering into his ear.

"Oh, all right."

She kissed him just below his ear, not a quick smack on the cheek, not the kind of kiss you'd give your mother. This was something wholly different, a lingering, purposeful contact that was suggestive of something else, something beyond my ready imagining. It was painful to watch, and yet it was magical, too, this power she seemed to have over others, over men, anyway — men and horses. It sometimes seemed they would do whatever she wished, whatever she said, whatever she didn't need to say.

Hilary stood back as the colonel shuffled around the car, fumbled with the front door on the passenger side, and then wedged himself into the seat there. I hurried over and swung the door shut behind him, then climbed into the back. Hilary slipped into the driver's seat and pulled her door till the latch clicked. She shifted her gaze to the right.

"Look," she said and nodded toward Quinton Vasco, who hadn't moved, still with his hands in his pockets, still watching us from the roadway in front of his house. "How long has he been there?"

"A few minutes," I said.

I raised my hand and waved, but he didn't wave back.

"Mysterious chap," said Hilary. "I'll give him that." She turned the key in the ignition, checked the rear-view mirror, shifted the transmission into drive, and carefully pulled out onto the shiny black street, with the trailer tottering gently behind us. I turned in my seat to look out the side window. Quinton Vasco was still there, still framed by the large oak trees in front of his house. Now he eased one of his hands from his trouser pockets, and waved at me. But this time I didn't respond. Instead, I turned around in my seat and fixed my gaze on the road ahead, the stone mansions off to the side, the lofty shade trees. Pretty soon Colonel Barker was making muffled snoring noises. He was sound asleep.

We were out on the open road by then, and Hilary glanced at my image in the rear-view mirror. "Congratulations, champ."

"Same to you." I smiled. "Champ."

And for two hours, until we got to Kelso, that was all that anyone said.

HILARY TIGHTENED THE CINCHES on South Wind's girth. Along with the two horses, she and Muletsi were both squeezed into a narrow gap between a pair of small cinder-block dwellings. "Do you trust him?" she said. She meant Mr. Ndlovu.

"I do," said Muletsi.

"But you don't trust anyone."

"Is that so?"

"Except me."

He nodded. "That's right. And my mother."

"But Mr. Ndlovu, too?"

"Shhh." He gave her a look.

She closed her eyes. What an idiot she was. He was right, of course. Nothing was private in this place, where everybody listened and everybody heard, a result of sheer physical proximity as much as anything else. No matter where you happened to be or how careful you were, it was practically a given that someone would overhear what you were saying — someone you didn't intend. So you never said more than was necessary. Muletsi had already explained this to her, but she kept slipping up. As for Mr. Ndlovu, they'd met with him the previous night.

The three of them had huddled together in a shebeen — really a pair of battered and repurposed old cargo containers. There, they'd sipped corn brew and debated in whispers the merits and demerits of her plan. Vile stuff, the corn brew, but never mind. She had spoken first. Clearly, Muletsi could not stay here. Eventually, word would get around, and the police would show up. It was inevitable.

More quickly than she'd expected, the two men took her side. They hadn't required much convincing. With no better plan in sight, they all agreed that a run for Basutoland made as much sense as there was sense to be made. Muletsi was not an accomplished rider, but he could sit a horse. As a boy he'd bestrode donkeys and ponies often enough. That part was not the problem. The problem was avoiding discovery, and the key to avoiding discovery was to set off as soon as possible. Five days the journey would take them — five days, more or less. Much would depend upon the weather, but with luck the skies would clear. It was Sunday now. They'd reach Qacha's Nek by the end of the week. Qacha's Nek. It was a mountain village in Basutoland near the border with South Africa. There was no migration post, or none that she knew of, but there was a nearby crossing. She'd worked out that much.

Mr. Ndlovu cleared his throat.

Muletsi turned to the man, frowned. "Yes …?"

Mr. Ndlovu shrugged. "It is only an idea," he said. "It might come to nothing." He lowered his voice, leaned closer to them both, spoke in a whisper. He proceeded to outline a proposal that was wholly unexpected, a thing that Hilary had never contemplated before.

When the older man was done, Muletsi leaned back and swore under his breath, an oath that was barely audible. "You can't be serious."

"Why not?"

The two words dangled in the smoky air, like the perfect counter-argument to any objection.

Hilary peered at the two men, first at Mr. Ndlovu, then at Muletsi, then at Mr. Ndlovu again. By all that was right and holy, the older man's proposal should have shocked her beyond words, and yet somehow it had not. She saw at once what he meant. Why not, indeed? Why the frigging hell not? This was war, after all — war and revolution. The normal rules no longer applied. Besides, there was a justice to it. Surely there was. Then, all at once, her mood switched, and her heart began to quake. What in God's name was she thinking? Now the idea seemed utterly untenable. The man could not be serious. What he had suggested just now, it was impossible to consider. In her mind, she heard a gunshot ring out, saw a man's body crumple and fall.

Again, she turned to Muletsi. He'd lost weight in prison, and he hadn't had much mass to spare. He was now without his eye-glasses, as well. They'd gone missing behind bars, and there'd been neither time nor money to replace the loss. That made her wonder, too. He wasn't exactly blind without his glasses — nothing as dire as that — but neither was he someone you'd trust as a marksman.

Muletsi seemed about to speak, but Mr. Ndlovu broke in. "No need to decide now," he said. There'd be time to reflect first. Besides, there was no guarantee the plan would be approved.

Hilary understood his meaning — approved by the ANC. Certain higher-up officials of the ANC would decide, one way or another.

Muletsi massaged the bridge of his nose, thinking. He let his hand fall away. His eyes blinked open and he peered at Mr. Ndlovu. "How will we know?"

Mr. Ndlovu smiled. "Oh, don't worry about that. You will know." He straightened the sleeves of his jacket and wiped his hands together, as if to say their meeting had reached its end.

It didn't seem he was prepared to be any more forthcoming than this. It was left to Hilary to say the last thing that needed saying before they retired for the night.

"So that means we go, hey? Tomorrow morning? First thing — is it? We just go?"

Muletsi swallowed the last of his corn brew and set his jar down on what passed for a table — really a wooden spool liberated from some construction site. He turned to look at her, his eyes fixed on her eyes.

"Yes," he said.

By now the shebeen was practically empty. She paid for their drinks with a small portion of her money, the money she'd got from her mother, and they ventured out on foot, out into the darkness. After a few minutes she and Muletsi parted company with Mr. Ndlovu.

"Good night, Uncle," said Muletsi.

It was an imprecise term; she knew that. An expression of respect. The older man tipped his trilby hat and gazed at them both in turn. He then set off on his own, proceeding in a direction apart from theirs. She and Muletsi made their way to a small, woebegone dwelling that belonged to a mate of his. They'd been invited to make their bed on a rug on the floor; it was all there was. A short while later she peered up at the sagging ceiling, listened to the sporadic barking of dogs outside. If she got through this, she'd never be afraid of anything again. That was what she told herself in the moments before she fell asleep.

When she was next aware of anything at all, she sensed another human being, kneeling above her in the morning darkness. Muletsi.

"Come, Hilary. It's time."

The sun had not risen, and yet it was morning. She was amazed she'd slept so well, amazed she'd slept at all. There was something to be said for nervous exhaustion, and here was proof. Muletsi said he had already been to see his mother to say his goodbyes.

"I said your goodbyes, too," he told her.

And that was that.

Within half an hour they were leading their horses along a narrow alley, gutted with pools of water from the previous day's rain. It was dry now but overcast and cold. This was the harshest winter she had ever known. Muletsi gave her a leg-up, and she settled herself in the saddle, gathered the reins. She watched as he prepared to swing himself up onto Welshman.

"Wait," she said. "You —"

He paused and looked up at her, his dark, oval face poking from the neck of a thick beige turtleneck sweater. He smiled. "Yes, Miss …?" Without waiting for an answer, with his back to Welshman's head, he gave the left stirrup iron a quarter twist, raised his left foot — clad in a takkie, no more — and slipped it into the iron. He bounced once, twice, on his right foot and then swung himself up and into the saddle. He slid his right foot into the stirrup on the offside, balancing on the balls of both feet. He took up the reins between the third and fourth fingers of each hand.

God in heaven. It was as if he'd been riding horses all his life, which she knew for a fact he had not. She inclined her head his way. "Where did you learn to do that?"

Muletsi smiled again. "That's easy. I watched you."

More fool, thou. This was what she thought, but she decided it would be better not to put the thought into words. Instead, she touched her heels to South Wind's flanks, coaxing him into an easy trot. Muletsi would do fine, it seemed — not that she had ever believed otherwise. You could call this the good news. She already knew the bad. The radio weatherman that morning was calling for a damp storm front to move in off the Indian Ocean and to continue bearing west. When it met the Drakensberg, the humid air would rise, cool, and likely turn to snow, at least on the mountain heights. Meanwhile, she and Muletsi would have to cope with rain, great dollops of the stuff, damnably wet and pissing cold. Goddamn the gods of weather. Still, there was no use complaining. The elements would attend to themselves. Besides, it was past time for them to get this journey started, and now at last they were off, aiming south toward Nottingham Road. They'd have to ride through developed areas for a time. As soon as possible, they'd bear west and enter the Lotheni reserve. There they'd go undetected; she was pretty sure. For a time, several days, they would travel in the shadow of the Drakensberg through what was mostly wilderness. Eventually, though, they would have to scale the Great Escarpment's southern face. Pray to God there wasn't snow. Still, either way, snow or not, the border would be unmarked and unmonitored. She had verified everything, first on a map and later at the little lending library in Mooi River. When they got to Basutoland, they'd be safe.

"Hilary," he said. "Tell me again. Why are we doing this?"

"So you can have choices. So you can be free."

He smiled, in that way of his, the way that suggested that maybe, just maybe, somebody was missing something here.

"Choices, is it? Freedom, hey? Is that it?"

She realized at once that she was talking rot. He had no choices. He wasn't free. She was about to reply, but he broke in.

"I'm sorry," he said. "You're right about one thing. I can't stay here."

That much was surely true, and they let the conversation lapse, at least for the time being. Off they went into the cold greyness of morning, the trek finally begun. She didn't worry that Muletsi might not be able to keep up. He would. She knew he would. He was a genius that way. On the other hand, she had a nagging sense that something wasn't right. It did not take long for her to work out what that something was. His glasses. He was still missing his glasses. They should not be heading off without his glasses. But they were.

MRS. BARKER PHONED THAT week with the news. I had made the Kelso team — both of us had, meaning Della and me. She said Edwin and Janet would also ride on the preliminary-level squad. Those two had been shoo-ins all along.

"After what happened on the weekend in Letham," she said, "we could hardly leave you off."

It was a short conversation, and once it was over, I marched straight out to the barn to let Della know. She didn't seem too surprised, but I hadn't expected she would be. I climbed up onto the grain bins and turned on the radio, tuned to CKEY. The Drifters were singing "Up on the Roof." I leaned back against the steel bars that marked the perimeter of Della's stall. In my tuneless voice, I sang along.

Hilary had easily qualified in the advanced division as an individual competitor representing the Mooi River Equestrian Club from South Africa. Many people in Kelso believed this idea to have been a reckless and ill-considered proposition from the start, especially considering the stain of scandal that clung to Hilary, but now they were stuck with it.

To celebrate our victories, Hilary and I met that Friday afternoon. We rode together down to the quarry ponds. There, as usual, we untacked our horses, replacing bridles with halters. I waited, holding Della and Club Soda by a pair of shanks, while Hilary slipped behind a grove of cedars to change. All the while, we talked about Quinton Vasco.

"When did you meet him?" I said. "In South Africa, I mean. Last year, was it? The year before?"

"He came out to my daddy's farm," she said from beyond the cedars. "Twice, actually. They were business gatherings. My father has plenty of meetings like that. At least, he used to. Probably still does."

"Is your father someone important?"

She laughed. "God, no. Just a farmer. A gentleman farmer, that's all." She was still beyond the cedars, changing.

Something about her answer struck me as strange, contradictory even. Was her father a businessman or a gentleman farmer? Or both? Then I remembered something else. That day in Letham, at Quinton Vasco's house, Hilary had referred to her dad as "the minister." I remembered it clearly. "The minister Daniel Anson." What kind of minister did she mean? The pastor of a church? And now she was saying her father was a farmer?

I noticed she had left her backpack on the broad ledge of rock. I thought at once of her gun, the Makarov. Supposedly, Bruce Gruber had the weapon now, but I wasn't so sure. He'd returned everything else.

"Say," I said, "did you get it back yet?"

"Get what back?"

"You know, the gun."

She was silent for a time. Then she said, "No. Not yet."

I kept looking at Hilary's bag. Its leather straps were loose, unbuckled, and it took me only a moment to reach down and peel back the canvas flap, to peer inside at a bunch of stuff, a small leather purse, a pack of Rothmans cigarettes, her copy of *Too Late the Phalarope*, a plastic tub containing some kind of ointment,

sundry other items of a personal nature — *and the Makarov pistol.*
Plain as day. There it was. She did get it back. Why would she lie?

"Hey …" Hilary emerged from the grove of cedars, barefoot,
wearing her blue two-piece swimsuit.

I swatted at the flap on her pack and straightened up. Had
she seen? "But you remember him?" I said. "Quinton Vasco. You
remember meeting him?"

"Yes. Who wouldn't?" She wrinkled her brow. "He's odd, don't
you think? Those black duds. Says unexpected things. I'd be sure
to remember him if only because of that."

It seemed she hadn't noticed me checking her backpack. "What
business did he have with your father?"

"Oh, very hush-hush. Always is." She wrinkled her brow. "Why
so many questions, hey?"

"I don't know. Just curious, I guess."

She nodded, apparently satisfied. "Come on," she said. "Let's
get these beasts into the water."

I handed Hilary the shank that was clipped to Club Soda's
halter, and she vaulted onto his back. At once, she urged him ahead,
and they both sailed from the limestone ledge, seeming to hang in
the still air for a moment before careening downward, colliding
with the dark-green surface below, where they were swallowed at
once. Soon a pair of horse's ears reappeared, followed by Club Soda's
head. An instant later, Hilary surged into view. The water sluiced
from her shoulders and down her back.

"Whoa!" she shouted. "That was a corker!"

I'd seen her perform this same manoeuvre countless times
this summer, but still I was impressed — impressed and relieved.
"Good one!"

"Come on," she said. "Come on in."

I swung myself up onto Della's back and started to rein her
around, to head over to the far side of the quarry pond.

"No," Hilary shouted. "Not that way. Jump in. From the ledge. Just don't drop her. Stay with her."

I rolled my eyes. It wasn't as if I hadn't tried this before. Still, something had changed. If there was one thing I knew by now, it was how to fall off a horse. Besides, this was only water, not solid ground — and, anyway, we had won first prize at Letham. What was I afraid of? I swung Della around and rode back toward the tall ledge overlooking the pond. This time I didn't hesitate. I pressed my heels into her flanks, urged her forward. By now she had seen Club Soda perform this same feat numberless times, and that must have had an effect. I guess it did. One way or another, she now took two strides, and I'll be damned if she didn't launch herself into the air with me aboard, clinging to her mane. For a moment, I felt as if we were both in flight.

"Wait ∴..!" I shouted, but the water exploded in a hail of crystalline splinters. Suddenly, I was underwater. It was as though we were being sucked toward the bottom, but the feeling lasted only an instant or two, and then we shot back to the surface. "Woo!" I shouted. "Woo!"

I held tight to Della's mane with one hand as she swam aimlessly about, first one way, then another, but never turning anywhere near the shore. She seemed almost as excited by what she'd just done as I was. Besides, the water was glorious. It was a sweltering day, after all — part of a late-summer heat wave — and the horses seemed content to swim all afternoon. After a while, I felt something soft and wet nudging against my left shoulder — a pale-blue twist of fabric. I realized it was the top of Hilary's two-piece swimsuit. Almost right away another piece of blue material floated past — the bottoms.

"Um, Hilary ...?" I said. "Your bathing suit?"

"I know. It just feels nice like this. Try it."

We were almost at opposite ends of the pond, separated by sixty feet or so. I didn't know what to say, so I said nothing. But, after a time, I did as she'd suggested, clutched Della's mane with one hand and reached down with the other to peel off my trunks. I let them float away, just as she had done with her own bathing suit. My head buzzed.

"Watch me," she said.

"What ...?"

I shifted around, still grasping Della's mane, and I looked on as Hilary urged Club Soda up the grassy ramp at the far end of the quarry pond, saw her ebony hair knotted behind her neck, saw her breasts, long legs, taut belly, slender arms, saw everything. Hilary guided Club Soda around the edge of the quarry pond and up onto the shelf of limestone. She halted just a few yards short of the edge and then dug her calves into her horse's flanks.

Club Soda tautened his legs, lowered his hindquarters, took two strides forward, and seemed to burst into empty space. Hilary's hair pulled loose and flared behind her as bolts of shattered water exploded all around. They vanished at once, she and Club Soda, the cool shadows of the pond devouring them whole. An instant later, they burst back into view, with Hilary laughing and waving at the trees with her free arm, like royalty on parade. Club Soda snorted and tossed his head, his ears twitching back and forth. I swore to myself that I would remember this moment, these images, for as long as I lived.

Later that afternoon Hilary and I huddled on a large slab of rock, our legs dangling over the edge. We had put our bathing suits back on, and she was reading aloud from her dog-eared paperback copy of *Too Late the Phalarope*. I listened to her plummy, singsong voice, so different from my own flat, utilitarian accent. The horses nibbled on green leaves and stubble in a thicket behind us, their shanks looped around a tree trunk and secured with safety knots.

I gazed at the soft down on Hilary's lower arms, so fine you wouldn't know it was there unless the sun's rays caught it just so. I still had an image of her in my mind, naked, as she and Club Soda plunged into the green water. The memory was utterly vivid, yet already I caught myself wondering whether it was really true. In a way, it seemed impossible to think that it had actually happened. It was the sort of vision I might make up. Maybe that was exactly what I'd done. Sometimes you want so badly for a thing to be true that you imagine it into existence. You can do that without even being aware. You can do the opposite, too. You can recoil from an experience so sharply that you wipe it out of your memory; you forget it completely. Or not quite completely. I suppose that a shadow always remains, a kind of pentimento. *Pentimento*. That was a new word I had learned. It refers to the traces of an older work just visible beneath a fresh layer of paint that has been applied to a canvas.

Pretty soon I started thinking about my own leap into the pond that afternoon. There was more than just pentimento there. I was sure it had really happened. I wasn't imagining things. Finally, I had done it, and that made me happy. At first, it did. Then I began to wonder why it had taken me so long to work up the courage to do something I should have been able to do all along.

"Hilary," I said. "Why am I such a coward?"

"*Qu'est-ce que tu as dit?*" She set down her book.

"Me. I'm a coward."

"You're nothing of the kind."

"I'm afraid to jump into a stupid pond."

"But you just did that very thing. I was watching." She frowned. "You're talking ball dust."

"It took me months to work up the guts to do it. Weeks, anyway."

"And now you've done it. Case closed."

We were both silent for a time, and then Hilary spoke.

"I'm serious," she said. "You're not a coward. You're just careful. That's a good thing — up to a point, anyway. You're a careful person. That's who you are. Unlike me."

"What kind of person are you?"

"Bold, hey. You hadn't noticed?"

"I want to be bold."

"And so you can — within limits." She sat up straight and looked at me. "We have to make do with what we are."

"We can't change?"

"We can, a bit. Look at what you did in Letham. You were careful, but you also took some chances, no? And so you won. And today you and Della leapt into the water. I'd call that a good week's work." She shrugged. "But you're still bound to be careful. That's you."

"I can't be different?"

She tilted her head, pondering. Then she shrugged. "Oh, who knows? Maybe."

"And you?"

She laughed. "Lost cause. Lost bloody cause."

"You couldn't be a bit less bold?"

"Could, I suppose. I could also be the next pope. But I don't think I will. I've come too far."

She reached for the book, and she opened it again. She took a deep breath. I thought she was going to say something else, but she didn't. Instead, she resumed reading aloud.

I listened to the rise and fall of her voice, but at the same time I thought of that gun, now mysteriously restored to Hilary's backpack. Why did she carry a gun? Why hadn't she told me it had been returned to her? Why had she taken so long to say that she had already crossed paths with Quinton Vasco even before she came to Canada? "I've come too far": I wondered what she meant by that. Back then, I had no idea. Now, all these years later, I wonder if it wasn't preordained that Quinton Vasco would die.

Just then, from somewhere along the wall of the escarpment, I heard the whine of the cicada, buzzing high and fading low, a warning that the fine weather was nearing its end, that autumn loomed — because it did. I knew it did. Already, I could sense the wraith of autumn in the dry rustle of the desiccated leaves overhead. I shut my ears to the sound, for it was summer still, and summer could lead to anything. Or at least I pretended it could, even as the doors of my world were edging shut. The cicada yowled again, but I ignored the sound. Instead, I clung to the rise and fall of Hilary's voice, as if her voice mattered more than anything — her voice and the nickering of horses nearby.

JACK SHIFTED HIS WEIGHT to the left and pressed his shoulder against Tempest's rear haunch. "Up. Come on, you. Up." Dutifully, the horse raised his near hind leg so Jack could pry away with the hoof pick. There. He set the hoof down. "There you go ..."

He sensed some disruption behind him, a shuffle of footsteps, a cough. He straightened up and turned around right quick, a boxer's instinct, ready for bear. "Eh, who's that?"

But it was only his old friend and secret accomplice, Everest Ndlovu. "Elephant," the name meant. Jack feigned surprise, but the truth was he knew full well why Mr. Elephant had come to call. The man had something to report, some information to impart. Right now Ndlovu stood at the entrance to the barn, framed in the dull light. He removed his trilby as if he had just entered a church, and now he clutched it at his chest with both hands. He was wearing a sloppy brown suit with a frayed white shirt and a smudged necktie. Food stains, it looked like.

"Mr. Jack," he said. He cleared his throat. "Fine horse there." As if he knew the first thing about it.

"The finest." Jack flipped the hoof pick into the equipment box and slapped his hands together. Time for business. In fact, it was well past time. He knew two horses were missing — South Wind and Welshman. Gone since Sunday. It was Tuesday now. He knew Hilly was gone. He knew they were upside down with worry up at the big house, or Mrs. Anson was, anyway. The boss man wasn't back yet from another of his business trips. Probably, he was on an airplane even now.

The police had been by already, the ones from Mooi River. But not much would come of that, not yet, not till Jack gave the word. He was that close to the chief, Walt van Niekerk. They kept each other informed, so to speak, an arrangement that suited them both. In this instance, Jack had decided to deal with matters on his own, and old Walt had said, "Good show, deal away. As you wish, you sneaky bugger." His very words. And Jack was grateful for that.

Still, it wouldn't do to behave in a reckless fashion. It would be best to take things slow, step by step. This was the approach he planned to adopt as regarded his old friend, Everest Ndlovu. One false move and the old coot might bolt. He might go back on the terms of their private agreement, their understanding. It was that delicate.

Jack nodded toward Ndlovu. "My compliments to your girl."

He liked to get that reference in at the start. Blessing was her name. Blessing Ndlovu. All of twelve years old. Be thirteen soon. He had her age committed to memory. He knew Everest Ndlovu understood that. He had been made to understand. The man also understood that it wouldn't take much to cause that girl trouble. Young people these days — they were forever getting mixed up in matters beyond their years. Politics, to put it plain. Subversion. It wasn't beyond the ingenuity of the police to find certain incriminating documents in a girl's bedroom. African National Congress — that sort of thing. Probably the documents were already there. All the young ones these days had them, the Xhosa at least. Granted, the girl was a minor. But that needn't make a difference. Subversion is subversion, and it is too serious a crime for any high-minded distinctions as to age. Everest Ndlovu understood this very well. Walt van Niekerk had explained it to him, and Jack had been on hand at the time. So it only made sense that Mr. Elephant himself now stood in the grooming bay at the Ansons' stable, with his trilby pressed to his chest. It was the most natural thing in the world.

"Well, now." Jack gave the man a wink. "Would you fancy a snort?"

Ndlovu seemed to hesitate but for only a moment. Then he nodded. A dram of the good stuff? Well, it just so happened that he might. So Jack put Tempest away, and the two of them repaired to the tack room, where they had one drink, then another, and soon enough they were well along on their third, both of them as snug as you like, chairs pulled up to the electric space heater, coils glowing bright red in the gloom. It wasn't long before Jack knew everything he needed to know. Qacha's Nek, the place was called, the place where they would cross. Funny-sounding name, but then again they all were. He knew the date, too. Give or take. It was all laid out for him, clear as glass.

"Well, well." He swallowed what was left in his mug of Glenmorangie. He had a taste for refinement, Jack did, no two ways about it. He tilted his head, gave Mr. Elephant his fiercest look. Make him buckle. The poor man would be stuttering before long — out of fear, plain and simple. "And you know all this for a fact?"

Mr. Elephant nodded. He fidgeted with his tie, cleared his throat, picked up his hat, and fanned himself. He was obviously not at ease. Nor would he be, considering what he was doing, betraying his own kind, not to mention what all of this might mean for the girl. Hilly.

"Another drink?" Jack said.

No reply.

"Eh …? I offered you another drink."

"Yes, *b-baas*."

Hah. He loved it when they said that word. *Baas*. He topped up Everest Ndlovu's glass. Everest … what the bejesus kind of a name was that? It was a custom with them, he knew. Strangest names you ever heard of. Everest. Blessing. Roller skate. Well, he'd made that last one up. He watched Ndlovu empty his glass of single malt. He'd take another, old Everest would. If you offer them something, they'll take it. Whatever it is. The reason is simple. They have no idea when they'll enjoy such goodness again. They're like dogs in that respect — either they accept your benevolence or they go without. No other way.

On this occasion, the question of money had also to be considered. Jack didn't begrudge the payment. Cash for information — nothing could be fairer than that. Besides, Walt van Niekerk would reimburse him for the cost, as he always did. He handed the envelope over, lickety-split. He watched as Ndlovu pushed the wad of legal tender deep into the side pocket of his forlorn suit coat, where it would be nice and warm. The poor man frowned and looked down at the floor. He said, "I feel ashamed for taking this."

"Oh, don't trouble yourself over that." Jack stood up. "Everyone's got to do what they can to get by. Besides, there's dependents to consider. Am I right about that …?" He let his voice trail off, gradual. He was thinking of the girl, Blessing. Wouldn't want anything untoward to happen in that department, would we? That was what he might have said, if he had deemed it necessary to spell the matter out. Instead, he let the sentiment rest for a time, like a chill in the air, unspecified but difficult to ignore.

"Well," he said. He clapped his hands to ward off the cold. "It's getting late in the day, and you've a long walk ahead of you. Miserable weather, ain't it?"

There'd been a time when he'd have offered old Everest Ndlovu a lift in the Land Rover. It wasn't far to Bruntville, or the outskirts thereof. It wouldn't take long. But that was when he'd still been working the man, gaining his trust, keeping him sweet. No need for that now. Now, thanks to good old Everest, he knew the name of the place — Qacha's Nek — and he had a good sense of the timing. That was all that he needed to know, that and the whereabouts of little Miss Blessing Ndlovu, of course. That was a given. He'd had his eye on her for a time now. He knew her particulars full well.

Ndlovu replaced his hat, tugged at his tie, to make it hang straight. With a nod of the head, he set out on his way. Jack accompanied him as far as the stable's big wooden door. From there, he watched him go — poor man shuffling down the macadam lane past the windbreak of poplars, a thin light threading in from the west. Pretty soon it began to rain.

THIRTY-SEVEN

Sam
Ontario, Summer 1963

"COME ON." HILARY CLIMBED to her feet. "Time to get a move on."

We quickly got ourselves organized, pulled jeans and shirts over still-damp bathing suits, saddled and bridled the horses. Soon we were riding west along Number Four Sideroad. Before long we jogged past the Quinton Vasco lands, where serious work of some kind was now underway. Construction machines of various configurations cluttered the ridge overlooking Number Four Sideroad. Stacks of concrete blocks stood nearby. For what purpose, I had no idea.

Just then, I heard a harsh grinding sound, a steel bucket dragging against a hard rock face. Something like that. Whatever was going on, I was against it. "I hated Quinton Vasco," I said. "Now I hate him even more."

"Why? Because now you've met him?"

"I guess."

I was thinking of Quinton Vasco as we'd seen him in Letham that weekend, dressed all in black, standing with his hands thrust in his pockets, watching as we drove away. I was also thinking about those two cannons we'd seen. They made no sense at all. What kind of real estate development includes pieces of heavy artillery stored under canvas awnings deep in the woods?

I had an idea that Hilary knew more than she was letting on. After all, she had made at least two questionable statements that afternoon, one about her father and the other about that gun of hers. And she obviously knew more about Quinton Vasco than she was saying. But what? What did she know? I wondered again why she spoke so rarely about her past and with so little detail. Still, I saw no benefit in pushing her to tell me more. If she wanted to, she would. If not, then nothing I said was likely to change her mind; I felt pretty sure of that. Either way, I was bound to go along if it meant being close to Hilary. I knew it, and I was pretty certain that she knew it, too.

When we reached Second Line, we both slowed to a halt. Hilary was heading south, toward the Barkers', while I would bear west and then north toward home. Only ten days remained before the provincial championships in Cardenden, and she said we should keep to our schedule — the schooling, the conditioning, the long afternoons at the quarry pond. I said that was fine with me, and it was. It was more than fine. I would have kept on like this forever if I could have, riding bareback at the Barkers', swimming with Hilary and our two horses down at the quarry, winning ribbons and silver plates at weekend competitions. I wanted the summer to last forever, and I felt a pang of dread that the present was already spilling into the past. There was nothing that I or anyone could do to stop it. But I didn't say anything about that, either.

Instead, we parted ways, and Hilary rode off, cantering south along Second Line through an archway of maple boughs. I watched her recede into the distance until she disappeared beyond a crest in the road, and the cicada whined again, that fierce, brittle sound.

I reined Della around and coaxed her into a trot. Soon, the gravel road jogged to the left beneath an assembly of maples, and I let Della break into a canter. She seemed to float, her stride less laboured than it sometimes was. The late-afternoon sunlight shot through the branches, alternating strokes of brassy warmth with patches of cooler shade. I hadn't ridden far when I heard an engine growl just a few horse lengths behind me. With no more warning than that, a pickup truck roared past, its horn blaring. The damned vehicle nearly forced us off the road before it fishtailed away, churning up waves of gravel in a sea of dust. The truck bore an inscription in black on its side: *SRC*. Those were the same letters we'd seen embossed on the crates of cannon shells in Quinton Vasco's sugar bush. The truck's driver must have been an employee of some kind.

"Idiot!" I yelled. "You stupid idiot!"

I hated everything about Quinton Vasco. He was ruining everything, cutting Kelso in half for some unknown but selfish purpose. What did he mean to do with those huge guns? As for Hilary, I wasn't to hear from her again for seven long days.

THE THIRD DAY WAS a good day.

In fact, it was better than good. It was one of those glorious winter days you often get on the high veldt of South Africa. Overhead, the clouds scudded across the sky, soaring over the Drakensberg. Rows of leafless poplars arched in the gusting wind. Muletsi thought there could be no land more beautiful than this, and he felt himself breathing freely at last, at least a little more freely. He shifted around, steadying himself in the saddle, and he waved at Hilary. She smiled, raised an arm, waved back. He straightened out, gave his horse a friendly swat. He was thinking he didn't feel so bad, after all.

From the very beginning he had been of two minds about this project. Simply put, he did not want to run away. On the other hand, what choice was there? It was either run or spend most of his life in prison. He'd had the good luck to escape — although, granted, it hadn't seemed like luck. It had seemed pre-arranged. The guards had been so incompetent you'd have thought their incompetence was deliberate.

At the time of the escape, the two wardens had been transporting Muletsi and two other inmates from the jail in Pietermaritzburg to another facility in Ladysmith. Who knew why? No one ever explained anything. Probably, it was just a tactic they had to keep inmates from forming alliances. Or maybe they wanted to move Muletsi even farther from his home, to impose an even greater hardship on his mother. Who knew why they did what they did? They simply did it.

Still, in some ways, the episode had seemed almost deliberately nonsensical. The vehicle that was used for the operation was a wobbly old bakkie, and Muletsi was put in the open bed along with the other two. No doubt the guards thought the shackles would be sufficient to constrain the prisoners. But then, in a town called Roosboom, when they stopped for coffee and a piss, Muletsi and his companions watched, slack-jawed, as the guards removed the chains, the lot, without a word of explanation. It was like an invitation for an escape. *Here you go, boys. Off with you, then.*

And what do you think happened next? Of course, as soon as the two guards disappeared into the little *koffiehuis*, the three prisoners — he did not know the others' names, and they did not enlighten him — heaved themselves out of the truck bed. They did some stretches right there, on the pavement, to get the blood flowing again and also to gauge the reactions of passersby, of whom there were few to none. They started to wander along the side of the road beneath a row of jacaranda trees. There was nothing to it. You'd have thought this sequence of events had been plotted out in advance. But why? And by whom?

Quick as they could, the three men got themselves off the main road. Reduce visibility — that was their watchword now. It wasn't long before they'd exchanged their prison coveralls for civvies — clothes they found in a second-hand bin. It was agreed at once that they had best split up. That way, at least one of them might escape undetected. There was no use in all of them being captured at once. So off they went, no one saying in what direction he was bound, that being the way they had, the way they'd learned in jail. Never trust anyone.

Muletsi put out his thumb and prepared to hitchhike down to Bruntville. After a time, a bakkie picked him up and a little later dropped him off. Before long, an ancient Morris Minor pulled onto the shoulder just ahead of him.

"Hop in," said the driver.

He was an elderly white man, hirsute and rotund, missing several teeth. He clung to the wheel of his sputtering, oil-burning contraption as though the vehicle were propelled by the sheer force of his will. The back seats were loaded with sacks of cornmeal. The driver didn't say much, and Muletsi said next to nothing at all. As they drove past Mooi River, he thought of Hilary. Of course, he did. But she was away at school in Johannesburg from what he understood. They proceeded to Bruntville in a continuation of the silence that seemed to suit them both.

Muletsi had few plans. He meant to re-establish contact with the ANC and go from there. None of this was personal. He had no scores to settle, not even with Jack Tanner. He meant to let those old dogs lie. He didn't think he would see Hilary again. That didn't make him happy, far from it — the exact opposite of happy. Still, a man has to face facts. White folks' business — that was what it had been. All of it. He would leave it behind and get on with his life. That was what he'd thought. But then Hilary showed up, that day by the soccer pitch in Bruntville. He hadn't meant to be drawn back into her orbit, but she had a way about her. She surely did. And then had come this madcap plan of hers. He had dismissed it at first, but Hilary was nothing if not persistent, and now here they were.

He was riding on horseback to Basutoland, to what was supposed to be freedom, with Hilary at his side in a dark-green parka, her eyes shining blue. He hadn't invited her back. She had worked her way there. At times, he wondered whether he wasn't guilty of the starkest betrayal. Not only was he running away, he was running away with a white woman. But what choice was there? And, besides, Hilary wasn't a white woman — or not only a white woman. She was Hilary.

Now the woman in question drew her horse alongside his and slowed to a walk. She gestured toward the distant heights of the Drakensberg, floating to the north like islands in the sky. "God, they're beautiful, hey."

He nodded. "Yes. I was just thinking that."

She laughed. "You were not. You were thinking, What am I doing here — I, Muletsi Dadla? What in God's name am I doing here? And with her, of all people, the crazy white girl? I know you."

And he laughed along with her because it was true, because it was exactly true.

"Come on," she said. "There'll be plenty of time to worry once you're safe."

She eased her horse closer and gave him a kiss flat on the lips, and he felt himself melting, as he always did.

"Come on," she said again.

They both broke into a loping stride that carried them across the high, slanting plain. Now he did smile, did breathe deep, because it *was* beautiful. You'd have thought you were riding across the roof of the world, except that the mountain peaks to the north were higher yet. She'd told him he'd be free. In Basutoland, he'd be free. But he knew better. Exile might bring safety, but it does not bring freedom.

And what about Hilary? Where would she go? Wherever he went? That was what she said, and he could almost imagine it might be so. Tanganyika. Or Sweden. Or Canada. They would go somewhere that would have him, somewhere that would let him carry on with his work, albeit from a distance. From exile. He bridled at the thought.

Still, this was a good day, and it is a sin to let good days go to waste. They cantered ahead, with Hilary a stride or two in front. The wind churned around them both, the clouds tilted against the high blue sky, and you'd have thought that this was the finest country in the whole wide world.

Only it wasn't.

THIRTY-NINE

Sam
Ontario, Summer 1963

"DAD ..." I SAID.

"Yes, Sam."

"Some people were talking at the riding club. They said you're working for Mr. Vasco. That's a lie, right?"

"Is it?" My father tilted his head and frowned. "That's pretty unequivocal, Sammy. I hope you didn't call your friends liars. That would be going a bit too far."

"No. I just implied it. They were wrong, right?"

"Well, that's a question of semantics." He got up to pour himself another Scotch. He paused at my mother's chair. Supposedly, she was working out another bridge problem, with the playing cards spread out on the table. "Mary ...? A refill?"

"What's that, dear? Oh? Oh, yes, please."

I could tell she was only pretending to be absorbed in her bridge. She was a terrible actress. My father clattered about in the kitchen, pouring Scotch, cracking ice from a tray.

"Dad," I said. "Are you working for Quinton Vasco?"

He returned from the kitchen with two glasses of Scotch with ice. One of them he placed on the dining table in front of my mother. He pulled another chair away from the table, turned it around, and settled on it backward, his legs straddling the stiles. He took a gulp from his Scotch and began to speak.

No, he wasn't "working for" Mr. Vasco, not in the sense of being an actual employee. But, yes, he was on retainer. Mr. Vasco had been a client for some weeks now and remained a client. This was not exactly the same thing as "working for." There was a semantic distinction. I barely listened to the words, something about the property-tax base, more money for the county, the inevitability of development, things being more complicated than they seemed. I didn't want to hear any of it. I stood up. I'd heard enough.

"Where are you going?" My mother looked up from her cards. "You haven't finished your dinner. Look, there's half a plate left and —"

"I'm not hungry."

"Sam ..." said my father. "You're not giving me a chance to explain."

I didn't care. I marched upstairs to my room. Once there, I planted myself on the windowsill and stared out at what would soon be the gloom of dusk. Just now, though, it was still a beautiful evening. The lilacs and apple trees caught the amber sunlight, and the grass glistened. After a while, I dropped down from the sill and changed into a pair of blue jeans. I already had on my Maple Leafs T-shirt. I pulled on my sneakers and clumped downstairs.

My mother peered up from her cards. "Where are you going?"

"Away." I meant to take Della for a ride. Who knew where? Maybe down to the quarry.

"It's late."

I didn't care. I strode out to the barn, saddled Della, and set off. Already, it was starting to get dark, and I had a feeling that maybe this was not the best idea I'd ever conceived. Still, I kept Della moving ahead at an extended trot. In the end, it took us nearly an hour to reach the Quinton Vasco lands, and we kept right on going. I was aiming for the quarry ponds. I didn't know what was drawing me there — or, yes, I did. Of course, I did. Hilary. I hadn't seen or heard from her in a week.

Della picked her way down the face of the escarpment, and we turned to bear right along the slender lane toward the quarry. Before long I halted. I dropped to the ground and ran up the stirrups on both sides of the saddle, tucking the leathers through the irons. I eased the reins over Della's head and guided her toward the main pond. I stumbled a couple of times against tree roots or jutting rocks, all practically invisible in the dwindling light.

Where the earth turned to limestone, I stopped to loop the reins around a maple branch. I left Della behind me and climbed up onto the rocky outcropping, the same one Hilary and Club Soda had leapt off only a week or so earlier, with Hilary wearing nothing at all. Now the sky was fading to a dull purple, and there seemed to be nothing beyond the limestone surface but a large and empty pit, a hollow space. I'm not sure what I was thinking — that Hilary might be there? That she might have fallen into the pond and drowned? It was nothing as melodramatic as that. What I felt was a general sensation of dread. It heaved deep in my belly, like a stubborn cramp. I noticed a ringing in my ears and then recognized its source — a barrage of crickets, screeching on all sides.

Even in that din, I could hear Della snuffling behind me, the snaffle rings clattering as she grazed, her nostrils muttering against the hard ground, her hooves clinking against rock. Every sound seemed magnified in the darkness. I really didn't want to be there at all. It was that exchange I'd just had with my father, his working for Quinton Vasco. I felt as if my head were on fire.

About then, I heard a car engine snarl, quite far away at first, then much closer. I heard a loud, grinding crunch — the chassis of a vehicle bottoming against stones and earth. The car was approaching along this narrow trail, approaching from the south, from the Base Line, the opposite way that I had come. Soon, the disruption seemed to be only a matter of yards away, a throbbing motor, a spray of headlights. Next, the motor cut out, its drone replaced by the slow pelting of cooling metal. I could hear everything, but I couldn't see much, blinded by the headlights' glare, knifing through the thickening dark. After a time, I heard a car door open and slam shut, then another, and, soon after that, a third door. I heard voices, male voices. They seemed to be advancing toward me. I heard something smash, a bottle dashing against a rock, then another bottle, then a jarring burst of laughter.

"Fuckin' Christ. Let me at 'er. Let me at 'er now."

"Fuck you."

"Fuck who?"

"You, stupid."

"Not me. Her. Do her."

"I'm gonna. But she's … ah, she's out of it. I … ah, Christ."

"Hurry. Come on, hurry …"

I loosed Della's reins and eased them back over her head. I slid the near-side stirrup iron back down the leather. It was no easy matter, on account of the way my hands were shaking. Quietly as I could, I swung myself up into the saddle. I really wanted to get away from this place.

"Ah, hell — lookit! She's throwin' up. Ah, jeez."

"Never mind. Here, put her over here. On top o' this. Turn her over. C'mon. There. That's better. That's all right. Jesus. Gimme the flashlight, will ya? Ah … lookit that. Fuckin' A."

I saw a pulse of light, several pulses. Flashlights, I thought. The beams seemed to scatter and shift in every direction, deflected by tree branches, catching against rocks.

"Wait," said another voice. I couldn't be sure, but it sounded like Davey Odegaard. "Her glasses. She's missing her glasses."

"So …?" This voice sounded like Bruce Gruber. "She doesn't need any glasses now, for Chrissake."

"Yes. She does. She's blind without them. They must have fallen off somewhere. They must be around here. Wait —"

"Shut the fuck up."

I touched my heels to Della's sides and headed her back the way we had come. The path ran through the woods, dark as a tunnel.

"What was that?" said one of the voices. "What the hell was that?"

I kept Della moving forward. The thing was, I really did think that I recognized a couple of the voices. One of them was Bruce Gruber's, I was pretty sure. Another was Davey Odegaard's. Maybe there'd been a third voice, too. Edwin's? Edwin Duval's? I should turn around, ride back, find out what was going on. I should do something. But what? I was all alone, and there were three of them. At least three.

"Ah, it wasn't nothin'. Just a bear or something."

"A bear …!"

"I'm jokin', moron. Give me the flashlight. Jesus, would ya look at that."

Before long, Della broke into a canter, and I had to keep my head down, to stay clear of overhanging branches. The woods swept past, a blur of shadows and tattered starlight. I tried not to think about what was happening back there by the quarry pond, but I couldn't help it. There was a woman there, or a girl, and she was drunk or passed out, and I had a terrible idea it might be Hilary. Then I thought, *no, it couldn't be Hilary*. She didn't wear glasses, for one thing. I was getting confused, my heart pounding so hard I could feel it stuttering in my chest. Maybe I had misheard the part about glasses. Maybe it *was* Hilary, after all. Part of me wanted to stop and go back and do something — I had no idea what — but the rest of me wanted to keep riding the other way. I knew what I was. I was a coward.

When we reached Number Four Sideroad, I reined Della to the left, to begin the steep ascent of the escarpment, and just then I remembered something Hilary had said. I slowed Della to a halt and let her stand there, in the centre of the road, surrounded by darkness. The roar of the crickets redoubled, or so it seemed, and I debated what to do. Hilary had been speaking about my being cautious — a cautious person — and her being bold. But I could change, she'd said, not a lot maybe, but some. Maybe it would be enough. Right now, if she were in my place, I knew that she would do something brave and heroic — something bold. I was sure of it. She certainly would not do what I was doing, slinking away like this. The realization hit me like a punch in the gut, and I decided that I wasn't going to run away. Not this time. I was going to go back, even though I had no idea what I would do when I got there. I would think of something. Somehow, I would. I reined Della around and aimed her back through the darkness toward the quarry pond. Pretty soon we veered off the gravel road and were clomping along the narrow trail. Okay. Maybe I *was* a careful person, but that didn't mean I couldn't take risks. Sometimes I could. If I had to, I could.

Before long, I heard the same voices as before. I couldn't really make out much of what they were saying, but it seemed they were still arguing. Another bottle crashed against a rock. Flashlight beams criss-crossed the branches overhead. Whoever they were, I was almost on top of them now. I sensed the dark outline of a car, Bruce's probably. In the glare of the darting flashlights, I could make out the glint of human faces. At first I had no idea what I meant to do, and then, the next moment, I did, as if some instinct had suddenly taken hold. I began to ride around and around in tight circles, and I started to sing. At the top of my voice, I belted out the first song that came into my head, one of the South African songs Hilary had taught me. "Yini Madoda," it was called. Its title meant "Why Men" in Xhosa, but I didn't understand any of the lyrics. I had simply memorized their sounds — some of them, anyway. I only pretended to do the clicks. Still, I roared the song out, loud as I could.

I didn't stop singing until I ran out of words. Then I started belting out another Miriam Makeba song, "Ndamcenga," which means "I Begged." I had to invent a lot of the sounds, but I knew the melody pretty well. All the time, I steered Della around in tight circles. I would have terrified anyone.

I kept on singing, bellowing out the melodies so loudly that I couldn't properly hear anything else. I did sense voices, though — male voices shouting and swearing. I think they were a lot more afraid of me than I was of them — afraid and bewildered. Pretty soon they were hurrying away. I could tell. I saw their shadows in flight. I heard car doors slamming. I wasn't sure, but I thought they'd taken the girl with them, or the woman — I didn't know which. A car engine roared, and I watched the vehicle totter away in reverse, its headlights careening wildly, glancing through the branches of trees.

I knew who it was back there. It was definitely Bruce's voice that I'd heard, his and Davey's. The other voice? I was fairly sure it was Edwin's. I stayed where I was, watching and listening, until there was nothing more to see or to hear. Whatever it was that I had stumbled upon, it was over now. Still, I checked to make sure they hadn't left the girl behind, whoever she was, and it seemed they hadn't. It seemed they'd taken her away. Maybe they were alarmed enough by now that they wouldn't do her any more harm.

I reined Della to the right and dug my heels into her sides. She sprang into a canter, and we headed off, back in the same direction we had come. When I reached Number Four Sideroad, I slowed Della to a trot and turned to the left, to scale the escarpment's wall. I knew what I would do next: I would ride straight over to Colonel Barker's, never mind the hour, and see if Hilary was there. If she wasn't, then that would mean I had to do something, try to find her. I didn't really have a plan beyond that. Maybe it had been Hilary back there, or maybe not. Maybe I wasn't thinking too clearly.

It took me half an hour to reach the old stone house. I cantered up the drive, only to find the place completely dark. Everyone must have gone to bed. I looked around to see if both the Barkers' cars were parked by the house, and so they were — the rental and the Cadillac. The pickup truck was probably over by the barn. That meant everyone was home. I thought it did.

I halted, yanked my feet from the stirrups, threw a leg over the cantle of the saddle, and dropped down to the grass. I was wearing only a pair of canvas sneakers on my feet, no socks. I eased the reins over Della's head and led her toward the house, my shoes squelching in the dew-slick grass.

When I got close to the front door, I peered up at the second storey. I was trying to figure out which window was Hilary's. That was stupid. Even if I located it, what would I do then? Toss pebbles at the pane, as if this were some old movie? Worse, my looking up at the second floor meant I didn't see the wrought-iron patio table until I had walked right into it, sending it toppling onto the flagstone terrace, upsetting a couple of wrought-iron chairs. Della shied and yanked back on the reins. She damned near dislocated my shoulder.

"Hey! Hey!" I shouted.

Almost at once, a light burst on upstairs, followed by a commotion of footsteps. Now a man's voice — Colonel Barker's — called down from a window.

"Who's there!"

"It's me."

"*It's who* …? Is that the Mitchell boy? Sam, is that you?"

"Yessir."

"What are you doing here? What time is it? Is that a horse? What are you doing?"

"It's about Hilary. She …"

"Hilary. Yes. What about her?"

"I think she's hurt … or something."

"No, no. I'm sure she's fine."

"Is she here?"

"No. Out. Is that a horse?"

"Yes."

"Good Lord, man. Go home. It's late. Hilary isn't here. Good night."

I turned and led Della away from the house, across the lawn, and out onto the drive. I shoved my left foot into the stirrup and heaved myself up and into the saddle. I was collecting the reins and straightening my shoulders, about to head off, when I heard the front door swing open behind me. I looked back, and there was Colonel Barker in a bathrobe and a pair of rubber boots. He was striding my way, across the sopping grass.

EFFING PIECE OF BLOODY English crap.

Jack pounded his fist against the wheel of his old Land Rover. Something had gone haywire with the steering mechanism. Damned thing had about thirty degrees of play to her, which made every turn a gamble. Just keeping the effing contraption on the road was challenge enough. Each vehicle lumbering up from the opposite direction was a bloody death sentence in the making. Plus three-quarters of the lot were piloted by kaffirs, none of which could drive worth a piss, as studies had shown.

But never mind. He knew he would manage somehow. Just now the Land Rover was stumbling north toward Ladysmith. From there he would head west and make his way toward Maseru, enter Basutoland from the north. He was well aware that Hil and that terro of hers would scale the Drakensberg from the southern side, but he had plenty of time. Even in this derelict old bus of his, he was sure he'd have no trouble finding his way to Qacha's Nek. Maybe he'd wait for them there. That was one plan. Another had him leaving Basutoland on foot and proceeding back into Zuid-Afrika, climbing down the mountains from the north. Either tactic would work.

His main source of worry was the prospect of losing his life along the way, a distinct possibility given the way these kamikaze imbeciles zigged and effing zagged along the road. He'd just have to keep his wits about him. That was the key to it. He reached over to his left and wrenched the cubbyhole open. He took a good peek at the Smith & Wesson revolver ensconced inside in all its glory, alongside a cardboard box of cartridges and a pair of field glasses he had lately acquired. Just checking. He pushed the cover back into place and resumed an erect position, both hands gripping the wheel.

Something out the windscreen caught his eye — a red bakkie careening his way. He managed to yank the steering wheel to the side, just far enough to avoid a collision. Instinctively, he glanced up at the rear-view mirror and watched the self-same bakkie groan away in a cloud of filthy brown smoke and with a load of firewood tottering high in the bed. It was as if nothing whatsoever had happened. Sweet Jesus, you'd think these people lacked nervous systems. Live out the day in comfort and safety or else perish in a crush of metal and firewood — it was all the same to them.

Ah, well. He'd just have to keep a careful lookout. Safety first. As he drove north to Ladysmith, he whistled a tune that had got into his head. "Pata Pata" it was called — one of these kaffir tunes. They had a way with music; you couldn't deny it.

At Ladysmith he pulled into a petrol station to refuel and pick up some grub, plus a Castle or two to steady his nerves, keep him company on his way. He asked the mechanic to have a look at the steering in the Land Rover, and he headed into the little café beside the garage to make his purchases.

When he emerged, laden with bundles, the mechanic ambled over to confront him. A lanky kaffir lad, he was. The boy said the problem with the steering was some serious stuff. There'd be parts and labour, and he couldn't say how long the work would take, as some of the spares would need to be ordered up from Pietermaritzburg.

In other circumstances he would have jumped to the obvious conclusion: this was some kind of a swindle. He'd seen it before. This time, however, he was inclined to credit what he heard. He'd been driving the damned crate, after all, and so he had a fair idea of the condition it was in. That was on the one hand. On the other hand, he didn't have time to wait for the parts to be trucked up from effing Pietermaritzburg. Hell, he could have drove to Pietermaritzburg himself if only he'd had fair warning. But had he? No.

"Can you fix her up temporary?" he asked.

The boy shrugged. He had a sparse curly beard, or not a beard really, just some coiled whiskers. Fat lips. Flat nose. Eyes that looked drugged. In other words, the usual thing.

"I could rig something up," the boy said. "It wouldn't last long. How far are you going, *baas*?"

"Far enough," he said. "Over to Basutoland." Bad idea, to mention that.

"What — Maseru?"

"Could be. So — they pay you to ask questions?"

"Sorry, *baas*."

"Are you saying I could make it or not?"

"I can't promise anything, *baas*. Might be you could make it that far."

"And might be I won't?"

The boy shrugged again.

"You have a boss, I take it?" The bags he was holding were growing heavy.

"Yes, *baas*."

"Well, maybe I should be having a palaver with him rather than wasting my time out here with you."

"He's just inside, taking a load off. I'll ask him. Just wait here, if you don't mind, *baas*."

"Fine. Fine and dandy."

Jack loaded his purchases into the back of the Land Rover and liberated a Castle, popped her open with the widget on his chain of keys. He had halfway drunk the brew when a portly gent sauntered out from the low brick structure by the petrol pumps, a white man with a proper beard, albeit grey with age and yellow from nicotine. Fat as all get out. Said his name was Jeremiah. Said the boy's name was Melvyn. Best mechanic in Ladysmith. "He'll have a look at your steering. See what we can do. Might not be much."

"I was thinking you might have a look yourself."

"Won't be necessary. If Melvyn can't deal with it, wouldn't be much I could do. You like coffee?"

For some reason, Jack flinched at the question. Was he being condescended to? He was drinking a beer, for Chrissake. "Coffee, yeah? What about it?"

The man named Jeremiah nodded back toward the little store. "Make a good cup over there. Have a gulp on me. Hell, have two. I'll let you know when Melvyn's done. Just don't expect any miracles."

"No," Jack said. "I won't be doing that."

An hour later, he was back on the road, and he'd be damned if the steering didn't work a treat. He was out a fair packet of rand, but he didn't mind that. Live and learn — that was all he could say. Live and effing learn. Just then, he had a sudden terrible thought. The gun. Quick as a sucker punch, he pried open the cubbyhole, and at once he felt his entire muscular system go slack with relief. There it still was, in all its glory, along with the field glasses he'd acquired just for this trip. The gun, the rounds, and the glasses, all safe and sound. Thank the effing Lord for that.

BEFORE LONG I WAS huddled at the table in the Barkers' kitchen.
At Colonel Barker's direction, I'd put Della away for the night in a
stall beside Club Soda's in the barn. Both he and Mrs. Barker were
up now, both drinking Scotch and debating which of them should
drive me home. Colonel Barker was still dressed in a terry cloth
bathrobe, but now he had on a pair of fuzzy brown slippers. His
legs were pale and skinny, riddled with varicose veins. Mrs. Barker
wore a housecoat over her nightgown. She looked about ninety
years old. Neither of them seemed to be in any hurry to give me
a lift. Meanwhile, I was still trying to explain what I had just seen
or heard down by the quarry pond. I tried to tell them what had
happened, which wasn't easy because I didn't really know myself.

"I heard men's voices," I said. "Boys' or men's. There were some
guys down there. They were doing something bad."

"You saw them?" Colonel Barker set his Scotch down on the
kitchen table and reached up to adjust his eye patch.

"Not really. Not very well. But I heard them. They ... they were
doing something bad. To someone. Maybe to Hilary. It might have
been Hilary."

Colonel Barker laughed. "Oh, I don't think so. Hilary is in *good
hands*, I can assure you."

He drew out the phrase — good hands — in a way that sounded bitter, sarcastic. I noticed it right away.

He looked up. "What would you say, Deirdre?"

"About what?"

"About what Sam Mitchell here has just been telling us — strange goings-on down in the quarry."

"I'm sure I wouldn't know what to say. You're the one who seems to know everything. What would *you* say?"

Colonel Barker reached for his Scotch. "Just youngsters — that's what I'd say. Just youngsters being troublesome. It used to be they got into trouble somewhere over on the Vasco property — parking in their cars and pitching woo and whatnot. But that's not on, anymore, so I guess it's the quarry instead." He rearranged his face in a sly expression. "Woof, woof."

Mrs. Barker rolled her eyes. "Well, you're the expert."

She stood up and eased a bag of oatmeal cookies down from a cupboard shelf. She placed a couple on a small plate and set it in front of me, along with a glass of milk.

"Thank you," I said. *Milk ...?* Did they think I was a child? I wouldn't have said no to a glass of Scotch. Scotch and Coke.

I turned to Colonel Barker and said that we should drive down to the quarry, he and I. That way, there would be two of us, enough to make a difference if necessary. We should go right now. What if it *was* Hilary down there? What if she was still down there now, hurt and bleeding, or who knew what? I was about to repeat these arguments, this time in a somewhat bolder tone, when a pair of car headlights flashed outside, scattering against the kitchen window. I heard a vehicle growl to a halt in the gravel parking bay.

Mrs. Barker glanced at her watch. "Must be little Miss South Africa," she said, speaking in a dull voice, as if she were musing on the prospect of rain.

And Hilary it was — a Hilary I hadn't seen before. She swayed into the kitchen, wearing a shimmering dress, sky blue, and with her black hair piled atop her head in what I recognized as a bun. Several locks dangled in front of her ears, and a circle of silver glinted in each lobe. I sniffed at the air — perfume. I'd never known her to wear jewellery or perfume before.

Not only that, but she wasn't alone.

A man ambled into the Barkers' house just behind Hilary. I recognized him at once and felt an immediate pang of jealousy. I felt as Della must have felt, hit by a spent bullet from a Makarov pistol. He was dressed entirely in black.

"Quint Vasco," the man said. He was talking to me.

"Uh. Right. Sam Mitchell. Uh, we met at your place."

"Not Hal Mitchell's son?"

"Uh. Yes."

"You certainly say 'uh' a lot."

"Oh."

It turned out that the two of them — Hilary and Quinton Vasco — had just returned from Toronto, where they'd attended a concert by Harry Belafonte and Miriam Makeba at the O'Keefe Centre. Miriam Makeba …? The South African singer …? I couldn't believe it. I'd heard nothing about any such concert. What was even worse, far worse, was that Hilary had attended it with Quinton Vasco, of all people. What was she thinking? My head felt hot, as if it were burning up.

"Sensational," said Hilary. She poured a Scotch for herself and another for Quinton Vasco. "Never to be forgotten."

"Agreed." Quinton Vasco sipped his drink and smacked his lips. "Those darkies can sing. I'll give them that."

I looked at Hilary, who closed her eyes. I looked back at Quinton Vasco. Some other time, I might have said something rude, made some biting remark. *They aren't darkies,* I might have said. *They're Africans.* I hope I would have said something like that. But I was just fifteen, just a jealous fifteen-year-old. Moments earlier I had practically convinced myself that Hilary, right that very second, was sprawled down by the quarry pond, a lifeless wreck, after suffering God knew what sort of abuse. Yet here she was looking perfectly fine — radiant, even — if wholly different from the Hilary I thought I knew.

Anyway, that wasn't what mattered, or so I told myself. What mattered was that someone else had been beaten up or raped — I wasn't sure which; maybe both — down by the quarry pond. She'd been unconscious, drugged maybe, or passed out from drink. Maybe she was down there still. It was possible. I was pretty sure I had scared those guys off and almost as sure they had taken the girl or woman with them, but who knew? I shook my head, trying to clear my thoughts. It wasn't easy — not with all that was going on. Why was Hilary dressed like this? Why was she doing anything or going anywhere in the company of Quinton frigging Vasco?

Colonel Barker drained his Scotch. He announced that he was going to call Hal Mitchell on the phone and ask him to come around and collect his son. It was damned late, far too late for me to be out riding horses all by myself. He wondered whose idea of parenting that was. It certainly wasn't his. He started for the phone, but Quinton Vasco waved him off.

"Nonsense, Colonel. I'll give the boy a lift. Why, it's practically on my way."

"Good show. That's awfully white of you."

Was Colonel Barker being sarcastic again? That was what it sounded like. I thought I understood why. It wasn't just me. He was jealous, too.

"No worries." Quinton Vasco took a swallow of Scotch, crunching the ice with his teeth. He winked at me. "We'll be off in a tick. Just want to bid a fond farewell to her nibs here."

Again, I looked at Hilary. "*Hilary* ...?" I said, in a voice that was louder, more urgent, than I had intended.

Now it was everyone else's turn to look at me, but I didn't care. I told Hilary about the uproar down by the quarry pond earlier that night. Whatever had happened down there, it was probably over by now, but you never knew. We had to go back there — just in case. I said something about the eyeglasses. Whoever the girl was, she'd lost her eyeglasses. At the very least, we had to look for them. Besides, I said, I had a pretty good idea who the girl was — Leslie Odegaard. Worse, her own brother had been down there, too. It was horrible to think of, just horrible. Her own brother! But we had to do something; that much was clear. And Hilary, being Hilary, agreed right away. She refused even to change her clothes; there wasn't time. She marched over to the entrance, kicked off her high heels, and pulled on a pair of tall rubber boots.

"Come on," she said. "Let's go, hey."

At first Quinton Vasco made a fuss. It was too late, he said, and, besides, Hilary was being unreasonable. Whatever might have happened down in this quarry place — it was nothing to get worked up about. There would be mud and dirt and God knew what else, and here he was, dressed in a bespoke business suit. The whole thing just wasn't on. But he was no match for Hilary. She was going down to the quarry, and I was, too, and that was final. As for Quinton Vasco, it was his decision. He could come or stay. It was all the same to her.

In the end, he came — complaining all the while. His complaints grew even more insistent as he nursed his car, a brand new BMW, along the narrow trail that ran off Number Four Sideroad, partway down the escarpment wall. I slumped in the back, amid piles of thick paper scrolls — blueprints or mechanical designs. Each time another tree branch scraped against the exterior of the car, Quinton Vasco let out another moan. Hilary kept urging him forward. Eventually, we had to stop. The way ahead was too narrow, too narrow and too rough.

"Keep the headlamps on," she said.

She and I climbed out of the car. Quinton Vasco emerged a few seconds later, but he stayed close to his BMW, using the open door as a sort of shield, not wanting to venture farther, worried about the shine of his shoes, I guess.

"Leave it," he told us. "Let's go. There's nothing here."

That was true in the sense that there was no other car hereabouts and apparently no other human beings, but Hilary and I kept probing through the undergrowth just the same. We were looking for those eyeglasses. The girl or the woman, whoever she was — she'd lost her eyeglasses. Leslie …? Could it have been Leslie? It was sickening to think of. I'd heard her brother's voice. Her brother's.

"Ye gods." Hilary was on her knees. "And you're sure it was around here?"

"I think so. It was dark. But, yes, I'm pretty sure."

"Hey," said Quinton Vasco. "It's past midnight. I've got an important meeting tomorrow morning. What are you doing out there? I can't see a damned thing."

"Ignore him," said Hilary.

I wanted to ask her what was going on. Why was she going on dates with Quinton Vasco, of all people? He was the arch-enemy, after all. Why hadn't she told me what was what? Why the big mystery? I also wanted to tell her she was breaking my heart. Did she know that? Did she care? But, of course, I said none of those things. Instead, I just kept shambling about on my knees, running both my hands through a riddle of dried leaves, saplings, and weeds, finding nothing.

After about ten minutes had gone by, Quinton Vasco swore he'd had enough of this, we were both dense as beasts, Hilary and I, and anyway he had work to attend to in the morning.

"Are you coming?" he called out. Then louder: "Are you coming?"

"Not yet," said Hilary. "Give us a few more minutes."

"The fuck I will."

"Ignore him," said Hilary. She raised her voice so that I'm sure he could hear her. "Maybe he'll go away. Racist prig." After that, she lowered her voice to a whisper. "Will someone please put a bullet in that man's cranium?"

It was a joke, of course. At least, I thought it was. Next, I sensed rather than saw Quinton Vasco's approach, a kaleidoscope of shadows in the glare of his car's headlights. He made straight for Hilary, leaned down, and without an instant's hesitation plunged his fist into her face, hard as he could.

"Who's a prig?"

She groaned in pain, slumped onto her side in the undergrowth, and he kicked her. He kicked her in the head, hard. Then he stood up, spat, and dropped something to the ground — Hilary's bag.

"Hey ...!" I shouted.

"That's what you get," he said. "Fuck with me, and that's what you get. Bear it in mind."

He turned and strode back to his car. He climbed in, slammed the door, and wrenched the vehicle into reverse. He backed away toward Number Four Sideroad, taking our only source of light. I turned to Hilary. She was on her knees now, her hands pressed to her face.

"Bloody doze," she said. Her voice sounded nasal and weak. She was trying not to sob. "I god a really bloody doze."

Just then, I let out a yell as my left hand brushed across something in the dirt. I closed my fist on whatever it was and held it up, barely visible in the darkness. But I could tell what I had found — a pair of eyeglasses.

As for Quinton Vasco, he was gone.

In the end, we had to walk only part of the way to the Barkers', both of us stumbling along in the middle of the road. Hilary had to keep her head back, because of the blood seeping from her nostrils. That guy had really conked her. I couldn't believe it, hitting a girl like that, as hard as he could. Kicking her. It was infuriating, but there was nothing I could do.

We kept walking through the night, the stars spiralling overhead. Before too long, a pair of headlights approached along Second Line. This turned out to be Colonel Barker in his Cadillac. He was just checking, he said, in case something had gone wrong. We both got into the car.

"Hilary ...?" he said. "What happened to you?"

She still had to keep her head back. She clutched a Kleenex to her nose.

Before she could reply, I answered for her. "A tree," I said. "She bumped into a tree. She hurt her nose."

I wasn't sure why I said that. But Hilary went along. She just shrugged and said nothing at all. Meanwhile, I slouched alone in the back, clutching the pair of eyeglasses we had found, along with Hilary's handbag, no doubt with her gun inside. By then it was past one o'clock in the morning, and the colonel drove both of us home — first Hilary, because she was the injured party, then me.

HILARY AND MULETSI SPENT the third night of their journey deep in the shadow of the Drakensberg, in a place called Umzimkhulu Township. There, a man wrapped in a blanket strode out to greet them. He had wisps of grey in his hair, his shoes did not match, and he walked with a stilted gait. He said his name was Champion Moyo, and he asked if they were ghosts.

"No," Hilary said. "We're flesh and blood. Thank God."

"Well, we don't get many people coming through on horseback, much less this late at night. Welcome just the same."

He said he would take them in hand, and he was as good as his word. He helped to put the horses away, in a stable yard protected from the wind and otherwise inhabited by goats. That done, he arranged a bed for these unexpected visitors in a cinder-block house. His house. His bed. He said he'd make do at his mother's home, along with his wife and their two kids.

Before they settled down for the night, Champion prepared a dinner of mealies with carrots and some kind of meat. Plates on laps, they huddled around a charcoal stove. Hilary elected not to inquire as to the origin of this meat, and Champion did not volunteer that information. When they were done eating, their host proffered a jug of corn brew, and Muletsi agreed to partake of it. Normally, Hilary couldn't abide the stuff, but she made an exception now. Her nerves were that taut. She needed a wee dram, no matter the source. After the jug had been passed around a sufficient number of times, she confessed that the concoction was not as foul as she had previously believed.

"Drink has that tendency," said Champion. "Improves with familiarity, hey?" He winked at Muletsi.

Muletsi merely nodded. He was turning moody again. She could easily detect the signs by now, and silence was surely one of them. He'd been high-spirited most of that afternoon, but later the same nagging question had returned to haunt him, along with its many subsidiary queries. Was he doing the right thing by leaving South Africa? Her own answer was simple: What else could he do? But she knew he didn't see it that way — or sometimes he did, sometimes he didn't.

Just then, they heard a fist pounding at the door, followed by a man's voice, loud but indecipherable. She set her mug of corn brew on the floor. Champion roused himself to see who was out there on a night this cold and blustery. The door groaned on its hinges, and a lone man swelled into the room, a large, imposing individual, square-jawed, sprouting an unruly beard. He wore a heavy parka and batted his upper arms with his gloveless hands to keep the circulation going.

He put back his head and erupted in a burst of basso profundo laughter. "Damned cold out this night," he roared. "Colder than the Virgin's tit." At once, he filled the room, partly as a result of his size but mainly on account of his drum-roll personality, large and pulsing. He seemed to glow. "Grand Central Station," he said. "Is that what this is?"

"Far from it," Hilary said. "Very far."

"Yes. You are undoubtedly right on the facts. But still. In two days, I've barely seen a human face — and now this. A multitude."

He said his name was Mandela, and he was freshly arrived from London.

"London, England …?" she said.

"You've heard of it, I think?"

She said she had. Remarkably enough, she had. But London was a long way from Umzimkhulu, in every conceivable sense.

"That is so," he said. "For better or for worse."

She introduced herself and also Muletsi, using only their first names. He saluted them in turn, using both his hands — one to cup an elbow and the other to grip a proffered palm. He looked each of them directly in the eyes and held their gaze far longer than was customary. When at last he looked away, she glanced at Muletsi, and she could tell from his expression that something was up.

"*Nelson* Mandela …?" he said.

The man smiled. "That is said to be my name."

"*Umkhonto we Sizwe?*"

The man named Mandela frowned. "I'm sorry. What is that?"

Muletsi smiled. This was evidently the right answer. "You will join us for a drink of corn brew?"

The man assented at once. Again, Muletsi gave Hilary a look, this time expressing what was almost disbelief. Mandela …? Nelson Mandela …? She knew the name, knew of it. He was one of the young firebrands of the ANC, part of a new generation of leaders, unencumbered by the burdensome compromises of their elders. He was a man who favoured aggressive tactics, even violence if necessary. Muletsi had spoken of him many times before now.

They stayed up a long while after that, all four of them, all talking about South Africa and the prospect of change. They used terms such as *Sharpeville* and *Malan*, words that she recognized now. The Sharpeville massacre, two years earlier, in which dozens of black people had been killed. D.F. Malan, the man who'd engineered apartheid. She had been aware before now that *Umkhonto we Sizwe*

273

meant "Spear of the Nation." It was the armed wing of the ANC, and Nelson Mandela was its commander. That was known. But here in this cramped dwelling, on this frigid night, he would not own up to having any relationship with the organization, none whatsoever. Still, here he was, travelling alone on foot from Basutoland, after long weeks in North Africa and Europe, seeking support for the cause of racial equality in South Africa.

It might have seemed strange to some that such a man would be journeying alone and on foot through remote territory, but this was said to be Mandela's special talent, a penchant for clandestine ruse, the gift of secrecy. Eventually, the talk turned to Muletsi, to his escape from prison and to his doubts concerning the future, his future. Should he stay in South Africa or flee?

"Go to Tanganyika," said the man named Mandela. He didn't seem to be in the slightest doubt. "Go to Basutoland first, then Tanganyika. We need you there, men with your education."

"What …? A degree in English literature from Fort Hare?"

"Don't laugh. That will carry you a long way — much further in Tanganyika than here. We need men who can communicate, who understand the power of words. You should proceed to Dar es Salaam. That's where the new South Africa is being constructed, in exile. They need people like you, people with talent and dreams."

Mandela said he had been in contact only days earlier with ANC officials in Basutoland, and he reeled off several names — Ezra Sigwela, Khalaki Sello, Robert Matji, Joe Matthews. He said he'd make sure they would be expecting Muletsi.

Hilary said little that night, content to listen, marvelling at the man's gift for persuasion. She was convinced already that he was right, and she could see that Muletsi was coming around, as well. If Nelson Mandela said he was better off outside South Africa, then how could it not be so? The man had an air of assurance about him, a will you could not doubt.

Eventually, they all grew drowsy, and the conversation took a desultory turn. Before long, Mandela hauled himself to his feet. He said he must retire for the night. It was late, and he had a long day of travel ahead of him. But first he wished to speak of another subject. He reached deep into the pocket of his coat and produced an object wrapped in foil. He removed the metallic covering to reveal another wrapping, a waterproof oilcloth, as he explained. He removed that, too. What remained was a gun. He nodded at Muletsi. "You recognize it?"

Muletsi said he did. "Russian-made. Makarov. Semi-automatic."

"You are aware of its workings? You can use it?"

"Yes. But why …?"

"I'm coming to that. But first: You understand its workings, is it?"

"Yes."

"Good." The man rewrapped the pistol in its two covers — oilcloth and foil — and proffered it to Muletsi. "It is loaded," he said. "I think you know what to do."

It was clear to Hilary by now that this meeting — apparently so random — had not unfolded by accident, after all. She understood that this man, this Nelson Mandela, must have been in contact with Everest Ndlovu, or else with his higher-ups, and here was the result. Here was the enactment of the plan she and Muletsi had discussed with Mr. Ndlovu in Bruntville on the eve of this journey. If all went well, they were to be granted possession of a gun, and now here it was. No sooner had this realization crossed her mind than Mandela all but confirmed it. He turned to her.

"You are Daniel Anson's daughter, is it? The minister of state security?"

"Yes."

"And yet you have taken up our cause?"

She nodded. Had she not, in fact, taken up the cause? She was not a bystander now, not any longer. She was a participant, a fighter in the struggle. She nodded again. "Yes."

"Well, you will find it difficult, I fear. A woman. White. Daughter of a government minister." He made a tsk-ing sound and shook his head. "Difficult. A difficult road. I wish you good luck, but I regret that this is all I am able to do."

She said she understood, and maybe she did.

With that, the man named Mandela turned and marched out into the night along with Champion, leaving the two of them alone.

"*Mandela* ..." said Muletsi. He set the pistol and its wrapping atop a saddlebag that rested on the floor. He shook his head, plainly amazed. "*Nelson Mandela* ..."

Neither of them said what both of them knew. The decision had been made. The plan that Mr. Ndlovu had spoken of — it had been approved.

BASUTOLAND …?

It was the worse effing place Jack had ever set eyes upon. Bar none. It was like a miniature South Africa, run by blacks. The good thing was, he'd got in. The bad thing was, he'd got in. Now here he was.

He spent the first night in Maseru in a sagging, fleabag hotel crawling with vermin. Somehow, he managed some sleep, despite the banging and crashing from below. He could've sworn they'd come to demolish the place, whoever they were. Instead, it was just some disagreement about a woman, followed by a round of fisticuffs. That, at least, was what he was told the next morning. He didn't have much time for exchanging local gossip, though. Instead, he was up early and away, for he had a bugger of a trek ahead of him — west to Mafeteng, south to Mohale's Hoek, and on to a place called Quthing. Who in bloody hell had dreamed up these names? Even when he completed that stretch, he would still have a muck of a ways to go before he reached his real destination.

Qacha's Nek.

He prayed to God he would manage the journey without some mechanical catastrophe befalling him, but he should have known that this hope, this minor, humble plea, was asking too much.

Halfway between Mohale's Hoek and Quthing, he heard a thump, followed by a terrible grinding sound and another thump. There you were — the effing steering mechanism was kerflooey again. Bloody hell. No surprise, maybe, when you considered the loopy madness of the roads in this damned place — not a straight stretch to be found. Just turn left, bear right, swing up, veer down. On the other hand, this latest cock-up was yet another sad object lesson in the quality of kaffir vehicular repair. Good for today. To hell with tomorrow.

Now here he was, swinging left and then right, high in the Drakensberg, with lethal cliffs plunging away to infinity at every turn. One false move and he'd be brown bread for eternity, no doubt about it. Still, there was nothing for it but to careen ahead, yanking at the wheel, first this way then that, narrowly escaping one brush with doom after another. There must've been fifty degrees of play in the steering.

It was damned cold, too. Not your South African cold. This here was different. Worst he'd ever known. And what did the cold bring? Dear Jesus, it had brought snow. Thankfully, it was melting now. Just the same, he kept the four-wheel drive engaged, and he ploughed through the slush. As for creature comforts, he had the heater pumped up full blast, for what little that was worth. Damned thing raised the temperature barely a notch. Still, he would get to Qacha's Nek one way or another, and then he'd figure out his next move from there, maybe find a good, secure lookout with a broad view of the mountain slopes and the land beyond. He'd hunker down and wait till he spied a pair of horses, each with a rider aboard. Even in the cold, this thought thrilled him to the core. Here was the secret, the thing that kept him going — the prospect of what was to come. He yearned for this.

To think, that kaffir boy had come at him without so much as a by-your-leave, armed with a bridle and a pelham bit. What species of treachery was that? Low animal cowardice was what it was. If only he'd been given fair notice, the outcome would have been far different. He'd have seen to that. He'd have put the kaffir lad in his place right then and there, that very instant, that very spot. He'd have savoured his recompense with none of this infernal dragging on. But events had taken a different turn, and now he was obliged to seek out justice by a different route.

He craned his head to look up through the windscreen, peering at the sky. The wind was up, and the clouds ran low, grey as mud with a rare rivulet of blue, like wrong-coloured blood dripping from a wound. This image raised his spirits and set his bile roiling, stirred by thoughts of what was to come. Pretty soon he felt as if he was driving across the very top of the world, his head close to nudging the sky. He could almost imagine he had Jesus himself riding alongside him, the good Lord in the flesh, long legs stretched out on the passenger side, smoking a fag he'd rolled with his own punctured hands.

And what did the good Lord say unto Jack? The words were a shock at first, a sacred bullet out of the effing blue. Kill the kaffir by all means, quoth the Lord, but also consider the girl. Just think. She was the one who'd defiled herself with that swine, the one who'd besmirched Jack's own good name. Consider what ought to be done with her. And there, in that moment, Jack recognized the truth. Praise the effing Lord!

Once again, the steering wheel lurched in his hands, and he yanked the mechanism the other way. Ah, well. He was past Mount Moorosi now, and that was the worst of it, or so he hoped. Even now it wasn't so bad. After all, he was barrelling east for Qacha's Nek on a snake-shaped road through the melting snow, with a hymn in his heart, a gun within reach, and the sunlight now bursting through the clouds overhead — all this, plus the holy word.

It wasn't the kaffir, or not the kaffir alone. It was that effing traitorous girl.

Had been all along.

FORTY-FOUR

Hilary
South Africa, Winter 1962

HILARY HAD UNDERESTIMATED EVERYTHING. She had surely underestimated the rain and the cold. How could anyone have known that the weather would turn so beastly? Not long after that night, when she and Muletsi had crossed paths with Nelson Mandela, it had again commenced to rain, and it continued to pour for two days without a break. That changed everything, all by itself, and then it only got worse.

Snow! In South Africa! It seemed unimaginable. But the stuff fairly pummelled down, piling onto the slopes of the Drakensberg. She and Muletsi rode through a chill rain that alternated with bouts of snow. He was a brick. For the most part, he was. She knew he was still haunted by doubts. That meeting with Mandela had galvanized him, for a time, but the effect was wearing off. She knew it was so. Frigging hell, he'd told her as much that very morning.

"The struggle is here," he'd said, "not in Tanganyika."

"If you stay here, you'll go to jail. Back to jail. It's just a question of time."

"That's a risk I have to take. Look at Mandela. He's not running away to Dar es Salaam."

"He hasn't been convicted of God knows how many crimes."

"Not yet."

"We can always come back, if things change. This isn't a death sentence, you know."

That seemed to settle him, the idea that he could come back, that they both could. They rode on.

Late that day they reached a township called Matatiele, and they spent the night there. The following morning, when she looked outside, she could barely credit what she saw. A deep cover of snow. The people said that this frozen whiteness was an unknown thing, at least in this abundance. They advised her not to go out. It was too cold, and the footing was deadly. The poor horses.

But she didn't listen, and Muletsi went along, putting his faith in her. They both elected to disregard the weather, which was bad enough. Even worse was the problem of Muletsi's glasses — or, rather, his lack of same. He'd been stewing about the matter in silence ever since the night when they'd met Mandela, when the great man had presented them with the Makarov pistol. The gun was tucked away in Muletsi's saddlebag now. But here was the fly in the ointment: without his glasses, Muletsi could not see, or not nearly well enough to be handling a firearm.

Hilary kicked herself for not having thought of this. It was so obvious. At least, it seemed obvious now. As usual, she had been too dense to connect the dots, and now here they were, the two of them, a nearsighted man and a girl who'd never handled a firearm, not once in her life. Here they were with nothing to be done. She brooded about this in silence and then looked up, looked at him. He was gazing at her. At first she could not interpret his expression, and then she could. It was clear to her now that he had been worrying about this for a time, for days. Now he said what he needed to say, the only thing he could say. He said it was up to her.

"No," she told him. "Not a frigging chance."

He replied with the only reply there was. "There's no choice, because I can't do it. It's you or it's no one."

"Well, I can't do it, either. I've never fired a frigging gun, not once in my entire bloody life, hey."

"It isn't so difficult. You'd be surprised how easy it is. I'll show you."

And that, it seemed, was that. It was true, what he'd said. There really was no choice. Even she could see it. Either she did the honours, or the honours did not get done. In a way it was a relief to have the matter out in the open. This was what had been causing him such torment — not some great existential question that no one could answer. That wasn't the problem. The problem was his glasses, his frigging glasses. Spectacles *in absentia*.

Initially, the realization calmed her. Then it did precisely the opposite. It unnerved her badly, caused her to quake in her boots, because there was no escaping what it meant, what it was now incumbent upon her to do.

"Here," he said. "You'd better keep it." He presented the gun, and she took it from him, wedged it among the contents of her saddlebag for one reason and one reason alone. There was no other choice.

They set out early that morning, never mind the cold. The horses were sore in the legs already, stiff as splints. Probably neither animal was properly sound, hadn't been for days, not after the beating they'd taken, the country they'd been ridden over — hard, rocky land, most of the time half frozen. They'd grazed poorly, scrounging for what dead grass the sheep and goats had spurned. With this covering of snow, they were even further reduced in forage. They needed rest, not additional punishment. She bloody well should have known better — should have but had not.

They pushed their way through the flurries of snow, nearly blinded by the onslaught, and then their luck changed, or so it seemed. Shortly past noon the snow let up, and what did you know? The frigging sun came out. They hadn't seen so much as a lick of proper sunlight for a matter of days, and now here it was, cascading all around, glancing off the rocks and flashing against the sparse leaves of the poplar trees, glinting like copper coins. Almost at once the snow began to melt.

Muletsi rode alongside her. He pointed at the canvas bag clipped to her saddle. "The gun. I'll show you now."

And he did. First, they tied the horses to the trunks of a pair of poplars, then strolled away a modest distance and got to work. It was perfectly evident he knew what he was about. He'd obviously had training himself. He released and reinserted the magazine, showed her how to engage and disengage the safety. There was no need to cock the hammer, he said. The first pull would do that, and then the hammer would recock itself. This was what was meant by the term semi-automatic. One pull, one shot. The first pull would be heavy — but after that, quick-quick. He fired two shots himself, to show her. Next, she fired two shots herself, thrilled at how simple it was — thrilled at first. Just seconds later, she felt the opposite way, not thrilled but horrified. So it was that easy, was it? That easy to kill?

Now the magazine was half empty. She wrapped the gun in its waterproof covering, the oilcloth and the foil, and pushed it back into her saddlebag. There. That was done. She tried not to think about ever having to use it again.

Instead she gloried in the weather, if only because it was impossible to do otherwise. The afternoon was sensational, even grander on account of the dreary days that had gone before. The Drakensberg reared overhead as if airborne. Those peaks made her dizzy, gleaming in the sun, taller than seemed possible and topped by the bluest sky she'd ever seen. She felt a surge of euphoria, couldn't help it. What pride she felt. She half-believed that she was single-handedly dismantling the whole system of apartheid — she, this stupid little self-centred girl from Mooi River. Why, she'd met Nelson Mandela himself. And here she was, guiding Muletsi to safety, with Mandela's blessing — all so that some wondrous thing could transpire.

And, yes, it was romantic. She wasn't inventing that. This was straight out of *Lost Horizon*. What was more, she would be the heroine. Dear God, she wanted that. And they were so close. That was what she imagined, or she did until they came within earshot of the Tsoelike River, where it flowed through a rocky gorge.

Up to that moment she had thought it really would be possible to ride to Basutoland. They would scale the Drakensberg and then sneak undetected across the border. But that was before she heard the river, the roar of its passage, before she realized that here was another obstacle she had failed to take into account.

When she came within sight of the water, she instantly pulled South Wind to a halt. Bloody, frigging hell. She could see already that the river had swollen to a ludicrous degree, and it was raging far above its normal banks — all that rain, that melting snow. The engorged waterway churned up mud and God knew what else, branches of trees, planks of wood. She saw the bloated carcass of some dead ungulate as it swept past. The water had turned brown except where it ran frothing with a thick, speckled foam. It was deep and fast and broad. More scraps of bric-a-brac raced by — clumps of grass, the detritus of old furniture, a splintered sheet of plywood. The flotsam rushed away, vanished downstream, giving her a pretty fair idea of how strong the current was.

"I don't think I can do it," Muletsi said.

He pulled up beside her, and they both peered down at the water heaving below.

"Of course, you can." Although she was far from sure herself. "You just have to try. It'll be fine." God, what a load of rot.

Muletsi turned and looked straight at her. "I can't swim."

What? What was this? He couldn't *swim* …? Who is unable to swim?

"You're not serious," she said, which was stupid. She realized this at once, tried to come up with something better. "Okay. Don't worry. You don't have to swim. Welshman can swim, hey. Just hold on. Hold onto his mane."

"That's not it," Muletsi said. "I don't think Welshman can do it, either."

That stopped her. Up to now, this journey had been a question of hope and spunk. If you believed that a thing could be done, then by God you could do it. Simple as that. But now this. This wasn't a question of belief. It was a question of sheer physical impossibility. Muletsi didn't think that Welshman could do it, and now, to tell the truth, she wasn't so sure that South Wind could do it, either — not given the hardship that these two had endured, days on end.

How that man Mandela had got across, she had no idea, unless he was like Jesus and could walk on water. Somehow, he had managed to ford the river. She supposed the waters had been a good deal lower then. Now the river was up, it was their turn to cross, and Muletsi was right — it didn't seem doable. If only she'd been wiser, she would have admitted defeat, and they both would have turned around and headed back the way they'd come, to suffer some unknown fate. If only she'd been wiser.

But she was Hilary Anson. Without stopping to think any further, she gave South Wind a right bloody booting in both his flanks, and — noble idiot that he was — he took several strides down a steep path that descended into the gorge, clattered onto an outcropping of rock, crouched at his hocks and knees, and then exploded, sprang straight into the Tsoelike, with her in the saddle. An instant later, they hit the water and went right under, both of them, and that was shocking. She thought she would drown, and at first that was all she could think of. She did not even register the cold, not at first. All she wanted was to get back to the surface of that river, get her head above water. At last, the daylight burst around her, she clutched Southey's mane, and it was only then that she remembered what she'd done. She'd bloody well forgotten to remove the standing martingale, the mechanism that held Southey's frigging head down, just as it was doing now, causing him to thrash and roll and swing his neck in all directions or to try. Nothing worked. He couldn't raise his bloody noggin. He couldn't breathe. The martingale was holding his head underwater. If she didn't get that damned thing off, he'd drown. Oh, for the love of God.

JACK HAD EXPECTED THERE would be lodging of some description in Qacha's Nek, some miserable excuse for a hostelry — nothing more than that. But what do you know? Nothing. No accommodation whatso-effing-ever. No place to get the wonky steering attended to, either. Nothing, nothing, nothing. Just a miserable, God-forsaken little crap hole without a single distinction to claim for itself except altitude and desolation. Behold: Qacha's Nek.

Well, never mind. He'd sort something out, one way or another. No grub, either. That was another thing. He was feeling more than a mite peckish, too. At some point, he'd probably have to cajole a leg of chicken off one of the denizens of the place, if chicken legs there were — that and a bed. Lord Almighty. No hotel, no garage, not even a place to eat. Quite the little tourist resort, Qacha's Nek. What a country this was.

Well, that was fine. He wasn't on holiday, anyhow. He was here to get a job done. He climbed back into the Land Rover, released the brake, pushed down on the clutch, and shoved the shift into first. He lurched out onto the bit of path that passed for a high street in this miserable locale.

He had to keep his wits about him to avoid colliding with sundry goats, mongrels, and pickaninnies, all of whom seemed to be beside themselves with joy to see him — a stranger in their town and, what was more, a white man. The tykes crowed and waved while he picked his way among them, marvelling at what a congregation of cuteness they were. What happened to the little buggers? They started out so well, so happy, so trusting, so prone to laughter, all bobbing up and down on their crooked little toes. But sooner or later they went bad. They all did.

He aimed the Land Rover down the lopsided path, past the children and the dogs. He had an idea that he could jimmy the vehicle into a protected spot somewhere on the downward slope. Once he'd got the Land Rover put to rights, he would get out and proceed on foot. He felt certain that a pair of travellers on horseback would be visible for a good long distance from up here.

He flung the wheel to the right, and the Land Rover wobbled over a rocky outcropping. Off to the left, some small, shaggy horses were grazing by a stand of eucalyptus trees. Ponies, really. Basotho ponies, as likely as not. Hardy creatures, it was said. Right away, he knew what he would do — get himself a proper mode of transportation, one suited to local conditions, as you might say. One of these ponies would do just fine, strong enough to carry a lean sort of man, which he was.

He fought off another lurch in the steering, spun the wheel, and that was when it bloody well happened. The disk seemed to fly from his grip, and the Land Rover tossed itself to the right. Before you could say, "Bob's your uncle," it broke free of the path and tumbled straight into a pile of rocks that was meant to be a fence of some kind. The vehicle came to an abrupt stop, and he kept right on going, square into the windscreen. He cracked his forehead against the glass and damned near blacked right out.

Effing hell. Meanwhile, the steering wheel had caught him full in the chest. And one of his legs had got twisted around somehow. The vehicle rocked back, and so did he, and now here he was, blood streaming down his face. Not only that, but he was having trouble breathing on account of what must have been a rack of broken ribs, plus a howling pain in one of his legs. Jesus effing hell.

He kept calm. Tried to. First thing he did was check the cubby-hole for the pistol, the box of shells, and the field glasses, all of which he salvaged and stuffed into the pockets of his anorak. That done, he jimmied open the door and toppled out onto the rocks and mud and patchy bits of dead grass, landed on his head. He was suffering a profound shortness of breath and, at first, he thought he was choking to death. You'd panic then. Any bloke would. Here he lay, flat on the ground, and he heaved and gasped, slowly recovering an approximation of his customary wind and mental acuity.

He tested himself.

Name: Jack Tanner.

Age: Thirty-nine.

Nationality: English-born, if it please your Lordship.

Dependents: None that he knew of. Granted, he hadn't been keeping track.

Current location: Qacha's Nek, or somewhere thereabouts.

He could have gone on, but he heard a man's voice from some-where not far off. He got himself twisted around a bit so that he could gaze straight up and saw a black mug peering down at him.

It said, "You all right, *baas*?"

Dear God, was it not apparent that *all right* was exactly what he was not? But in the interest of moving matters along, he said that he was passably fine — and that was how he made the acquaintance of Yul Brynner Dlamini, so named because he was without facial hair of any kind.

"It's a nickname," he said. He hadn't been born Yul Brynner. It was a moniker acquired much later in life, for reasons now appar-ent. He was all for taking Jack over to his nearby abode in order to attend to these fresh injuries. His spouse was a midwife, he said, which meant she possessed nursing skills of a kind. Jack was briefly tempted to take the man up on his offer, but on the whole he believed he should push on. What he needed was a four-legged means of conveyance, and one of these sturdy creatures would meet his requirements, if Yul Brynner Dlamini happened to know how such a transaction could be effected.

As it happened the man did. He said so at once.

Jack had thought as much. Nice to see the old familiar gears still working in unison. "Fine," he said. "That's just fine."

Half an hour later, having supped upon a bowl of something that narrowly passed for soup, he was on his way once again, this time slumped upon the back of a particularly brawny grey gelding. Either the creature didn't have a name or Jack had forgotten what it was. Elvis was the label he settled on, in recognition of the animal's squiggly way of moving, like the King himself. Jack peered at the trail that wound below him and noticed a sort of natural belvedere, a rocky ledge covered with moss and flanked by a few barren shrubs. He would make for that. He would dismount down there, find himself a good spot for a piss, then set up a lookout. Take his bearings. Catch his breath.

When he reached the indicated spot, he eased himself off Elvis's back. At once a stabbing pain pierced his chest. Mother of effing Christ. But there was nothing to be done save grin and withstand. He looped the reins around the branch of some kind of acacia shrub, and old Elvis seemed as happy as any four-legged creature could ever be, poking through the slats of snow to feast on wrinkled brown leaves, clumps of lifeless grass.

Jack managed to attend to his business and even to button up his trousers when said business was done. He got the field glasses out and peered through the lenses. He fiddled with the focus, and the land below sprang into clearer view. Here and there, the afternoon sunshine broke through the clouds like spotlights. He felt as if those shifting rays were doing just what he was doing himself, searching across the terrain for a pair of riders. He was sure to see them if they approached this way, and he was just as sure they would. He took a deep breath, gasped at the stabbing pain. Come on, you effing Berkeley Hunt, you and your effing slut.

Just you come.

FORTY-SIX

Muletsi
South Africa, Winter 1962

"HILARY ...!"

Muletsi did not stop to think. He drove his heels into Welshman's flanks, and the old codger did what no sentient creature had any business doing — certainly not an animal of Welshman's sober and cautious instincts. He slithered down the rocky path, scrambled onto the outcrop of stone, arched his back, and hurled himself into the air. A moment later he plunged into the swirling brown waters of the Tsoelike River. Muletsi clamped his mouth shut and staunched his breath just before the water hit him like a series of blows. He struggled to hang on, one hand clenching the pommel of the saddle, the other grasping at Welshman's mane. He felt himself go under, and he gritted his teeth, pursed his lips, to keep the water out. Finally, a light erupted, and his head burst above the river's surface. He rolled over onto his back, gasping for air, still clinging to Welshman's mane. The current dragged them both downstream.

"Hilary!" he shouted. "Hilary!"

Welshman swung his head to the side, and his great body listed, his legs struggling for purchase against the river's pull. There was nothing Muletsi could do but hold on. For a few moments it felt as if they were not moving at all, both of them motionless in the churning swell. But that was an illusion. He caught sight of the muddy banks and scrub trees that marked the far shore. The land raced by, shockingly fast. He shouted Hilary's name again, and then he was pulled under once more, gagging and flailing about. He fought to get his head up and into the air, terrified at what might happen if he lost his grip on Welshman. He could not swim.

Gradually, he managed to steady his breathing. He peered ahead, above the river's spinning surface, straining for a glimpse of South Wind or Hilary or both of them together. But he could make out nothing except a brown rush of water, a spiralling froth, the sight of Welshman's head. On his own he would have had no idea what to do. He could have done nothing but let this current bear him where it would, to some cold and lonely end. Thank God for horses that had some wit and muscle, more of both than he'd ever possessed. Welshman kept beating against the water with his huge legs, striding through the river, crossways to the current. Before long, even Muletsi could sense it. Foot by foot, they were working their way across the water, not directly but on a long, curving course that was aslant to the river's flow. It seemed that Welshman knew exactly what he was doing. Muletsi ceased to struggle, just held on. *Stop thinking.* He allowed Welshman to do what horses can manage for themselves far better than the fools who ride them. Get out alive.

Closer to the far shore, the current slowed and gyrated in eddies that carried both of them nearer and nearer to land. When Welshman found some footing at last, he heaved himself up toward the bank, far faster than Muletsi expected. He wasn't quick enough to position himself in the saddle and so lost his grasp on Welshman's mane. He felt the river bottom with his feet. He tried to stand, but the current was still too strong. He reached out blindly and somehow managed to close his grip on the saddle's knee roll, just as Welshman clambered ashore, dragging Muletsi with him.

He kept hold of the saddle for as long as he could, then loosened his fingers, too cold to hang on. Under his own power, he clambered up through the scrub trees, dead grass, and mud on the bank and soon collapsed onto his front side. He sprawled there, chest heaving. Meanwhile, Welshman scrambled onto a forested bank that ran alongside the river's flow and proceeded to amble further downstream, as if he needed a little time to be alone, to reflect on what had just happened here. Muletsi raised his head and watched the horse, too tired at first to do anything else, too tired and too stunned. Then he remembered — Hilary.

He climbed to his feet and peered downriver, where the racing water veered to his left. He could make out nothing that resembled a woman or her horse. It seemed the only thing to do was to retrieve Welshman, climb back into the saddle, and ride along the river's shore, hoping to find Hilary somehow. What an idiot she'd been to urge South Wind into the drink like that. But never mind. He turned to make his way in Welshman's tracks, and only then did he truly realize how cold he was, how frigid and wet, how drenched to the bone. He'd be lucky not to perish of hypothermia. Neither of them had thought of that.

Soon his limbs began to shake, and he found he could not stand. He collapsed into a sort of crouch, trying to marshal whatever strength he could find. After a time he managed to raise himself to his feet once more, and he stumbled over toward Welshman, who had come to a halt. The horse lifted his great head, perked his ears, and gazed back, as if vaguely surprised to see Muletsi again and not altogether happy at the sight.

Now it got complicated. No sooner did Muletsi advance within several feet of the horse than Welshman loped a few paces further away. This sequence repeated itself over and over, like a succession of turns in a futile dance. Each time Muletsi got near the animal, almost close enough to lunge ahead and snatch the draggled reins,

Welshman scooted off several paces more, as if they both had all the time in the world. Muletsi made another stab at the reins, landing on his knees, empty-handed, as Welshman trotted away yet again, this time putting considerable distance between himself and his former rider. It wasn't long before he disappeared beyond a thicket of trees while Muletsi remained out in the open.

"Christ. You miserable bugger. Come back!"

The words had barely left his mouth before he became aware of some other movement, something quite apart from Welshman. A change of shadow and light on the margins of his vision — that was all he sensed at first. He looked up and blinked, straining to see, despite being deprived of his glasses. Before too long he was able to make out a blurry but strangely familiar figure approaching down a rocky slope amid scraggly grass and sharp pillars of stone — a man riding a stout grey pony and looking for all the world like the angel of death. Muletsi said nothing, merely waited as the image drew near.

"Well, well, well," said the man, now only a few yards away. "What have we here?"

Muletsi recognized him, of course, despite his own imperfect vision and never mind the man's wretched condition, his blood-encrusted face riddled with cuts and bruises. He slouched on the pony's back as if his frame had collapsed, as if his collarbone and most of his ribs were bust.

"Hold hard, Elvis," the man said, his voice strained and creaky. "Why, what do we have here? Ha. If it ain't my old friend Berkeley. Berkeley Hunt to the cognoscenti." He laughed and shook his head, groaned at the pain he must have been feeling. He really was in a bad way. Now he rummaged in the pocket of his coat. When his hand reappeared, it was clutching a gun. Muletsi stiffened at once. He thought he should turn and run, but what was the use? He would never get away.

Besides, it seemed that this was just a warning on Jack's part, this brandishing of a weapon. He didn't seem to be in any hurry. He told Muletsi to stand up. Stand up like a man. Slowly, unsteadily, Muletsi did as Jack Tanner bid. Muletsi stood, and he waited for what would come next, wondering if it would come soon. But the man seemed more interested in talking than in shooting. He seemed willing to take his own sweet time, rambling on in a sorely laboured voice, making little or no sense, cursing this, blaming that. He seemed to be halfway out of his mind, a condition that no doubt resulted in part from his many injuries. Time passed, and more time passed until even Jack seemed to grow tired of his verbosity. He raised the firearm and pointed it at Muletsi's forehead, from not a dozen feet away.

In that moment, or in the moment that followed, Muletsi remembered something he had read somewhere, or maybe it was something that someone once said. You do not hear the shot that kills you.

FORTY-SEVEN

Hilary
South Africa, Winter 1962

HILARY WAS SO COLD she could barely control the movement of her hands. She thought she would perish from exposure if she didn't drown first. Meanwhile, South Wind struggled with the current, pacing against the river's flow. Somehow, he'd got his head swung out to the side, got his nostrils clear of the river's flow. In brief, frenzied snorts, he managed to breathe the only way that horses *can* breathe, through the nose. Meanwhile, he kept striding sideways through the water's rush, and it worked. By God, it worked. Gradually, stroke by stroke, he managed to shoulder his way through the surging water. But it was hard going. Southey could barely breathe, and it was a good question how long he could keep his head twisted around like that. He was bound to tire before long, tire and then drown.

By now, Hilary had got her left hand around the noseband on Southey's bridle. In her other hand, she clutched his mane. Numb though she was, she fumbled at the buckle, tried to release the noseband, tried to free the martingale so that Southey could raise his head clear of the water. Damn. Damn. Damn. She couldn't bloody well move her fingers, and she could get no purchase, cold as she was, borne downstream with only a horse's mane to hold on to.

Oh, Southey. Oh, you poor beautiful boy. He coiled his shoulders and damned near performed a cartwheel in the water before flopping again onto his belly, his head again beneath the roiling surface. He thrust his shoulders up again, freed his muzzle, and shrieked into the cold air, a sound she'd never heard a horse make before, a wail of panic or of anger. *Sever this frigging leather. Remove these fetters from me.* That was what he was trying to do. *Tear these leather straps that dare to restrict my glorious head.* He jerked and thrashed, sprayed spouts of frigid water that arched through the grey daylight. But he could not hold his nostrils clear. She knew it, and somehow he must have known it, too. Still, he kept kicking through the water, even as his muscles burned, even as his neck began to weaken and wilt.

Hilary realized they were advancing almost to the banks on the far side of the river. Before long, she felt her shoulders brushing against the low, drooping boughs of trees. She thought she might be able to grasp one of those branches, and possibly pull herself to safety. The idea raced through her head like a phantom, like a thought that wasn't really there. In that same instant, she remembered the gun, the one they'd got from Nelson Mandela. She stopped struggling with the martingale. She knew she could never work it free. Instead, she thought of the gun. She frigging well needed that gun. She released her grip on Southey's noseband. She swung herself around, still gripping Southey's mane. Somehow, despite the crazy trembling of her fingers, she managed to yank the weapon from the saddlebag and then shove the pistol in its water-proof cover into a side pocket of her parka. The riverbank rushed by, and she caught sight of a tree branch racing toward her, just overhead, bending low over the water. Without pausing to think, without actually making a decision, she thrust out her right arm. *Oh, Southey. Oh, my splendid one.* She snagged the branch with her raised arm and then hurled herself up, wrapping both her arms around that blessed limb, praying it would hold. She wasn't sure

South Wind even knew what she had done. He would never know that she had betrayed him in the end, left him to drown after he had saved her. She caught a last glimpse of that wondrous beast, dwindling with the current, his head still flailing from side to side, his shoulders yawing, his neck lowering in what must have been a state of monstrous exhaustion, and she never set eyes on him again.

Inch by inch, she shimmied along the tree branch, like some waterlogged hybrid of human and sloth, until she could hold on no longer, and so she fell, fully expecting to be plunged into the river again. Instead, she landed on the bank itself. At once, she patted the side of her parka, to make sure the gun was there — the first thing she thought of. For several moments she just lay where she had fallen, panting for breath and wondering what in God's name had ever possessed her to make this infernal trek. Then she remembered.

She raised herself to her knees and climbed to her feet, surprised that she was whole and that she could actually stand. She glanced around herself, trying to get her bearings. That done, she set out on foot, tending back the way she had come. She kept as close as she could to the river's edge. Either Muletsi and Welshman were in the water by now or else they were still stranded somewhere back on the southern side. At first she failed to notice how cold she was, but it wasn't long before the trembling and the chattering took hold. Never mind. Never you bloody well mind. She kept on going, keeping to the river's edge, picking her way through thickets of trees, mostly yellowwoods, ash, and stinkwoods.

Keeping close to the trees, it turned out, was a stroke of luck. As a result, she could easily see without being easily seen. And what she saw, before long, was dear old Welshman poking through the bush on her side of the river. Where was Muletsi? Nowhere that she could make out. For his part, Welshman seemed distracted, not bothering to graze, breaking into a trot every now and then, moving clumsily among the trees. She noticed he'd got the reins looped around his near foreleg, which worked almost as a hobble.

She was about to whistle for him and call out his name, but something stopped her, some sixth sense — and a damned good thing. She peered beyond Welshman and caught sight of a slump-shouldered man mounted on a shaggy grey pony. The pony was loping along a footpath, down toward the river, with the massive heights of the Drakensberg soaring to the north, like a wall of churches. She figured the man must have ridden down from those heights, and then it struck her like a kick to the head. It was Jack frigging Tanner. All this time she'd been expecting him to show — and now here he was, and she hadn't even recognized him, not at first. She surely recognized him now.

The next thing she saw was Muletsi himself, about a hundred yards away. He was perched on his knees, which was probably why she hadn't located him before now. She could tell he was soaking wet, and he was staring up at the man on the pony. He probably wasn't able to make out very much, on account of his missing glasses. Still, he wasn't quite blind. He would be able to see enough. She watched as Jack Tanner halted about a half-dozen yards from Muletsi. Even from this distance, she could tell that her old nemesis was in a bad way, just pathetic, lop-shouldered, flumped in the saddle, awash with what looked like blood smeared across his face. He must have suffered a crack-up of the worst kind. But that wasn't what most caught her attention. What most caught her attention was his right hand, a slow movement of his right hand. He reached down, so that his hand vanished from her view. When the appendage reappeared, it was holding a gun. Seconds later, as if obeying orders, Muletsi staggered to his feet.

Just then, she sensed some disturbance on her right, and good Lord if it wasn't Welshman, come to snuffle at her pockets, hoping for an apple or a lump of sugar, neither of which she possessed. "There's a good man," she whispered, thinking for the umpteenth time how much she loved horses. There isn't a good turn they won't do, if only they know what that good turn is. South Wind had saved her life — and now this. She hunched down and nudged Welshman's foreleg up, to work the reins free. Without needing to think, she looped the lengths of leather over his head and neck and swung herself up into the saddle, suddenly knowing exactly what she meant to do.

She meant to ride up the way Jack had come, keeping under a cover of trees. When the time was right, she would swing around into the open, to approach Jack from a blind spot, from behind. Judging by his doleful appearance, she thought he might be less than fully alert. His guard might be down. Besides, he seemed focused on Muletsi just now, which was no surprise, considering what had gone on between them. She expected he would stretch these moments out. Jack was like that — not one to rush events. He liked the feeling of power, the sensation of control.

That was lucky for her, or it was now.

After weaving through the trees for a distance of a hundred yards or so, she swung Welshman out into the open, reversing direction. She kept him to a walk, stalking through the grass, avoiding the worn surface of the footpath, where a careless hoof striking a rock might give her away. Here, all was quiet. She was pretty sure Muletsi could see her now, even without his glasses. He'd have identified Welshman. He'd have identified her.

She was alert — aroused without being anxious. Her breathing was steady. She did not feel the cold. Now she reached down into the side pocket of her parka and eased the Makarov out. With her free hand, she managed to remove the gun from its wrapping. She hoped the cover had kept the weapon passably dry, but she had no control over that. Either it would fire or it wouldn't.

She kept her eyes fixed on Jack's shoulders, which were rounded in a way she had never associated with him before. Usually, he sat straight as a lord in the saddle. Say whatever else you might say about him, he could surely ride a horse. Everything she knew about these glorious creatures, he had taught her — he alone. A monster in most other ways, he was as gifted an equestrian as she had ever encountered, although you would not have guessed it now. He must have suffered at least a couple of broken ribs, to be sagging the way he was. She felt almost sorry for him and realized at once she should not be thinking this way. These were not the kinds of thoughts to be troubling herself with now. And yet she couldn't seem to help it. She had known the man so long, even loved him for a time, back when she was merely a girl. Bad as those years were, they were what she knew. They had fashioned her into the person she had become. She was starting to feel that same misery again, that bedraggled sorrow that always overcame her around Jack. She was now just a dozen yards or so from the rump of the grey pony, and she heard Jack speak. She could not make out what he was saying, but she saw that he was raising his gun.

That was that.

She released the safety on the Makarov, urged Welshman into a canter for three quick strides, and stopped dead beside Jack Tanner.

"Goodbye, Jacko," she said.

She raised the weapon, she aimed, and she squeezed the trigger — a long, slow pull. The gun recoiled, the hammer recocked by itself, and she fired again.

FIRST, THEY HAD TO dispense with Jack's body. Hilary helped Muletsi drag and then roll the thing into the river. Off it went, headed east. It was awful, just awful, but to be honest she was too cold to think about what she had done only minutes earlier. Killed a man. Two bullets to the head. That was bad, a mortal sin no matter how you looked at it. But she didn't look at it now. They were in a perilous way, she and Muletsi, no doubt at all. They were drenched and in danger of perishing from the elements. They might very well die out here, and this entire adventure would count for nothing.

It was around then that they heard the first warble of a cowbell, followed a few seconds later by another and then another. They peered off to the east, and within moments they saw a pair of Basotho herd boys striding down along a faint trail, guiding their charges — a half-dozen bony cattle, plus a smattering of goats. Both of the boys were barefoot, enfolded in thick blankets draped over their shoulders. Neither of them looked to be more than thirteen years of age.

"We heard shots," said one, speaking in laboured English. "That was you?"

She said it was.

The other boy frowned. "Your clothes are wet. Like this, you will die."

In broken English, the herd boys said they were both heading for a place where they customarily sheltered for the night. It wasn't much, a derelict stone-walled structure that had an old tarp for a roof. Their sister was up there now, they said, tending the fire. "Come with us."

Hilary and Muletsi agreed, of course. What else could they do? Muletsi rode Welshman while she straddled the Basotho pony, its dense grey coat now matted in places with Jack Tanner's blood. She didn't think of that or of what had been done. All she thought of was how cold she was. Her hands and feet were the worst. They felt ready to fall off.

"Do this," said one of the boys. "Watch."

One of the cattle had just defecated, and now the youth made straight for the steaming pad of muck. He plunged his bare feet into the thick of it, howling with pleasure at the sudden warmth.

"Primo!" he shouted. "Primo!"

Where did they get these words?

She swung her right leg over the pony's head and slid to the ground, shuddering at the twin stabs of pain when her feet hit the dirt. She yanked off her boots and socks. When the opportunity arose, she did just as the herd boy had done, buried her feet in cow shit — disgusting but heavenly. It was just processed grass, after all.

Soon, Muletsi did the same.

They spent that night with the two herd boys and their younger sister, all wrapped in blankets and huddled near the fire in the tumbledown stone hovel they used as a shelter. Their clothes — Muletsi's and hers — were stretched over rocks to dry. The following morning, hungrier than cold, they said their goodbyes and set out on a steep, winding ascent of the Drakensberg.

Muletsi rode Welshman, and she contented herself with the Basotho pony previously ridden by Jack. She kept shifting around to peer behind them, thinking that some sound she heard might be South Wind, magically restored to their company. But she was mistaken each time. Drowned and dead, her father's finest horse. Late that afternoon, she and Muletsi straggled across an invisible border into Basutoland, near the lofty mountaintop village of Qacha's Nek.

Here they made a gift of Welshman and the Basotho pony to a man they met — a baldpated individual who said his name was Yul Brynner Dlamini, strangely enough. The following morning they rode in the bed of a smoke-spewing bakkie down to Maseru, the main city in that land. It was not long before they made contact there with some of the men Nelson Mandela had named, ANC officials living in exile. Comrade revolutionaries that they were, these men welcomed Muletsi with open arms. But Hilary was a woman — what was more, a white woman, and the daughter of a government minister to boot. They wouldn't have her, flat out refused. Mandela had been right, it seemed, when he'd said her prospects would be difficult. Evidently, it didn't matter that she'd shot a man in the name of the struggle, shot him twice. They didn't say so, not in so many words, not to her face, but it was clear they did not believe her. As likely as not, she'd simply made that story up. They needed proof, and she had none. Muletsi debated with them, debated with her, but it was no use. Their paths had diverged, hers and his. She saw it, and he would come to see it, too. She had only to convince him.

"Look at it, man," she said. Whereas he himself was where he belonged, she, quite evidently, was not. It took a good while and much draining effort for her to counter Muletsi's many objections, but in the end she won out, if you could call it that. She left him in Maseru and returned to South Africa on her own on a bus, meaning to remain in the country only for a time, only for as long as it would take to turn her life around.

She told her father an outright lie — insisting that Jack Tanner had killed Muletsi Dadla and then absconded for parts unknown. Maybe he believed her. Maybe he did not. Either way, what Daniel Anson most feared was scandal, which explained why he sent her packing. First he shipped her off to England, to serve her penance at a boarding school in Kent, a place called Cobham Hall. For months, she bided her time, plotting her escape. At last, she got it sorted. Toward the end of term, she cabled her father to say she meant to spend that summer in Canada, of all places, rather than dwell beneath the thumb of some distant family connections they had in London, as previously planned. She had a reason for this — the Canadian man with the Liverpool accent, the one named Quinton Vasco, inventor of massive guns — but she kept all this to herself. Of course, she did. By actions, not words, would she be judged. The ANC would learn to set greater store by her name than it had so far done. In the end, her father relented, probably because Canada was even further away than Albion.

In her suitcase she packed the Makarov pistol, the very weapon she and Muletsi had received from none other than Nelson Mandela. By this time the great man was locked away in a South African jail. She also packed a box of nine millimetre by eighteen millimetre shells that she'd purchased at the shop owned by Henk Viljoen, the pot-bellied gun merchant in Mooi River. All these long months, she'd kept them a dark secret — the gun, the munitions.

A week later, thanks to the money wired to her from Canada, she boarded a Trans-Canada Air Lines Douglas DC-8 that landed in Toronto on Thursday, June 6, 1963. The man she knew only as Colonel Martin Barker met her at the airport, dressed in riding breeches, desert boots, and a green military-style jumper. He wore a patch over one eye. They were not related to one another in any way and, in fact, had never met before. She had simply responded to an advertisement he'd placed in *Horse & Hound*, looking for an

English girl to work as a groom for the summer at his estate in Kelso County, Ontario. Hilary wasn't English, of course, but Colonel Barker was happy to make an exception in her case. She was of the empire, after all.

He was waiting for her in the arrivals area after her plane touched down in Toronto.

"Hip, hip!" he said before rounding up a porter to deal with her bags. He led her out to the parking lot, where his Cadillac Eldorado awaited. "To horse!"

She wondered why he spoke with an English accent. Wasn't she supposed to be in Canada? Did they not have an accent of their own in this country, hey? Well, it didn't matter. She was here now, and she had a plan to carry out. Lord, did she ever.

Three months spiralled by, and then it was done.

On that final evening — the night that turned out to be her last in Canada — she drove to the outdoor bioscope with that boy, Sam Mitchell, the one who'd been her loyal friend all that summer long. They paid their admission at the entrance and drove on in, an outing that would establish an alibi. It was just the two of them this time, Hilary Anson and Sam Mitchell.

Her treat.

FORTY-NINE

Sam

Ontario, Summer 1963

HILARY SWITCHED ON THE right-turn signal, slowed down, and peeled off the highway toward the entrance to the Newburgh Drive-In. I was in the passenger seat. At the ticket gate, she rolled down her window.

"Two," she said to the girl in the booth.

The girl was plump with a round face, her lips a thick smudge of ruby-red lipstick. She was chewing bubble gum, making a little popping sound each time the inflated membrane burst.

"*Two* ...?" the girl said, laying stress on the word, as if there were some discrepancy between that number and the quantity of people in the car.

"Yes," said Hilary, just as emphatically. "That's right. Two." She turned to me. "Sam, sit up. Let the nice lady see you."

I did as she said, as always.

"See ...?" said Hilary. "Two of us. See?"

"Hold your horses. I heard you the first time. No need to make a capital case."

"What's your name?"

"What ...?"

"Your name. Mine's Hilary Anson. This here's Sam Mitchell. What's yours, hey?"

"Bonnie."

"Bonnie what?"

"Just Bonnie."

"All right then, 'Just Bonnie.' Two tickets, please."

In due course, the tickets appeared, and Hilary handed over way too much money.

"Keep the change," she said.

"What …? This is too —"

"Never mind. I'm feeling generous, that's all."

"Fine. Thanks." The ticket clerk rolled her eyes, shrugged. She popped another bubble of gum and snatched the membrane back into her mouth with her tongue before returning her attention to her magazine, devoted to celebrities in Hollywood.

"Pleasure," said Hilary. She pronounced it *plezha*, something like that. "Well, bye." She waited for a response. "I said goodbye, hey."

Only now did the girl at last look up and fix her gaze on Hilary directly, eye to eye. She glanced at me. Then she delved back into her magazine. "Fine," she said. "Bye. Happy now?"

"You see?" Hilary made a face. "Was that so difficult?"

But the girl did not respond.

Hilary eased the car into the large outdoor theatre with its rows of individual parking bays, each equipped with a wired speaker mounted on a metal post. After manoeuvring into a space at the back, near a smattering of other cars, Hilary announced that she craved a cheeseburger. With chips.

"Fries," I said. There was a ringing in my head that wouldn't go away.

"Hey …?"

"We say fries. French fries, really."

"Oh, right. Actually, I knew that."

We both trudged across the lot toward the snack bar. There, Hilary got into a strange discussion with one of the servers, having to do with the proper way to order french-fried potatoes. Was it acceptable, Hilary wondered, to say "chips"? The server had his hair in a net and didn't seem to have any idea what she was getting at. He asked Hilary if she wanted chips. He pointed along the counter to a display of foil packages containing Humpty Dumpty potato chips.

"No, not crisps," she said. "Chips."

Finally, it got sorted out, and we both carried our purchases back to the car.

When I look back on that evening now, I have the clear impression that Hilary was trying to draw attention to herself and to me, to ensure that we both were noticed and, I suppose, remembered. I didn't really dwell on it at the time. It seemed puzzling; that was all. I didn't figure it out until later, when it ceased to seem puzzling at all.

Besides, I had other matters on my mind. Just that morning, I had retrieved the pair of eyeglasses, the ones Hilary and I had found down in the quarry. I already had a suspicion about whose they were, but I asked Charlotte all the same. She and Leslie were school chums, after all.

"Where did you get those?" she said. "They're Leslie's."

"You're sure?"

"Of course. D'you think I'm a total idiot? Where did you get them?"

"I don't remember."

Later, I rode my bike into Hatton to turn in Leslie's glasses at the store. I'd expected to find her at the counter, where she seemed to have spent most of her time that summer, but there was no sign of her. Instead, her father was alone in the store, tottering back and forth on his game leg, occasionally pausing to straighten a box or jar that seemed out of alignment. I doubt he was more than forty years old, and yet he walked with a limp. Something to do with the war.

I offered him the glasses. "They're Leslie's, I think."

He didn't take them, or not at once. Instead, he stared at my outstretched hand for what seemed a very long time, saying nothing but clearly upset. Then he took the glasses from me. He proceeded to turn them over and over in his hands, as if to be sure they really were what they seemed. I noticed the knuckles of both his hands were abraded and raw, the skin broken in places. I wondered about that. I wondered if he had been hitting someone or something. I wondered if he had been hitting Davey.

"I found them in the quarry," I said, meaning the glasses. I started to explain what had happened down there, what I had seen and heard, but I could tell this was not welcome information. I was thinking that one of the voices I'd heard that night had belonged to Davey. Her own brother. I was pretty sure of it. I was thinking that such a thing could not possibly happen, not in this world or in any other. And yet it seemed it had.

After a while, Mr. Odegaard spoke. "You're the singer?" he said. "The singer on the horse?"

I guessed he meant the South African songs I had belted out that night. Someone must have told him about that — Leslie, maybe, or else Davey. That had been dumb, my singing those songs, but at the time it had been all I could think of. And maybe it had helped. At least, it had stopped whatever had been going on, and that was something.

"*Well* ...?" he said.

"Yes." My throat was dry, and it was hard to swallow. "That was me." After a pause, I said, "I hope Leslie's okay."

Again, he looked down at his daughter's eyeglasses, and now he shrugged. He said he hoped so, too. He said that time would tell.

I remember he was wearing a brown windbreaker, even though it was still summer. He slipped those glasses into the side pocket of his jacket.

"Thank you," he said. He hesitated, and then he did something completely unexpected. He reached out with his injured right hand and took mine in his. He shook my hand. "Thank you," he said again. "It was brave, what you did."

I wasn't so sure about that, but it didn't hurt too much to hear him say it. I didn't know what else to say, so I just said thank you. I told him again that I hoped Leslie would be all right. Then I turned and left the store and rode away on my bike.

Now, at the Newburgh Drive-In, Hilary rolled down her window and reached for the speaker, suspending the device on the half-open pane. She turned the sound level down, cutting off a bunch of advertising prattle about the food and drinks available at the snack bar. I had thought she might have a broken nose, from the blows she'd taken from Quinton Vasco that night in the quarry, but her nose seemed to be okay. She had another black eye, though. Probably, the punch was responsible for that, the punch or the kick.

"Do you want to listen?" She turned and looked at me. "I don't, really. I just want to watch."

"That's okay," I said. "Whatever you like."

Actually, I did want to listen. The feature film was *The Pink Panther*, starring Peter Sellers. It was supposed to be hilarious. Maybe it would take my mind off all the stuff that was whirling around in my head. But, as usual, I went along with Hilary. For a while we just slumped there in silence, staring up at the giant screen. Before too long it began to rain — just drizzle at first. Then it started raining harder, and finally it began to pour. You couldn't make out much of anything on the movie screen, just an assortment of human faces, all seeming to melt in the glaze of water slithering down the windshield. Hilary switched on the wipers. A few minutes later she turned them off. Right away, the glass was transformed into a slurry of hazy celluloid images and splattering rain. She ground out a cigarette in the ashtray.

"Come over here."

"What ...?"

"You heard me. Come here."

"Okay." I shifted my weight to be closer to her. "Like this?"

"More or less."

She ran a hand through my hair, and my scalp tingled at the sleekness of her touch. A cold pulse rippled up my spine.

"Remember that day?" she said. "That time in the sugar bush? You were looking at my breasts."

"I ... *what?*"

"I saw you. I'm right, am I not?"

"I don't know," I said. But the words were barely audible, even to me. I tried again. "Yes."

"Wasn't that nice?"

"I ... I mean —"

"You mean it wasn't nice?" She stroked my hair again. "How can you say that?"

I stammered something, some words. I didn't even know what they were.

"Do you want to see again?"

I closed my eyes, not quite believing what I was hearing. I opened my eyes again. "Yes."

"Here." She reached up and undid a button of her blouse, then another. "Here. You can look. Just look. That's all."

I was shivering all over, every part of my body, my hands, everything.

She removed her blouse, one sleeve first, then the other. Next, she reached behind her back, shifted her shoulders to the side, and the white fabric of her brassiere fell loose, tumbling from her breasts. She slipped off the straps.

I felt a buzzing in my head, as if I were dizzy, as if I were about to faint.

"Do you like them?"

I couldn't speak. My head felt as though it were trying to spin through space, as though it might snap free of my neck at any instant and simply hurtle away, never to be seen again. I didn't know what to say. I couldn't stop staring at her breasts. At first, I couldn't. Then something made me look up, and I saw that she was crying. She was actually crying. Even in the dim light, I could make out the glow of the tears sliding down her cheeks, and then I realized that I was crying, too.

"I'm evil," she said.

I swallowed. "No, you're not."

"I am. I swear I am."

"Maybe you're just upset."

She shook her head, gave a bitter laugh. "I'm what …? What did you say?"

"You're upset?"

"Upset, am I? Is that what I am? Upset? What makes you say that?"

I shrugged.

She nodded, as if my shrug had some kind of deep meaning. She was practically sobbing now.

"I'm sorry," I said.

"You're sorry …? Why?"

"I just am. For everything."

"I'm sorry, too."

I said, "Maybe you should … I don't know. Maybe put your …"

"My clothes? Put my clothes back on?" She sniffled, half laugh, half sob. "It's true. You're right. I should." She struggled with her brassiere but finally managed to put it right. She slid her arms into the sleeves of her blouse, first one then the other, and refastened the buttons. "There. Is that better?"

"I'm not sure." I put a hand to my brow, checking for dampness, which there was. I swept some of it away and shook my head. "I think I'm too young for this."

"I think I am, too. I think we all are." She tried to wipe her tears away with the heels of her palms. "As for you, my boykie, I think you're wise beyond your years."

"That's not true at all. I'm average."

"No, Sam. You're not. Average is the one thing you most certainly are not. If you remember anything I've ever said to you, please remember that."

"Okay." I said nothing for a while. Then I said, "Do you think we could watch the movie? I mean, just, you know, as friends?"

"Yebo," she said. "I think we could do that."

She reached over and switched on the ignition. Then she turned on the windshield wipers. The rain had slowed, and now you could see.

"Here," she said. "Come over here. It's okay. I won't bite."

I did as she said. I settled myself against her side.

"Volume …?" I said.

"Oh, right."

She raised the volume, and then she put her right arm around my shoulders, and I rested my head on her chest. We both stayed like that, both of us watching Peter Sellers in *The Pink Panther* on the huge outdoor screen, in the rain. After that night at the Newburgh Drive-In, I would never see Hilary Anson again.

As for Quinton Vasco, they found his body the next day.

PART FOUR

RIGHT FROM THE OUTSET, the police fixed their attention on
Bruce Gruber. That was no surprise. He'd had run-ins with the law
before. Besides, it turned out that there'd been a series of unexplained incidents in Kelso that summer — livestock being shot
while grazing. Bruce was already under suspicion on that account,
thanks to one or two eyewitness reports. I already knew that he, or
Edwin or Davey, was responsible for the bullet that hit my horse.

The police obtained a warrant to search the Grubers' home on a
tumbledown farm a mile or so outside Hatton. Bruce was still living
with his parents at the time. The search turned up an unlicensed
Makarov pistol along with a box of cartridges that matched the
rounds used to kill Quinton Vasco. The weapon itself was smeared
with Bruce's fingerprints. Not only that, but he also confessed to
the crime, and nothing would make him recant. He said he had
stolen the gun and shells from Hilary Anson and had shot Quinton
Vasco out of jealousy, pure and simple. He was guilty, he said —
and that was that.

As for Hilary, she was gone. Colonel Barker drove her to the
Malton airport just outside Toronto only a day after our outing at
the Newburgh Drive-In. She must have known she would be leaving

the next day, yet she said nothing. She left no message or, anyway, not for me. She simply stepped aboard an airplane and vanished. No phone call. No letter. At first I thought I would go out of my mind, and maybe I did. It was around then, after all, that I started to have these panic spells of mine. Anxiety attacks, I guess you'd call them — something I had never suffered from before. For a time my mother drove me down to Toronto once a week so that I could talk to a man there, a therapist, who taught me some calming techniques. Eventually, they seemed to help.

Still, after Hilary nothing was the same. I'm not saying it has been so terrible, my life. Just different, I guess. No Hilary, hey. I liken the experience to the lives that I imagine anosmics must lead. Anosmics: people who lack a sense of smell. It wouldn't be so horrible to be anosmic. You could still see beauty, hear music, touch skin. But something would be lost, something you would miss.

The provincial championships went on as scheduled that year, and our team won the preliminary division, no thanks to me. I scraped through the three days of competition without being eliminated — and without saying a word more than necessary to Edwin Duval — and then my score was dropped, in keeping with the formula in use at the time. As the two leading riders on the winning team, Edwin and Janet went on to compete in the national finals, held that year in Alberta. I seem to recall they did pretty well.

Not long after that Bruce Gruber was convicted of Quinton Vasco's murder, just as everyone had expected. I learned he was just seventeen years old, and that came as a surprise; he looked older. On account of his age, he was sentenced to ten years' imprisonment, the maximum allowed for a minor. Around this time the Odegaards sold their store and moved away. Before long the Duvals moved away, too. Rumours circulated for a while — something about a rape, possibly involving the Odegaard girl — and then died down. This was the way scandals were dealt with in Kelso in those days.

You went someplace else, and in time things blew over. You hoped they did.

As for those two massive cannons that Hilary and I had discovered, hidden away deep in the Quinton Vasco lands — that part of the story was eventually cleared up, too. Quinton Vasco was a sort of renegade inventor, with a specialty in ballistics and a penchant for right-wing politics. Eventually, the *Toronto Star* conducted a big investigation of the man's operations. His original plan had been to establish a testing site in Kelso for a long-range weapon he had designed, a howitzer called the GC-45, which meant "Gun, Canada, 45-calibre." The two cannons Hilary and I had stumbled upon were prototypes for the device, which was being developed under contract to the South African government. The project was delayed following Quinton Vasco's death, but it did not stop. Years later, during the 1970s and 1980s, the GC-45 would prove to be an especially deadly part of Pretoria's arsenal in its long war against Cuban and government forces in Angola. You can look it up. It's all part of the public record now.

Meanwhile, Quinton Vasco's company — known as the Space Research Corporation — relocated its testing operations to a huge tract of land sprawling across the international border between Quebec and Vermont. Around the same time Vasco's properties in Kelso were sold off for potential development as housing estates. Probably, that had been Plan B all along. In the end, the man's death made little difference. The weapons project went ahead just the same. But who could have known that then?

For my part, I did the only thing I could do. I went back to high school in Alyth, back to my gloomy teenage existence. Each day, at the end of class, I boarded a bus for the long journey home, aching with emptiness. Could she not have written? Just a paragraph? A few lines? One afternoon as I was about to climb aboard the bus at the end of another day of boredom, I noticed a group of boys in scrappy shorts and T-shirts. They were assembling outside the school gym, and they soon set off at a run, aiming toward the high drumlin that loomed above the town to the west. Something about them fired my imagination, how independent they seemed.

Before long I, too, was training every afternoon, along with a dozen or so other cross-country runners. Each day after classes we'd set off from the school grounds, headed for the drumlin. We dashed along the shaded streets of the town and then scaled a succession of footpaths that wound toward the heights of that great hill, rearing high above Alyth. We traced the drumlin's eastern summit, darting among the rocks and then racing each other through newly mown hayfields before beginning our descent.

I knew that I was neglecting Della. I knew, as well, that Charlotte had outgrown her pony, so I did what seemed the obvious thing. I handed Della Street over to my sister. When it came to horses, Charlotte had far grander ambitions than I had ever entertained, not to mention more courage and talent. It was not very long before important horse owners — people with expensive, European-bred animals — were seeking her out to ride their pedigreed equines in high-level competitions. Charlotte never quite made it to the Olympics, but her name was always in the mix. She got damned close.

As for me, I was done with horses. The decision had a lot to do with Hilary Anson, I'm sure. I was like one of those bird species — penguins or kiwis or dodos — that perversely renounce the ability to fly, preferring to skitter among the pebbles and hedges on the ground, flapping their stubby little remnant wings.

In my second year on the Alyth cross-country team, we battled all the way to the Ontario finals, where our school finished in second place. The next year we won. After that, I earned an athletic scholarship in the United States, so for four years I ran on the cross-country team at Purdue. I returned to Canada with premature arthritis and an undergraduate degree in English literature. I was determined to carry on in that field, focusing on contemporary writers of the African diaspora. I'm sure I was thinking of Hilary and her fascination with South African writing. I completed a graduate degree at the University of Toronto, followed by a doctorate at Rutgers. Eventually, I found a job as an assistant professor of English at Syracuse University in upstate New York.

During all that time I received not a word from Hilary Anson. I still thought about her, though — about her and Quinton Vasco and Bruce Gruber and that long-ago summer. For a time, while Bruce was still in jail, I wondered whether he would change his story, assuming it was only that — a story. Surely, he would recant his version now. Why stick to it any longer if it was a lie? What good would it do?

When Bruce had been eight years behind bars, I took it upon myself to visit him in a correctional facility located a couple of hours' drive east of Toronto. We met in a characterless, antiseptic room furnished with institutional tables and tube-metal chairs. He had aged badly — not that I cared. I still loathed him. Even so, it was impossible not to feel some pity for the guy. Eight years behind bars? Eight years and counting? I fully expected him to deny his guilt, even to incriminate someone else. He had no good reason to do otherwise, not now, not anymore.

But he stood by his tale. He still swore up and down that he was the killer and that he acted alone. He didn't implicate anyone else, Hilary least of all. Instead, he repeated what he had insisted all along: he shot Quinton Vasco out of jealousy and hate. I asked him if Hilary had played any part at all, any direct role. Had she encouraged him in some way, goaded him into the crime? But he said no. He insisted that he alone was responsible, and he seemed to swell with pride as he spoke. But I knew that at least part of his version was a lie, the part about Hilary, about her not being involved. He virtually admitted as much.

Only seconds after protesting that he acted alone, he drew closer to me, his chair chattering against the tiled floor. In a low voice he pleaded for news of Hilary. Anything. Anything at all. She had promised to wait for him, he said. She had sworn an oath. When he said that, I sat up straight in my chair. I felt the vertebrae shiver in my back. This was more like it. An oath. She had sworn an oath. Any other time I would have pushed him for more details. There was so much else I wanted to know. *What kind of oath? What had she said? What words exactly?*

But I saw his eyes were welling up, and I couldn't bear to put him through more pain. I almost started weeping myself, thinking of Hilary and that summer and the emptiness she'd left behind. So I let Bruce Gruber be. He had clung to his story for so long that he had probably convinced himself it was true. That was enough for me. Besides, there was the law of parsimony to consider. I was thinking once more of Professor Lisgard, my philosophy teacher from my undergrad days. It was he who introduced me to the logical principle also known as Occam's razor. Expressed in its classic form, it goes like this: "Entities must not be multiplied beyond necessity." In other words, don't overcomplicate things. When you are faced with competing explanations for some occurrence, it's generally best to go with the simplest account — and Bruce's version took that prize, hands down. He'd stolen a gun and killed a man for the most shopworn reason going: good, old-fashioned jealousy. What could be simpler than that?

Finally, there was at least one other unusual wrinkle to the case. Call it cosmic justice. Even if Bruce Gruber had not killed Quinton Vasco, he belonged in prison just the same. I thought of that terrible night down at the quarry pond, the assault on Leslie Odegaard. For that crime, Bruce had gone unpunished. And so there was a certain rightness to his being in jail, whether he'd killed Quinton Vasco or not. In the end, he got what he deserved — ten years behind bars.

I sometimes wonder what became of him after his sentence was served and he walked free, but I have never bothered to find out. I lost interest in him after that.

And the years ground past. Shortly before his seventieth birthday, my father fell ill — some unsteadiness of the heart. I drove back up to Kelso for a visit. Charlotte was going to be there, too. I hadn't set eyes on either of my parents for a year at least, and I was troubled to see how much they had aged. Charlotte was living in Alberta now, training at a big equestrian centre they have out there, a place called Spruce Meadows.

When the weekend was over, I drove back down to Syracuse, where I had recently gone through what would prove to be my first divorce. I buried myself in my work once more — my teaching load, plus a book I was working on about literature and radical politics. A few years after that I married a second time, but that venture ended in a breakup, too. There were no children in either case.

I know what a therapist would say: "Hilary Anson rides again." And maybe that would be right. I thought about her still. I wondered what I had meant to her and why she had remained silent for so very long. I hadn't heard from her in all that time, not once since she had left Kelso. Not a phone call. Not a letter. Nothing. For twenty-seven years.

FIFTY-ONE

Sam
En Route to South Africa 1994

I TRIED TO FIND her. For a time, I did. I ran down every clue I could find, but there were precious few of those, and they brought me no closer to learning Hilary's fate. Nothing changed on this front until 1994, when I was in my forties.

With a sabbatical year coming up, I decided to travel to South Africa myself. I planned to do research for a book I had in mind, a study of literature and courage — writers in sub-Saharan Africa practising their craft in the face of economic hardship and political upheaval, challenges I could barely imagine. I was lucky enough to obtain funding for the project from a philanthropic institution in New England. God knows there was nothing on the domestic scene to hold me back. I figured I could carry out both missions — conduct research for the book and also try to find Hilary or some vestige of Hilary. It had been thirty years. No, wait — it had been thirty-one.

I bought a bucket-shop ticket that took me on a roundabout route. First I flew on a small regional airline to New York City, where I had a three-hour layover at JFK before I boarded a VARIG flight, non-stop to Rio de Janeiro. There, I wandered around the departure hall at the Galeão International Airport for hours on end until finally I dragged myself aboard a South African Airways jet bound for Johannesburg. I had a window seat, and I nursed a Scotch — the first of several — as we arched high over the Atlantic, bathed in the deep, bronze light of the setting sun.

Inevitably, I started to brood once again about Hilary and the little I knew of her life before I met her. There'd been a man named Jack Tanner, who had preyed upon her and who later killed her African boyfriend or lover, a political activist named Muletsi Dadla. At the time, the two of them — Hilary and Muletsi — were trying to flee South Africa, setting off from a township called Bruntville, where a man of some authority also dwelled, a man named Everest Ndlovu. That was about all I knew. Oh, and Hilary's tale about Nelson Mandela. Supposedly, it was he who had given her that Russian gun. At age fifteen, I hadn't even known who Nelson Mandela was, and now all of humanity celebrated his name. He was the president of the whole damned country.

But at the centre of it all was Hilary. What had become of her? Did the Anson clan still live on a horse farm near a town called Mooi River? Was Jack Tanner ever put on trial for murder? If so, did Hilary testify? What became of her then? How did it all turn out? Did she ever think about me?

The drinks trolley rolled past, and I secured myself another Scotch, a double. I peered out the window, staring at a vacuum of darkness that seemed to extend in all directions. What happened? That was what I wanted to know. What the bloody hell happened?

FIFTY-TWO

Sam
South Africa, Summer 1994

I SPENT A COUPLE of days in Johannesburg, decompressing at a small guest house located in a bohemian part of town, a neighbourhood called Melville. This was the new South Africa. Apartheid was finished and done, at least in principle. Everyone had a vote, and all were equal. In theory, there was no colour bar. But it was apparent at once that matters were more complicated than that.

I did little during those first two days but walk, something I do with a cane owing to this arthritic hip of mine. I took note of everything — the children strutting along the streets in their starched school uniforms; the couriers decked out in blazers and ties as they clipped through the city on their motor scooters; the whiteness of people's teeth; the bustling newspaper vendors; the shiny Mercedes sedans; the crowded, fume-spewing bakkies; the evangelical women parading along the shaded streets in robes of white; the high, forbidding walls that seemed to enclose every dwelling, every office; the razor-wire barriers; the jacaranda trees; the electric gates.

After two days and three nights in Joburg, I flew to Durban. It was summertime in the southern hemisphere, and flowering trees festooned the streets. The sun beamed down. I rented a car and drove, very cautiously, on a course that took me out of Durban en route to Mooi River, into the very heart of that town. This was my first experience of driving on the left-hand side of the road, and I suffered one or two perilous moments. Somehow I made the trip without killing myself or anyone else. Once I was safely in Mooi River, I parked the car in a central lot and clambered out. For a time I just stood where I was, peering around, amazed that I was standing where Hilary herself might have stood.

I got straight down to business, putting questions to the people I encountered on the street — black men in threadbare jackets and cheap fedoras; black women with babies slung on their backs in knotted shawls; elderly white couples tottering along the sidewalks, the men in short pants, desert boots, and knee socks, the women in cheap floral dresses and sun hats.

I explained that I wanted information about the white folk who lived around here, the rich white folk. But I had no luck. People just shook their heads. Oh, there may have been horse farms hereabouts once upon a time, but not anymore. As for someone named Daniel Anson, people merely nodded and told me a man with such a name had been a force around here in olden times, but no longer. Gone to England, most likely — that was what they said. Gone to England along with the rest of them, the rich ones. To England or to Oz.

After a couple of hours of getting nowhere, I climbed back into my car and headed off through the hill country that surrounded the town. I didn't know what I was looking for, some pulse of recognition, I suppose. And, sure enough, the landscape matched Hilary's description, or my memory of her description — broad summits and plummeting valleys criss-crossed by narrow macadam roads, like loops of black ribbon. It wasn't difficult to imagine there might once have been vast equestrian estates hereabouts — in fact, several remained — but it seemed that none belonged to a man named Daniel Anson ... or at least not any longer.

I spent that night in Mooi River itself, in a tired little inn adjoining a bar that jittered with African pop music until 2:00 a.m. The next morning, I drove down to Pietermaritzburg and found my way to the offices of the *Witness* on Longmarket Street, said to be the oldest continually published newspaper in South Africa. I wanted to rummage through their files if they would let me. Somewhat surprisingly, they did.

"Why, certainly, Mr. Mitchell." A middle-aged woman in a red skirt and white blouse guided me straight into the paper's small, musty library. "Why not sit yourself down here?"

She said her name was Blessing Ndlovu, and she explained that the paper's files were not fully computerized and possibly never would be. Instead, she brought me several reels of microfiche from the early 1960s and patiently showed me how to feed the film through the reading machine.

I spent three hours that day hunched over a scratched wooden table, peering at decades-old film. I came across about a half-dozen references to a Daniel Anson of Mooi River. It seemed he was both a businessman — a mining magnate — and a politician. He had been the minister for national security, no less. For all his power and influence, he seemed to have kept a remarkably low profile, just a brief speech here and there, a couple of international trips on government business. I supposed that a lot of his activities would have been kept secret, not the sort of thing you would read about in the press. Still, what little information appeared in the *Witness* was enough to prove the man existed. *Had* existed.

I kept feeding the film through the reading machine, and finally I found the story I was looking for, or — let me put it another way — what I found was the story I was *not* looking for. I had hoped to find an article or two that recounted the murder or disappearance of a political dissident named Muletsi Dadla, employed as a stable hand at the farm belonging to Daniel Anson. But I didn't find that.

Instead, I stumbled onto a report about the death of Jack Tanner, the transplanted Englishman who had long tormented Hilary.

In July of 1963 a man's badly decomposed remains were discovered by a group of young herd boys in South Africa, near the border with Basutoland, then a British protectorate and now an independent country called Lesotho. They came upon the body where it had snagged itself by a wooded embankment bordering the Tsoelike River. After its discovery, the corpse was conveyed to Durban, where the British consulate got involved.

Forensic experts used dental records to identify the body while an autopsy determined the cause of death — two gunshots to the side of the head. As for suspects, the article in the *Witness* said there was just one — Muletsi Dadla, an escaped convict who had earlier been jailed after an attack on this same individual, Jack Tanner. But Dadla's whereabouts were unknown. According to the newspaper's account, he'd simply disappeared.

I found one other article that mentioned Muletsi's name — an earlier story from mid-1962 reporting the man's escape from jail. That was it. I searched as carefully as I could, but I did not come across any other news items that provided any further information. It seemed the story of Jack Tanner's death simply stopped in its tracks, and I wondered whether someone — someone with the wealth and sway of a Daniel Anson — might have put pressure on the papers to ignore the whole business. Surely, Daniel Anson would have wanted to keep his daughter out of the picture.

I stood up to stretch my legs, and I gazed through the window at the street outside. A black man in a fedora rode past on a wobbly bicycle. A pair of elderly white men stood on a nearby corner. They seemed to be engaged in a heated argument, waving their arms and berating each other in a muffled tongue that I took to be Afrikaans.

I looked back down at the table and the spools of microfiche. None of this made any sense at all. Jack Tanner had been murdered?

By Muletsi Dadla? Hilary had told me the exact opposite, that Jack Tanner killed Muletsi. Why would she lie? I shook some of the stiffness out of my legs and then set about reorganizing the spools of microfiche. Before long the woman named Blessing passed by.

"You found what you were looking for?" she said.

"In a way. I found something."

And I had. I just didn't know what it meant.

FIFTY-THREE

LET'S FACE IT: I am not a private investigator. I am an assistant professor of English literature at a university in upstate New York. I decided I had better get started on the work that had ostensibly brought me to this continent, which was to conduct interviews and carry out research in the subject area of my academic discipline. I had decided to focus on three countries — South Africa, Zimbabwe, and Nigeria — so chosen because they possessed a wealth of novelists, mostly working in English and against a backdrop of political and social unrest. South Africa was just emerging from the long night of apartheid rule, Zimbabwe was in the throes of oppression and economic mayhem under a virtual tyrant named Robert Mugabe, and Nigeria was, well ... *Nigeria.*

My adventures and mishaps during the next three months could easily fill a pair of volumes — not only the serious work of scholarship that had brought me to Africa but also another book, partly dark comedy and partly a reflection on hope and fear, a memoir that I still mean to write one day, the reflections of a naive, middle-aged white man, at loose and alone on a turbulent continent in an unsettled time.

One way or another I got through it. In fact, I thrived. When my work was done, I returned to Durban on the east coast of South

Africa. Only a couple of days remained before my departure, and I meant to spend those days searching for Hilary. I had one last idea that might help me determine what had become of her, and it meant venturing into Bruntville, the black township that neighboured Mooi River, a two-hour journey to the north.

Rather than get behind the wheel myself — a foolhardy enterprise, as I'd learned by now — I hired a car and driver, a voluble and perspicacious individual named Foster's Moyo, who spelled his first name out carefully, to be certain I understood.

"Foster's?" I said, to make sure. "Apostrophe-ess? Like the beer?"

"Exactly." He laughed, and the metal in his teeth glinted. "Just like the beer. From Australia." He hesitated. "The beer, that is. Not me."

There were two people I wanted to seek out in Bruntville, assuming either of them was still alive and dwelling there. One was Muletsi's mother. The other was a mysterious gentleman named Everest Ndlovu, who'd been a local authority of some kind, according to Hilary. I had a feeling that if anyone knew what had become of her, it would be one of these two.

The problem was I had no idea how to locate either one of them except by bumbling around, asking anyone I met. Foster's said he had a better idea.

"The barber-man," he said. "Everybody has got to get his hair cut sometime, isn't it? So if there is news, then that is where the news must come — to sit for a time, just like everyone else."

If there had been just one barbershop in Bruntville, my task might have been easier, but they seemed to be everywhere. All appeared to be hole-in-the-wall joints, each with a stool of some kind for the client and several tilting wooden or metal chairs set outside on the street, where patrons might sit while awaiting their turn, smoking cheap cigarettes, sipping corn brew, and chatting. We turned up nothing at the first place we visited, same as at the second place.

On our third try Foster's sallied into the fray, soon ingratiating himself into the ebb and flow of a conversation already underway. A quartet of men were gathered around a shaky wooden table in the gauzy shade of several flamboyant trees. Foster's informed me in a whisper that the matter under debate was tigers. Had tigers ever dwelled in Africa? The men were speaking in Xhosa, apparently, so Foster's had to translate the exchange for my benefit. The outlook of the assembly, he said, seemed to be evenly divided. Yes, tigers had once lived in Africa. No, they had not. He turned to me.

"They want to know what you think, mistah," he said. "As a white man. From the United States of America."

I didn't bother to specify that I was actually Canadian. I adjusted my hat, a straw fedora I'd picked up at a safari outfitter on First Street in Harare during my sojourn in Zimbabwe. "What should I say?"

"Whatever you like," said Foster's. "It's a free country now, isn't it?"

One of the men in the gathering climbed to his feet, offering his chair to me. "*Baas* ..." he said, no doubt out of long habit.

I thanked him in English and said I was happy to remain standing. As for the question of tigers, I said I doubted there had ever been any such creatures in Africa, but I wasn't sure. I had expected Foster's to translate my words, but that proved unnecessary. It turned out that all these men spoke English perfectly well.

"No tigers ...?" said one man, the one who had offered me his seat.

"Not as I understand it."

"And previously?" he said.

I repeated my initial comment. "I don't think so. If they had found the skeletons of tigers, then that would change things. But I don't believe they have."

"Just because a thing isn't proven," said another man, a large, imposing individual who spoke in a deep, reverberating voice, "that doesn't mean it cannot be true." He smiled. "After all, it is impossible to prove a negative."

I nodded although I disagreed. The supposed impossibility of proving a negative is a common fallacy in logic. In fact, we perform that very feat all the time. For example, to show that Hilary Anson did *not* kill Quinton Vasco, it would be sufficient simply to demonstrate that someone else did. Of course, if she *did* kill Quinton Vasco, then that would be a different proposition altogether. I briefly debated whether to mention any of this. Instead, I merely shrugged and deferred to his judgment. "Or so they say."

He gave a broad smile. Case closed, it seemed. He inclined his head, densely bearded with mixed filaments of black and grey. "And what has brought you here, *monsieur*, into our august company?"

I got straight to the point. I said I was trying to locate a woman named Mrs. Dadla or, failing that, a man named Everest Ndlovu. I briefly explained why. For a time after I had finished speaking, this arch and self-confident fellow remained silent, as if ruminating on a broad range of complex or elusive thoughts. Finally, he inclined his head once more and smiled again.

"Everest Ndlovu," he said. "At your service."

FIFTY-FOUR

Sam
South Africa, Summer 1994

I HAD SOMEHOW ENVISIONED Everest Ndlovu to be a meek sort of fellow, frail and deferential — a very different proposition from the portly, talkative, and even somewhat theatrical gentleman who appeared before me now, the one who had made the hypothetical case for tigers in Africa.

Now he spread out his arms in a gesture of welcome. "I am the man you seek."

Somewhere in his midseventies, he wore a bright, voluminous shirt in the manner of Nelson Mandela himself, as well as a pair of loose black slacks and brown tasselled loafers. With some effort, owing to his generous girth, he hauled himself to his feet. He reached for a grey trilby, which he clamped upon his large, round head, and then fumbled about for a gnarled walking stick. He brandished it at the other men.

"I will relinquish my position in this never-ending queue," he said, then glanced at me, at my cane, with what seemed a look of fellowship. "Come. We have much to discuss."

At a tottering gait, Ndlovu led us to his home several blocks away, a small cinder-block structure roofed with sheets of zinc. Flower boxes decorated the windows, which were protected by iron grates. An elderly cream-coloured automobile — a Vauxhall Astra, I determined — occupied a cramped space beside the little house.

"Behold, my humble estate." Mr. Ndlovu called out for his wife, Marimba, by name. "Come, my dear, and meet our visitors."

Before long a woman shuffled out to greet us, a slender, dignified figure in a coiled head scarf and a long African robe. Meanwhile, the three of us arranged ourselves outdoors, Foster's, Mr. Ndlovu, and I, lowering ourselves into an assortment of unstable-looking chairs arranged around a low table consisting of a repurposed wooden door mounted on cinder blocks. Soon enough Ndlovu's wife plied us with coffee and chicory served in mismatched china cups. A pair of tulip trees provided a patchy sort of shade.

Ndlovu explained that the other individual I had hoped to locate — Muletsi's mother, Mrs. Dadla — was, unhappily, no longer among us, the victim many years earlier of TB. As for himself, he said that he now served as a local organizer for the ANC, a post that afforded him certain modest perquisites, including the ownership of a private vehicle. He gestured toward the Vauxhall, then replaced his coffee cup in its saucer, and folded his arms at his chest. He turned to look at me.

"So," he said, "you have come to inquire about Muletsi Dadla."

"And Hilary Anson."

"Just so. You have come a very long way."

I said that I had a dual purpose in my mission and explained a little about my literary investigations.

"I see. And you have sought me out because …?"

"Because you knew them both, I think. Because …" I hesitated, then decided to get straight to the point. "Do you have any idea where they are now? Do you know what happened to them?"

He nodded. "It is possible that I do. But, first, tell me what you know."

"Not very much," I said.

Still, I told him what I could. I had known Hilary for just three months or so, the time she had spent in Canada during the summer of 1963. Possibly, she had been sent to Canada by her father to avoid scandal here in South Africa. Or maybe, for all I knew, the ANC had dispatched her on a mission to assassinate Quinton Vasco. Here, I shrugged and rolled my eyes, as if this version of events could not possibly be true. I briefly explained about the arms maker and his death, but I had a feeling that Everest Ndlovu was in possession of this information already. As for Hilary, at the end of that summer, as far as I knew, she had simply disappeared.

Mr. Ndlovu stroked his chin with its thick brush of stubble, like some African oracle. He continued to peer at me but said nothing, so I kept right on going.

I told him about the news report I had found in the archives of the newspaper in Pietermaritzburg — the *Witness*.

"Ah," he said. "My daughter works at that place."

I nodded. I realized now that I had probably met her that day in Pietermaritzburg. The librarian who helped me — her name had been Ndlovu. Something Ndlovu. I was pretty sure of that. I nodded again and went on. According to an article I had read, it was Jack Tanner who had died and Muletsi Dadla who had supposedly killed him — the very opposite of what Hilary had told me. The report had contained no mention of her at all.

Throughout this monologue, Foster's, my driver, said nothing. He merely let his gaze shift back and forth between Mr. Ndlovu and me, his mouth agape. He hadn't bargained on this — these tales of death and mystery.

"You seem to be in a fix," said Mr. Ndlovu.

He shook his head in what I took to be amusement and then scratched his jaw for a time. When he spoke next, it was to call for his wife to bring more coffee. "Or would a stronger libation be preferred? I believe we have a carton or two of iJuba in the refrigerator. You have sampled our traditional beer?"

In fact, I had. In Zimbabwe on one memorable evening, I had tried to drink the stuff. Chibuku, it was called in that country. I could not say I had enjoyed the experience.

"Maybe just coffee?" I said.

Again, Mr. Ndlovu laughed.

I waited for a beat or two and then posed the question. "Who shot Jack Tanner?"

Mr. Ndlovu closed his eyes, smiled to himself, and opened his eyes again. "That is one question. Surely you know the answer already, or you can guess. The next question is who killed the other one, this, uh, this Quinton Vasco. Who was the killer there?"

He peered at me for a time, then shrugged and looked away. Soon he shifted in his seat and again fixed his gaze on me. He kept me in his sights while his wife brought more coffee. Then he shrugged again and smiled and asked me to wait where I was. I watched as he hauled himself to his feet. Clutching his cane in his right hand, he lumbered into the small house. When he returned several minutes later, he was carrying a crumpled manila envelope. He held it out to me.

"I believe," he said, "that this is for you."

I took the parcel from him and placed it on my knees. I could tell at a glance that it was addressed to someone, but I had to fumble for my eyeglasses before I could discern whose name was written there. At once I started in surprise, the hackles rising on the back of my neck. Of all the possible addressees, this was the least expected. The name that was written on that envelope was mine. *Mr. Sam Mitchell, in care of Mr. Everest Ndlovu.* The following lines contained a Bruntville address. I glanced at the postmark — Maputo, Mozambique. There was no return address, and I could not make out the date stamp. I peered up at Mr. Ndlovu with what must have been a look of bafflement.

Again, he laughed. "I am something of a clutter-bug, I fear — the bane of my beloved's existence. I have kept this for you during so many years. It was all that I could do. I didn't know where else to send it. I didn't know you from Adam. But now you are here."

I was about to tear the parcel open right on the spot, but Mr. Ndlovu put out his hands and ordered me to desist. His tone was suddenly urgent.

"Forgive me, but I have lived in southern Africa in darker times than these. You might easily be opening a parcel bomb."

"A what ...?" I glared down at the envelope on my lap. The package suddenly seemed to glow, it seemed hot to the touch, as if it really might contain an explosive of some kind. I was tempted to fling it away, but I fought off the urge.

"Very well," he said and nodded at me. "I am no doubt guilty of excessive caution, but I have not survived all these years in this country by taking unnecessary risks. If you are going to open that parcel, I would request that you do so alone — and some distance from here. Even that might not suffice. I am far too old to be mopping up the residues of overly impetuous men."

I swallowed. "All right. I understand."

After a time he began to swirl what remained of the coffee in his cup, as if contemplating what to say or do next. "Come," he said at last. He set down the cup and clambered to his feet. "I have something to show you. It isn't far."

He called out to his wife, to inform her that we were off. Then, listing upon his cane, Mr. Ndlovu led Foster's and me on a short walk that soon brought us to a pair of narrow, intersecting streets — just lanes, really, uneven and overgrown.

"Look."

He pointed to a pair of wooden signs, already cockeyed and fading, that marked the intersection of these two forlorn-looking alleys. In fading, hand-lettered script, one of the signs said *Sonya Abrahams Road*; the other, *Wilson Themba Street*.

These, he said, were the names by which Hilary Anson and Muletsi Dadla had come to be known — known to some. I took note of the inadvertent play on words in the name *Sonya Abrahams Road*. Yes, she did. She rode like an angel, if angels could ride.

"I seem to recall that there is a bench hereabouts," said Mr. Ndlovu. He gazed around. "A place where a civilized man might sit."

And so there was, a wooden park bench, squatting awkwardly amid the unkempt grass, large enough and sturdy enough to contain us three. We arranged ourselves there, with Mr. Ndlovu in the middle. He was silent for a time; then he began to speak. Regarding the murder of Jack Tanner, he said, the entire affair had been a set-up, one that he himself had devised, with the eventual approval of the ANC leadership. It was he who put Jack Tanner in the know, informed him of Hilary and Muletsi's whereabouts, of their planned escape from South Africa on horseback. As a result, Jack ceased to be the hunter and became the prey. Why, even Nelson Mandela had gotten involved. After that, said Mr. Ndlovu, the only surprise was the identity of the shooter, the one who fired the shots that killed Jack Tanner.

"Muletsi Dadla," I said. Surely this was known.

Mr. Ndlovu shook his head. "No. On the contrary."

"*Hilary...?*"

He nodded, then laughed. "None of us could believe it. A girl ...! A *white* girl ...! Daughter of a government minister! No, no, no. Impossible to credit. And yet it was so." He heaved a loud sigh and fixed his gaze on me. "What do you make of it?"

I was unsure what to say or whether to say anything at all. *Hilary...?* It had been Hilary? Even before she'd appeared in Kelso, long before that, she had already done this? Murdered a man? Killed Jack Tanner? By rights, I should have been horrified. Instead, I was amazed. Thrilled, even. I shook my head. I had nothing to say.

Mr. Ndlovu smiled — glad to be the purveyor of unsettling news, I suppose. After a short pause, he picked up the reins of his narrative and carried on. When he was done talking, the man let his shoulders slump. He said that I myself would have to fill in the rest. Perhaps the contents of the manila envelope might help me. Perhaps they would blow me to kingdom come.

As for himself, he could use a carton of traditional beer, a carton or two. His throat was that dry. He hauled himself upright and led us on foot back to Foster's's car. From there, we gave the man a lift to his home and soon left him behind us, with his wife and his memories and his stock of iJuba beer.

Foster's drove me south to Durban. Somewhere along the way, he cleared his throat rather more loudly than was strictly necessary. He asked me if he might revisit the conversation of that afternoon.

"If you like."

"About this Quinton Vasco chap ..."

"Yes?"

"You did not answer the question."

"What question?"

"Who it was who killed him? You were asked, but you did not say."

"You are very curious."

He nodded. "I have been told so before."

At first I didn't answer. I gazed out the window at a riddle of decrepit shops and slanting makeshift houses, all speeding past in the dwindling light. My head was on fire. The manila envelope seemed to scorch my hands. Who killed Quinton Vasco? Finally, I told him that I did not know.

We passed the rest of our journey in silence. It was seven o'clock in the evening and almost dark by the time Foster's drew up outside my hotel, near the end of my African adventure. The following morning I would board a plane to begin the long journey back to

Syracuse. Now I stood at the hotel entrance and watched as Foster's drove off. Dead, of course — Hilary and Muletsi. Both of them dead. I turned and walked into the hotel.

Upstairs, in my room, I placed the manila envelope on the bed, where it seemed to glow. By now my muscles were cramped from tension. My pulse was racing, and I was close to hyperventilating. I was that worked up. During the drive back to Durban, it had been all I could do to restrain myself from tearing this parcel apart, bomb or no bomb. All these years I had dwelled in a sort of gloom-ridden slough, not only because Hilary had vanished, but also because she had made no effort to communicate with me — no letter, no phone call, no hastily scribbled note. If nothing else, surely, she had owed me that.

And now, this package. It had somehow remained intact through all these long years. I was certain it was Hilary who'd sent it. Who else? I raised the envelope to my nose and sniffed at the sealed flap, an absurd gesture, I know. Did I think I could identify an explosive by its smell? Besides, was it likely that Hilary would send me a bomb? Why on earth would she do such a thing? It was ridiculous to think that this package contained a weapon of any kind. Ndlovu had a gift for melodrama, that was all. Oh, hell. I didn't care. I took the envelope in both hands, and I tore it open.

THREE WEEKS AFTER I returned from South Africa, my parents moved into new quarters, a two-bedroom condo in a newly constructed building in Hatton. Condos in Hatton! It seemed like a contradiction in terms. I remembered the place as a small farming village with a car-repair shop and a single store. But this was progress, I suppose. Anyway, the move proceeded without incident, and my presence was required for only a couple of days, long enough for me to drink too much Scotch, get in my mother's way, conduct several aimless conversations with my father, and say my goodbyes.

It was late morning when I climbed into my car and drove off, aiming south toward Mississauga and the Queen Elizabeth Way, on a journey that would take me around the western reaches of Lake Ontario and then eastward into New York State and on to Syracuse, a five- or six-hour drive. I was feeling downhearted, as I had been for days, ever since I got back from Africa. I was also feeling old, and my father's dwindling health had only added to my sorrows on that account. Age. Age and its afflictions. That wasn't all. For years now, I had resented my father, considered him a traitor of sorts, all because he had once worked for Quinton Vasco. I no longer felt that way. I understood now that he must have had his motives. I had learned, for example, that he'd once scraped through a lean patch, after some investments of his went sour. He'd been *that* close to declaring bankruptcy. It seemed he had gone to work for Quinton Vasco for the oldest of reasons: he needed the money. He'd done what he thought was best, and that was it. I had to let it go.

Not far south of Hatton, I surrendered to a sudden impulse. I was still thinking of Hilary, of course — of Hilary and Quinton Vasco and everything else. I flicked on my left-hand turn signal, slowed down, and peeled off onto Number Four Sideroad. The next leg was shorter than I remembered. In a matter of minutes, I reached the Quinton Vasco lands, or what had once been the Quinton Vasco lands. That large tract of terra firma presented an entirely different aspect now. I pulled over onto the shoulder of the road and stopped the car.

For a time I merely stared out the windshield. The chain-link fences were gone, of course, but so were the open fields, broad slopes, and the vast phalanx of maple bush. I barely recognized what I was seeing. Once, green hills had rolled like waves through a sea of grass that churned to the distant edge of the escarpment, bordered by a shoreline of trees. Now I saw only serpentine asphalt drives, fanciful street lamps, two-car garages, and houses.

The houses were massive, all constructed in an ersatz Cape Cod style that seemed weirdly incongruous here in rural southern Ontario. But I suppose Kelso isn't truly rural anymore. It's practically a suburb of Toronto. I eased myself out of the car and continued on foot. I wanted to take a closer look at this startling transformation. I had so many memories of this place, yet for decades I had avoided coming back, owing to events or circumstances I preferred not to recall. Now something had changed. Some blockage had been cleared from my mind. Probably, I could blame my trip to Africa for that. It had shed new light on everything — or not light exactly. Different shadows. Still, one way or another, I now knew that Hilary and I had been even closer confederates than I had ever imagined. Maybe for that reason I was now willing to confess — at least to myself — what I had kept bottled up for so very long.

I wandered for a time along these twisting streets, most of them bearing twee monikers such as Heartfelt Crescent or Sweetdreams Parkway. Eventually, I found Quinton Vasco Boulevard — was I the only individual in this drama never to be immortalized by a road? — and I turned to plod along a portion of its length, as if drawn by some irresistible force. I had to make careful use of this cane of mine, for my balance is apt to be shaky. I tramped on until I reached a high point two hundred yards or so north of Number Four Sideroad. Here, I drew to a halt.

More than three decades had crept past since that afternoon in late August 1963, the afternoon when I had last stood here, at this spot or very near it. Now I took a deep breath and peered around at all these houses with their dormer windows and pastel hues. It wasn't long before my head began to swim. I felt dizzy, a haze of vertigo, as if I might fall right down. I managed to steady myself with my cane, and my thoughts slowly cleared.

I wondered if the people who lived in these houses had any idea that Quinton Vasco was murdered right here — or right *about* here. I found it difficult to fix the location exactly. So much time had passed, so very much had changed, the view not least of all. The view was stunning, or it used to be. Even in my roaring panic — with Vasco's body prone upon the grass beside me, his skull and face disfigured beyond recognition, the blood — I had felt compelled to keep still and to take stock of the view. Even now, all these years later, I can remember it perfectly well, the riffling grass and cerulean sky, the fleets of platinum clouds. My ears had been ringing, yet I had stood my ground, transfixed, unable to do anything but watch as that vast panorama seemed to detach itself from my shrinking world, detach itself and drift away, luffing into the past, stealing my boyhood with it and scuttling all the possibilities of that summer, possibilities that once had seemed endless.

I remember that Vasco's body had suddenly jerked or twitched — some involuntary post-mortem spasm, I guess — but it had seemed for all the world as if he were coming back to life. He would have to be killed again! The prospect so horrified me that I could think of nothing else.

After the second shot, I turned and began to run. I kept on running, through that field of alfalfa grass, out the unlocked gates, and then south along Second Line toward the Barkers' place, toward Hilary. I remember how deafening it all seemed — the pealing in my ears, the crazy whine of the cicada, the panting of my lungs. I ran and ran, and I suppose that I have kept on running all these years, ever since that pre-lapsarian afternoon in August 1963, when my world changed forever.

Now, from somewhere nearby, I heard a screen door slap shut. A lawn mower buzzed in the distance then faded. A woman's voice called out to some child to "stop that, stop that this instant." I reached up with my free hand to massage my forehead. I felt a headache coming on. Pulling the trigger — that had been the easy part, strange as it may seem. The hard part had come several days earlier, in the back seat of Colonel Barker's car, when I removed the Makarov pistol from Hilary's bag. After that, everything had seemed to carry me along as if I were being propelled by some force of nature, a fast-flowing river that bore me downstream. It had been no great feat to goad Quinton Vasco into meeting me in that field. Where the enticement of sex is concerned, it seems a man will do almost anything. Once there, I knew what to do. I'd seen enough Perry Mason episodes to understand the basic working of a gun. Meanwhile, I had somehow convinced myself that I had a lofty purpose to uphold — to seek revenge for an African's death, to defend a woman's honour.

What nonsense it was, what drivel. Who was Muletsi Dadla to me, alive or dead? His supposed murder was a lie that Hilary told because it suited her to tell it. Now I understood the truth, and the truth was this: I had avenged a falsehood. I had wagered my life for no good reason, for nothing at all.

Well, not for nothing. For Hilary.

That night down by the quarry ponds, when Quinton Vasco punched Hilary in the face and then kicked her — it was then that I made my decision. I knew what I was going to do. "Fuck with me," he'd said, "and that's what you get." And I had thought *Oh …? Oh, really?*

Two days later, when I found her at the end of my harrowing foot race from the Quinton Vasco lands, Hilary did not seem shocked at all. She was lounging on the patio, reading a book, wearing only a bikini. I babbled uncontrollably, yet she took it all in, as if my words made perfect sense. What was more, she seemed to know exactly what to do next. It was as if she had worked everything out in advance.

"Give me the gun," she said. She quickly engaged the safety, something I had neglected to do. "Wait here."

She hurried inside to dress. Later we drove to Bruce Gruber's place, and Hilary delivered the weapon to him while I waited in the car, keeping my head tucked out of sight. After that we headed up to Newburgh, where we watched *The Pink Panther* on the big outdoor screen, attracting as much attention as Hilary deemed necessary. Either I was her alibi or she was mine. And then she was gone.

And that parcel? The one that Hilary sent me from Mozambique, in care of Mr. Ndlovu? It did not contain much, but what it did contain represents everything that I now possess of Hilary Anson, everything that I ever will — a dog-eared copy of *Cry, the Beloved Country* inscribed to me, along with a one-page letter written in her cramped and slanting hand.

In it, she admitted what I already knew to be the truth. It was she who had shot Jack Tanner by the banks of the Tsoelike River, she who helped to roll his body into the water's flow. I suppose he'd had it coming. Of course, he did. Still, it stunned me to know she had been a murderer even then, even before I first met her, before she first set foot in Kelso County. Maybe I should be repelled by that knowledge, yet, strangely, I am not. Just the opposite, in fact. She lived her life for a cause, and that is vastly more than I can say for myself. The truth is, I honour her for what she was and for what she did. I always will.

In her letter, she explained the silence she had maintained for all those years. It was simple, really. Any communication between us might have been monitored by the Canadian authorities and could have incriminated me. This would remain true, she wrote, at least until the statute of limitations ran out — which practically made me laugh. She was dead wrong there. In Canada, there is no such statute, not for murder. I will dwell beneath this thunderhead for the rest of my days.

I wonder, did she cast some brand of spell on me? Did she work some hoodoo with my mind, just as she seemed to do with Bruce Gruber, just as she so easily did with horses, bending their will to her own, sans saddle, sans bridle? I wish I knew the answer, but I understand now that I never will. Because there *is* no answer. You might as well ask if free will exists. Maybe it does. Maybe it doesn't. Either way, the sensation is the same. Either way, we believe that we are free. But we can never truly know.

She made no mention in her letter of Quinton Vasco, not a word. Still, she told me she remembered that last day, that final night, just the two of us in Mrs. Barker's rented car at the Newburgh Drive-In. She ended with a trio of sentence fragments split by ellipses. *If I had been younger … if you had been older … if the world had been ordered a different way …*

If. If. If.

Her letter was dated December 3, 1976 — nearly two decades ago. She had signed it, *Love, Hilary.*

And now here I was, back at the scene of the crime for the first time in three long decades. All those years I had tortured myself with one question above all others: Had I meant anything to Hilary Anson at all? Now I suppose I had an answer — an answer of sorts. She wrote that letter, after all. She trusted that one day I would embark upon an African odyssey of my own. In a way, she reached from beyond the grave to renew contact with me. I must have mattered to her, at least a little, for her to do that. I must have lived in her thoughts for a time.

That night in Durban, back in my hotel room, after my session with Mr. Ndlovu, after I learned what had become of her, I had wept. I sobbed like a child, without shame or restraint. It was only to be expected, I suppose. Hilary Anson had been at the centre of my life for so long, ever since that summer when I was fifteen years old. And then, in an instant, she was gone. Finally, I could mourn. Now here I was in Kelso once more, on a street named for Quinton Vasco. I sensed my eyesight beginning to blur yet again. I clasped my cane to my side with one arm and reached up with my free hand to dab the dampness away. My vision cleared a little, and I gazed out at what remained of that shimmering view, now mostly obscured by houses and sidewalks, by street signs and parked cars.

Well, people have to live somewhere.

A vehicle approached along the roadway, and the driver slowed, ducking his head to squint up at me. I could tell what he was thinking. Here was a stranger, a man who did not belong in this place, a trespasser arousing suspicion. I had no wish to disturb the peace, so I turned to trudge back to my car, thinking of the long drive ahead, across the border and on to Syracuse. I remembered what awaited me there. I had a book to write. I did have that. In all my brooding over Hilary these last days, I had almost forgotten about this other project, the reason I had travelled to Africa in the first place. A book. An important, even necessary, book. I felt the tug of it now, like a pang in my gut.

As I walked toward my car, I heard a once-familiar sound — the clip-clop beat of horse hooves drumming along a blacktop road. I looked up just in time to see a pair of teenaged girls on horseback, striding eastward along Number Four Sideroad at an extended trot. They wore sneakers, blue jeans, and T-shirts, their long hair rippled behind them, and they were tending in the direction of the old quarry ponds. Both of them were laughing, maybe on account of something that one of them had just said or maybe because it was springtime in Kelso and laughing was what you did. What some people did.

I held these two riders in my gaze for as long as I could manage, but soon they vanished beyond a blind of Cape Cod houses and maple trees. They disappeared from my view, just as everything eventually does, just as everything finally will. I shuffled back to my car and climbed inside. I started the engine, eased the vehicle around, and drove off along the fresh-paved road, aiming for someplace like home.

ON A SWELTERING NIGHT in midsummer, a South African couple drives out along the Marginal, the arching boulevard that snakes along the seacoast, dividing Maputo from the Indian Ocean. Their car is a second-hand Renault sedan, which the driver parks outside a quaintly named establishment, O Restaurante Mini-Golf, famed for its prawns in piri piri sauce. The two stroll across the terrace and find a table by the pool. She wears bell-bottomed blue jeans and a beige halter top, and her bottle-blond hair is tied in a loose ponytail that barely brushes the back of her neck — a relief in this seething climate. Her skin glows with a glaze of perspiration, for the air practically steams even now, well after sunset. She doesn't care. She loves this languor, this stillness, this heat.

Her companion wears leather sandals, tie-dyed jeans, and a grey T-shirt with a likeness of the Fab Four stencilled on the chest. He points over his shoulder toward the bar and raises his eyebrows, posing a question. He means beer.

She smiles. "*Por favor.*"

He grins in return, then rises to his feet, and ambles over to the poolside bar, its roof fashioned of thatched palm fronds. She watches him stride away, his arms glistening in the heat, his shoulders square, his back tapered. She shivers, despite the humid and stultifying air. To distract herself, she turns to peer out into the darkness, punctuated here and there by the pilot lights of fishing boats returning late to harbour. The heat ploughs back, and she vainly fans herself with the restaurant's one-page menu, laminated in plastic.

For two years now these two have lived in this Portuguese-speaking city overlooking the Indian Ocean on the east coast of Africa. Already, most of the Portuguese settlers have fled, taken the so-called chicken run, all thrown into a panic following the collapse of the Marcelo Caetano regime in Lisbon. That long-feared calamity led to this territory's sudden independence under majority rule. *Black rule*. Almost overnight, the armed rebels of Frelimo paraded in triumph into the capital, discharging their automatic rifles into the sultry blue sky, waving from the armour-plated turrets of their commandeered tanks. Once known as Lourenço Marques, the city has been rechristened Maputo, and now this mixed-race South African couple are residents here. Residents in exile. After all, it is safe in this handsome seaside town — relatively safe — or so it is said. Of course, in this treacherous portion of the world, *relatively safe* means not very safe at all. A war is underway, a brutal counter-revolutionary war, and spies are everywhere. Spies, saboteurs, assassins. It is said the presence of a revolutionary government in Mozambique will hasten the demise of apartheid in South Africa. That very fact is what makes this place so dangerous, for South Africa's agents are on the prowl everywhere, picking off their enemies one by one.

It is for this reason that the two of them have established themselves here. As a front, she runs a travel agency, a small office with a basement flat that serves as a clandestine safe house for her compatriots, ANC freedom fighters shuttling in and out of Mozambique. Nor is that all. At times she and her companion have been required to undertake secret operations themselves. They have killed; both of them have. She recalls the dates and the circumstances, but almost never the names. That makes it easier, or anyway less wrenching — not to recollect the names. She learned that much from the first one. Jack. She'd had no choice, yet the memory pains her still.

Now her companion returns to the table with two bottles of Manica, both sweating with condensation. He settles back into his chair, stretches out his long legs.

They spank the heels of the bottles together, raise the rims to their lips, swallow the rising foam. She is happy and she knows it — happy not in spite of the wars and the dangers but because of them. Conflict rages all around: the struggle against apartheid in South Africa; the bush war here in Mozambique; the fire burning just inland, in Rhodesia; the battlefields of Angola. Everywhere you look, men are killing each other, which is terrible, a sickening waste. But it is necessary, too. Nothing is going to change without a fight. *A luta continua!* Almost everywhere you cast your gaze, armed liberation outfits are bristling, in nearly all the frontline states. They are fighting against white oppression and for black freedom — Frelimo, SWAPO, ZANU, ZAPU, MPLA, ANC. She sounds the abbreviations in her mind, thrilling at the muscular impression they make.

The waitress shuffles over in flip-flops, a halter top, and a short black skirt. They both order prawns — huge Mozambican prawns with piri piri sauce, accompanied by hot, salted chips.

"*Duas mais cervejas,*" she says.

"*Sem.*" The waitress turns and heads back to the kitchen.

He winks at her, and she knows he means her Portuguese. After only two years' practice, he now speaks the language almost as though it were his mother tongue. Meanwhile, she struggles to order a beer or to ask directions in the street. She finds she can get by, more or less, in English.

Later they share a final round of beers and a third plate of prawns, and only then do they totter out into the parking lot. Behind the wheel, he guides the car along the mostly empty streets that tunnel beneath the arching branches of the jacaranda trees. Before long, he pulls up to the gate at their home, on a high spit of land with a view of Delagoa Bay.

As usual, she climbs out of the car first so that she can unlock the wrought-iron gate. Now she swings it open and stands back as he manoeuvres the car inside, onto the small cobblestone pad with its flimsy shelter of corrugated zinc. She steps through the gate, pulls it shut, fastens the padlock. He slides out of the car, quickly checking to make sure all the doors are locked. They both stroll past the small yard in front, surrounded by tall brick walls and sheltered by a Bauhinia tree, its ivory flowers glimmering in the murky garden light. They trace the flagstone walkway around to the side entrance.

The house is a low, whitewashed bungalow built in the Cape Dutch style, protected by iron bars at every point of ingress or egress. The bars cover each window, each door. Once you are inside the house, it is a job to get back out. If a fire were to strike, good luck to you. The precautions are a nuisance — everyone agrees about that — but it is taken for granted that robbery is the greater threat, robbery or worse. They have learned the hard way that it really is better to be safe, never mind the retrograde politics of it. A fortress mentality, it is called. You deal with it as best you can.

She opens the iron grate, followed by the sturdy wooden side door. She steps inside and, almost immediately, she stops.

"Love," she says.

"Yes, pet?"

"Look." She nods toward the wooden counter that forms a border between the kitchen and the dining room. Someone has placed a large poinsettia atop the counter. It squats upon a china plate.

"Where did that come from?"

He reaches back and switches on the overhead electric light. She winces in the sudden glare and then refocuses her gaze. The countertop. The unexplained poinsettia. She walks over to inspect the plant more closely, to see if there is a card. She probes the branches but turns up nothing.

"Where did it come from?"

"I don't know," he says. "It must have been João."

True enough. It must have been João. He is the houseboy — an absurd misnomer, considering the man is fifty years old at least. Anyway, there is no other explanation for the plant. João must have put it here. But why?

"We'll sort it out in the morning," he says. "I'm sure there's a good explanation." He hesitates. "Or maybe it was Lisa. Lisa and Ham."

He means Lisa and Hamilton Bennett, a couple of Americans they know, both employed by a research-and-documentation centre that promotes women's rights and social justice. The four of them have been good friends for a year or so, pretty good friends. Maybe they dropped by, unannounced, bearing a gift. Maybe they left it with João.

"Okay," she says. "All right."

The poinsettia makes her think. It reminds her of something she read one time, a tale of horrible customs in a country ruled by generals. In that land, dissidence was not tolerated, and death squads were dispatched in the night to silence those who spoke out. It was an evil business, but one with an odd quirk. Before launching a lethal mission, those same death squads first observed an unlikely drill, almost genteel in its way. They arranged for daffodils to be delivered to the targeted address, along with a card inscribed with a single chilling remark: *Flowers in the desert die.* Fair warning, it was called. If you received those flowers and that card, you knew what you had to do. You had to flee the country — Guatemala, was it? Otherwise, you were dead.

Funny. Why has this strange, unexplained poinsettia made her think of that eerie ritual in some faraway land? Who put the poinsettia here? Surely there is some harmless explanation, yet she wonders, *A poinsettia? Why a poinsettia?* From somewhere in her memory, she feels a long-forgotten stab of fear.

"Come," she says. "We'll ask João in the morning. Now let's go to bed."

That night she sleeps poorly, which probably explains why she hears the thump, a muffled impact of some kind. If she'd been asleep, she never would have noticed it, but she wasn't and now she has. She remains where she is, peering up at the tin ceiling tiles, barely discernible in the darkness. She tells herself it was nothing, the sound she heard — or not nothing. Anything. It could have been anything. She decides to ignore it, but just as quickly she realizes she will never fall asleep now, not with this doubt in her mind. She thinks of waking him, but he is dead to the world, his breathing slow and rhythmic. Leave the poor man alone.

She climbs from the bed and glides out into the hallway barefoot, dressed only in a slip. She crosses the hall and steps into the living room, thinking that the sound came from here or maybe just outside, beyond the window, where the car is parked. Just then she sees something strange — a faint illumination, visible through the window. As quickly as it appeared, it vanishes. She takes a step closer to the window.

Seconds later, she sees it again — a pale glow inside their car. What is it? Not a torch. Nothing so bright as that. The light flickers and goes out, but she is certain she's seen it and just as certain she's seen something else, too. A man's face, hey. The outline of a man's face. She waits for the light to reappear, and so it does, first flaring, then fading. It is a match, the thin light of a match. This time, she can make out the silhouettes of at least three faces — three men's faces in the car beside the house.

Her heart pounds, but she realizes at once what they are. Radio thieves. They have broken into the car using a blanket of some kind to dull the sound of the window as it crumbled beneath the blow of a brick or a rock. Then they climbed inside. This has happened before, twice before. A bloody nuisance is what it is, but not surprising, not when you consider the poverty and unemployment here. Regarded in that way, it is a wonder their car isn't vandalized every single night.

The break-in is an aggravation, of course, but it isn't the end of the world. The thieves will steal the radio, nothing more, leaving an empty slot in the dashboard along with a dangling cable, and off they will go. There is nothing she can do about it now, nothing that he could do, either. It is like a mugging in the street — better just to let it happen, to suffer through. You never know where a confrontation might lead. She waits and watches. Before long the men creep out of the car. There are three of them, just as she thought. They trot back toward the yard, three ghostly shapes, doubled over. She crosses the living room so she can watch as, one by one, they vault over the front wall. It seems they've put down blankets to counter the broken shards of glass embedded there. In a flash, they are gone.

She wonders once again whether she ought to wake him but decides against it. There is nothing to be done now. In the morning, there will be a broken car window needing replacement, not to mention a radio. But that is tomorrow's concern. Now she will simply return to bed. She will tell him in the morning, tell him what she has seen.

Several hours later, right on schedule, the sun explodes over Maputo, and the two of them bustle about, showering, dressing, preparing breakfast. The poinsettia still rests on the countertop. *Dear God, what is it doing there?* When João turns up, dressed in his customary beige work clothes, she asks him, "Where in God's name did this come from?"

He shrugs. Speaking in his broken English, he says it is a mystery to him. He found it on the concrete stoop the evening before, on his return from some errands at the shops. No card. No nothing. Just a plant. He wonders how it got past the gate. Whoever brought it must have found a way.

"All right," she says. "That's fine. We'll sort it all out in due course. Still, it is curious. Right bloody curious."

Just now, it is time to be off, she to the travel agency that she runs, located in a small unit at a commercial mall downtown. From there, he will take the car to the garage, see to the window and the radio. On second thought, maybe it would be better to dispense with the radio, once and for all. It is an invitation to thieves.

She struggles with the clasp of her brown-leather briefcase, stuffed to overflowing with tickets and brochures, memos and bills. *Why a poinsettia? Why that, of all flowering plants?* He waits as she fusses, then holds the door open for her. Meanwhile, João trots out to the front gate, releases the padlock, pushes the barrier open, and stands there waiting, shoulders thrust back, like a soldier on parade.

Once she is settled in the passenger seat, he closes the door and strides around the bonnet to the driver's side. He gets in.

"Beautiful day," he says.

And she smiles. It is a joke between them. In Maputo, the days are almost uniformly beautiful. It isn't really necessary to remark upon the weather.

"Perfect," she says and watches as he slides the key into the ignition and starts to turn the switch. She has a sudden terrible thought. "*Wait —!*"

She catches the sound of her own voice but hears nothing after that. Neither of them does. They say you never do.

AUTHOR'S NOTE

SWIMMING WITH HORSES is a work of fiction, and all of the events and characters described in its pages are either wholly imaginary or else recruited from the real world to serve imaginary but credible purposes. For example, the novel includes a cameo appearance by Nelson Mandela himself, a turn that some readers might find somewhat disconcerting, for it is at this point that Mandela issues Hilary and Muletsi a Russian-made Makarov pistol and gives the go-ahead for Muletsi to assassinate Jack Tanner. This scene is an invention, of course, but it is not out of sync with the real world as it was at that time. Mandela, who died in 2013 at age ninety-five, is now all but universally regarded as having been a beacon of peaceful struggle in the long campaign against apartheid in South Africa. But that is not the whole story.

Certainly, in his later years, Mandela was a champion of non-violent protest, but it wasn't always so. As a leader of the African National Congress's youth wing in the late 1950s, he advocated far more aggressive tactics than those favoured by the organization's sclerotic old guard. In the wake of the infamous Sharpeville massacre in March 1960, Mandela concluded that the struggle could no longer be waged by peaceful means alone. The following year he became the founding commander of *Umkhonto we Sizwe* — or Spear of the Nation — the ANC's military wing. Unfortunately, he was captured roughly a year later. Following the Rivonia Trial, he was sentenced to life in prison; in fact, his incarceration lasted twenty-seven years. As a result, it is difficult to say for certain which forms of violence he might have endorsed had he remained at large. Still, I don't think it's too much of a stretch to think he might have approved the assassination of a villain as toxic as Jack Tanner, had the occasion arisen at any time, whether before or during Mandela's imprisonment. Prior to his capture, Mandela himself sometimes carried a gun — the very same Makarov pistol that is put to murderous, if fictional, use in the pages of this book. That weapon was real, a gift presented by Haile Selassie, the Emperor of Ethiopia. The gun probably still exists, possibly buried under a house in a suburb of Johannesburg, as one version has it. I have given the pistol a different fate.

The same goes for another possibly unexpected element of the plot — the tale of the two huge howitzer cannons that Hilary and Sam discover when they venture onto the Quinton Vasco lands one afternoon in late summer. I have taken several liberties here, but the essential ingredients of my made-up account are derived from the true story of one Gerald Bull, a Canadian arms inventor who is the model for the fictional Quinton Vasco. The real-life Bull developed a hyper-accurate, long-range cannon called the GC-45 while heading a company called Space Research Corporation, which operated a testing range along the Quebec-Vermont border. The weapons were eventually sold to South Africa and played a prominent and deadly role in the war against Cuban and government forces in Angola in the 1970s and 1980s. Not unlike Quinton Vasco, his fictional avatar, Bull came to a violent end, shot to death outside his Brussels apartment in 1990. Some say he was gunned down by an Iraqi assassin. Others insist he was dispatched by an agent of Mossad, the Israeli foreign intelligence service. Nearly thirty years after his death, the truth remains a mystery.

ACKNOWLEDGEMENTS

DURING THE WRITING OF this novel, I received invaluable advice and encouragement from friends and colleagues who include Don Gillmor, Adrienne Kerr, and Jackie Kaiser, my agent, each of whom read the manuscript multiple times and had plenty to say, not all of it positive by any means but all of it helpful. Either way, they kept my spirits alive. Cynthia Villegas provided an island of support during some disheartening stretches that finally ended on an otherwise dreary November afternoon when an email hopped into view on my computer screen. It was from Scott Fraser, acquisitions editor at Dundurn Press, and it began with the magic words: "I want to make an offer ..." My thanks to him and to all the devoted literati at Dundurn, including Kathryn Bassett, Michelle Melski, Kathryn Lane, Jenny McWha, and Tabassum Siddiqui. Freelance editor (and violinist) Kate Unrau turned the dreaded editing process into a collaboration of pure pleasure, while David Drummond conjured the stunning cover literally out of the blue. My thanks to them both.

Meanwhile, Sandy Mattison of Cape Town generously addressed many of my questions about South African expressions in English.

In a less bookish vein, I want to express my gratitude to all the grown-ups — many long gone — who made the lives of their children a paradise on horseback during the fresh springs, sun-dazed summers, and crisp autumns of my youth. Finally, here's a shout-out in memoriam to my quadruped soulmates of long ago, the indispensable Sheba, the gracious Woody, the unstoppable Fred. They swam with humans.

OF RELATED INTEREST

This Shall Be a House of Peace
Phil Halton

Chaos reigns in the wake of the collapse of Afghanistan's Soviet-backed government. In the rural, warlord-ruled south, a student is badly beaten at a checkpoint run by bandits. His teacher, who leads a madrassa for orphans left behind by Afghanistan's civil war, leads his students back to the checkpoint and forces the bandits out. His actions set in motion a chain of events that will change the balance of power in his country and send shock waves through history.

Amid villagers seeking protection and warlords seeking power, the Mullah's influence grows. Against the backdrop of anarchy dominated by armed factions, he devotes himself to building a house of peace with his students — or, as they are called in Pashto, taliban. Part intrigue, part war narrative, and part historical drama, *This Shall Be a House of Peace* charts their breathtaking ambition, transformation, and rise to power.

BOOK CREDITS

Project Editor: Jenny McWha

Editor: Kate Unrau

Proofreader: Ashley Hisson

Cover Designer: David Drummond

Interior Designer: Jennifer Gallinger

Publicists: Michelle Melski and Tabassum Siddiqui

DUNDURN

Publisher: J. Kirk Howard

Vice-President: Carl A. Brand

Editorial Director: Kathryn Lane

Artistic Director: Laura Boyle

Production Manager: Rudi Garcia

Publicity Manager: Michelle Melski

Manager, Accounting and Technical Services: Livio Copetti

Editorial: Allison Hirst, Dominic Farrell, Jenny McWha, Rachel Spence, Elena Radic, Melissa Kawaguchi

Marketing and Publicity: Kendra Martin, Kathryn Bassett, Elham Ali, Tabassum Siddiqui, Heather McLeod

Design and Production: Sophie Paas-Lang

dundurn.com
@dundurnpress
dundurnpress
dundurnpress
dundurnpress
info@dundurn.com

FIND US ON NETGALLEY & GOODREADS TOO!

DUNDURN